SOPHIE BEING SINGLE

by

Sheila Norton

Sheila Norton lives in Essex and has been writing ever since she discovered it was the only thing she was good at in school! She enjoys writing contemporary relationship fiction and has been published under the name of Olivia Ryan as well as her own name. She also writes short stories for magazines including Woman's Weekly, Yours, The People's Friend, etc.

She worked for most of her life as a medical secretary, until retiring early to concentrate on her writing.

Sheila enjoys hearing from readers and can be contacted through her websites:

www.sheilanorton.co.uk or www.oliviaryan.com

3

A Sunday in June

My name's Sophie and I'm an alien. Well, most people seem to think I'm an alien anyway – but from my point of view I become one every Sunday afternoon: an alien in a scary foreign world. It's the world of my friend Polly, who grew up with me, went to school with me, and now lives a life so different from mine that I find myself floundering and gasping with shock whenever I visit her.

Today, Polly opens the door with her short dark hair standing on end, wearing her pyjamas with the top on back to front.

'Bad day?' I ask.

'The worst. I've been up since before six, but I still haven't managed to have a shower. He keeps on, constantly …' A wail goes up, interrupting her, making her clutch her head in anguish. 'Screaming,' she finishes, closing her eyes and swaying slightly.

I haven't got through the front door yet. She stands aside to let me step into the narrow, brightly-painted hallway that always reminds me of the corridors of a primary school. I kiss Polly on the cheek and head for the source of the noise.

'Sit down,' I call back to her. 'Or have your shower. Whatever. Where's Gracie?'

'I'm here,' says a little voice, suddenly, at my elbow. 'What's the matter with Mummy, Sophie? Why is she crying again?'

The *again* makes my heart constrict with pain and fear. Polly never cried like this when Gracie was a baby. Admittedly she often looked as if she didn't know what had hit her – but she never looked like she was falling apart or wanted to run away. This has all happened since Ethan was born five months ago. I wonder vaguely, and anxiously, about things like postnatal depression. What do I do if she's got that? Suggest she gets some pills for it? Why am I so ignorant of things that other women seem, instinctively, to understand? I've managed to reach the same age as Polly – thirty-four – without acquiring even a smidgeon of an idea about what goes on beyond the moment of conception. To be honest, even the thought of *that* makes me shudder.

'Mummy's just tired,' I tell the little girl brightly. 'Very, very tired, because Ethan keeps her awake at night.'

'Ethan is a bloody pain,' says Gracie fervently, following me upstairs to the nursery.

'I don't think Mummy would like you to say that.'

'But Daddy says it. All the time. He says ...'

'It's not a good idea to copy what Daddy says, Gracie.' I can feel my jaw tighten and the familiar knot in my stomach. I don't want to talk about Leon, not even to his daughter. I always try to come round to see Polly when I know he'll be out – Sunday afternoons, he goes to play golf with his mates, regardless of his wife or his family, regardless of his responsibilities.

'Now then, young man!' I'm in the baby's room, looking into the cot at the red and bawling infant, whose open mouth seems to fill his whole face, and whose tiny fists are punching the air with rage. 'What?' I shout above the din. 'What *is* it all about?'

Needless to say, I've got no idea. Despite the number of babies suddenly being produced by my friends, family and sundry acquaintances, I'm as clueless about how they work as I ever was. As we all used to be, in fact, back then when everybody I knew was single – when we all, together through our teens and our single, rowdy twenties, swayed on bar stools with pints of cider in our hands, tottered home from nightclubs on terrible heels, arms linked, singing, calling out to the men. When being still in our pyjamas halfway through the day would have been because of a hangover from the night before, not because of the demands of a fractious baby.

'He's probably hungry,' suggests Gracie.

Ethan, suddenly becoming aware of me leaning over his cot, gives a hiccup of surprise and stops crying for a moment. He breathes jerkily, in pitiful gasps as if it's as much as he can do to hold back more blood-curdling screams. I reach into the cot and pick him up.

'Let's go and feed him, then,' I tell his sister, trying to sound confident about it. 'Where does Mummy keep his bottles?'

'No, not bottles.' Gracie puts her hands on her hips and shakes her head at me, amazed at my lack of knowledge. 'He doesn't have bottles.'

'Food, then?' I know about jars of baby food. I remember seeing my sister spooning orange muck from one such jar into my nephew, when he was a baby, and marvelling at the baby-bird open-mouthed speed of its demolition. Baby Rice with Apricots, it was. 'Rice?' I suggest hopefully, heading for the stairs.

'No, silly!' Gracie's convulsed with laughter now. 'Babies don't eat rice! They don't eat *food*!'

I experience one indescribably awful moment of terror that this is what's wrong with Ethan. That Polly, in her postnatal madness, has stopped giving the baby any food, that she's starving him without being aware of her actions, and that I might actually have to do something serious, like call an ambulance and Social Services. But fortunately Gracie stops laughing at my idiocy for long enough to go on: 'Mummy has to stick her boobies in his mouth. Don't you know *anything*?'

'Apparently not.' I thought Polly said she'd stopped breastfeeding. I look at the baby suspiciously. What age do they get teeth? I suppose it's OK to still be

7

breastfeeding them at this age? After all, you do hear stories about people still breastfeeding toddlers – two and three year olds who apparently like to wash down their chicken nuggets and chips with a quick swig from their poor mothers' wrung-out tits.

'Go on then,' demands Gracie. 'Do it. Or he'll start crying again.'

'OK – I suppose we'll have to take him in to Mummy, then, if she's finished her shower.'

'But you said Mummy was tired,' Gracie reminds me sternly. 'Why don't *you* stick *your* boobies in his mouth.' She looks me up and down critically. 'Or haven't you got any?'

Ridiculously, I find myself sticking out my chest, looking down at myself, feeling wounded.

'*I* haven't got any yet,' Gracie confides, lifting her pink bunny-rabbit T-shirt and showing me the flatness of her Mothercare vest, 'because they won't grow till I'm older. Perhaps yours haven't growed yet either.'

Not wanting to get into a sex education situation with a four year old, I just give her a vague nod of agreement and, swallowing back pre-pubescent feelings of inadequacy about the size of my breasts, knock on the bathroom door with the baby in my arms.

'I think he might need feeding!' I yell, taking credit for Gracie's diagnosis of the problem. 'Are you out of the shower, or ...'

'Shit!' says Polly, pulling open the door and appearing naked in a cloud of steam. 'Again? Are you sure?'

'Well, I ...' The kid's screaming again, and I'd really like nothing more than to drop him in Polly's arms and run, especially as he smells very unpleasant and there's a dampness spreading through his Babygro into the arm of my cardigan. I try not to look too disgusted as I add as an afterthought, 'Or he might need changing.'

'Shit!' Polly says again, appropriately, before covering her mouth and glancing guiltily at her daughter. Luckily Gracie either doesn't realise this is a naughty word or has heard it too often to be surprised. 'Could you do me a favour and change him for me, Sophe? Just to give me five minutes to dry off and get dressed? The nappies are in the bottom drawer in his room, and there's a changing mat … and some bum cream. Gracie will show you.'

Gracie could probably do it herself, I think uncharitably, wishing I could suggest it. For a split second I consider putting the baby back in his cot, lying down on the floor and pretending I've fainted. But I can't do that to my best friend, can I. I'm happy to help her. If only it didn't involve this one thing, of all the things she could ask.

I look at Gracie, who looks back at me with challenge in her eyes.

'OK then,' I say through gritted teeth. 'Let's do it, kid.'

I am definitely, *definitely*, never going to have children.

A little later, we're sitting together in the lounge while Polly feeds the baby. I'm feeling pretty chuffed with myself. I managed the nappy, somehow, although the clean one didn't look too secure the way I fastened it, and I've made us both a cup of tea and a drink of something purple for Gracie.

Gracie's playing with her dolls now, wrapping them in blankets, telling them to be quiet and go to sleep. She looks up at me, big blue eyes wide with curiosity.

'My daddy's a virgin,' she announces. 'What are you?'

I'm choking on a mouthful of tea – almost dropping the cup in my lap.

'I'm a bull,' the child goes on calmly. 'Mummy's a lion, but she only just missed out on being a virgin, didn't you, Mummy?'

'Yes – by a couple of days.' Polly gives me a grin. 'It's best if we call it Virgo, Gracie.'

'Why? You *said* Virgo was a virgin. You said it means a young lady. It's funny, my daddy being a young lady, isn't it, Sophie?'

I nod, dumbly, wiping spilt tea from my jeans.

'What are you?' Gracie repeats. 'Are you a virgin too?'

'No,' I say, ignoring Polly's snigger. 'No, I'm not. I'm a crab, unfortunately.'

'Ugh. I don't like crabs. They go like this.' She demonstrates, skipping sideways across the room, barging into her mum and making the baby's eyes fly open with shock. 'Have you seen one? We saw one at the beach, didn't we, Mummy. It was going like this.' She gallops back again, waving her arms in the air. 'It was going to pinch me with its pinchers!'

'Claws,' says Polly. 'Gracie, why don't you see if your cartoons are on the TV now?'

'Yeah!' shouts the child, crab-skipping across the room to the TV, where she bounces down onto a beanbag and cuddles the remote control in one hand, a blanket-swaddled doll in the other.

'I was never going to do this,' says Polly quietly. 'Never! No child of mine was going to be fobbed off with a TV programme just because I couldn't cope.'

'You *are* coping. Don't be so hard on yourself.' I lean closer to Polly and ask her quietly, 'Is everything all right? Should you see the doctor, if you're feeling really low?'

'No. No, I'm fine, really. Just tired. Nobody warns you how tired you're going to be with the second one. I thought it'd be easier, you know, now I'd got the hang of it? When Gracie was born I didn't know which end was up. But actually, that was a doddle compared with this.'

'Is it because you're still feeding him? Weren't you going to stop? Put him on the bottle?'

'I was,' she sighs. 'But I think I'd feel such a failure. Like I was putting myself before my baby. I fed Gracie till she was nearly a year old.'

'But like you said – you didn't have two of them to look after, then. Hopefully it'll all get easier when she starts school.'

'I know. And when Ethan starts sleeping through the night.'

I'm not bothering to ask when she expects that to happen. Clearly, I know nothing whatsoever about infant development. For all I know, he could still be waking up for a breastfeed when he's fourteen. Yuck.

And I know I shouldn't say this, either, but I can't help myself:

'It'd be a lot easier too if Leon played his part.'

'So what am I supposed to do? Chain him to the house? Stop his pocket money? He'll do whatever he wants to do, at the end of the day – how do I make him *want* to spend more time with his kids?'

'I don't know,' I admit. You see? I shouldn't have said it.

'What would *you* do, Sophe? In my position? I mean, I do love Leon, but he's just no bloody use to me at all – you know?'

'What, are you thinking of leaving him, then?' I cross my fingers and hold my breath. 'Could you manage – on your own with the kids?'

'Of course I couldn't! Of course I'm not thinking of leaving him! It's never even crossed my mind.' She frowns at me. 'I can't believe you said that!'

'Sorry.'

'I just wanted some advice, that's all. You're always so sensible, so practical. I thought you might know how I can ... change things.'

I try not to sigh out loud. Why does everyone always want my advice on subjects I know nothing about, like husbands and children? In my opinion the only way Polly can change things is to boot that great useless lump of a husband out of the door, the sooner the better, before he breaks her heart as well as refusing to meet his responsibilities. But because I can't suggest that, I just say, gently:

'Let him see how exhausted you are, Polly. Stop being so brave and noble. Tell him you're too knackered for sex. That'll make him take notice.'

'You don't think that might just make him look for it elsewhere, though, do you?' She's trying to make it sound like she's joking.

I pretend to laugh, pretend to think this is ridiculous, a ridiculous joke.

'Why would he look anywhere else, when he's got you?' The words leave a sickly taste in my mouth. I put down my empty cup and change the subject.

'Are you coming out with the girls next Saturday night? Come on, Polly. Get him to babysit. It'll do you good.'

'I don't know.'

'Emma and Jo are coming. It'll cheer you up.'

'I *am* cheerful.' She looks hurt, insulted. 'I'm just tired, that's all. Honestly, Sophie, life isn't all about going out with the girls and getting rat-arsed any more! We're thirty-four, for God's sake!'

There's an irritation in her voice that makes me flinch.

'I do know how old we are!' I try to keep the tone light. Polly and I have been friends since school. We were in the same class, back home in Devon and she moved up to London a year or two after I did. We shared a flat, did everything together – right up till Polly gave birth to Gracie and gave up a good job to stay at home and be supported by the prat she married – and pretty much gave up her life at the same time.

'Yes, well, sometimes I think you forget. You can't live like a teenager for ever, Sophe.'

I want to ask why not, but decide it's better not to go there. Polly is probably feeling moody and regretful. Who wouldn't? How dreadful it must be to be stuck at home with two crying children, changing dirty nappies every day, while everyone else is out there enjoying themselves, earning money, spending it however they want.

'I'm not really interested in coming out on Saturday nights,' she goes on. 'It's just not my scene any more.'

'But it could be! You could have some fun again.'

She looks at me blankly, shakes her head.

'I don't want *fun*, Sophe. You don't get it, do you? I love being a mum. I might moan about being tired, and about not coping – but that's all part of it. I don't miss anything about my old life at all.'

'You don't? Not your job? Your friends?'

'I've got my *children*!' She lifts Ethan up onto her shoulder to get his wind up, and he eyes me balefully over his mother's shoulder. 'Sorry, Sophie, but I sometimes wonder if you're still trying to party like mad because you *haven't* got anything.'

I've got my own business! My own flat! My friends! My own money! No-strings sex! A fucking life! I think, indignantly. But I don't say this, not any of it. I might have done – maybe – but just as I'm considering it, I hear Leon's key turn in the lock.

'Right – I'm off,' I say abruptly, getting to my feet and kissing Polly goodbye. I stroke the top of the baby's head and blow a kiss to Gracie who's engrossed in the TV. 'See you next week. Give me a ring if you need to chat.'

'OK. Thanks for your help with the nappy.' We smile at each other, and I'm glad I didn't rise to the bait. I don't want to fall out with my best mate over nothing.

'Bye, bye, Crab!' calls Gracie.

'Hello, stranger,' says Leon as I pass him in the hall.

'Hi, and goodbye.'

'You're off already?' He smirks unpleasantly. 'Was it something I said?'

'No,' I mutter, without looking back. Just loud enough for him to hear. 'It's something you *are*.'

The air outside feels fresh and sweet. It doesn't smell of milk or baby sick, and better still, it doesn't smell of Leon.

The next Friday

Of course, when you work in the wedding business, Fridays and Saturdays are always the busiest days, and Wedding Belles is no exception. I love my work, and I'm happiest when I'm busy. This is my own territory; this is where I feel in control. But this morning's not going well, and I haven't even got started on the first head yet. Hilary's been here half an hour, and all we've done is talk. She's upset.

'Don't you think Daniel's being selfish, Sophie?' she says, pleading with her eyes for me to agree with her.

What am I supposed to say? I look back at her in the mirror, trying to consider the question seriously.

'I guess *all* men can be a bit selfish,' I suggest gently.

'A *bit* selfish!' Hilary drops the magazine she's been holding. It falls on the floor and she treads on it, creasing the cover so that the beautiful model bride pictured on the front suddenly looks like a one-eyed screwed-up monster with Hilary's shoe kicking her in the mouth. 'Would you call it a *bit selfish* if *your* fiancé did it? Or would you think he was a totally thoughtless, uncaring, heartless, callous pig?'

I don't actually know Daniel, and Hilary's not exactly making him sound very appealing. All I really want to do is get on with her hair, but this is what so often happens: I end up spending more time trying to sort out my clients' problems than I do sorting out their hair.

'Well, I haven't got a fiancé myself,' I tell her, apologetically.

'Then you don't know how lucky you are!' Hilary exclaims with satisfaction.

Actually I do. I know *exactly* how lucky I am. But I just nod agreement and run my fingers through Hilary's hair, encouraging her to sit still and calm down.

'It'll all sort itself out. Trust me. Everyone has a few ups and downs just before the wedding.'

'Sophie, listen to me, darling. Inviting his rugby team to the wedding at the eleventh hour, when the catering's all been booked, the numbers finalised and the bloody *table plan*'s been printed,' – she makes the table plan sound as if it's equal, at least, in significance to the actual wedding ceremony – 'we're not just talking *ups and downs* here. We're talking *outrage*. Total, unforgivable outrage.'

'I'm sure his rugby mates will have realised he was drunk. They won't have taken him seriously. And their wives, girlfriends, whatever, will *definitely* realise.'

'He didn't invite any wives or girlfriends! Just the blokes! Typical – just what you want at your wedding reception, isn't it – a table full of raucous, hairy-arsed, rugby-song-singing, foul-mouthed, evil-smelling …'

'Evil-smelling?'

'They must be, mustn't they. What with all those communal baths. *Anyway*, I've told him. I don't care what he's said to them, he'll have to unsay it. He'll have to un-invite the lot of them. Otherwise the whole thing's off.'

'Fair enough,' I say, to humour her, although in fact you know what? I've heard so many hysterical threats to call off weddings at the last moment, I don't take any notice any more. Most of my bridal clients seem to threaten it at least once during the lead-up to the wedding – usually because of something unforgivable their other half's done.

'Oh, Sophie,' wails Hilary now, closing her eyes and sighing as if the pain's too much to bear. 'What should I do? Tell me honestly? What would *you* do?'

Here we go again. I try not to sigh. This is what happens, you see: I enjoy chatting to my brides while I'm working on their hair and their make-up. I try my best to listen impartially to all the worries they inevitably pour out to me, try to be sympathetic without getting dragged in to venture an opinion. But it never works. It always comes down to this: *What would* you *do, Sophie?*

What would I do? How the hell should I know! The truth is that I wouldn't have agreed to marry Daniel in the first place. There wouldn't be a *whole thing* to call off, or the myriad and costly arrangements to cancel. I wouldn't be wearing his mega-expensive diamond-and-sapphire engagement ring and I wouldn't be sitting here, having my eighth practice for my wedding hairstyle and crying to the hairdresser about him! But I obviously can't say that to Hilary.

Anyway, let's face it – Hilary doesn't really want my honest opinion. She just wants me to smile reassuringly and say:

'Give him another chance, Hilary – that's what I'd do. He's probably suffering from pre-wedding stress himself, you know.'

'Do you *think* so? *Really?*' Her eyes implore my reflection in the mirror, wanting my permission to make excuses for Daniel's selfishness.

'Yes, of course. That's probably why he got so drunk – and I don't suppose he even realised what he was saying when he invited them all to the reception.'

'Maybe they could just come to the evening? That would be a compromise, wouldn't it?'

I smile at her. 'I think that would be incredibly generous of you. Probably most of them won't even end up coming.'

Hilary looks pleased at this. Now's the time to change the subject; now she's looking less upset; now she's lost the indignant squawk to her voice and started to notice me fiddling with her hair. 'How about,' I suggest, 'we try it *this* way: pinned up like this, at the back, with the sides curled?'

Hilary has lovely hair: thick and straight and shiny. I'm sick with envy. Mine is curly, mousy and the texture of fuse wire. It needs straightening every day and the administering of three or four different conditioning products just to tame it into some sort of style that doesn't look completely mad. *And* she's naturally blonde, the sort of blonde that looks like she's just been sitting out in the sun and developed highlights without having to try. I change my own colour regularly, from chestnut to aubergine, rich mahogany, plum – anything to try to shock it into looking more interesting. It's currently Shade 15a – Warm Copper – which has somehow, on me, ended up looking like rust. Perhaps that's why I enjoy doing other people's hair – people like Hilary, who are easy to make look beautiful. I almost feel guilty about taking money for it, but this *is* her eighth appointment.

'Sophie, you are *such* a treasure.' She beams, everything apparently all right again. 'I knew I could rely on you for advice. I feel so much better now that's all sorted out. And I think having the sides curled would be *absolutely perfect*.' She swings her hair happily, watching herself in the mirror. 'I think today might be the day I make up my mind, Sophie – at last! I think today's style is going to be *The One*. The one I'm going to have for the *Actual Day*!' She clasps her hand over her mouth, looking like she's going to burst with girlish excitement at the thought of the wedding she has, only five minutes ago, threatened to cancel.

'Let's get started, then.' I check my watch. Listening to the Daniel saga has already put me behind schedule, but rushing things, now Hilary seems committed to the idea of making a decision, could be fatal. Of course, there's been a different Daniel saga on every one of the seven previous occasions that Hilary's been here, but the wedding is now only two weeks away and things can't be allowed to drift on like this.

'Today's Decision Day,' confirms Hilary, sitting up and smiling at me. 'Make me look wonderful, Sophie. I need Daniel to be struck dumb with amazement when I walk down that aisle.'

And of course, I'm going to do my best. Even if Daniel's going to be too hungover from drinking with his rugby mates to notice.

'I don't know how you do it,' says Charlie, as always, over dinner later when I tell him the story of Daniel and the rugby team. He shakes his head and laughs. 'I wouldn't be able to keep a straight face and tell her what she wants to hear.'

'She'd go ahead and marry him anyway, whatever I said, so there's no point upsetting her.'

'I guess you're right. I suppose you're in a privileged position, really, aren't you – hearing all this stuff. Like a psychiatrist or a counsellor. It wouldn't do for you to tell them all to get a life and dump the bums.'

'There'd be nobody getting married at all, if I got started on that!'

'And no kids being born! The population would die out!'

This is my point exactly. I'm the first to admit that the whole marriage-and-babies scenario scares the life out of me. It isn't what *I* want, but that doesn't mean I can't sympathise with all the other people falling over themselves in their rush to commit to it. *Sympathise*. Like I'd sympathise with people with mental health problems. Not much difference, as far as I'm concerned.

'It's not that I'm cynical about it,' I say, a bit defensively.

'No?'

'Well – not in the sense that I just take their money even though I think they're mad. I do actually want my brides to be happy.'

'*My brides!*' he teases gently, sipping his wine, smiling at me across the table

'But how can I *not* be cynical about marriage in general? When I hear so many disastrous stories?'

And when I see so many of my lovely, excited brides-to-be crushed by the disappointments of their marriages within a year or two of their fairytale weddings.

'It's not just Polly's marriage that's put you off completely?'

'Don't start me on that,' I say, gloomily. 'Even if I'd had any ideas of settling down and getting married before, I'd have changed my mind the minute I realised what sort of a husband Leon's turned out to be.'

'I know.' He touches my hand across the table. 'It's hard for you – that situation. But don't you ever want to ask girls like Hilary why they're getting married at all if they think their other half's so selfish or whatever? Don't you think people like Hilary talk themselves into something that obviously isn't right?'

'She just wants to be happy, Charlie – that doesn't make her wrong.'

He smiles. 'I sometimes think you're kind of like an atheist who enjoys cleaning churches and making them look beautiful.'

'That's it, exactly!' I laugh. 'There's something, well, *rewarding* about seeing a bride looking all lovely and glowing. I *like* weddings – other people's weddings! I like elephants, too, but that doesn't mean I want one of my own.'

'You don't need to get all defensive with me, Sophe! I agree with you. Especially about the elephants!'

Charlie knows me well. And he's such a lovely guy – the closest thing I've got, or want, to a boyfriend. We don't exactly have a relationship. We don't have rings on our fingers, or a shared home, or any form of commitment whatsoever. What we have is fun, and respect for each other, and nice dinners like this, at Chez Monique, our favourite restaurant. Nice, easy, adult conversation without any hidden agendas. And incredibly good sex – whenever we fancy it. Charlie's funny and kind, intelligent and gorgeous-looking, but he's never made demands on me or expected me to give anything up for him. We understand each other.

Well, mostly. The one thing I don't think he quite understands is just how difficult and wearing I find the whole agony aunt stuff.

'It's bad enough that all my clients pour out their hearts to me,' I try to explain. 'It's my sisters now, too! They both keep calling me to complain about their husbands and kids and ask what I think they should do! Like *I'm* the one to advise them!'

'You're obviously such a good listener,' he says, laughing. 'You should be flattered. They value your opinions.'

'Why? They shouldn't! *I* wouldn't!'

It's beyond a joke. All my friends, too, seem to have the impression that I've only been put on this earth to listen to their problems. And random people strike up conversations with me in supermarkets, and want to tell me about their horrible husbands and their bastard boyfriends. I've been trying, recently, to rearrange my face so that I don't *look* like someone who might be a good listener, before women in bus queues and behind post office counters start telling me their life histories.

'I think it's just become a habit for you,' says Charlie, seriously, topping up my wine glass. 'You're so used to listening to your crackpot brides, making sympathetic noises and trying to keep them happy – you do the same thing when anyone else bends your ear with their problems, without even realising you're doing it.'

'Do I do it with you?' I ask him, slightly surprised. 'Is that what you like about me? The fact that I sit here with my care-in-the-community face on, trying to sound understanding when you whinge about your job, or the traffic, or whatever?'

'No, Sophie,' he says, giving me a grin that starts to melt my insides. 'That's not what I like about you. Not the only thing, anyway.'

'Good,' I say softly. 'I'm glad about that.' I gulp down the rest of my wine. 'Let's pay the bill and go. You can stay over at mine tonight if you like?'

'Haven't you got any clients turning up in the morning?'

'Not till ten o'clock. We can have a bit of a lie-in. I'll throw you out at nine – OK?'

'OK,' he says. 'Sounds good.'

Actually, you know what? It sounds perfect.

Saturday

My first client today is Barbara Fine. It's only the second time I've met her – she came to see me a few weeks ago to book this appointment, and today she's having her hair coloured and cut for her wedding this afternoon. No fuss, no trials – just coloured and cut, and that's it. Barbara is about sixty and this'll be her second marriage.

'I didn't really want to get married again,' she confides as I put the colour on her hair. 'It was Dennis's idea. He kept on, and on, and on – and in the end he got on my nerves so much, I agreed.'

Not the most romantic engagement story I've ever heard, but who am I to judge?

'You must be very much in love with him, though,' I say, smiling at her encouragingly in the mirror.

'No. Not really. To be honest with you, Sophie, I've never stopped loving Graham.'

Graham? Who the hell is Graham?

'My first husband,' she explains with a long drawn-out sigh. 'We were married for thirty-one years.'

'Oh – I'm sorry. I didn't realise you were a widow.'

'I'm not. He didn't die, although admittedly he did come close to it. I tried to stab him with the bread knife, but he ducked out of the way. Then I hit him over the head with the iron. But he only had concussion.'

'Blimey!' I look at her with new respect. 'What had he done?'

'Had an affair with a twenty-two year old veterinary nurse. He chatted her up while he was supposed to be getting some ointment for my poor old pussy.'

I can't think of a single word to say to this, so I just make a sort-of grunt that I hope sounds sympathetic.

'I wouldn't have minded so much,' she goes on sadly, 'but he told me he'd fallen in love with her and was going to live with her in her caravan.'

'Her *caravan*?'

'Yes – with bunk beds and a chemical toilet. And he was always such a stickler for nice furniture.'

'That must have been really hard for you, Barbara. I'm surprised you still have feelings for him.'

'You never get over your first love,' she replies solemnly, reminding me strangely of stories in girls' picture magazines that I read when I was a teenager. 'And also, he was a bit of a sex bomb.'

I nearly drop the foil I'm using to wrap her coloured streaks.

'Really?'

'Oh yes. A real tiger between the sheets, he was. Used to go at it like a dog on heat. Made me howl like a hyena.'

Enough with all the animals, here! I'm struggling to get a picture of this – and not too sure that I even want to.

'So what about Dennis?' I say brightly instead. 'Is he as ... um, nice as Graham?'

'Of course not,' she retorts quite crossly. 'He's only fifty-four, anyway – these youngsters have no stamina. But at least he does the cooking.'

'Oh, that's ... well, that's something in his favour.'

'Yes. And the shopping.'

'Great!'

'And the cleaning.'

'Blimey! Good for him!'

'And he cleans my car once a week, mows the lawn, does the laundry, brings me tea in bed every morning and buys me chocolates and flowers.'

'Wow! Barbara, I'm really impressed – he sounds like a superhero!'

24

'Yes,' she says gloomily. She shakes her head at me so that the foils rustle and shiver. 'At times, though, he just gets on my fucking nerves.'

'So why's she marrying him?' Jo screams at me over the noise of the music. 'I mean, that is just *so* hilarious! I can't believe she's still hankering after having sex with her ex!'

I know, I know – I shouldn't have told the girls about it. It's true, after all, that being a hairdresser is like being a doctor. Or a barmaid. You get told all this stuff in confidence – you shouldn't really repeat it and laugh about it on a drunken night out with your friends. But it was too good not to share. And they're never going to meet Barbara, anyway.

'She says it's just for companionship. He's no good at sex, apparently, but he mows the lawn.'

'Well, let's face it,' says Emma, 'at her age, she's going to choose the lawn.'

'Never mind her age – so would I!' laughs Jo. 'You can always get a vibrator, but they can't do the gardening.'

'Poor cow, though,' I point out, feeling a bit defensive about her. At the end of the day, she's one of my brides, and I want her to be happy. 'After all those years, being dumped for a young bit of stuff with a caravan.'

'Yeah. Men can be such bastards.' Emma takes another swig from her drink.

'Even Stefan?' I tease her. Stefan's the latest boyfriend. They never last long, with Emma, but she's actually moved in with this one. I don't suppose for one minute it's really serious, but she's been looking very pleased with herself lately.

'Well, maybe not Stefan,' she amends with a funny little grin. 'Actually ...'

'I suppose Stefan would *never* do anything like that! I suppose he's different,' I carry on teasing, getting into my stride. I'm a bit drunk, so I don't know when to stop. 'I suppose he *lurves* you and you *lurve* him back. I suppose he's the man of your dreams, and ...'

'Yes, he is.'

'... and next thing you know, he'll be asking you to *marry* him, and you'll be wearing a bloody great rock on your finger and .... oh. Oh shit.'

She's holding her left hand up to show me – a bloody great rock on her finger.

'I've been trying to tell you, but you wouldn't shut up! We're engaged. We're getting married.' She smiles again and I wonder why I didn't realise it before. It's *that* smile – the one I see on my brides' faces when they talk about their husbands-to-be. Well, most of them, anyway – Barbara was probably the exception. It's a sickly, dopey kind of smile, like someone with a terminal illness who's nevertheless trying to be gracious and wonderful and thank all the nurses while pretending to be happy and brave for everyone else's sake. 'He asked me last weekend.'

'Did he?' I say, stupidly. 'And what did you say?'

'She said Yes, of course, Sophie – what do you think she said!' Jo squawks at me indignantly. 'Look at her ring! Isn't it gorgeous?'

'Oh – um, yes, it's lovely. Well done, then, Em. I mean – sorry, congratulations, and all that. When are you actually, um, doing it?'

'Next April! We've booked the venue already! And the caterers. You have to get in quickly, you know, otherwise they all get booked up. We're talking to photographers tomorrow.' She's on a roll now. I can feel my eyes glazing over. 'And then it's the florists. And, of course, Sophie,' her voice takes on this strange, coy tone as if she's going to say something a little bit risqué, 'I don't have to ask you, do I? You'll do my hair, of course, won't you? And my make-up?'

'Of course I will.' I'm recovering myself, just in time. 'What date in April? Tell you what – send me an

26

email tomorrow so I can get it in my diary, yeah?' I give her a hug and a kiss on the cheek. 'I'm *so* pleased for you, Em. It's brilliant news.'

'I know – I'm just *floating* up *there* somewhere, right now,' she gushes, pointing to the ceiling, the soppy grin intensifying.

That'll be the morphine, then, I think, uncharitably.

'So – we'll be the only two left, soon!' I shout at Jo as the music suddenly goes up by a few hundred decibels. 'The last stand of the Single Army, eh!'

'Yes, I suppose so!' she shouts back.

'Wannanother drink?' I yell. 'Whaddya want?'

'Vodka and tonic, please, Sophe,' Emma shouts. 'Thanks.'

'Orange juice, please,' says Jo.

'You driving?' I demand, crossly. 'Whaddya wanna drive for, on a Saturday night? We *never* drive on Saturday nights, do we, girls. Saturday nights are for getting pissed and having a bloody good time, a bloody good laugh, a bloody good – ' I grab her arm suddenly, making her jump. 'I've got a bloody good idea. Leave the car here!' I wait for her to gasp in amazement at the incredible cleverness of my very original, very cunning plan. 'Whaddya say? Leave it here and get in the taxi with us. And *come back for it* tomorrow. Yeah?'

'I didn't bring the car, Sophe. I don't like driving in the dark. I'm getting in the taxi with you.'

'Oh, brilliant! So you can have a drink, then! Great!' I'm almost beside myself with excitement. 'So! Whaddya want?'

'Orange juice, please,' she says again.

'It's not all about getting pissed, Sophie,' says Emma reprovingly, sounding exactly like Polly did on Sunday in fact. She's only just got the engagement ring on her finger and already she's sounding like a middle-aged vicar's wife in the middle of Lent. 'It *is* possible to have a good time without getting out of your skull.'

'Is it?' I'm annoyed now. Annoyed to suddenly, apparently, be cast in the role of a loose-living, gutter-dwelling, alcoholic slut, by the very friends I've always fallen into the taxi with at the end of every Saturday night, carrying our shoes and singing at the tops of our lungs. 'Since when, exactly?'

'Since I did a test yesterday,' Jo says quietly, with a very similar little sickly smile to the one Emma's still wearing. 'Since I found out ... I'm pregnant, Sophie. I'm having a baby! Isn't it amazing? I'm actually going to be a mummy!'

And I actually think I'm going to be sick.

I go to the bar and order myself a large Becks with a double vodka chaser. I want to pass out before I have to listen to descriptions of morning sickness and antenatal appointments. It looks like our Saturday nights might soon be a thing of the past.

'And if it's a boy,' Jo's twittering away in my ear, 'then I'm thinking, maybe *Harry* or perhaps *Jack.* But what I'm not sure about is, shall I ask them to tell me the sex of the baby when I have the scan? Or shall I wait? What do you think, Sophe?'

'Mm?' I'm leaning against her, in the back of the taxi, and I'm half asleep. Emma looks like she's already out for the count.

'I said, what do you think, Sophe? Shall I find out, or shall I wait till it's born?'

See what I mean? Yet again, my opinion is being sought on something I have absolutely no knowledge or experience of, and quite frankly, no interest in.

'Well, um, I guess that's your decision to make, really, isn't it? Yours and the baby's father's.'

There's a sudden frosty silence. Whoops. I open my eyes and blink at Emma, who's also wide awake now and staring at me, horrified. None of us have yet broached the subject of the baby's father. Partly because Jo herself hasn't mentioned him; partly because we've kind of gathered he's not exactly in the picture, but mainly because we have no idea who the fuck he is. If I hadn't been drunk, half asleep and frankly fed up with hearing baby talk almost non-stop all evening, I'd have stayed off the subject until the kid was born and I'd had a good look at it to see if it reminded me of anyone I knew.

'The baby's father is irrelevant,' says Jo, crossly, as if it was preposterous to suggest that a mere man could have had anything to do with her situation. 'This is *my* baby, and any decisions are *my* decisions.' She pauses for a minute, and then adds calmly: 'So what do you think I should do?'

'I think you should probably, um … make your own decision,' I tell her, trying not to yawn. 'That would definitely be best.'

I phone Charlie as soon as I get in.

'Guess what? Emma's got engaged to that dickhead Stefan, and Jo's having a baby with no father.'

'Bloody hell,' he says. Then, 'It must have a father.'

'No. I think it was an immaculate conception. And she was on orange juice all night and asked me what I thought about finding out the baby's sex.'

'Poor you.' He laughs. 'What *do* you think about it?'

'I think it's the most uninteresting question I've ever been asked.'

'That's a bit harsh,' he says, still laughing.

'Well, yes, I suppose it is. She *is* my friend, after all. Well, she was. But now I suppose she'll stay at home on Saturday nights and knit bootees.'

'Do people still knit bootees?'

'I don't know!' I retort. I sit down, still holding the phone, feeling suddenly, ridiculously, like crying. 'All my friends are turning into wives and mothers and things,' I whine pitifully. I know it's the drink talking, but I can't help it. 'It's not fair!'

'*I'm* not,' he reminds me. 'I don't think I'd make a very good wife. Or mother.'

'No.' I wait, for a moment, picturing him sitting in his flat, which is just round the corner from mine. He's probably just got in, like me, from a night out with his friends. He's probably wearing his jeans with the black T-shirt that shows off his muscles, and he's probably, like me, just a little bit, ever-so-slightly drunk. And tomorrow's Sunday, and neither of us have to get up early.

'Do you want to come over?' I ask him softly.

'I'm on my way,' he says.

Thank God for that.

Sunday

'So – when?' My sister Debra's voice has taken on its usual badgering tone. I hold the phone away from my ear slightly so she doesn't hurt my hangover-head too much. 'When *are* you coming down to see Mum and Dad?'

'Soon.' I think about getting my diary out, finding a free couple of days, making a promise – but I haven't got the energy. 'Soon, Debs – OK?'

'You've been saying that for months.' There's a pause, while she waits for me to digest this. '*Months*, Sophie. You haven't been home since Easter.'

'That was only a few weeks ago. Don't exaggerate. And it's not that I don't *want* to. You know how it is.'

'Do I?' she says with irritation in her voice. I don't like that irritation. I'm not in the mood for a row. I just want to get back into bed with Charlie and bury my head under the pillow.

'I'm sorry. Tell Mum and Dad I'm sorry, I love them, I'll see them soon.'

'Tell them yourself! Phone them! When did you last ...'

'OK, OK – I know. I will. Yes, today. Yes, I promise. I'm really sorry, Debs, but you know how it is – with my work.'

'We all have to work,' she says – which, actually, is crap, as she doesn't. I mean, not in the sense of going out to work, doing an actual paid job – although she's always quick to point out that looking after their (large) house and her (difficult) children and (challenging) husband is a job in itself. 'But some of us still like to put our families first.'

'Yes, and I'm very grateful that you're down there, living so close to them, doing such a brilliant job of holding the family together between my visits. I'll come down soon, really. As soon as I get a couple of clear days with no weddings.' Her silence resonates with disapproval. 'How are things with you, anyway?' I say, to change the subject.

'Oh – you know. Much the same.' She sighs. I've got a horrible feeling I'm going to regret asking. 'James is never home ... he works all hours.'

'Well – that's what doctors do. You knew that, when you ...'

'Yes, yes, I knew that when I married him. But sometimes I wonder if he actually has any interest in coming home at all. I mean, I work so hard to keep the house lovely for him, cook lovely meals for him, try to keep myself looking ...' She sighs again and I can picture her, shaking her head, trying to pretend she's not bothered, it doesn't really matter.

'Looking lovely,' I finish for her, gently. 'You *do* always look lovely. And you do all those things for him. I'm sure he appreciates it – he's just busy.'

'You think so? You think I should just put up with it? Not complain? Even though I hardly ever see him, I'm on my own all day, wondering what he's up to.'

'I'm sure everything's fine, Debs.'

'You think I'm just being silly? What would *you* do?'

Oh, *God*. I don't know! I don't know, I don't know, I don't know!

'Maybe just talk to him,' I say, desperately. 'Tell him how you feel.'

'Perhaps you're right. Oh, Sophe – I do miss you. I can't talk to Millie – she's got enough on her plate with Tom being such a bastard. I wish you didn't live so far away!'

'Families are always like that,' Charlie tries to comfort me when I finally get back into bed after another fifteen minutes of listening to what my other sister Millie's been

32

putting up with from her bastard husband, and finally a tearful ten-minute farewell with Debra, who makes me feel like I might as well be living in Australia rather than London, and that I might not be going to speak to her again for another five years.

'Are they? Is yours?'

'God, yes. I think the nagging's even worse for me, actually, being an only child. Mum tells me every time I see her, about the shawl in the attic.'

'The shawl in the attic?' I repeat, surprised. 'What shawl?'

'I've never mentioned it to you,' he says, looking a bit embarrassed. 'I know you hate hearing about stuff like this. But apparently, Mum's kept the shawl she used when I was born, to carry me out of the hospital. It's wrapped in several layers of tissue paper and plastic bags, up in the attic, and she keeps asking me to get it down.'

'Get it down? What for?'

'So she can give it to me,' he admits. 'She seems to think, if she gives me the shawl to look after, she'll somehow be passing on to me the genetic blueprint for making babies. Making a grandchild for her.'

'Jesus! Who does she think you're going to be doing *that* with?'

'You, of course,' he says, laughing. 'She refers to you as my *nice young lady* and thinks we're practically engaged. I don't like to disillusion her.'

'Well, you should!' I sit up, throwing off the duvet, looking at him crossly. 'No, I'm sorry, Charlie, but you really *should*. It isn't fair, letting her carry on with those sort of delusions – she's only going to be upset when she finally realises it's never going to happen.'

He shrugs. 'I've told her we're just friends. But she thinks I'm being coy. She's even told me she doesn't mind if we sleep together in her guest bedroom if we go and stay with her.'

33

'Well, that's really bloody good of her! Considering it's never going to happen...'

'Sophie – she's my mum, I can't just tell her flat-out that she's got no chance in hell of ever seeing her dreams come true. Don't look like that. She wants a grandchild – I'm her only hope of getting one – and I can't bear to take that hope away from her. Not yet. She'll realise eventually that it isn't going to happen.'

'Well, sorry but I think you should be more straight with her. I did think it might be nice to meet her one day, but that's completely off the cards now. I'm not going through that – having baby shawls thrust at me and questions asked about my fertility.'

'Nobody's going to ask ...' he begins, laughing at me. He tries to pull me back into bed but the mood has gone.

'I'm having a shower,' I tell him. 'I'd love a bacon sandwich if you fancy making them!'

'I'll pop out for the papers first.'

Good. I'd rather discuss the latest corrupt politician; I'd even rather discuss yesterday's football results, than continue this sudden and very alarming conversation about his mother and her unfulfilled aspirations of grandmother-hood. Bad enough that I might have to change baby Ethan's nappy again when I visit Polly this afternoon. Sunday mornings are for lazy lie-ins, cosy breakfasts, adult conversation – *not* whispered confidences about baby shawls, thank you very much!

'I've heard about Emma!' squeals Polly before I've even closed the front door behind me. 'And Jo! Isn't it exciting!'

'Yes, it is, isn't it.' I smile at her. It's good to see her looking so much more animated – and dressed – than last week. 'Wish you were with us last night, to join in the celebrations.'

'It's OK. They both popped round this morning.'

'Did they?' I feel, unreasonably, left out and hurt. 'Why?'

'To tell me their news, of course! Isn't Emma's ring *gorgeous*!'

'Yes, it's lovely.'

'And Jo's feeling sick nearly every morning!' she says with peculiar satisfaction. 'And her mum's absolutely over the *moon* – you can imagine! Her first grandchild!'

'Yes, I've, um, heard some mothers get quite enthusiastic about that.' I fight back the unwelcome mental image of Charlie's mum, holding up a crocheted baby shawl, smiling at me knowingly, gesturing to her spare bedroom where Charlie's sitting up in bed waiting for me like a reluctant bridegroom. Was my own mother hysterical with excitement about my sisters getting pregnant? I'm ashamed to say I didn't really notice. They were all down there in Devon, and I was here, getting on with my work, getting on with my life.

But I do visit them. More often than Debra makes out. Whenever I get the chance, I'm down there, of course I am. I do love my family. I've got no reason whatsoever to feel guilty.

'Did Jo say anything to you about the baby's father?' I ask Polly, to stop myself from thinking about my family and feeling guilty. We're sitting in her lounge now, where Ethan's lying on the floor, kicking his fat little legs and swiping his fists at a collection of toys suspended from some kind of scaffold that seems to have been erected over him.

'Ooh, no – we mustn't ask about the father.' Polly giggles slightly. 'She doesn't want to talk about him.'

I consider this for a minute.

'She wasn't ... I mean, you don't think she was, you know, *raped* or anything like that, do you?'

'Sophie!' Polly gasps and stares at me, big-eyed. 'What a terrible thing to say!' She looks round to check that Gracie's still occupied with her crayons. 'Honestly! What on earth made you think that?'

'Well – just the fact that she's so reluctant to talk about him. Either she hates him, in which case why did she think it was a good idea to get pregnant with his baby, or she actually doesn't know who he is. Not that I'm implying she sleeps around or anything, but you know – she hasn't got a regular boyfriend.'

'OK, if you really want to know.' Polly lowers her voice and looks around her again, as if she's worried the neighbours might be peering through her windows and listening. 'The truth is, she got herself inseminated.'

'Well, obviously ...'

'No! I mean *artificially*. You know – without having,' she drops her voice to a whisper, 'actual sex.'

'Now I know you're joking. You're not trying to kid me that she's a virgin?'

'Of course not, but ...'

'Daddy's a virgin, isn't he, Mummy!' Oh-oh. Big mistake to think four year olds' ears stop working when they're sitting quietly drawing pictures of stick men and suns with legs on.

'Yes, dear. A Virgo,' says Polly without missing a beat. She's too into this story to stop now. She leans closer to me and goes on earnestly, 'Jo says she realised she was never going to meet the Perfect Man.'

'There's a surprise,' I say sarcastically. 'Most of us realised round about the age of fifteen that he doesn't exist.'

'Well, you know – *The One*. She says she's spent her entire life searching for the right person.'

'You'll be telling me next she still believes in Father Christmas.'

'I do!' squeals a little voice. Gracie jumps down from her chair and runs straight at me, bounding onto my lap. 'I do believe in Father Christmas, Sophie! He brought me my bike! Didn't he, Mummy?'

'Yes, dear,' she says again, still leaning confidingly towards me. 'SO – she finally realised she was never going to meet The One before her clock stopped ticking.'

'Clock? What clock?' I'm confused now, and Gracie's digging her elbows in my stomach, wriggling, singing something right in my ear about wheels on buses. How do mothers of small children ever manage to have a sensible conversation?

'Her *body* clock!' Polly sighs with exasperation. 'Keep up, Sophe!'

'Yeah, keep up, Sophe!' mimics Gracie, giggling. She jumps off my lap again and almost trips over Ethan.

'Watch out, you'll knock his scaffold thing over,' I warn her.

'It's a baby gym!' Polly and Gracie both stare at me in utter astonishment. How could anyone be so ignorant? Doesn't everyone know that?

'Of course – baby gym. I forgot what it was called,' I apologise lamely. 'So anyway – she went and got herself artificially *done* because her clock was ticking? Is that what you're saying?'

'Absolutely. And good for her – I mean, she could afford to pay for it, so why not? What's wrong with that?'

'Nothing! Don't look at me like that – I'm not arguing!'

'She just wants what every other woman wants, at the end of the day – well, most women, anyway,' she adds quickly, giving me a look that acknowledges my absolute peculiarity. 'And this was the only way she could see herself getting it.'

'She's only thirty-three. Not fifty. She still had time to meet someone she might have considered suitable, before she hit the menopause, surely.'

'She wasn't prepared to compromise, Sophe. She didn't want to wait, getting gradually older and more desperate, and end up having a baby with someone who might not have been a very good father, who might have ended up leaving her on her own.'

I stare at her. 'But she's on her own anyway. The father didn't even get as far as having sex with her before he left her! He didn't even know her! How much more of a crap father could he be – just donating his half of the baby's genes and clearing off without even knowing who the mother is!'

'She doesn't consider the sperm donor to be the baby's father,' says Polly rather primly. 'She's still hoping, eventually, to meet Mr Right – and he'll adopt the baby and …'

'And they'll live happily ever after,' I say, with a shrug of disgust. 'Sorry, Polly. I don't mean to be nasty about this, but what *is* she playing at? Aren't you worried about her?'

Polly seems to consider this for a minute. Ethan starts to grizzle and she bends down to pick him up, pressing her lips against his head as she does so. He stops crying and rewards her with a huge gummy grin.

'To tell you the truth, Sophie, I'm more worried about you.'

'Me?' I laugh in surprise. 'Why the hell would you be worried about me? I'm the *last* person you need to worry about.' She doesn't reply, or even look at me; she's jiggling the baby on her lap and he's gurgling with laughter at her. '*I'm* not having some stranger's baby and bringing it up by myself!' I go on, and then, because she's still not answering, 'and I'm not wearing myself out looking after two kids, without any help from my husband, either!'

'You only ever talk about the negatives,' she replies, finally. 'Can't you see that what Jo's doing is making her happy? And what *I'm* doing is making me happy?'

'If you say so.' I shake my head, unconvinced.

She laughs, suddenly.

'You and Charlie should get married. No – don't look at me like that! I mean it – you're so obviously right for each other. You've been seeing each other for – how long? Two years? And you don't even have arguments!'

'That's because we don't live together. We give each other space. We respect each other. We enjoy each other's company without trying to own each other.'

'You love him.'

I blink at her in surprise. 'We don't bother with all that stuff.'

'Why not? What are you frightened of?'

Frightened? Me?

'Nothing. I just don't want to spoil it. We *do* get on well, and neither of us sees any need to change the way it is. Make it more demanding. Difficult.'

'So you're *not* in love with him, then?' She looks at me sadly, like I've disappointed her.

'Apparently not,' I say lightly, wanting to change the subject. 'Did I tell you about this client of mine – Barbara? She's about sixty and she's just married this guy who does everything for her – cooking, cleaning, everything! But she still hankers after her ex, who shagged her like a steam train every night and left her for a veterinary nurse in a caravan.'

'No!' Polly squeals with laughter. 'Put the kettle on, Sophe, then you can tell me the whole story. You do get some mad clients, don't you!'

All of them, in my opinion. Every last one of them.

The first Saturday in July

It's Hilary's wedding day and, although I say it myself, I've made her look absolutely incredible. OK, she's beautiful anyway – but I'm really chuffed with her hair, thank God, after all those endless changes of style – and her make-up. And more importantly, she's chuffed too, and she seems happy, and surprisingly calm.

Which is more than can be said for the bridesmaids.

Bridesmaids! Most of them are lovely. Look, I've been a bridesmaid three times myself – to both of my sisters, and to Polly – and I enjoyed every minute of it. And I like to think I was of at least some use, somewhere along the line, to each of the brides, even if it was only helping them to do their dresses up and chatting to them to stop them getting panicky.

But every now and then I come across a bridesmaid who's such a Prima Donna, you'd think it was her own wedding or in fact you'd think it was her own *royal* wedding – and today I've got two of them, competing for the title of Bridesmaid-Pain-In-The-Arse of the Year. To say nothing of the Mother of the Bride, who hasn't stopped squealing since I arrived at her house this morning and is so seriously getting on my tits now, I think I might actually have to strangle her.

Chief Bridesmaid is the bride's best friend, and if she was my best friend I'd probably kill myself. I mean, surely Hilary must have a better friend than this somewhere, anywhere – someone who could at least make the effort to smile occasionally, instead of walking around with a face more suited to a funeral than a wedding?

'How's that?' I ask her now, putting the finishing touches to her hairstyle, which again, although I say it myself, looks beautiful.

'All right, I suppose,' she says sulkily.

What is it with her? Is there somewhere else she'd rather be?

'Do you want more spray? Another clip just here?'

'No. It's OK.' She gets up from the chair, without thanking me, and calls out to the other bridesmaid, the groom's sister, a loud, bossy girl with difficult hair, 'Your turn, Melissa,' before throwing herself down in an armchair, sighing with apparent boredom.

'Yes, yes, come along Melissa!' shrieks Mum of the Bride, fluttering her hands at her. 'Come along, come along, don't keep Sophie waiting. She's still got *my* hair to do, don't forget!'

As if anyone possibly could.

'How about you go and make us all a nice cup of tea, Mum,' says Hilary with admirable coolness, 'while you're waiting.'

'Yes – tea all round! Great idea!' Melissa booms. 'OK, Sophie, do your worst! I'd like mine the same as Hilary's. But no hair products, please. I've got *Allergies*.'

She makes this sound like a rare and noble condition, on a par with a war wound, that she's understandably proud of. Great. So I've got a head of mid-length crinkly hair with a half grown-out fringe, that I've somehow got to coax into an approximation of the bridal hairstyle, without using any products. Last time I checked, I was a hairdresser, not a magician, not a miracle worker.

'OK to use hair straighteners?'

'Oh, God, no! Please! I don't want my hair *ruined*!'

Sometimes it's just *so hard* to think of a thing to say.

I'm halfway through my struggle with Melissa's hair when she begins to open up to me. Well, to everyone in the room, really, since her voice is so loud, but she appears to be addressing me in the mirror.

'I nearly got married myself last year, you know. Had the date booked, the caterers, everything. Dress is still hanging in the wardrobe. Waste of bloody money.'

'What happened?' I ask with my mouth full of pins.

'Bastard dumped me. Two months before the wedding. Said he'd got cold feet. Cold feet, my arse!'

I ignore the unpleasant anatomical picture this conjures up, and make sympathetic noises. I'm good at sympathetic noises.

'Thing is,' she goes on, attempting to drop her voice to a discreet bellow, 'The bastard wants to go out with me again now. Says he misses me. *On your bike, sunshine*, I told him. But you know, I keep wondering. Maybe it'd be better than nothing. For the sex, you know. He's no good for anything else. Well, none of them are, are they?'

'Um. No, I suppose – sorry, could you keep your head still?'

'So what do you think?'

'Pardon?' Think? Me?

'Do you think I should? Have him back?'

'Oh. Um, well, I don't know. It sounds as if he treated you badly.'

'See! You're right, of course. I'll stick to my guns. Tell him to sod off. Thanks for the advice.'

'You're welcome,' I say weakly. 'What do you think of the hair?'

'Yeah – that's fine. Cheers.' She stomps off to find Mum of the Bride, leaving me with a headache and the feeling that I should definitely, definitely, have become an agony aunt. *Why* do people always think I can answer their problems? It must be my face. I need to try looking less

42

interested. Perhaps I could look bored out of my skull, like Chief Bridesmaid.

'Are you OK?' I find myself asking her now, as she's sitting with her head between her knees, risking complete ruination of her hairstyle, and her face looks as white as a sheet.

'She's just feeling a bit faint!' squeals Mother of the Bride enthusiastically. 'It's all the excitement! It's all got too much for her!'

'I can't help myself,' mutters Chief Bridesmaid in the same bored monotone. 'I always get like this at Important Events. I'm Highly Strung.' Highly strung? If she was strung much lower she'd be underground. 'My doctor thinks I should take sedatives. But I don't want to be turned into a zombie. Especially at times like today, when I'm needed so desperately. What do you think, Sophie?'

I close my eyes for a minute. What am I – a medical advisor now, as well as an agony aunt? Next thing you know, I'll be expected to check everybody's blood pressure while I'm doing their hair.

'I think you'll be just fine,' I tell her briskly, 'if you get up and go outside for some fresh air. And concentrate on looking after the bride. And,' I look around the room and decide to go for it, 'if everyone keeps nice and quiet.'

'Well done, Sophie,' says Hilary, touching my arm and smiling at me. 'I couldn't have put it better myself.'

'And were they all OK in the end?' Charlie asks me, pouring out more wine.

I can laugh about it now. I can always laugh about it all, with Charlie. He always makes me feel better, makes me realise that however stressful the day might have been, it's all turned out OK again, as usual, and as long as I've ended up with a happy bride and no major hair or make-up disasters, I've actually done well.

'Yes, they were better than OK, to be honest. Hilary looked amazing, Daniel wasn't drunk, and even the bridesmaids seemed to rally round in the end. The bride's mum still squealed a bit but I suppose I can forgive her for that.'

'Mums do get excited at their daughters' weddings,' he says, smiling.

'And how would you know that?' I laugh. 'How many mothers of brides have you known?'

I'm getting just a little bit drunk. It's a Saturday evening again and I should, by rights, be out with my girlfriends, hitting the clubs, having a laugh, dancing, enjoying ourselves, like we always do. *Did.* But one by one, they've cried off with different pathetic excuses. Their boyfriend or husband wants to take them out for a romantic meal to celebrate their engagement or anniversary or the dog's birthday or whatever. They're feeling sick because they're pregnant. They're feeling sick because they're not pregnant. Their baby's feeling sick. Their toddler's swallowed something. The list of domestic dramas is incredible. Sometimes I wonder if they just don't *want* to come out, but I can't quite bring myself to believe that. How ridiculous would that be? Anyway, tonight it's finally happened. I've been let down by all of them: every last one. Up till now we've always managed to get a quorum of … well, at least two, often three or even four … of the original group of about ten Saturday-night-clubbers. This is the first time I've been left, like Billy No Mates, sitting at home on my own.

Fortunately, Charlie never minds being used as an afterthought. We have this agreement, you see: when either of us is on our own and feeling fed up, or let down, or just plain suicidal, we can ring each other, no questions asked, no excuses needed, and we'll end up together with a bottle of wine and a takeaway.

'You're right, I don't know any mothers of brides, or even any brides,' he admits, 'but from what you've always said, it's a big day for the mum, I guess.'

'Yeah. Tell me about it. My own mum was totally *ecstatic* when Debra married James. Must have been a bit of a coup – daughter marrying doctor from rich family.'

'Ouch. I'm sure she was just happy to see her daughter being happy.'

'Yeah. I guess.' I yawn. 'Oh, that reminds me, Debra phoned again earlier. She keeps nagging me about going home to see Mum and Dad.'

'Well, it does seem ages since you went.'

'Don't you start! It wasn't that long; I've been busy. I must remember to give Mum a ring, though. Debs said she hasn't been very well. One of those viruses that's going around, I suppose.'

'Give her a ring now, then, Sophe. Go on – I'll clear up in the kitchen.'

'That's OK. I'll phone her tomorrow. I'm a bit tired.' I nudge him suggestively. 'Could do with an early night.'

'Well, now you're talking.' He kisses me, slowly, gently, just the way he knows I like. 'I can't stay over, though, Sophe.'

'What?' No Sunday morning lie-in together? 'Why not?'

'I told you already: I need to make an early start – I'm going to visit *my* mum.'

'Oh yes. Watch out for the cot blanket or whatever it is.'

'Shawl.' He grins at me. 'She's probably got it parcelled up all ready for me. She's nothing if not persistent. And my cousin's just had a baby girl, so she'll be full of it, telling me all the gory details about the birth, probably. '

'God. Don't start getting ideas.'

He laughs and starts to kiss me again. Thoughts of baby shawls and gory birth details recede swiftly from my mind and I pull him to his feet.

'Come on. Bed.'

But we haven't even reached the bedroom door when my phone starts to ring.

'Leave it. Voicemail,' Charlie says. 'Bound to be a client.'

I stop, just briefly, to listen to Voicemail clicking in. It's not a client. It's my other sister, Millie, and she sounds strained. Or cross. Or something.

'Sophe – it's me, Millie. Look, Mum's not at all well. I know you're busy, but can't you get away just for one day, to come and see her? She'd really appreciate it. She says she hasn't heard from you for a while, and she doesn't like to ring you because you're so busy. Honestly, Sophe – I … well … for God's sake. Talk to you soon. I hope.'

There's another click and we're left, holding onto each other, at the edge of the bed, listening to the suddenly-weird silence ringing with the echo of her voice.

'Call your mum,' says Charlie again. 'Or call your sister back. She sounds upset.'

'Tomorrow. I will, tomorrow. She's OK. She just gets arsey because of her bastard husband. I'll send Mum some flowers to cheer her up. Now then, where were we?'

'Round about *here* somewhere,' he says softly, pushing me down on the bed.

Phone calls. Flowers. Tomorrow. I must remember, I think. And then I forget about thinking, completely.

Monday – a week later

Mondays are often quiet. I have weddings on pretty much every day of the week now, but very rarely Mondays. It's just not a day that anybody likes, and who can blame them? So I try to fill it with last-minute requests for hair trials. Most brides will take a morning or afternoon off work to have a hair trial, especially if they've left it to the last minute and I haven't got any evening appointments left.

But today I've got Emma. Yes, my friend Emma – even though she's not getting married for another nine months – has booked herself in for a hair trial and she's almost delirious with excitement.

'I'm *so* glad you could fit me in, Sophe,' she babbles as she plonks herself in the chair. 'I've got this week off, you see – we both have – Stefan and I.' She adds this with a little shy smile, like I'm supposed to be surprised and touched to hear that she's spending her week off with the guy she's living with. 'So we're trying to sort out as much as possible, for the wedding, while we've got the chance.'

'Of course,' I say, smoothly. 'It's better to start early, isn't it.'

I'm not being facetious, here. I've had brides, in the past, who've left everything to the last minute and then come to me in tears asking what they can do because they can't get a DJ or a photographer or the right shoes for the bridesmaids, or whatever – like I'm supposed to be a wedding organiser.

'What do you think, Sophie?' she asks, grabbing a handful of her thick, dark hair and holding it high on her head. 'Shall I have it up? Shall I have it curly? Shall I wear a veil? What about a tiara?'

'Whoa! One thing at a time,' I say, laughing. I'm going to enjoy doing Emma's hair. She might have turned into a Bridezilla overnight, but I've known her for years – she's zany and fun and at least she's not likely to get flaky on me and start pestering me about whether she's doing the right thing, whether all men are bastards and whether she's going to regret getting married. 'I'll show you some pictures of my most popular styles. You can have as many trials as you like, so don't panic if we don't make a decision today. OK?'

'OK,' she agrees, with a grin. 'I'm looking forward to this, Sophe.'

'Me too.'

'Sophe?'

'Mm?' I'm flicking through my portfolio of photographs, looking for the styles I think will suit her best. I stop and look round. 'What?'

'You do think I'm doing the right thing, don't you?'

What?

'I'm joking!' she adds quickly, bursting out laughing at the expression on my face. 'I *know* I am. I can't wait to marry Stefan. I've never been more sure of anything in my life.'

Well, thank God for that. Let's just hope it stays that way!

She's so thrilled with the first style I try on her, she doesn't want to try any more, and she doesn't want it taken out.

'I'm going to show Stefan! I don't care if it's bad luck!' she squeals, turning this way and that to see her hair from every angle.

'Well, I'm sure it's not bad luck, but don't forget, you might change your mind and want to try something different.'

'No! I won't! This is *it*, Sophie – I love it, I just *love* it!' She gives me a soppy smile before going on, in a rush, 'You know, when you're sure about something, there's no point in keeping on looking, is there? Just like I was sure about Stefan.'

Pass me the sick bucket.

'Of course – I know what you mean,' I lie. 'It's so nice to see you so happy, Em.' That part isn't a lie. She's totally glowing. I *am* pleased for her.

'Thanks, Sophie.' She looks at me slightly pityingly. 'I just wish *you'd* meet someone special, someone you could settle down with, before …'

She stops herself, but it's hovering in the air between us, unspoken: *before it's too late.*

I laugh. 'I'm happy as I am. Honestly.'

She ignores this. 'If Charlie's not The One, then you need to move on,' she says quite severely. 'Really. I hate to see you – well, wasting your time. Especially now *I'm* not going to be around so much, and Jo's going to be off the scene.'

'Why? Where are you going?'

'I'm *engaged* now, Sophie!' she says, reprovingly. 'And Jo's pregnant! We've both got new lives to look forward to!' She makes it sound like they're both emigrating. 'We won't be able to keep going out *clubbing* and such like.'

'Why not?' I don't get it. I really don't. What happens to people like Emma when they get a ring on their finger? Why do they seem to think it means they've got to suddenly start acting like they're ten years older? 'You'll be going to garden centres next,' I say, a bit sulkily.

'Yes. That's what we're doing tomorrow, actually. We're thinking *azaleas* for the back garden, and a few bedding plants in the front. What do you think about pansies?'

'I don't know any, personally.'

'Sophie, you are funny! Look, I must get going. I'm meeting Jo later; she wants me to go to Mothercare with her, to look at prams. Do you want to come with us, if you're not busy?'

I'd rather fry my own organs in olive oil.

'Sorry. Can't. Got another client in half an hour. Give Jo my love, though.' I hesitate, and then add, 'Has she told you anything about the father?'

She gives me an appraising look.

'You know? She's told *you*?'

'No. Polly told me. I was pretty shocked.'

'Well, I can understand it, though. I mean – if I hadn't been lucky enough to meet the love of my life, my future husband, the future father of my children …'

'Who?'

'Stefan, you daft moo – keep up! If I hadn't met him, I might be getting worried myself by now.'

'What about?'

'My *body clock*, of course!'

'Oh yes – tick, tick.' I laugh. 'I forgot.'

'I don't know why you find it so funny,' she says, slightly aggrieved. 'One day, you'll wake up and realise you've missed the boat. You won't stay fertile for ever, you know.'

'Thank God for that,' I say, with feeling.

'All I'm saying, Sophie,' she adds more gently, 'is think about it.'

'I have, thanks. I know you think I'm strange. Perhaps everybody does!' I shrug. 'But I don't want to get married. I don't want babies. I really don't, and I'm not going to change my mind. And fortunately, Charlie feels the same.'

She's shaking her head at me as she waves goodbye.

Charlie's invited me round to his place tonight. He's cooked for me, too: three courses – salmon, steak and a lemon tart from Sainsbury's. Well, he cooked the steak himself.

'This is lovely,' I tell him. 'What a nice surprise on a Monday evening.'

'Well, I thought I should do something special. It *is* our anniversary.'

'Is it?' I look at him blankly. 'Anniversary of what?'

'Two years we've been ...' he hesitates. We've been what? What do we call it? Going out? Seeing each other? Being each other's fuck-buddies? 'Together,' he finishes quietly, even though we're not – strictly speaking – even together, are we.

'Is it really?' I don't mean to sound so astonished. I did actually realise we'd been ... seeing each other ... for about two years, but I'm astonished that Charlie knows the actual date. I'm astonished that he thinks it's significant. I'm astonished – shit, I'm *very* astonished – that he's looking so serious about it, all of a sudden.

'Happy anniversary,' he says, softly, raising his glass to me.

I giggle. 'Yeah – happy anniversary.' It sounds silly. Like we're two kids, playing at being grown-ups.

'I've bought you a present,' he goes on, still looking serious and still talking in the same softly-softly voice.

'Shit. I mean – sorry, Charlie, but you shouldn't have done that.' I feel vaguely alarmed now, and vaguely guilty. 'I didn't buy you anything. I didn't realise.'

'That's OK. I didn't expect you to. I just wanted,' he shrugs awkwardly as he passes the little package across the table, 'well, I just wanted to let you know how I feel about you.'

This Is Weird.

I sit, looking at the package lying on the table between us, and I feel hot and trembly with nerves. I don't like this new serious, soft-voiced Charlie. I don't like the way he's looking at me, I don't like him buying anniversary presents, and I really, *really* don't like him telling me how he feels about me. Not that he has, yet. I think he's waiting for me to open the present first.

I pick it up, turn it over, tentatively. Sod it, what's to worry about? He's being nice. I should just smile and be grateful.

I look at him, smiling, grateful, and rip off the wrapping paper. Inside is a box, and inside the box is a bracelet. One of those new ones, with charms on it. It's chunky, and lovely, and it must have cost the earth.

'Oh!' I get up and go round the table to him, put my arms round him, kiss him. 'Charlie, it's *gorgeous*! I really wanted one of these! Thank you so, so much!'

'You're welcome. Here – let me put it on for you.' He holds my arm out, studies the bracelet on my wrist. 'It looks lovely,' he pronounces.

'You really shouldn't have! I mean, it's not like it's my birthday.'

'No.' He pulls me onto his knee. 'But I wanted to show you that I think our anniversary's special, too.'

'Well, that's a really nice thought. I really appreciate …'

'I want it *always* to be special, Sophe.' He looks at me pointedly. 'To both of us.'

'Always?' I repeat it as though it's a foreign word I don't understand. 'We don't talk about *always*, Charlie. We said we never would.'

'I know. But I'm starting to find it more difficult.' There's a silence between us – a silence that makes me suddenly aware of little things around me. The candles flickering on the table. The piece of lemon tart I didn't quite finish, turning sticky on the plate. The hum of traffic on the road outside. The big clock ticking on the wall – tick, tock, tick, tock, like somebody's body clock.

Somebody's, but not mine. 'I think I'm changing my mind, Sophie,' he goes on, touching my cheek very gently with his fingertips. 'I think I'm beginning to want more.'

I need to answer him. I know I do – I can't just sit here, well, *perch* here really, on his knee, like a life-size ventriloquist's dummy, my heart racing with panic, wearing his bracelet, listening to him wanting more, and not say anything.

'More what?' I squeak, and I flinch at the sound of my voice. It's the voice of someone who's got no idea what the fuck to say. I want to say *What – more lemon tart? More wine?'* and make him laugh – get back to our normal, easy, bantering way and forget he ever looked at me like this, gave me an anniversary present and started talking about always. Forget it before it's too late, and the easy banter's gone for ever.

'Don't look so frightened!' he says gently. 'Don't you … well, don't you feel at *all* ready to even consider it, Sophe? Moving things on a bit? It's been two years, after all, and – well, you must know how I feel about you.'

Stop it, stop it, stop it! I push his arms away and get, unsteadily, to my feet, turning away from him.

'We always said we wouldn't!' I try to remind him, but I'm aware that I sound slightly hysterical. 'We said we'd never do this! We *agreed*! You always agreed with me, Charlie! We were never going to make this *serious*.'

'I know. But I've realised, just over the last few weeks I suppose – I've just suddenly realised that I've been fooling myself. It *is* serious. I'm serious about you, Sophie. I love you, and I want more from this relationship.'

I close my eyes. I want to run away and cry. I'm losing him. My best friend, the only guy I've ever met who saw things exactly the way I did. How could he suddenly have changed his mind? It's not fair. I don't want to lose him.

'You don't feel the same way, do you,' he says quietly, stonily. He rubs his hand across his face.

'Forget it!' I turn to him quickly, try to take hold of his arm, but he shakes me off, looking at the floor. 'Let's just forget you said it! OK? It doesn't matter, we'll just carry on ...'

'But it *does* matter. I can't ... I can't carry on like this, now – that's what I'm trying to tell you. I can't, now I've realised how much you mean to me. I can't just pretend it's OK, pretend I'm happy being – what? Your friend? Your date? The guy you have sex with when you've got no mates to go out with? If you don't feel the same, if you're *never* going to want a serious relationship with me, I don't think I can go on like this. It's ...'. He stops, looks at me, and I can see it in his eyes. How have I not seen it before? What's the matter with me? Have I really been so selfish, so blind, so determined that he was going to agree with me about everything, that I've never noticed it before? 'It's *hurting* me,' he says flatly.

'I'm sorry.' I feel like crying now. I can't bear this. 'I don't want to hurt you.'

'I know you don't. It's not your fault.'

'I'd ... better go, I suppose.' He doesn't answer. I pick up my bag. It'll be best if I do – go home, leave it till tomorrow, maybe even leave it a couple of days, for him to get himself together. Then we can try – I'm sure we can try to pretend it hasn't happened. He'll be fine. We can still have sex. 'Do you want the bracelet back?' I ask sadly.

'Don't be stupid. It was a present.'

'I'll see you tomorrow, then? Or ...?'

He rounds on me suddenly, looking – angry? I take a step back. I've never seen Charlie angry – not with me, anyway. What have I said?

'You're not hearing me, Sophie. I'm telling you, I can't go on with this – this *pretend* relationship. I can't pretend any more! I want – fuck it, all I want is what everybody on the planet wants – everybody except you, it seems! *Everybody* except you!'

I take another step away from him. I can feel my lower lip wobbling. I don't want to cry – not now, not yet, not till I get home and get the duvet over my head.

'I'm sorry,' he says at once, looking distraught. 'I didn't mean to shout. I'm so sorry, Sophe. But if you won't even *consider* a serious relationship, then it's got to be over. That's it.'

And that, I tell myself as I walk back round the corner to my own flat, tears beginning to burn my eyes, shock beginning to make me tremble, is that.

Now I've got nobody.

Tuesday

'You've still got me.' Polly, alarmed by my drunken and tearful phone call late last night, has left the children with a neighbour and turned up on my doorstep at half past eight this morning. I'm still in my dressing gown, last night's make-up all over my face, and I've got to get my arse in gear: I've got a client at half past nine. 'Can't you cancel?' she adds, looking me up and down critically. 'Say you're ill?'

'No! It's a new client. I can't afford to mess them around like that. Especially now – now my career is the only thing I've got left,' I add dramatically.

She opens her mouth and then closes it again, apparently deciding it's not a good idea to start arguing with me right now about what I have, or haven't, got left in my life. I know I'm being ridiculous. For a start, she's right – I've still got my friends, even if none of them do want to come out clubbing with me any more. She's still turned up in my hour of need, hasn't she. And I also know I'm being ridiculous because, let's face it, I was never in love with Charlie, I never wanted a relationship with him, so what am I crying about? Not having sex – probably not in the foreseeable future, and possibly not ever again, as all the men under eighty who aren't gay seem to be married now? Has it really come down to this – I'm crying and throwing tantrums because I might not have a sex life any more? From what I hear, that pretty much seems to happen to everyone who gets married and has kids, anyway, so it's not like I'm alone.

No, I know what I'm really upset about. It's losing the last person I could talk to about my lifestyle, without being ridiculed or told my body clock's going to start ticking as soon as my back's turned. Charlie and I were supposed to be soul mates. We were supposed to think the same way, understand each other, agree about everything. Well, about staying single and not having kids, anyway. We had endless conversations about it – how we enjoyed our freedom, how we never wanted to settle down and commit ourselves to anyone. Or did we? I'm beginning to wonder if I imagined it. Was it just me having those conversations, while all the time Charlie was listening and wishing I'd just shut up and get pregnant?

'How could he have changed his mind?' I demand, as Polly makes me another strong cup of coffee. 'Just like that, so suddenly? How can he have gone from agreeing with me, to deciding he's in love with me and can't be my friend any more unless I love him back? It's not fair! He can't just *do* that!'

'It must have been a gradual thing,' says Polly, sitting down opposite me and taking hold of my hands. 'And he's probably been trying to pluck up the courage to tell you, for a while. It would have been difficult for him, knowing how strongly you felt about staying single.'

'Difficult? Never mind it being difficult for *him* – how does he think *I* feel?' I mutter into my coffee cup.

'Perhaps you should feel flattered. He's a lovely guy, and he's taken a huge gamble, telling you he loves you.'

'Well, he shouldn't have! I didn't ask him to! I don't feel flattered at all! I feel let down! Betrayed! Cheated!'

She shakes her head. She doesn't know what to say. She probably thinks most girls would sell their souls to be in my position, and here I am, hungover and blubbing like a baby.

'It's all his mother's fault,' I tell her, morosely. 'The bitch.'

'Why? What's she done?'

'She's been putting pressure on him, trying to force crocheted shawls on him and offering to let us sleep together in her spare bedroom. I *knew* it was getting to him. He went to see her last week, and she spent about an hour telling him about his cousin's new baby. That's what's done it. The bitch!'

'Sophie, I don't think any of that would have affected him in the slightest, if he wasn't already feeling the way he does. Come on, love – if you're really sure you're going to keep your appointments today ...'

'I know. I'll have to get dressed.' I make no effort to move. I wonder if I can see my clients in my dressing gown. Why should they care?

'Have a shower. Wash your hair.' My hair? I'd forgotten about my hair. I feel it, nervously, wondering if I'm going to have time for a full blow-dry and straightening session. It's all right for all these brides with their thick, shiny, heavy hair. As a hairdresser, my crazy mop's a source of embarrassment to me at the best of times. I normally spend the first hour of every morning making myself look a little less like someone who you couldn't trust even to put in a hairclip. 'I'll be making you some toast, and some more coffee,' Polly goes on, giving me a hug as I lumber unwillingly to my feet. 'Come on, Sophe. You'll get through this. You're the strong one, remember? You're the one who holds all the rest of us together! You always cope.'

Yeah. Good old Sophie. The one with all the answers, the one who always listens to everyone else's problems – when the reality is that I don't have a clue. I've somehow become the local relationship guru, when I've never had a decent relationship myself and as soon as I get offered one, I run away crying. What a sad, pathetic cow I really am.

'My fiancé's parents are *so* demanding,' my new client, Eleanor, shouts at me as I clip sections of her hair up on top of her head. Her voice is shrill and her chatter

58

relentless. I feel worn out with listening to her and trying to keep the polite, interested expression pasted onto my face. 'His mother drives me *mad.* She's trying to take over the whole wedding. She wants everything done *her* way, and Gavin's just useless – I can't get him to stand up to her. How do I get through to her, Sophie? How do I get her to see that it's *my* wedding – well, mine and Gavin's, of course – not hers, and she should just, well, not to put too fine a point on it, mind her own fucking business?'

I nod, trying to look concerned.

'Any advice?' she yells, a little more shrilly, if that were possible. I'd forgotten there was a question in there somewhere.

'Well. Um, perhaps, er …' I stumble awkwardly, trying to remember what she's asked me. Advice? Bloody advice, from me, the dedicated spinster, the born-again virgin, the only person left in the universe who's refused to pair up and breed? What a joke. What a bloody joke. 'No,' I say abruptly, dropping the rest of the pins on the shelf with a clutter. 'No! I haven't got any advice. I've run out of it.'

'Run out?' She stares at me, perplexed, as well she might do. A hairdresser with no advice to offer? What's the use of that?

'I haven't got any advice left. I've given it all away, already. I'm not a good person to ask for advice, not at all. Sorry.'

'That's OK,' she says, faintly. At least she's dropped her voice by a few hundred decibels. She's still staring back at me in the mirror and I realise I'm holding on to the clump of her hair that I've just clipped up. She can't move her head without suffering severe hair loss.

'Sorry!' I say again, letting go of the clump and trying to pull myself together.

'Are you all right?' she asks somewhat anxiously. 'You don't look well, to tell the truth.'

Oh God. All I need now is to start losing my clients because I'm not concentrating, not giving out advice, pulling out clumps of their hair and looking slightly unhinged.

'I'm fine, thank you,' I say, trying to sound brisk and business-like. 'I just ... well, I'm just ...'

What? What feeble excuse am I supposed to give? I'm just suffering a mega hangover because I drank myself to sleep after my boyfriend told me he loved me? I'm just feeling sorry for myself because nobody understands me and I've got to go clubbing on my own?

Eleanor narrows her eyes at me. 'It's boyfriend trouble, isn't it, Sophie? Yes, I thought as much!' she goes on immediately as I drop my eyes in embarrassment. 'Poor love,' she croons. 'Tell me all about it. Has he dumped you? Is he a *complete* bastard?' As opposed to what – just a partial one? Jesus, this woman is a total stranger to me! What is it with women and other people's relationship problems? Eleanor's eyes are alight with excitement as she leans encouragingly towards me, eager to hear some nice juicy gossip about someone's rotten love-life that will make her own seem idyllic by comparison. 'What did he do?' she repeats.

'Nothing,' I admit miserably. 'Really – nothing. He just wants us to be in a committed relationship.'

'And ...?'

She raises her eyebrows, beckons me on. *And the problem is ...?*

'And I don't.'

'You don't?' She frowns, uncomprehending. 'So – what? He *is* a complete bastard?'

'No. He's not, at all.'

'He drinks too much? Flirts with other women? Snores? Farts in bed?' I'm shaking my head, feeling like crying again. This is awful. I wish she'd shut up and just let me finish her hair. 'Is he ... well, you know,' she touches my hand, looking at me sympathetically like I've recently been orphaned or buried my favourite cat, 'Is he *not very good at it*?'

'No. I mean yes, he's actually very ...' Shit! What am I *doing*? Am I really about to start discussing my sex life with a woman I've only just started styling? Who hasn't even paid me yet or made a definite booking for the wedding?

'So what is it then, love?' she purrs. 'No job? No money? He's mean? Lazy? Leaves his dirty underwear on the floor?'

'No.' I give myself a shake, pick up the hairspray and cover her eyes with my hand while I spray her. More than she needs, really, but it's giving me a few minutes to pull myself together. 'No, he's none of those things,' I tell her, firmly. Let's put an end to this right now and get on with booking her next appointment. 'He's actually lovely. He's a lovely, gentle, intelligent, kind, generous man and he was my best friend, and he understood me, and ...' Bugger, bugger, shit. The hairspray's gone in my eyes.

'Don't cry,' she says calmly, standing up and patting me on the shoulder. 'I'm sure he'll ask you again. Why don't you just go and see him tonight? Tell him you've changed your mind?'

I try to smile gratefully. Is this really me? Me, being given advice by a client? What's going on?

'OK,' I say hoarsely, wiping my eyes. Bloody hairspray. 'Thanks.'

But the thing is, of course, that I won't. I won't, because I haven't changed my mind; I can't, I won't. *He* needs to change *his* mind – to stop all this stuff about getting serious – just stop it and go back to how we were!

One thing, though. Eleanor must have enjoyed feeling sorry for me. She's given me a really good tip. Perhaps I should discuss my problems with clients more often.

The evening is terrible, and endless. Polly phones to ask if I'm feeling any better, and I lie to her, say I'm fine, because I don't want her worrying when she's already having sleepless nights with the baby. Emma phones to tell me about the azaleas she and Stefan chose for the garden. Jo phones to tell me she's chosen the pram. I listen to them both, and make the right noises, and they don't ask me how I am, and I don't tell them about Charlie. How can I? They already think I'm an alien, a strange unrecognised species of woman who hasn't got a body clock. They'll have me committed if I tell them Charlie's finished with me because I've refused to be in love with him. And then to make matters worse, my sister Debra phones again.

'I sent Mum flowers,' I tell her quickly, before she can start criticising me. 'And a Get Well card. Is she better?'

'You should be asking her yourself.' She sounds odd, kind-of depressed. I suppose James is out late again.

'I know. I'll ring her tomorrow, definitely.'

'You said that last week.'

'Well, I've been … there's been a few things …' Shit, I'm not telling my *family* about this, that's for sure. 'I've been really busy,' I add desperately.

'Sophie, do you know what?' My sister's crying. She's actually crying! James must really be pissing her off. God, I don't think I can deal with this right now. I try to think of an excuse to hang up, but I can't. I'm sitting here, transfixed, gripping the phone, staring at my feet, listening to her cry.

'What?' I ask, feebly.

'You're *so selfish*. So *bloody* selfish!' she sobs.

What? Where's *this* coming from?

'Look, Debs – don't be like that. I know, I *know* I haven't been very good about keeping in touch, but …'

'Huh!' She makes an extreme noise, like a dragon snorting fire. 'That's the understatement of the year!' Then, very quietly, she adds, in a strangely calm, clear voice, like she's spelling something out to me in a foreign language: 'Mum's *very* ill, Sophie. She's in hospital. You understand? She's got to have an operation.'

Very ill ... hospital ... operation.

The words are echoing in my head, beating like a pulse. I'm trying to get a hold of them, make sense of them, but I can't.

'It's not just a cold, then? Just a virus?'

'No. Did I ever say it was?'

'It's ... serious?' My throat's gone dry now. My tongue feels too big for my mouth. I can't talk properly. 'Why didn't you *tell* me?' I whisper.

'Because, like always, Sophie, we've all been pussy-footing around you, trying to protect you, trying not to worry you, trying not to make you think you need to spare five minutes from your *precious bloody business*!' She's spitting the words at me down the phone. I gasp, recoil, feel the sudden relief of hot tears in my eyes. Then, just as suddenly, she's crying again herself. 'You're right!' she sobs. 'I should have told you it looked serious. But we've only just got the test results. We've only just found out she needs an operation. Oh, Sophie, I'm so frightened! We're all so frightened!'

'I'm coming home,' I hear myself squeaking, my own fear rising up and threatening to overwhelm me. 'I'm coming home right now, this minute.'

In fact it takes five minutes to pack a case and throw it into my car; another five minutes of sitting in the driving seat shuddering and shaking before I acknowledge to myself that I'm not fit to drive to the end of the road, never mind all the way to Devon. And about five seconds to make the phone call.

'I'll be with you straight away,' says Charlie. 'I'll drive you. Of course I will.'

This is my old bedroom. It's warm already today at only half past eight, the sunlight pouring through the gap in the curtains, and I'm lying on top of the bedclothes, staring at the furniture, which hasn't changed from my earliest memories. There's still a mark on the side of the wardrobe where I ripped down my poster of Wham when I went off them in favour of Jason Donovan. There's still a crack in the corner of the mirror where I threw my make-up across the dressing table when I was upset about being dumped by Ian Wilkins in Year Ten. I remember Mum rushing into my room when she heard the crash, seeing the damage and opening her mouth to shout at me, before turning to look at me, my face buried in my hands, sobbing with the agony of my first broken heart, and instead, taking me in her arms and rocking me like a baby.

Mum, in the hospital, having an operation. The fear, panic and guilt fill my chest again so that I have to sit up and take deep breaths. I should have been here. I should have listened to what my sisters were trying to tell me. I should have visited more often. I should have been a better daughter, more caring, more grateful, less selfish. What did my stupid hairdressing business matter? What did my friends in London matter? I should have been *here*.

There's a tap on the door, and it opens at once, before I have a chance to say 'Come in'. Charlie's standing there with a cup of tea in his hands. Ridiculously, I try to cover myself with the duvet, as if he hasn't seen me naked hundreds of times over the last couple of years.

'Forgot to bring any PJs,' I mutter, without meeting his eyes.

'Me too.' He's pulled on his jeans – just his jeans. As ridiculous as it is to cower beneath the duvet from someone I was having sex with a few days ago, I'm also trying to avert my eyes from his beautiful bare chest.

He sits down on the side of the bed. 'I met your dad in the kitchen. He asked me to bring you this,' he says, putting the mug of tea on the bedside table.

'Thanks.' I swallow hard. 'Thanks for everything, Charlie.'

'Don't be ridiculous.'

We sit in an awkward silence, like a couple of strangers thrown together by both witnessing something traumatic: a road accident, a fight, a murder. A horrible illness.

'If there's anything else I can do,' he goes on, 'if I can take you or your dad to the hospital, or do anything here ... shopping, whatever ...'. He spreads his hands, helplessly.

'No. You've done more than enough already. Honestly – you get back to London. You're already missing work this morning.'

'Sophie, it's fine. I told you, it doesn't matter. I've called them. It's no problem. If you need me, if I can do anything ...' He reaches out, touches my cheek, lightly, gently. The touch of a friend. 'What I said the other night ... look, it doesn't count right now. This is something different. You know that.'

I nod. We had this discussion last night, driving down here. Well, it wasn't exactly a discussion. It was more a case of Charlie listening patiently to my hysterical wails of fear and regret about Mum, interspersed occasionally by my abject bitter apologies for calling on him, of all people, to help me out in my time of need – when he'd only just told me he didn't want to see me again.

'This is different,' he kept telling me. 'Of course I'll always be here for you for anything like *this* – what do you think I am?'

66

'I don't know!' I wailed. 'I don't know what you are, any more. I thought you were my friend!'

'I am, Sophie. Of course I am.' He took his hand off the wheel briefly to pat my leg, as one would a poor little dog. 'Try to close your eyes. It's a long journey.'

Unbelievably, I must have gone to sleep for about an hour. When I woke, I offered to drive for a while but he wasn't having any of it.

'You must be tired,' I said.

'I'm fine. We'll stop at the next Services and get a coffee.'

It was three in the morning when we arrived at my parents' house. Dad had stayed awake waiting for us, dozing in the chair downstairs – which made me feel even guiltier, if anything could. Charlie put my bag down in the hall and went, tactfully, on the excuse of finding the bathroom while Dad and I hugged and cried together.

'Is Mum going to be all right?' I gulped, tasting cold fear in my mouth.

'We don't know yet, love. It depends what they find when they operate tomorrow. But the lump ... well, it's definitely cancer.'

He stumbled over the word, the word nobody ever wants to have to say, least of all in connection with someone they love; and hearing it made me nauseous with dread. Dad suddenly looked old and gaunt, and I felt as if the solid foundations of my world were crumbling beneath my feet. It was several minutes before I became aware again of Charlie, hovering behind us, coughing discreetly.

'I'll be going, then,' he said when I turned round.

'No! Of course you're not going anywhere! Dad, he's driven me all the way from London and – oh, God, I'm so sorry, Charlie – I haven't even introduced you.' And I haven't, even, ever brought you to Devon to meet my family. Not once during the two whole years we've been seeing each other. Or going out together. Or having whatever kind of weird relationship we seem to have been having together. Not once! I hung my head, and mumbled. 'Dad, this is Charlie, my ... um ...'

'I'm a friend of Sophie's,' Charlie took over at once. 'I'm very sorry to hear about your wife's illness, Mr Jennings.'

They reached out and shook hands, as if it was a pleasure, as if they were meeting at a conference or a formal dinner.

'You can't drive all the way back to London, boy,' Dad said firmly, making me blink at the use of the word *boy*. 'Charlie can have Debra's old room, Sophie,' he added, turning to me, 'unless ...?'

The meaning of the *unless*, my dad's questioningly raised eyebrows, hung tauntingly in the air, bringing me a renewed blast of pain. The first time we've visited my family together, and it's already all over between us.

'Debra's room would be good,' Charlie replied calmly. 'Thank you.'

I cook breakfast while Charlie showers. Bacon, eggs, tomatoes, mushrooms – the works. When it's on the plates, none of us seems to feel like eating it.

'I'll head back, then,' says Charlie. 'Will you keep in touch?' He gives me a direct, sympathetic look. 'Let me know?'

I duck my head as if he's chucked a missile at me. *Let me know*. The breath catches in my throat and I can't answer him.

'Thanks for your help, lad,' says Dad, shaking Charlie's hand again. 'Drive carefully.'

We wave to him from the door. Everything so polite. Everything so correct, so normal. So surreal.

We can't go to the hospital this morning. Mum's operation's scheduled for eleven o'clock. I'm tormented, tortured, by the thought that if this turns out to be really bad, as bad as the fear inside me is threatening, then I might have left it too late. This awful, terrifying thought is there the whole time – while I'm going through my diary calling my clients for the next few days to cancel their appointments, while I'm calling Polly to explain where I am, while I'm talking to Dad, catching up on all the stuff I've missed. Stuff I should have known about if I'd phoned home more regularly, come home more often, returned my sisters' calls. Behaved like a proper member of this family instead of an estranged and distant relative.

'You should have told me,' I rebuke Dad, gently. 'I know it's my own fault, but even so …'

'What are you talking about?' he retorts, staring at me. 'Nothing's *your* fault, Sophie! This thing has been so sudden. None of us had a clue. Your mum found the lump a couple of weeks ago. Even then, Dr Benson wasn't too worried, didn't think it was anything …'. He stops, swallows, holds onto the arm of his chair as if it'll stop him from falling. 'Nobody thought it was this serious,' he goes on quietly. 'Until we got the biopsy result.'

'You weren't keeping it from me? Trying to protect me?'

'Of course not!' he says, almost crossly. 'I asked Debra to phone you yesterday, as soon as we got the result. As soon as we knew your mum needed the operation. We weren't expecting the surgery to be this quick, but apparently they had a cancellation, and the consultant offered it to us. Your sisters have both been … well, obviously, they're worried. Distressed. I should have phoned you myself.'

'No. I should have picked up on what Debs was saying. She hinted to me last week that there was something wrong with Mum. I should have called. I'm so sorry, Dad. I've just been …'

I stop, shake my head. I can't say *so busy*, can I. How can I possibly, ever, have thought I was too busy with my life, my friends, my clients – OK, or with Charlie? – to pick up the phone and talk to my family. I'm *never* going to let that happen again. Never. If Mum can only come through this OK, I'll never, ever, make those excuses again.

Debra turns up at lunchtime.

'I couldn't sit at home, worrying,' she says, grabbing hold of me and immediately starting to cry. 'Thank God you've decided to come.'

Decided to come. It rankles slightly – the implied criticism, the suggestion that I might equally, having been told about Mum's operation, have decided to carry on with my life regardless. Then I remember that I deserve all the criticism she can throw at me.

'I just wish you'd told me what was wrong with Mum,' I say, to cover my own shame.

'Oh, like that would have made any difference!' she shoots back, immediately on the defensive.

'Yes, Debra, it would have done! If you'd said Mum had found a lump, rather than fobbing me off with euphemisms about her *not being very well...*'

'And that stopped you phoning her, did it? I thought it might be enough, Sophie, to tell you Mum wasn't well. Enough to make you concerned – make you want to find out more for yourself.' She's angry now. I know I deserve it, I know she's right to be angry with me. I should leave it alone, but ridiculously, I want a fight. The adrenaline is helping to keep the horrible fears at bay for a while.

'How can I be concerned, when you make it sound like little more than a headache? Like she had a sore throat, or just a *cold*? How am I supposed to know it's serious, when you're on my case all the time, phoning me up, whining to me about this or that ...'

'*Whining*?' she repeats in a screech. '*Whining*?'

'Yes – whining, all the time. Whining about James, mostly, even though you've got everything you ever wanted – big house, nice life, kids, dogs, three toilets – you're *still* whining because he works too hard, because he's never there when you want him. Like anyone could blame him, listening to you whining!'

I've gone too far, and I know it.

'You *cow*,' she says, slowly and deliberately. She's gone white, and she's trembling slightly. 'Why did you even bother coming home? Piss off back to London, go on. Piss off back to your stupid *hairdressing*.' She spits out the *hairdressing* as if it's something slightly disreputable that I'm getting up to. 'Anyone would think it was important,' she adds with a snort of derision.

'At least I work for a living. At least I'm not being *kept* by someone who doesn't even ...'

'Girls!' Dad's standing in the doorway, looking from one of us to the other, shaking his head. 'What on earth?'

The words are caught in my throat: *someone who doesn't even love you.* I close my eyes, shocked at myself, relieved I didn't say it. But when I open them again, I can see in my sister's eyes that she knows what I was going to say. She hates me.

'Sorry, Dad.' She goes to him, puts her arms around him, begins to cry again. 'I'm sorry. Sophie and I ...' She looks at me balefully over his shoulder. 'We're just a bit agitated.'

'Of course. I know.' He strokes her hair, kisses her forehead. I watch, feeling like an outsider, like the naughty child who's pinched her sister's arm and taken her toys away. 'We're all upset, we're all feeling tetchy. But we need to support each other, don't we?' He's looking at me.

I nod, shame-faced, and look away. 'We can't afford to fall out with each other right now. Mum would hate that, wouldn't she.'

'I know that,' says Debra piously. 'I'm sorry if I snapped at you, Sophie,' she adds in the self-righteous tone of the child who wants to be seen in a good light. Teacher's bloody pet. 'Let's agree to put all this aside for now. For Mum's sake.'

I nod again, not trusting myself to speak.

'Good. Because I came in to tell you,' says Dad, 'that I've just phoned the hospital. Mum's had her operation. It went well, and they think they've got it all.' His eyes suddenly fill with tears and I feel my whole body starting to shake. 'They think they've got all the cancer,' he says in a wobbly voice that doesn't sound like my dad at all. 'She's got to have treatment: radiotherapy. But they think she'll be OK.'

'Oh! Oh!' I can hear myself saying. But this doesn't sound like me, either. I can't seem to say anything else. Just 'Oh! Oh!', over and over, like an annoying record that's got stuck. My nose is running. My legs seem to have given way. 'Oh! Oh!' I keep going.

And then my sister's suddenly holding me up. Literally holding me up. And I'm holding onto her, and we're, strangely, kissing each other.

'Sorry,' I finally manage to mutter against her hair. 'Jesus, Debs, I'm so sorry.'

'Shut up, you fool,' is all she says.

It's enough.

Saturday

'And the *children*,' Debra raises her eyebrows, shakes her head, tuts with exasperation. 'They're so demanding these days. They have to have it all – mobile phone, their own computer, all the latest fashions – it's a job to keep up with it all.'

'Tell me about it,' says my other sister, Millie. 'The girls are a nightmare. They'll only wear certain brands of trainers, carry certain bags to school and even certain pencil cases. Trouble is, by the next term it'll be different ones in fashion. God, it's a nightmare – so expensive, especially with two of them so close in age.'

'James says it doesn't hurt to give them the things they want – after all, that's what he's working so hard for. But I don't know. I wonder if we're in danger of spoiling them. You know? What do you think, Sophie?'

Oh, God: not again. I've been hiding behind the paper, hoping I won't get roped into this conversation. It's not like it has anything to do with anything I understand. I've been down here for three and a half days now, and I'm beginning to feel like a visiting exchange student who can't comprehend a word of the host family's language. I try, from time to time, to turn the conversation around to other things: politics, sport, music, books, even the weather. But every time, every single bloody time, it comes back to husbands and kids; and *what do you think, Sophie?* Like I'd have a clue!

'Yes, what do you think, Sophie? About the trainers?'

I suppose I should make an effort. At least they're trying to include me. Perhaps I should, really, be flattered that they bother to ask my opinion on these subjects that seem to totally consume them. You see – the thing is, I'm the eldest. Despite our role reversals, with me being the

Cinderella who hasn't found her prince (and doesn't even want to), my sisters are both younger than me. Both married, both mothers of school-age children, both playing their proper parts as members of the adult community, while I, Big Sister Sophie, who they looked up to with envy and admiration when I got my first bra and my first boyfriend, seem now by comparison to be suffering from arrested development.

'Um.' I turn the pages of the newspaper thoughtfully, playing for time. Trainers? What the fuck? I don't think *anything* about kids' trainers. I'm not even sure that I've ever seen any. 'Well, um ...'

'Don't you think it's scandalous?' Millie prompts. 'The cost of these things? The way the manufacturers advertise them, so they get all the kids pestering their parents for them?'

'So why don't you just say no?' I suggest. I feel quite proud of myself. I think that's actually a good suggestion. Why Millie hasn't thought of it herself, I can't begin to imagine.

'*Say no*?' she repeats, in tones of disbelief.

'Huh!' says Debra, dismissively. 'You can tell she hasn't got any experience with kids, can't you, Mills?'

'Yeah!' Millie laughs. '*Say no*! Right, like it's that easy, eh, Debs?'

'Well, you know I haven't got any experience!' I retort, somewhat aggrieved. 'So why do you always ask my opinion?'

They look at each other, raised eyebrows.

'Well,' says Millie, in the gently admonishing tone she might use to the kids when they've been naughty but they're upset about it. 'We don't want you to be left out of the conversation, do we. We want to include you.'

'We don't want you to feel any worse than you probably do already,' says Debra sadly. 'You know. Not having ... what we've got.'

What they've got includes, unfortunately, a husband each, of whom neither of my sisters ever seem inordinately fond. When the Saturday morning conversation turns inevitably to the listing of the husbands' various faults, including those manifesting themselves particularly in the bedroom, I decide it's time to take a walk.

I always forget, between visits, how much I love this part of Devon. Today the weather's perfect – warm and sunny with a gentle breeze off the sea. It's only a five minute walk to the beach, and I'm now stepping out along the walkway that calls itself, rather too grandly, The Promenade. I'm swinging my arms and breathing in deeply the wonderful scents of salty air, seaweed, wet sand and something else, something indescribably sweet and sticky. It's possibly candyfloss, or ice creams, or fizzy drinks – or probably a mixture of all those things inevitably sold by the little cafés and kiosks along the prom – and it brings back to me in a rush all my treasured childhood memories of summer life in a small English seaside town.

We hardly used our back garden when we were kids. As long as the weather was fine enough for us to be outdoors – and often even when it wasn't – we'd be at the beach. Dad taught us all to swim in the sea, long before school swimming lessons at the pool in the next town caught up with us, and we'd spend whole days down here, completely immersed in our games – building forts in the sand, or elaborate pictures with shells, stones and sticks. Or paddling for hours in the rock pools, searching for crabs, anemones, shellfish and strange, unidentifiable pieces of claw or bone that used to have us scuttling home with our trophies in our buckets.

Later, of course, as teenagers, we'd be down here to strut our stuff in our bikinis and sunglasses and try to pull the holiday boys. I like to think we broke a few hearts. Strangely enough, for three sisters fairly close in age, there

75

wasn't much rivalry between us. Whenever any of us had a proper boyfriend – which always meant a local boy, not someone who was going to bugger off home after two weeks – they just dropped out of Beach Flirting for a while, being welcomed back on the scene when the boyfriend was dumped. And the boyfriends always got dumped fairly quickly, because we preferred the fun of Beach Flirting. Just think about it: a whole new townful of boys delivered virtually to your doorstep every two weeks! We weren't in any hurry to get serious and settle down.

So what happened? What the hell changed? How did I end up being the only one who *still* isn't in any hurry, who *still* prefers having fun to getting serious and settling down, while my two little sisters have both become wives, mothers, and – OK, I'll come right out and say it – boring whingers?

I'm out of breath by the time I reach the pier. Like *Promenade*, *Pier* is really a very grandiose term to describe what's actually little more than a jetty with a few seats on it, but this too was one of our favourite haunts. We'd mingle with the holidaymakers strolling in the sunshine, loiter around the fishermen leaning on the railings at the end of the pier, and out of season we made use of the boardwalk as a roller-skating track. I sit, now, on one of the green wooden benches, looking out to sea, consumed with thoughts of the old days and how little everything has changed here. Next to me on the bench is a couple, probably in their forties, who are sitting with their arms entwined, looking at each other and laughing as a young girl of about thirteen who I presume to be their daughter is leaning against the railings, taking their photo.

'Smile, Dad!' she shrieks. 'Look happy!'

'We *are* happy, Ellie!' laughs the mum, nudging her husband so that he laughs again too.

'Couldn't be happier!' he echoes, smiling for the camera as the daughter takes the photo.

Snap, snap. Recorded for posterity. Mum and Dad, as happy as it's possible to be, Sand Bay Pier, July 2009. My heart, suddenly, fills with a grief so unexpected, so terrible, that I have to get up and walk away. Sometimes, and for no particular reason, other people's happiness just seems too much to bear.

'You and Mum,' I say to Dad, later, in the car on the way to visit Mum in the hospital. 'You always seem so happy. You always did, when we were growing up. Was it real?'

'What on earth do you mean?' He turns to me, looking puzzled and amused. 'Why would it not be real?'

'I mean – *all* the time? It wasn't, like, just an act? For us kids' sake?'

'Of course not!' He shakes his head at me now as if I'm slightly weird. A child asking odd and disturbing question that nevertheless have to be faced and answered. 'We always *have* been happy together, Sophie. Of course, we've had our arguments, disagreements, but ...'

'But never – I don't know, never got fed up with each other? Wanted to walk out? Wanted a *change*? In all these years?'

'No. Never.' His expression is more serious now. 'We're still in love with each other. We're still each other's best friends. OK, there have been some sticky patches, but neither of us has ever considered jacking it in. That's what marriage is supposed to be about, isn't it.'

'Not for everyone.' I think of my sisters, constantly moaning and complaining about their husbands' faults – but I'm obviously not saying this to my dad. 'Lots of people are unhappy in their marriages,' I point out, instead.

'Yes. So I guess your mum and I have just been lucky. Or maybe we've learnt to overlook each other's faults,' he adds with a grin that makes me, ridiculously, want to cry. 'Maybe *that's* what it's about.'

'Maybe,' I agree. How would I know?

We drive in silence for a while, and then suddenly, as if he's just commenting on the weather, Dad says:

'Charlie seems a nice boy.'

'He's thirty-five, Dad. And we're just friends, OK?'

'OK.' He shrugs to himself and whistles a little tune through his teeth. 'OK, I get the message.'

I wish to God he hadn't mentioned Charlie, because for the last few days my head's been so full of concern about Mum, I've forgotten to feel sorry for myself. I phoned him the other night, as promised, to give him the good news that Mum is expected to make a full recovery. And he offered, rather less than enthusiastically, to drive down to Devon again to pick me up when I'm ready to go back – but I said no, I'd get the train. The whole conversation was carried out with pleasant politeness, and I was left wondering, after I hung up, whether this was really the same person that I'd been having sex with for two years. The thought of it being over between us, finished, so completely over that we're not even supposed to be seeing each other as friends any more, seemed faintly ridiculous – the distance between us at the moment probably helping to numb the pain and make everything feel unreal. Now, though, I'm sitting in the passenger seat, listening to Dad whistling to himself as if he knows a secret, and I'm filled with a foolish urge to shout at him: *We were lovers, OK? We were lovers, but I didn't love him, so now he's dumped me! So stop looking at me like that!*

Thankfully, I manage to resist the urge.

'You'll need to be getting back to London,' says Mum matter-of-factly. She's propped up on the pillows, smiling at me. She looks good. It's hard to believe she's had such a serious operation just a few days ago. 'It was lovely of you to come, but I didn't expect it.'

See! I'm such a bad daughter, even in these extreme circumstances she expected me to quite happily carry on with my selfish little life rather than rushing down here to see her. I hang my head.

'Sophie,' she goes on gently, 'I'm not criticising you. I know how things are. I know you can't just drop everything, when you've got your own business, and come to see us on a whim every few days like your sisters do.' She pauses and then adds: 'It's different for them. They need me more.'

'*They* need *you* more?'

'Of course. They've got their own families now, their own children, and all the worries and problems that children can bring – as well as the pleasures. It's not till you've got your own children that you begin to find your place in life. You begin to see how you fit into the grand scheme of things, the pattern of the generations – the whole point of *families*. You'll see, one day,' she adds, looking at me a little sadly.

'Perhaps.'

I don't know what else to say. I want to change the subject – talk about the weather, or my job, or the hospital food, or anything, really, rather than this very scary and unwelcome venture into the realm of mothers and families. But to do so now, when Mum and I are alone in her side room, seems crass and somehow disrespectful. Mum's holding my hand and looking at me with that very tender, very special look she used to adopt when she was explaining why I couldn't have a new bike for Christmas, or why I ought to be careful when snogging strange boys after dark on the beach. Just as then, I find I can't meet her eyes and I'm dreading what comes next.

'I hope so,' she says quietly. 'For your sake, Sophie – I do hope so. Do you know what? When I found out that I had this cancer, there were so many things that went through my mind.'

'Well, of course! I can understand ...'

'Not just things about myself. I thought about Dad, and how he'd manage if I didn't survive. I thought about all of you – my children, my grandchildren, how hard it would be to leave you all, how difficult to know you'd all be sad, and that I wouldn't be able to make it better. Mums are always supposed to be able to make it better, aren't they – but I wouldn't even be here to do it.' She wipes a tear away from her eye, quickly, before I'm able to protest, or stop her from going on: 'But you know one of the things that concerned me the most, when I realised I might be going to die? It was the thought that you still weren't settled. No, don't look at me like that. I know you're happy with your life, your career, your independence. I know all that, I understand it – in some ways I suppose we all even envy you occasionally. I think your sisters do. I think that's why they give you a hard time.' She stops, smiles at me, while I splutter for feeble words of protest. 'I know they do,' she says, patting my hand. 'But they mean well. We all do, Sophie. We all have your best interests at heart, darling, because deep down, we just want you to be happy. And even if you always choose to live in London, if you always put your career first, and you always keep your independence – they're all *good* things, I know that! – but if you never find your *one special person*, Sophie – well, how can you be truly happy without experiencing what I've had with your dad?'

I want to tell her she's got it all wrong. I want to say that I don't believe in *one special person* – never have done. That she just hit it lucky, with my dad – that they both just happened to be two particularly lovely people who, as Dad said himself, learnt how to overlook each other's faults, and that's why they've always been so happy. That it doesn't always work like that – that Millie and Debra are good examples of women who married their so-called *special person* and have ended up miserable and resentful.

But I can't, can I. She's lying here in her hospital bed, telling me she was thinking of my happiness when she was waiting to find out if she was going to die – and she's probably the most important person in my life, and there's no way I'm going to upset her. Not now, not ever, if I can help it.

I squeeze her hand, lay my cheek against hers.

'I love you, Mum,' is all I can manage.

Monday

They've all come to the station with me to wave me off. Dad's driven me here, even though it's less than a ten minute walk. He's insisted on carrying down to the platform the ridiculously inadequate bag I brought here with me, containing none of the necessities I actually needed but an assortment of odd clothes I threw in at random without stopping to give it any thought. I've had to go out and buy myself a couple of pairs of knickers and some T-shirts while I've been down here.

'It's not heavy, Dad. Give it to me.'

'No, I'll take it. If I can't carry a bag for my own daughter, it's a poor show.'

I'm on the point of asking him how he thinks I manage to conduct my entire life in London without his assistance but I realise this won't be helpful or even kind. Instead, I take his other arm and say, quietly,

'I'll be back again in a few weeks.'

'No need,' he says. 'We appreciate you being here this week, but …'

'Dad, I *want* to. I want to see how Mum's getting on. OK? I'll sort out my diary, move a couple of appointments, and as soon as I can, I'll be back.'

'I know it's difficult for you, love.'

'Yes. Difficult, but not impossible. I'll come. I'll call you.'

It's not exactly like I can make up for lost time. But I'm never going to stay away from my family for so long again. I've found out the hard way what can happen when your back's turned.

'Take care, Sophe.' Debra's crying. For God's sake, I'm not going to Afghanistan or Iraq. 'Give us a call to let us know you've got home safely.'

82

'People do travel in and out of London all the time, you know, without getting mugged or murdered,' I tell her gently. She's thirty-two and still has the country girl's fear of big cities.

'Take care,' Millie echoes sadly. 'It's been lovely seeing you, although not for the reason, you know, with Mum,' she adds quickly, looking away.

'Catch up again soon on the phone!' Debra says desperately as my train pulls in. 'And give our love to that gorgeous man you're dating!'

'I'm not ...'

'Yes, it must be serious,' Millie joins in. 'He drove you all the way down here, in the middle of the night!'

'It's not ... he's just ...' Shit. Why – why now? They've managed to keep off the subject all week. We've had hour-long discussions about children's trainers, unsatisfactory husbands and even touched on different types of mortgage repayments and how to avoid getting swine flu. But my love life (or lack of it) has, amazingly, not been subjected to sisterly scrutiny, until now, now that I'm just about to grab my bag of inappropriate clothes out of Dad's hands and kiss them all goodbye.

'Sophie tells me he's just a friend,' Dad announces calmly, treating Debra and Millie to one of his best fatherly *Don't argue with me* looks. 'So let's leave it at that, please, girls.'

'Right,' says Debra, looking disappointed.

'Sure,' says Millie, eyeing me suspiciously.

But they don't argue with Dad. We might all be in our thirties, but he's still Dad, at the end of the day.

'Thanks, Dad,' I say, hugging him first and then the girls. 'See you soon. Give Mum another kiss from me.'

And I'm on the train, watching them all waving – smiling at Debra's silly tears, raising my hand to wave back as the train begins to pull away from the platform, mouthing *Bye! Bye!* until they're out of sight, and I'm left staring stupidly into the eyes of the elderly lady sitting opposite me. And it's not till she gives me a funny little sympathetic smile that I realise I'm crying too.

Daft cow.

'Oh! You're back! I've missed you!' squeals Polly as soon as I call her from my flat. Then she remembers to drop her voice to a discreet tone of concern, and adds quickly: 'How's your mum now?'

'Doing OK, thanks. Well, you know – what's the expression? As well as can be expected, in the circumstances. But look, I'll tell you everything properly later on. I've just called to say I've got one appointment this afternoon – another new client that I didn't really want to cancel – and then I'll come round. Is that OK?'

'Of course it's OK. Leon won't be home till late tonight.'

'Good. I mean – ' Whoops. 'I mean, good, we can have a long chat.' And good, I won't have to see his nasty, smirking face or pretend to be polite to him.

My new client today is called Nina and she's probably about my age, and has brought her brat of a seven year old daughter, Bluebell (yes, that's right – *Bluebell)* along with her because the brat is going to be her bridesmaid, and the brat wants her hair done *just like Mummy's*, and so, apparently, has been allowed to take the afternoon off school in order to have a hair rehearsal *just like Mummy*. She's telling me, in her very loud, very self-assured and irritating little madam's voice, that she's having the exact same dress as Mummy, except that Mummy's will be ivory, and hers will be pink.

'And smaller,' I point out, thinking that little girls like to be teased. Big mistake. She looks at me with something approaching real disdain.

'Of *course* smaller,' she says, shaking her head at me and nearly getting a hairclip in her eye. '*And,*' she goes on, getting back into her stride, 'Mummy says I can have the exact same shoes as her, too – with *heels*.'

If I'm meant to be impressed by this, I have no idea how to show it.

'Oh,' I say, holding her head still so that I can get another clip in. 'That's nice.'

'*And*, I'm going to carry the exact same roses as Mummy, and wear the exact same necklace.'

'Wow.' I smile at her in the mirror, mainly because I think I've made a good job of her hair. 'Nobody will be able to tell which one is the bride and which one is the bridesmaid!'

Whoops, done it again. Little girls obviously don't like jokes like this. This time, I get a full-on glare of disgust.

'Of *course* they will,' she says imperiously, aware by now that she's addressing a half-wit. 'The *bride* gets to wear a ring on her finger.'

'Oh yes. I see.' I catch Nina's eye and she smiles at me, clearly thinking I'm entranced by her daughter and having the time of my life.

'Kids, eh!' she says. 'They're so grown-up these days! She wants to be the centre of attention – don't you, Bluebell?'

'Yes. I want to look like a Princess,' says Bluebell, studying herself critically in the mirror. 'I *think* my hair looks OK – do you, Mummy?'

I can feel my face beginning to set into a snarl.

'Yes, darling, you look beautiful,' says Nina. 'Now then – can Mummy have *her* hair done now, do you think?'

'Well, I suppose so,' says the child, making no effort to get out of the chair. 'As long as it doesn't take too long, only you *did* promise to take me to the nail bar as a special treat. Remember?'

Like this isn't a special treat? Missing school to get your hair done like a princess? She's tipping the chair back now, holding up her hands, studying her nails, which already look perfect – painted a delicate shade of pink, needless to say. A bit *too* perfect for a seven year old's nails, if you ask me. Why aren't they bitten, or chipped from playground scrapes, stained with paint or mud or the petals of flowers she's crushed to make pretend perfume? *Why* aren't little girls enjoying being little girls any more? I don't get it!

I straighten her chair, before she tips it over, and ignore the glare.

'OK, Bluebell,' I say cheerfully. 'Up you get. It's your mum's turn now, and as we both know, *she's* the bride, isn't she. It's going to be *her* big day.'

'And *mine*,' she says, jutting her lower lip out at me mutinously. She looks at the time on her pink princess watch. 'Don't be too long doing Mummy's hair, will you. We're going to the nail bar.'

'So I heard.' I try hard not to bare my teeth at her as she flounces off to throw herself dramatically on the sofa. 'Now then, Nina.' She's seating herself, much more daintily than her daughter, in the chair and smiling at me slightly timidly. 'What look are we aiming for?' I ask her encouragingly.

'Oh, well, exactly like Bluebell's, I suppose,' she says apologetically.

Silly me.

I've almost finished the adult replica of the Princess hairstyle when Nina starts to open up to me.

'We were on our own together for six years, you see,' she says in little more than a whisper.

'You and your husband-to-be?'

'No!' She glances over her shoulder to make sure her daughter isn't listening. No worries, she's plugged into some earphones. 'No, Bluebell and I. Her father left me when I was pregnant.' She dips her head as if this is something she's profoundly ashamed of. 'So she grew up having me all to herself.'

'I see.'

'And then ...' Her eyes light up and a smile transforms her face, making her instantly beautiful. 'Then last year, Simon came into my life. I met him in Sainsbury's – he helped me with my wonky trolley – and he asked me to marry him on our second date.'

'Ah, that's nice. Romantic!' I say, smiling back at her. I'm good at this. I *like* other people's romances. It's not necessary to believe in something, to find it charming. After all, I like Mickey Mouse, too. And Father Christmas.

'Simon's absolutely wonderful.' She sighs, a dreamy look in her eyes. 'I love him so much! It's just like … well, a dream come true! An amazing love story! A fairytale!'

OK, steady on.

'We were meant for each other! A perfect match! It's like he was dropped from Heaven, just for me!'

Right, I think we've now passed *charming* and we're heading for *sick bucket.*

'There's just one thing,' she says – and the smile of ecstasy begins to fade slightly. 'Just one little problem.'

Oh, God. Please don't say we're going to start getting the details of his sexual perversions. I've listened to descriptions of most fetishes in my time in this job, but if it involves rubber gloves or black bin liners I'm afraid I do switch off.

'It's Bluebell,' Nina says urgently, and then clamps her hand over her mouth, checking over her shoulder again. The child's engrossed in whatever's coming through her earphones. 'Oh dear. I shouldn't have told you that.'

'It's OK. I'm like a doctor – you can tell me anything, and it doesn't get repeated.' Well, only to the girls on Saturday nights – not that we seem to do Saturday nights any more. And only to Charlie – not that I'm going to be seeing him any more either. So yes, it's a pretty safe bet that nobody ever finds out why Bluebell is a problem, not that it takes much imagination to guess.

She gives me another wan, nervous smile.

'It's just that she's a *teeny* bit jealous, you see. Because of having me to herself for so long. It's understandable! It's only natural!' she gabbles, as if I'd said otherwise. 'So I suppose, what I'm doing is, I'm kind-of trying to make it up to her, you see?'

'With the little treats? The hair, the nail bar ...'

'The new clothes, the computer, the phone, the new fitted bedroom, the parties for her little friends, you know, just to keep her happy, really. Just to show her I still love her.'

'Well, as you say – if that's what you need to do ...'

I'm totally out of my depth again here, of course.

'To show her she's still Mummy's best little girl,' she goes on, looking like she's going to cry. 'And to stop her wrecking my relationship with Simon,' she adds in a whisper, looking down at the floor.

Oh.

'Oh. So it's more a case of ... a little bit of bribery,' I suggest, gently. I wait till she looks back up at me in the mirror. 'Is it?'

'Simon says it's more like blackmail,' she admits. Suddenly she looks ten years older. I wish she hadn't told me, now. I want her to go back to looking beautiful, telling me how Simon's absolutely wonderful. I'd even prefer to hear her saying he'd dropped from Heaven, if it keeps her happy. 'He says if she's still carrying on like this after the wedding, I'll have to start being firmer with her.' She appeals to me with her eyes. I can't imagine her being firm with anybody, least of all that spoilt little madam. I can't even imagine her being firm with a jar of pickled onions.

'Oh dear,' I say. I think I need to change the subject.

'What can I do, Sophie?' she asks me wretchedly, wiping a tear from her eye. 'What would *you* do, if you were me?'

And here we are again. As always.

I consider my options. *Drown her in the bath* doesn't seem like an acceptable suggestion. *Sell her on E-Bay* could be marginally better, although I don't think she'd take me seriously.

'Perhaps ...' I begin, thinking desperately. What would I do? What would I, honestly and seriously, do? 'I think I'd stop all the treats, Nina. Take away her phone, her iPod, all the new toys, whatever – and tell her she'll only get them back when she starts behaving herself and being polite to Simon. That's what I'd do.'

I suppose I've said the wrong thing. I've probably offended her now and she won't book me for the wedding. I open my mouth again to backtrack, to tell her I'm being an idiot and that's not a good idea at all.

'Actually,' she admits quietly, 'that's what Simon says I should do, too. *Exactly* that. Thank you, Sophie. I'm very grateful to you for being straight with me. Do you know what my mum always used to say? *If you want good advice, Nina, don't ask your friends – ask a hairdresser.*'

She books me for the wedding. And gives me a good tip. I don't suppose she'll actually manage to stand up to her domineering little princess when it comes to it, but you never know.

Ask a hairdresser? Tell me about it!

Tuesday

So this is what Polly told me yesterday afternoon when I'd finally got rid of Bluebell and her mum, and went round for a morale-boosting chat with my best friend: *Sophie, she said, you're going to end up a sad, miserable old bag with no friends.*

Well, OK, she didn't say it quite exactly like that. And she didn't just come straight out with it, apropos of nothing, like she thought it was a good idea to kick me while I was so far down I had no hope of getting up again. It just *felt* like that. It just felt like everyone else was against me, nobody understood me, and now even Polly was getting in on the *let's all have a go at Sophie* act.

In fact we'd been working ourselves up to it gradually. It started with me telling her that my dad thought Charlie seemed a nice boy, and her saying that well, he is, isn't he, after all he did drive me all the way to Devon less than twenty-four hours after I'd broken his heart. I didn't like the bit about the broken heart, but I didn't say anything. But then we went on to the question of my mum saying all that stuff about wishing I was settled down, when she was wondering if she was going to die – and Polly said yes, well, mums never stop worrying about their children, and it was only natural for her to be worried that I was unhappy.

'Why? Why is it only natural? Why should she think I'm unhappy?'

'Because you *are*, Sophie. Aren't you,' she said, with an irritating calmness.

'No! Well, OK, yes,' I amended grudgingly, because I was close to crying again so it seemed a bit pointless to pretend I was full of the joys of spring. 'But

90

only because everyone's being so bloody *horrible* to me, all of a sudden.'

And if you think that sounds like a self-pitying whine, you're absolutely right, it was. Can you blame me?

'Charlie was being horrible to you by falling in love with you?'

'Well, no, but he shouldn't have said anything. He should have just kept it to himself, so we could carry on the way we were, and ...'

I ran out of steam, but Polly was ignoring me anyway.

'Your mum was being horrible to you by telling you she was so concerned about you, her dying wish would have been about your happiness?'

'All right, don't make me feel even worse! *You're* being horrible to me!'

'By telling you the truth? Isn't that what friends are supposed to do?'

'Polly, I don't need this right now, OK? I don't want truth. I just want you to be nice to me. For God's sake – my mum's just had an operation, my sisters are both using me as their personal marriage guidance counsellor, my best man-friend doesn't want to see me any more – I'll probably never have sex again for the rest of my life, and end up in a convent or something.'

'No, you won't. Don't be ridiculous. And I'm trying to be nice to you, but you're so full of shit about yourself, you're not making it easy.'

'Well, thanks a million! That's just great, coming from you! When I think about all the times I've sat here with you, listening to you crying ...'

'Because I was fucking *tired*, is all! And hormonal! And emotional! Not because I was sorry for myself! Not because I was pretending it was everyone else in the world who'd got it all wrong!'

'Well, in that case, I'd better just go,' I said, huffily, getting to my feet. 'I'll go home and feel sorry for myself on my own then, shall I, if that's what you think?'

'You might as well, Sophie. You'll be spending *all* your time on your own, if you carry on like this. You'll drive everyone else away! If that's what you want, sure – stay on your own, be miserable all your life!'

And so I did. I went home, on my own, and stayed miserable all evening, and made up my mind I *would* be lonely and miserable all my life, have no friends and wouldn't care. The three large glasses of wine I downed didn't help. But this morning I've woken up wondering what it was all about, how I managed to get into an argument with Polly – Polly, of all people! And I'm starting to panic that she's going to refuse to see me again, like Charlie – like it's somehow catching, a kind-of Dumping Sophie virus. And I'm grabbing my mobile as soon as I'm out of bed.

Sorry, sorry, sorry! I text her frantically, and jump with surprise when the phone bleeps just as I press Send.

Sorry, sorry, sorry! says her message to me.

Simultaneous identical texting. It has to mean something, doesn't it? We're laughing together about it on the phone a minute later. And I can't even remember who phoned who, or who apologised for what. At least she says she didn't mean it – about me ending up lonely and miserable, that is. She probably meant all the rest.

The trouble is, obviously, Polly hit a nerve – well, several nerves, to be honest – with the stuff she was saying. Especially about my mum. If you want to know the truth, it's affected me more than I care to admit, knowing Mum was worrying about me like that when she thought she might be going to die. I've never made any pretence about the fact that I don't want to get married or have children – and if I ever had any doubts, I'd only have to spend a few hours with either of my sisters, to be convinced all over again. They make marriage, and their husbands, sound the way people describe the British weather – unreliable, usually unpleasant, but something to be borne stoically because they can't see any alternative.

Mum and Dad's marriage is different. They've always seemed to enjoy spending time together, rather than putting up with each other grudgingly. If I was making an advert for marriage, not that I ever would in a million years, I'd choose Mum and Dad every time over any of the gooey romantic brides I see every day. Most of them will be complaining about their grooms before the honeymoon's even over, and half of them will end up hating each other and getting divorced. Don't blame me – it's a statistic! But when I stop and think about Mum and Dad – and about other couples like them, because even though they're a rarity, the exception to the rule, I'm not silly enough to think there can't be other happy, solid, dependable long-term couples who have survived the years and still love each other – when I stop and really think about those couples, I suddenly feel like I'm floundering in my convictions. If marriage can work like that, even very rarely, even with one couple in a hundred, say – then who am I to say it's a crock of shit?

What makes it worse is that Polly thinks she's in one of those happy, solid, dependable marriages. When in fact she's married to the biggest heap of garbage since the dustmen went on strike.

Today's much like any other day: another two new excited brides, gushing about their dresses and their venues and their flowers. It's good for me, believe it or not. I listen to their stories, and their enthusiasm rubs off on me. Their simple faith in the random selection of a partner for life by means of some bizarre direction of Cupid's arrow never fails to touch me, to stop me in my cynical tracks and keep me aware that it's a good thing for the world that people like me are in the minority. And their equally bizarre belief that hairdressers are put on this earth to give advice on personal relationship issues does at least force me to take an interest in something other than my work and what's on TV tonight.

Jo comes round to see me this evening. She's only two months pregnant but she sits down carefully, holding her stomach as if she's already massive and the baby's about to be born.

'How are you, Sophie?' she asks, eyes round with concern. 'Polly told me. About your mum. And about Charlie.'

'Oh.' I sigh. Well, no point having friends if they can't gossip about you, I suppose. I'd do the same – in fact I have been doing the same, haven't I, about Jo and her self-service pregnancy. 'Well, Mum's getting over her operation, and has to have lots of treatment now, which is horrible for her, but we're all so relieved that they think she's going to be OK.'

'Yes. Your poor mum. And poor you.' Her eyes fill with tears. 'Oh, sorry, Sophe!' She fumbles for a tissue. 'It's my hormones – you know? I get so weepy about everything.'

I nod sympathetically, pretending to look as if I have a clue what she's talking about.

'It's not that I'm not happy,' she goes on, tears beginning to stream down her face. 'I'm over the moon about the baby – I'm so excited, so looking forward to it! And my mum – you can imagine, can't you!'

I nod again, sagely, pretending to imagine.

'Knitting already!' she sobs.

Baby shawls. I shudder, and then feel like crying myself, remembering Charlie's mum.

'I'm so happy!' Jo howls, blowing her nose and covering her face.

I wait for her to pull herself together.

'So why are you crying?' I ask eventually. Come on – hormones are one thing; full-on bouts of hysterical, shuddering weeping are another. 'What's wrong?'

'It's the circumstances,' she says darkly, without meeting my eyes. 'The circumstances of the pregnancy.'

There's a silence for a moment while I pretend I'm not sure what she means. Then: 'Polly told me,' I admit. 'About the artificial insemination.'

'Right.'

'By a donor,' I add, just to make it clear I know the whole story.

'Yes.' She sniffs, blows her nose again. 'Don't get me wrong. It's not that I'm ashamed of it.'

'Of course not. Why should you be?' To be honest, it makes more sense to me than the traditional method, but then I realise I'm probably not the best person to comment.

'I wanted a baby. Nothing wrong with that, is there?'

'No! Nobody thinks there's anything wrong with it – do they?'

'Maybe not.' She shrugs. 'I don't know. I don't know, to be honest, Sophie, what my family would say.'

'You haven't told them?'

'No. I've only told friends. Friends are different from family.'

Again, I nod solemnly as if in agreement. Well, she's got a point. Friends don't start knitting shawls at the first sign of a pregnancy test kit, at any rate.

'I suppose your mum and dad are asking questions about the father?' I suggest.

'Yes!' Oh, God, what have I said? She's crying again. I shuffle up next to her on the sofa and put my arms round her. 'Yes, that's just it,' she blubs. 'They want to meet him, they want to know why I'm not living with him and whether I'm going to marry him! What am I supposed to say?' She looks up at me, desperation in her wet, red eyes. 'What shall I do, Sophie? What would *you* do if you were me?'

Looking back later, I can't think how we got there. She came round to talk about *me*, and *my* problems, to ask how *I* was, and within five seconds she's crying, I'm trying to comfort her, and as always, I'm finding myself trying to give advice on a subject I know less about than I know of the surface of the moon. It's not that I mind. I don't resent it. It just bewilders me. How does it happen, every time, every single time I have a conversation with anyone? Do people take one look at me and find themselves gripped by an overwhelming urge to divulge their feelings, their problems, their insecurities? And do I give off some sort of vibes, some sort of pheromone perhaps, that convinces everyone I know the answer to every human dilemma under the sun?

I don't!

I know less than they do!

I know *nothing* about *anything*!

Maybe, if I'm going to go through life giving out this impression to everyone that I'm some kind of all-knowing white witch, I really ought to do something about it. Take a counselling course, or a psychology course, or at least a GCSE in how normal people who have normal relationships think, because I'm sure as hell never going to find out for myself.

'Jo seems upset,' I tell Polly on the phone, rather inadequately, this evening.

'Does she?' Polly sounds astounded. How can anyone be upset when they're pregnant? 'She seemed fine to me when I saw her. Full of excitement, telling me how her mum's started knitting ...'

So it must be me. You see? It's just me. Everyone cries when they see me, and everyone wants me to tell them what to do. I'm wasted as a hairdresser. I'm going to write a self-help book. It'll sell in its thousands, make me a pot of money, and when everyone's read it they'll all know how to sort themselves out, and leave me alone.

Always supposing that's what I really want!

A Saturday in August

It's warm and sunny – a perfect day for a wedding. Just as well, as I've got two of them today – one this morning (Julie, short brown hair, full make-up, marrying Mark, taking on his two young children from a previous marriage, asking me how to cope with step-children who don't respect her), and one late this afternoon (Sandra, straight blonde bob, light eye make-up only, marrying Nathan, a policeman, wanting advice on how long after their marriage she should break it to him about her criminal record for drugs offences). I've got time, between the morning bride and the afternoon one, to nip up to the Broadway for some shopping and grab a quick sandwich in Subway.

And that's where I bump into Charlie.

It's not like we've been avoiding each other. Correction: *I* haven't been avoiding *him*, although it's strange that we've barely even seen each other at waving distance since Devon – especially as we live so close. Even when we *have* seen each other at waving distance, he seems to have been either rushing into his flat or rushing out of it, with no time to stop and talk, so that I've become slightly paranoid that he hasn't just finished with me, he's decided to wipe me off his memory, delete me from his consciousness and pretend we never knew each other. Is that what you do when you supposedly love someone and they don't want to love you back? I might be perverse, but I find it hurtful. I've been close to phoning him a couple of times, to tell him how hurtful I find it, but I've stopped, halfway through punching his number into the phone, thinking that if I phone him he'll assume I've changed my mind and decided I love him after all.

Of course, I do want him back; oh, yes, I admit it. Seeing him, now, standing at the counter, and smiling at the assistant (young, pretty, smiling back) and choosing the filling for his Sub (steak and cheese), I realise how badly I want him back. But only as a friend, and in bed, and not necessarily in that order.

'Charlie!' I shout.

He turns round, and there's a look on his face, just fleetingly, before he corrects it and smiles, that could be interpreted as panic.

'Sophie. How are you?' he says quietly, without moving.

I walk over to him with a concentrated, careful lack of haste or eagerness. Inside, I'm flustered, trembling, weak with the kind of nerves you feel when you're fourteen and talking to the boy you've fancied all term. But this is ridiculous: this is Charlie, for God's sake, and the worst thing I could do would be to give him the wrong impression, the same wrong impression he'd have got if I'd phoned him. It wouldn't be fair. I need to keep my voice neutral, my face impassive, my body language that of a casual acquaintance ...

'Oh, God, Charlie – I've missed you *so much*!' I squawk, close to tears, as I throw myself at him, arms round his neck, hands raking through his hair, mouth instinctively seeking his. So much for neutral. So much for impassive. Shit, I'm only human.

It isn't anything he says or does. In fact it's his total lack of response that makes me draw back, hold him at arm's length and look up at him. He's not even looking at me. He's looking over my shoulder. I turn round to follow his gaze – and look straight into the clear green eyes of a tall, blonde girl in a short red dress who's standing behind me, holding two Diet Cokes.

'I'll have the tuna Sub, please,' she tells him in the clipped staccato tones of someone who's not liking what they're seeing.

And that makes two of us. I continue to stare at her, while she stares back, and the girl behind the counter makes up their rolls and looks at me with raised eyebrows and I tell her thank you, but I don't want anything, I don't feel hungry any more. Charlie pays for the two Subs and two Diet Cokes, and all the time he's avoiding meeting my eyes, and Red Dress is looking increasingly hostile, and then we're outside, all three of us, and Charlie's stopped at a table on the pavement and he finally looks at me, helplessly, and says:

'Sophie, this is Helen.'

She's standing with her hands on her hips, waiting for a proper introduction. Her figure is so perfect, the red dress clings everywhere it should, and hangs like folded velvet everywhere else. Her legs are brown and smooth, and go on forever. Her hair shines in the sunlight. Her red glossy lips match her dress. I hate her.

'Hello, Helen,' I say, trying not to snarl. 'I'm Sophie.'

'Sophie's ... an old friend of mine,' says Charlie quickly, as if he thinks he'd better make it clear that I'm an old friend before I try to claim I'm really his wife, that he's left me and my five hungry children at home and is masquerading under a false name. But he hesitates just long enough over the *old friend* bit, to make Helen look back at me, sharply, eyes narrowed with suspicion.

We've got each other's measure. I hate her, and she hates me back.

Hate away, lady. Suspect whatever you like. He might be going out with you, you might be his rebound date, his sympathy shag, you might think you're in with a chance, but you're not. It's *me* he loves, *me* he wants a relationship with, *me* he's had to finish with because I've broken his heart. *Me* that he'd take back given half a chance. I'd only have to say the word, Madam, Miss Lady-In-Red, and he'd be back with me like a shot and you'd be

100

yesterday's news, you'd be running backwards faster than your lanky legs could carry you.

'Helen,' says Charlie, still barely meeting my eyes, which shows just how difficult he's finding it to control his feelings around me, 'Helen is my fiancée. We're engaged, Sophie. We got engaged last Saturday.'

OK, I'm perfectly in control, here. I'm walking away. I'm unlocking my car. I'm driving to the afternoon wedding venue. I'm wondering, seriously, if that was all a dream. Or a nightmare. It just can't be true – can it? Nobody goes from loving somebody to getting engaged to someone else in – what? – four, five weeks? It's just not realistic. It's just not possible. I can't believe it. I won't!

I'm so stressed out about it, I tell Sandra-the-policeman's-bride that he's probably looked her up on the computer system already and knows all about her dodgy druggy past, and then she starts hyperventilating while I'm straightening her hair, and I have to calm her down by pointing out that he's marrying her anyway despite it all. And I find myself wishing somebody loved *me* enough to overlook my faults and take me on for life, warts and all.

But I don't mean it, do I. If I did, I'd still be with Charlie, and it'd be *me* that he was calling his fiancée. And Hateful Helen would never have got a look-in.

'You can't have it both ways,' Polly points out, infuriatingly. I've driven straight to her house from the wedding and she's poured me a cup of tea and a glass of red wine. The cup of tea was her first thought, the glass of wine came afterwards, when I started crying and swearing all at once. 'You didn't want him.'

'I did, I did! Just not on those terms!' Those forever-commitment, stick a ring on my finger and call me something different, terms.

'But they were the terms he was offering, Sophe,' she says more gently, taking hold of the hand that isn't gripping the wine glass. 'What did you think? That because you weren't prepared to commit, he'd stay single for ever? Join a monastery, perhaps?'

'No.' Yes. If I'm honest – yes, why not? If he really loved me so much, why wouldn't he stay celibate for life if he can't have me? I look back at Polly miserably. 'No, I know that's unreasonable. But for God's sake! It's only been a couple of *weeks*! It's almost indecent! I've only just got out of his bed, before she's got into it. The sheets were probably still warm!'

'Oh, please. Too much information,' says Polly. 'Look, I can see that it must have been a shock, finding out like that. And seeing him with someone like *that* – so obvious, so tarty, so tall and blonde and shiny ...'

'All right, don't rub it in.' Then I pause, looking at Polly in surprise. 'I didn't tell you she was tall and blonde. I didn't say anything about what she looked like.'

'You must have done,' she says, colouring slightly.

'No. I didn't. Polly! You *knew*, didn't you! I don't believe it! You knew, and you didn't tell me! Do you *know* her? Is she ... what, a friend of yours, or something?'

'No, of course not. Look, calm down. I don't know her, I had no idea who she was or what her name was, or anything. I've just ... seen them together. Once. For all I knew, she could have been his sister, or ...'

'He hasn't got a sister. When did you see them together?'

'Oh, I don't know!' She waves a hand, vaguely, looking uncomfortable. 'A few days ago.'

'Where? What were they doing?'

'Does it matter?'

'Yes! I want to know why you didn't tell me! You'd normally tell me if you saw Charlie! What were you trying to hide from me? Why ...?'

'Oh, all right – look, I didn't tell you because it was obvious they were *together*. OK? And they were looking in a jewellery shop window. At rings. Get it?'

I gasp. 'You *knew* they were getting engaged!'

'No! I didn't *know* anything! I just had a suspicion. It looked kind-of serious. I didn't think you'd thank me for telling you.'

'I'd rather have heard it from you, than finding out the way I did! Face to face with her over a bloody tuna Sub!'

'I know – I can see that now. I'm sorry. I wish I *had* told you, Sophe. I was only thinking of you; I didn't want you to be hurt.'

'Well, I am hurt,' I tell her, huffily.

'I know. I'm sorry.' She sighs. 'Look, it might be for the best, in the long run. If he's with someone else, if he's getting married ... then at least that kind-of draws a line under it, for you, doesn't it? You can't go on hankering after him, wishing things had been different.'

'I can. I *am* hankering! Oh, Polly, he looked so gorgeous. I just wanted to grab him and kiss him, and I've missed him so much! Why did he have to dump me like that? *Why*?' I'm crying again. I feel so sorry for myself.

'Because he wanted something you weren't going to give him.'

'So he goes straight out, finds the first available, desperate old scrubber and ties himself to her for life?'

'I don't suppose that's quite the way he sees it.'

'I'm going to phone him.' I jump to my feet. 'Where's my phone? Where's my bag? I'm going to call him and ask him what the fuck he thinks he's doing.'

'No you're not!' Polly pushes me back in the chair, quite forcefully. A wail goes up from Ethan, who'd been asleep in his cot upstairs. 'Now look what you've started! I'd better go and bring him down.'

'Sorry.' I look at her properly for the first time. 'Sorry, Polly. Are you OK? I haven't even asked you – where's Gracie?'

'Playing at a little friend's house. I have to pick her up in half an hour.' She runs up the stairs two at a time and returns with a red-faced, hiccupping baby in her arms. 'I'll have to feed him first. Sorry, you're welcome to stay, but I need to get on. Leon's going to be home soon, and I haven't prepared his dinner or anything yet.'

'Can't he do it?' I say, crossly – but I'm getting up to go, anyway. I'm not hanging around if he's on his way home.

'You know what he's like,' she says with an indifferent shrug. 'He's not going to change.'

Pity. A change of any sort – into a dog, a cat, a pig – anything would be an improvement.

'I don't suppose you're coming out tonight?' I ask her without much hope as I head for the door.

'No. I've got the ironing to do. And, you know, he doesn't like having to look after the kids.'

'Doesn't he realise they're his too?' I ask tartly, and then immediately regret it when I see the look on her face. I give her a hug. 'Sorry. I just wish he'd help out, give you a break.'

'I'm fine. Things are getting better all the time. Easier. I'm not so tired now.' She jiggles the crying baby in her arms. 'I don't need him to help. It's not worth the aggravation.'

I'm shaking my head to myself as I leave. How can it be aggravation to expect the kids' own father to get involved in their care? But then again, what would I know about it? I'm looking at a situation that's so alien to me, I'm never going to experience it in a million years. Thank God.

But I still feel like crying.

104

I know I shouldn't do it.

I've been sitting in my kitchen, holding my phone, hitting Charlie's number in my contacts, waiting for it to ring and then cancelling it quickly. I've done it five times now. I keep telling myself to put the phone down, get off my backside, make myself something to eat and get ready to go out for the evening. Jo and Emma have agreed, for once, to come out for a drink. I should be looking forward to it. I should be putting on my clubbing gear, my make-up and my killer heels, and preparing to hit the town. But instead, I'm sitting here, paralysed, like a zombie, hitting his number, staring at it. Picturing him with that Helen bird. Kissing her. Shagging her. Buying her an engagement ring. Hitting the number, letting it ring, cancelling it. Finally, I do it. I'm shaking – actually shaking! – but I do it: I let it ring until he answers it.

'Sophie,' he says. Hearing his voice, I start crying again. Quietly. He can't hear me, he can't see me, he won't know I'm crying. 'I thought it might be you. Don't cry,' he says.

'I'm not crying.'

'OK.' There's a silence. I'm sniffing. A person can sniff, can't they, and not be crying. 'Look – I know that wasn't the most ideal way for you and Helen to meet, but …'

'Ideal?' I sit up straight in shock, almost overbalancing and falling off my kitchen stool. 'Ideal? Charlie, there is *no* ideal way for me and Helen to meet. The only ideal situation, as far as me and Helen are concerned, is for you not to be going out with her.'

'That doesn't make a lot of sense,' he says. I can hear him smiling. I can picture him smiling. I don't want him smiling at me right now. This is serious.

'What are you *doing* with her?' I'm shouting. In fact, to be honest, I'm screaming. He's probably having to hold the phone away from his ear. 'Why? *Why?* Why the hell are you *with* her?'

'I'd have thought that was obvious.' The smile has gone from his voice now. 'Calm down, Sophie.'

'I don't want to calm down,' I retort, childishly. 'And it's not obvious at all! It's ridiculous! We've only just split up! How can you have met *her*, already, and decided you want to marry her? You can't tell me you're in love with her!'

'Can't I?' he says, stonily. He sounds hostile, different, not like my Charlie at all. 'Why not? Because you don't believe in it? You don't want anyone else to settle down and be happy, because *you're* not going to?'

'You never wanted to either, before!'

'People change. They grow up, change their minds, want different things. Most people don't stay for ever in a kind of protracted adolescence.'

I gasp, feeling like I've been slapped.

'You never used to talk like this, Charlie. What has she done to you? Has she talked you round?' And suddenly, something occurs to me – something I haven't thought of before. 'Were you already seeing her? Is that it? You were seeing her when we were together?'

'No! Of course not! I wanted *you*, Sophie. You turned me down, if you remember.'

'You were! You were already seeing her, and she talked you round, talked you into wanting things you never wanted before! That's why you've changed! It's nothing to do with you growing up, nothing to do with your mum and her blanket, shawl, whatever the hell it is. Nothing to do with your cousin's baby. It's *her* – Helen – she's a fucking witch! She's *changed* you! Dump her, for God's sake, Charlie, or the next thing you know, she'll be pregnant …'

The line goes dead.

He's hung up on me.

I throw the phone on the floor and stamp on it.

Sunday

I think I'm going to die.

My head! My head's going to burst!

My eyes! Where are they? Have they disappeared into the back of my head? I can't feel them, can't open them, can't see! Help! I've been struck blind!

Oh, oh – my throat! I want to shout, but I can't. I can't even manage a croak. How am I going to get anyone to come and help me, if I'm blind and I've lost my voice? I'll die. I'll just lie here and die.

But I think I'm going to be sick first.

I try to get up, out of bed, but it's no good – it's just not going to happen; my head's too heavy, I can't lift it off the pillow. Oh, God, no – I can't be sick in bed. Not now, at my age, whatever my age is – I can't remember, but I'm sure it's too old to be sick in the bed. Last time that happened, I was fifteen and my mum nearly killed me. Mum! I want my mum now! Where is she, when I need her?

I seem to be making some sort of groaning noise. The noise seems to be coming out of me without me doing it. It's not my voice. I try to listen, try to concentrate, try not to think about wanting to be sick. Is it my stomach, groaning? Or my chest? Or is the bed groaning under me? I roll over, to see if the bed groans when I move – and roll straight into a body.

'Shit!'

'Fuck!'

The body and I both sit bolt upright on the bed. My eyes have jumped back into the front of my head and they're wide open now in shock, although the room's spinning too fast for me to see the body properly. But it was warm, and it's groaning. That's where all the noise is coming from.

'Where am I?' it's groaning.

'*Who* are you?' I try to yell at it, but the yell won't come out of my parched mouth properly, and I end up making a strangled noise that sounds like 'Ooooh-ah'.

'Am I dead?' the body whispers. It's holding its head and swaying. 'Please tell me I'm dead.'

Hold on.

Hold on, hold on, it's starting to come back to me. Oh – my – God, I remember now. I roll over again, away from the body, and let myself fall off the edge of the bed, where I lie for a minute, wondering whether I'd rather die here on the floor, or on my own in the bathroom, and then – deciding on the bathroom, where I can at least be sick relatively decently until I die – I crawl on all fours across the bedroom, out of the door, across the hall, and finally slump in a naked, shivering heap on the bathroom floor and wait for death.

It went like this.

When Jo and Emma knocked for me to go out at half past eight, I was still sitting in the kitchen, drinking endless cups of coffee and feeling sorry for myself. I told them I wasn't going out, I just wanted to stay at home and be miserable, but they weren't having any of it.

'*You're* the one who's always nagging us about coming out on a Saturday!' said Emma.

'We've made a special effort tonight, to come out with you!' said Jo.

'Yes – I've thought about what you keep telling me, about keeping my girl friends, so I've left Stefan *all on his own* tonight,' – she made it sound like he was a two-month-old puppy with special needs, who'd had to be tethered to a post and left with only crusts and water – 'just to come out with you.'

'And I've come out, too, despite being *exhausted* by this baby,' – Jo rubbed her tummy, for all the world as if she was in the final stages of labour. 'We've put ourselves out to spend the evening with you, Sophie, so this is no time to let us down. Come on – we'll give you five minutes to get dressed and do your hair.'

'Well, she might need ten, if she's going to do her hair,' Emma amended, trying to be funny, but I wasn't in the mood. 'Come *on*, Sophie. Remember what you've always said to us, in the past? No man is worth it?'

That did it. It was true. I was supposed to be the independent single girl around here, wasn't I. I was the one who'd always scoffed at silly, soppy women who lay around pining after men, being weak and pathetic and letting themselves get walked all over. I was *not* going to let Charlie and his stupid *fiancée* get me down. I was *not* going to spend any more time crying about him. If he wanted to go out and marry some desperate old slapper, why should I care? I still knew how to enjoy my life, I did! I'd bloody show him!

So I went out to the club without having anything to eat. Well, I'd forgotten about that. I actually hadn't eaten since breakfast, which was stupid Helen's fault, because coming face-to-face with her in Subway had put me off the idea of lunch. And so I started drinking on an empty stomach. And the more I drank, the more it was getting on my nerves listening to Emma prattling on about how much in *lurve* she was with Stefan, and how much in *lurve* he was with her. And the more it was driving me mad hearing Jo droning on about the how many centimetres long the baby was now, and how far its brain had developed, and how it could probably hear what she was saying, and how important it was to create the right environment for it, playing it classical music and talking in Shakespeare sonnets to it. It was a wonder I wasn't actually sick before I'd even had my second vodka-and-Coke.

After approximately the *seventh* vodka-and-Coke, I remember taking off my shoes and walking onto the middle of the dance floor. I vaguely remember dancing, completely on my own, waving my arms above my head and singing the wrong words to whatever music was playing, and laughing hysterically.

And then I remember – horribly clearly now, now I've been sick, and the bathroom has stopped spinning around quite so frighteningly – someone holding me up when I started to stumble. Someone with nice brown eyes and a deep dark voice to match. I remember him asking my name and saying I was a good dancer. He bought me another drink and laughed at my jokes. I waved goodbye to Emma and Jo and I stayed with him until the club closed. We got a taxi back to my place, and I brought him inside, and undressed him, and took him to bed, and called him Charlie by mistake, but his name was Oscar.

Oscar.

The body in the bed is called Oscar.

I hold my head again and groan to myself softly. I've spent the night with a man called Oscar. We had wild, passionate sex – at least, I suppose we did – there are some memories tugging urgently at my consciousness, very noisy memories. We might have been competing with each other to see who could make the most noise. Or we might just have been enjoying it a hell of a lot. Oh, God – how embarrassing. How can I get out of the flat without facing him again? If I stay here in the bathroom for long enough, will he have disappeared by the time I go back to bed?

I must have passed out for a while. When I open my eyes again, I'm aware that there's a banging on the bathroom door. Who the hell's that, and what are they doing in my flat? I scramble to my feet, look down at myself. Shit, I'm totally frigging naked.

'Can I possibly use the toilet?' shouts the person on the other side of the door.

Oscar. The man I had (apparently) fantastic sex with. Bugger, he's still here. Why hasn't he gone? Anyone with a shred of decency would have gone by now.

'I'm terribly sorry,' he says, sounding so polite I feel bad for thinking he didn't have a shred of decency, 'but I need a piss quite badly, and I'm not going to make it home. Would you prefer me to go in the kitchen sink?'

'No!' I throw the door open, remembering too late that I haven't got any clothes on and grabbing the nearest towel (small, inadequate), with which I try unsuccessfully to cover at least one of the more personal parts of my anatomy. 'I don't allow strangers to piss in my sink,' I tell him haughtily, thinking rather ridiculously that this makes me sound slightly less common. Less common than a drunken slut who picks up strange men in nightclubs and brings them home for wild sex.

He rushes past me, pausing only to pull the door half-closed behind him before grunting with obvious relief as he ... well, relieves himself. I take the opportunity to return somewhat unsteadily to the bedroom where I wrap myself in the duvet. There are shoes, trousers, knickers and ... well, that's a relief – several condom wrappers ... strewn around the bedroom. I rush around, trying to pick things up while holding onto the duvet.

'You don't need to hide the evidence from me,' says the deep, dark voice I remember from last night. Oscar's leaning against the doorway, looking more relaxed and more sober than I feel. 'I was there. I know what happened.'

'Lucky you,' I mutter. 'My memory of it all is a bit of a blur.'

There's nothing I can say that will make sense of what happens next. Nothing that can make me feel any less ashamed, astonished, in fact *aghast* at myself. Still swaying with the devil's own hangover, still trying to piece together the story of last night, still coming to terms with the fact that this rather nice, in fact very nice-looking, very suave, very *sexy* stranger is here in my bedroom with me at all – never mind the fact that he's apparently made love to me several times already and is looking at me now in a manner I recognise only too well – I watch, mesmerised, as he comes towards me, smiling, takes hold of the corners of the duvet I'm sheltering under, tosses it aside and runs his hands confidently down my body.

'Shall we endeavour to recap?' is all he says.

And next minute, we're on the bed again, going at it like a couple of demented, sex-starved tigers on heat. And the noise I'm making is definitely as loud as the noise he's making. And I don't care. I'm loving it. I'm absolutely fucking *loving* it!

So stick *that* where the sun doesn't shine, Charlie Dawkins!

We stop for breakfast in bed; we stop again much later for some baked beans on toast, which is all either of us fancy, and it's not till we're sitting on the bed, still naked, not caring any more, eating the beans on toast that he asks me:

'So, what's the story?'

'Story? Story about what?'

'Charlie,' he says calmly, ignoring the fact that I immediately choke on a mouthful of toast. 'Who's Charlie?'

'Nobody,' I mumble.

'Come on, Sophie,' he says, laughing. 'You called me by his name at least three times last night. I think the least you can do is tell me whether he's your boyfriend or your husband. Or your cat!'

'Neither! I mean, none, I haven't got any. I don't have boyfriends, or husbands. Or cats.'

'So what's the story?' he repeats, shovelling in another mouthful of beans. And then, when I just shake my head instead of answering, he goes on, gently, 'Let's put it this way. I've known you for less than twenty-four hours, and for most of that, we haven't even been dressed, but you don't strike me as the sort of girl who gets drunk out of her skull and spends the night' – he checks his watch and adds – 'and most of the next day, having sex with a stranger.'

'I'm not,' I assure him indignantly. 'I've never ...' But I stop myself, and shrug. It's a bit ridiculous to be indignant about it in the circumstances. 'Anyway – so what?'

'Absolutely. God, don't get me wrong, I'm absolutely, totally, all-out in favour of being unexpectedly picked up by a beautiful woman in a nightclub, invited back to her place and seduced to within an inch of my life.'

'*I* seduced *you*?'

'Yes, and you were very good at it. Thank you very much!' he says, teasing me with his eyes, making me want him all over again. What's the matter with me? I'm not usually this rampant! 'So – what's the story? With Charlie?' he insists.

'What does it matter to you?'

He swallows another mouthful and waves his fork at me. 'It doesn't – apart from wanting to know whether you're still with him, whoever he is. If you are – well, one drunken night with someone else's partner is something to regret and move on from, I suppose. But I wouldn't want to make a habit of it.'

'And if I'm not? If I'm not with anyone?'

He smiles again. When he smiles like that, I'm having trouble keeping my hands off him.

'If we're both free agents, I'm up for starting a habit. If you are.'

'I'm a free agent,' I say quickly. 'I was never anything else. Charlie was …' I hesitate just a second too long. 'A friend.'

'I see,' he says, nodding slowly, watching my face.

'I don't suppose you do. We were friends, but we were also … kind of … sometimes … together. And eventually he wanted more.'

Why am I telling him this? Why is it any of his business? Why does he need to know my personal history, just to have sex and baked beans with me?

'Can't blame the guy,' he says, putting his plate on the floor and pushing me back on the bed. 'He'd have been mad not to want more.'

And I don't even realise, until much, much later, after he's finally gone home, that despite giving me the third degree about my past sexual history, he hasn't told me the first damned thing about himself.

Monday

'His name's Oscar, he's tall and very dark, with amazing brown eyes, the most gorgeous voice, and …' I stop, feeling silly. 'And that's about all I can tell you.'

Polly's on the phone at lunchtime demanding to know the goss, which is understandable since Jo and Emma were both apparently texting her within minutes of leaving me smooching with him at the nightclub, and since I cried off going to see her yesterday afternoon because I was *busy.*

'What do you mean, that's all you can tell me?' she screeches. 'Don't be ridiculous! You could be describing anyone! You could be describing Charlie,' she adds, 'as a matter of fact.'

'He's nothing like Charlie!' I retort. Then I consider this for a minute. 'Well, OK, actually I suppose there are some similarities.'

'Hah! I knew it!'

'So I've got a *type*. Everyone has a type! Don't start doing any amateur psychology on me! And anyway,' I add, smiling to myself, 'he must be about ten years younger.'

'*What!* Ten years *younger*? What, than you? Than Charlie?'

'Yes! Both, since we're the same age! What's so shocking about that?'

'Nothing, nothing whatsoever!' She's still shrieking. 'Oh my God. What's it like? I always fancied having sex with a younger man.'

'Polly, you weren't much more than a teenager when you moved in with Leon. If you'd been having sex before that, with anyone younger than you, you'd have been arrested!'

115

'Don't change the subject. I asked you what it was like. With your new man – or should I say, new *boy*,' she adds mischievously.

'He's not *my new* anything. It's just, well, we just …' I stop. 'It was fantastic!' I admit, sniggering. 'I'm worn out!'

'Wow.' She sighs. There's a world of envy in that sigh. 'I can barely remember what that feels like. Well, I can, of course, remember what it's like to feel worn out, but not by sex. Leon doesn't really seem to fancy me these days. He says it puts him off – you know, my body being different, after having the kids.'

'He had something to do with that!' I say, indignantly. I feel so angry with Leon, on her behalf, I'm gripping the phone hard enough to break it. If only it was his bloody neck. 'How dare he!'

'Well, what am I supposed to do?' she says, sighing again. 'D'you reckon I should dress up?'

'Dress up in what?' My brain's a bit slow today. I'm thinking party frocks and necklaces, jackets and hats.

'You know.' She drops her voice to a whisper. 'Kinky stuff.'

'Oh! Well, I, um … I couldn't say. I've never been into that, but sure, why not, if it turns you on?'

'It doesn't,' she says, miserably. 'Not in the least. But I thought it might work on *him*. What do you think, Sophe? Should I give it go?'

How did we arrive at this point again? Don't get me wrong – I'm relieved, in a way, to be honest: at least it's taken the heat off me, regarding what I know, or don't know, about Oscar. But how do I always end up – even when my friends phone *me*, to ask *me* stuff about *my* love life – being asked for my advice with their own problems? Just for once, I don't think I can be bothered to make any pretence about it. I'm going to tell her what I really think.

'Actually, no, I don't think you should give it a go, Polly. I think you should tell Leon straight that if he doesn't still find your body just as beautiful now, after it's been through the trauma of producing his two children, then there are plenty of people who would, so he can just go and fuck himself.'

There's a stunned silence for a moment. Then:

'You wouldn't really say that, would you, Sophie?'

I sigh. 'No. Not really.' Actually I *would*, but it's not helping her, is it? 'Maybe just try a basque and suspenders, eh, Polly?'

Jo and Emma are next. They arrive together, pretty much straight from work, having phoned first to make sure I haven't got a client with me.

'Oh my God!' squeals Emma as soon as I open the door to them. 'Who *was* he?'

'You didn't sleep with him, did you?' demands Jo, coming in and looking round the flat as if she half expects to find him still here, in his underwear. Then, without waiting for an answer, 'Was it good?'

'Yes, and yes,' I say, grinning – which starts them both off squealing in stereo.

'Who *is* he?' repeats Emma, plonking herself down on the sofa, ready for a long gossip. 'Come on! Tell all!'

'Oscar.' I fiddle with my hair, thoughtfully. 'Want a drink? Glass of wine, Em? Orange juice, Jo?'

'Oscar who?' Jo sits down next to Emma, looking at me expectantly.

'Where's he live?' says Emma. 'What's he do?'

'Um. Red wine or white?'

'Sophie!' says Jo.

'*Tell* us!' says Emma.

I hang my head.

'There's nothing to tell. His name's Oscar, he's lovely …'

'He's about twenty, by the look of him. Did his mother know he was out?' says Jo.

'Not as young as *that*,' I protest weakly.

'And you don't know anything else about him, do you?' There's a thrill of shock in Emma's voice. 'You brought him back here, had sex with him …'

'All right, all right!' I spread my hands in defeat. 'Yes, I did, and no, I don't know anything else about him. I kind of forgot to ask.' They both giggle. Well, it's more of a titter. I give them a look of annoyance. 'Come on – we've all done it, haven't we?'

'Yeah, we have,' Jo laughs. 'One night stand, then – right?'

'Well, no. Actually, he's coming back tonight.'

'Bloody hell!' They both jump up like they've been shot.

'It's all right – not yet! Sit down, finish your drinks, for God's sake! He's coming round about eight, with a takeaway.'

'And his toothbrush?' Emma says cheekily, nudging Jo.

'I hope so!' I say – and we all burst out laughing.

Actually, just before he arrives, I get a sudden fit of nerves. Or something. I'm just doing my make-up when I stare at myself, in the mirror, and say to myself, out loud:

'*What the hell are you playing at, Sophie?*'

I drop my mascara and shake my head at myself. Only a couple of days ago I was crying, distraught, because Charlie told me he was engaged to someone else. You can't be that upset, and then almost immediately start something with somebody new, can you? It's not supposed to work like that. Surely the least I should have done would be to cry for a couple more days, on my own, before jumping into bed with the first lovely, fit, sexy, amazingly athletic man who comes along? What's the matter with

118

me? Forgotten Charlie already, have I? Or what – am I trying to retaliate? Is that it – a case of whatever Charlie can do with Hateful Helen, I can do with someone much younger, much more often, and without having to buy a bloody diamond ring?

'*No,*' I tell my reflection, quite calmly, quite deliberately, picking up the mascara and finishing off my eyes. '*It's nothing to do with Charlie whatsoever. It's just sex, OK? Just sex, and plenty of it. Nothing wrong with that, is there?*'

And what's more, I'm going to be sober this time.

My sister Debra phones me just before he turns up. We've been talking at least once a week since I went down to Devon, and I've been phoning Mum every few days. I'm never getting into the situation again of not knowing whether she's in or out of hospital, in or out of serious operations with serious consequences.

'She's doing OK,' says Debra tonight.

'Only OK? She told me she was absolutely fine, when I spoke to her the other day.'

'Sophie, don't panic – yes, she's fine, but she's still recovering from the surgery, and the treatment isn't going to be a picnic, you know? The drugs have side-effects. She's not going to be jumping up and down shouting with excitement about it all, not for a long while yet.'

'No. Of course not. Do you think I should come down?'

'There's nothing you can do.'

'I'm coming next month, definitely. I've cleared a week in my diary.'

'I know – you said. That'll be great. But look, Sophe, I know I said stuff, before – about you not caring, and all that – but I didn't mean it. I was just worried about Mum, obviously. I know you're not exactly just round the corner.'

'No, but I could have come down sooner. I should have ...'

'We've been over all this, haven't we. Let's forget it, now. Let's just concentrate on Mum getting better. If there's ever a need for you to worry, again, I promise I won't mess around – I'll tell you outright to get your arse down here.'

'Good.' I smile. 'That's a relief.'

'How's Charlie?' she says then, so suddenly, so out of the blue, that I reply without giving it a second's thought:

'Engaged.'

'*What*?' she shouts. '*Engaged*?'

'Not ... no, Debs, no – not to me! To some bird called Helen that he's only just met. Desperate, or what?'

'He dumped you?' she squawks indignantly.

'No. It wasn't like that. I told you – we weren't an item. We weren't even together. He didn't ...' I stop, sigh. 'Yes,' I admit, wearily. 'He dumped me.'

'The bastard!' she shouts.

'No – look, he's not a bastard. He actually dumped me before I even came down to Devon, but he still drove me all the way down there.'

'He didn't dump you for the Helen bird?'

'No. He dumped me because I didn't want a serious relationship.'

There's a silence. I can actually hear Debra breathing. It's a very strained kind of breathing, like she's trying to force herself not to shout at me.

'You're bloody mad, do you know that?' she says finally.

'Why? Because I didn't agree to something I don't even want? Because I don't want to be tied to some bloke for life, take his name, become his property, have his kids, and end up resenting him? Like you do with James?'

'James and I have a perfectly adequate marriage,' she says.

'Listen to yourself, Debra. Just listen to yourself.'

'At least I'm not alone and lonely!'

'And nor am I.' Dead on cue, the doorbell rings. I find myself smiling as I add, 'Sorry, love – got to go. That'll be Oscar – with a takeaway. And his toothbrush, I hope.'

'*Oscar*?' she yells. 'Who the fuck is Oscar?'

But I'm cutting off the call.

And turning off the phone.

'I need to ask you,' I tell him later, much later, when we've eaten the takeaway and gone back to bed and woken up halfway through the night to start again. 'Before we go any further …'

'I haven't got an STD,' he says, deadly serious, 'if that's what you're worried about.'

'No! God, sorry – thank you, neither have I – I suppose that should have been something we got out of the way first, shouldn't it. Before we got started. Before we even …' I stop, swallow, flounder. Funny how you can shag someone senseless for hours on end without a twinge of embarrassment, but start talking about the possibility of any diseases you might give each other, and suddenly you can't meet each other's eyes.

'Even before we got out of the taxi,' he finishes for me, smiling.

'Yes. But we were both a bit drunk. And the thing is …'

'It's OK. I've used a condom every time. In case you were too drunk to notice,' he says, politely.

'I know. It's not that. It's just …'

'And I don't expect you to marry me to make an honest man of me.'

'Well, that's a relief!' I laugh. 'But …'

'What is it, then?'

'I don't know the first thing about you! I don't know where you live, or what you do, or even what your surname is! I don't know how old you are! I don't know, even, if you're already married,' I gabble.

There's a silence.

'Shit.' I sit up, horrified. 'You're not, are you? Please tell me you're not!'

'I'm not,' he replies, smoothly. 'And in answer to everything else: I live in Putney. I'm a sound engineer. My surname's Mitchell. And I'm twenty-five.'

'Oh!' I grin with relief. 'Only nine years. I thought it might be ten.'

'Sorry?'

'Younger than me. You're nine years younger than me. Do you mind?' I add quickly.

'Of course not. It's a turn-on.'

'Is it?' I ponder this for a moment. But before I have time to ponder it for any longer than a moment, he goes on,

'And while we're on a roll with the life stories, I should also say that although I'm most definitely not married, I did used to be.'

'Used to be what?' I repeat dreamily, still trying to get back to happy pondering of the whole age turn-on thing.

'Married. I used to be married. I was married for five years.'

'Blimey!' I sit up again. 'Blimey, Oscar – are you sure?'

'Well of course, I'm sure!' He's laughing again. But this is no laughing matter.

'You must have been married when you were about twelve!' I protest.

'Maths is obviously not your strong point! I got married when I was eighteen. Too bloody young, yes, of course – it was a stupid mistake. I've been divorced for three years now.'

'Oh. Well, phew – at least you won't want to make *that* mistake again.'

'Not in a hurry,' he agrees. 'Especially because of the children.'

'Yeah, absolutely. You wouldn't want to have any *children* and then get divorced.'

He props himself up on one elbow. 'That's what I'm saying, Sophie. We did. We did have children.'

Oh shit.

'Three of them.'

Oh, triple shit.

'Benjamin's seven, and the twins are five.'

'Twins?' I say, hoarsely. 'Oh. Lovely.'

And I close my eyes while he, lovingly, starts to describe his lovely three children.

Tuesday

My youngest sister Millie's on the phone to me before I've even finished getting dressed this morning.

'Who's this Oscar?' she demands, her tone reminiscent of the strict mother of a wayward teenager. The jungle telegraph in Devon is obviously alive and well.

I smile at *this Oscar* across the bedroom.

'I'll phone you back later, Mills.'

'No! Now, Sophie – come on, the whole story, please! Debs says Charlie dumped you because he wanted to get engaged, and now ...'

'Yes. And I'll talk to you *later*,' I say, pointedly.

'Shit. He's there, isn't he!' she hisses. 'He's stayed the night!'

'That's absolutely correct.' And I'm watching him now, walking naked across my bedroom, heading for the shower. Gorgeous. A picture of perfection. I'm almost licking my lips.

'You crafty old *cow*!' says Millie, her voice dripping with envy and admiration. 'You don't waste any time, do you?'

'And talking of time, I'm going to have to scoot, OK? I've got a client in less than an hour.'

'OK, I get the picture, I'll call back later. And I want *all* the details!' she warns me.

Well, I think to myself grimly. I may leave out one or two little details. Or maybe three: seven year old Benjamin, and two five year old twins.

I think about it, on and off, during the day, while I'm crimping and curling and pinning and clipping, while I'm moisturising and toning and lip-sticking and eye-lining. I'm convincing myself it doesn't make any difference. Well – it doesn't, does it? I mean, as far as I'm concerned,

124

his kids are irrelevant. They're part of his past. We've all had things in our past, haven't we. So, he's had a seven year old son and twin girls, and I've had… a hamster called Clive, and a ginger cat called Nutty who's actually buried under a rosebush in my parents' garden. I do know a little bit about love and loss, you see. So, he married very young, probably had the kids by mistake, and now they're just part of a package of regrets he obviously has to live with. It really doesn't have any impact on our enjoyment of each other whether he has three kids, or three hundred. It's fine. It's just a nice, civilised, sexual thing between consenting adults – no strings, no responsibilities, fun while it lasts, see how it goes. Just the way I like it. It's helping me get over Charlie, keeping my mind off him. I'm still upset with him, but I think I'm missing him less already. He was *far* too serious for me.

'You're quiet, Sophie,' says my client, Annabel. Annabel is a colleague of Jo's – a special recommendation – the story is that Annabel's family has pots of money, Daddy's paying for the wedding and whatever Annabel wants, nothing will be too much trouble, so I really want to make a good impression. She's a nice girl, too, which helps. 'Are you OK?'

'Yes, yes – of course. Fine. I'm just concentrating – trying to make your hair look as perfect as possible.' I smile at her in the mirror. 'What do you think?'

'It's lovely. You're so clever. Jo said I wouldn't regret coming to you, and she's quite right. Would you be interested in doing my bridesmaids too, Sophie, on the day? If you've got time? I'm having six of them – all children – but they're very nice, very well behaved kids.'

Six bridesmaids. I'm doing a few sums. This could be a very profitable booking. As long as they *are* nice kids, not like that little brat Bluebell the other week.

'Yes, that'll be fine,' I tell Annabel calmly. 'And if they're under twelve they get a special rate, of course.'

'Oh, don't be silly. They've all got long hair, so it's just as much work for you, Sophie, no matter what age. I insist on paying the normal rate for them all.'

'Well, that's very generous, but honestly ...'

'No, I absolutely insist!' She smiles. 'I expect you love doing little girls' hair, don't you? It must be so lovely for you – seeing them all excited, in their bridesmaids' dresses, their little eyes shining – ah, kids are so lovely, aren't they? I can't wait to have my own!'

'Mm,' I say, forcing a smile.

'Ideally, I'd like to try for a baby straight away, as soon as we're married,' she gushes on. 'But Jeremy wants to wait.' Her smile drops. 'It's the only thing we disagree on.'

'Well, at the end of the day, there's still plenty of time, isn't there.'

'No, Sophie!' She's looking really upset now. Shit. Why did we have to get onto this subject? 'No, there's *not* plenty of time. I'm already thirty-seven! Do you *realise* how few eggs there are left in my ovaries?'

'Um, no. I must admit ...'

'Every month, my chances of conceiving naturally get less and less. It's all very well for *him* – he can father children right up till he's eighty or ninety, not that anyone will still want to be having sex with him at that age, of course – that's what I keep telling him. But to be honest, Sophie, if he doesn't change his mind about starting a family straight away, after we get married, I'll think I'll just have to come off the Pill anyway. What do you think?'

'Oh! Well, er, I don't know if that's really a good idea. It's ...'

'Starting married life with a deception, isn't it? Say it, go on – yes, I know you're right, Sophie, but let's be honest, when a woman's desperate for a baby, she'll do anything, won't she?'

'I suppose so.'

'After all, look at what Jo's doing. Do you think that's a reasonable thing for a woman to do? Even though she's on her own? Having her own baby – without bothering about a man? What do you think, Sophie – would *you* do it?'

'No. No, *I* wouldn't,' I admit, 'but then, I don't want children.'

'You don't …?' She blinks at me. 'What – not for a while yet?'

'No. Not ever. Not at all.'

'Oh, *Sophie*!' Her eyes have actually filled up with tears. 'Have you really thought this through? You see, when I hear people say things like that, I feel so *worried* for them. So worried that they'll suddenly wake up and realise what they're missing when it's too late. Have you thought about that, at all?'

I want to say *Yes, I have bloody thought about it, and don't patronise me!* But I grit my teeth and reply as calmly as I can: 'We're all different, you know. Having kids isn't right for everyone.'

'I've never thought about it like that,' she says, wonderingly. 'Well. I suppose it takes all types, as they say.'

She goes quiet for the rest of her appointment, no doubt thinking about what planet I might be from, and whether I'll be able to cope with her six bridesmaids without tying them all up by their long hair, when I'm apparently such a committed child-hater.

Well, as she quite rightly says, it takes all types.

Jo rings me later.

'How did you get on with Annabel?'

'Great, thanks. Thanks for the introduction. I'm doing her six bridesmaids as well, on the day. Good one.'

'That'll be all her nieces and second cousins or whatever. The whole family is heaving with kids,

127

apparently – she's the only one who hasn't got any yet. She's desperate to have her own.'

'Yes. She was telling me.'

'Understandable, of course. That was exactly how I felt, myself.'

'But – sorry, Jo, but I don't ever remember you saying you wanted kids! You never mentioned it! You were ...' *Perfectly normal,* I was going to say. But by all accounts, it's me who's not perfectly normal, isn't it. 'You were enjoying yourself just fine the way you were,' I finish instead, slightly resentfully.

'I wasn't. I was pretending. All those nights out – all those boring, stupid nights when we had nothing better to do than hang around in nightclubs chatting up the men and getting drunk ...'

'Boring!' I gasp. Chatting up men and getting drunk is boring, but staying home every night on your own, feeling sick and knitting baby bootees isn't?

'Yes. It might be fun for sixteen year olds, Sophe, but at our age, sorry, it's boring, and it's sad, and immature.'

'So *that's* what's wrong with me!' I say. 'I'm immature!'

'Well – in a nice way, of course!' she says, laughing.

'Well, I've been called worse things.' Actually, at any age over twenty, I think it's quite a compliment. I look at myself in the mirror. Do I *look* young for my age? I hope so. Especially now I'm having sex with a twenty-five year old.

'You'll probably end up being one of these old women who want babies when they're about seventy,' she says, exploding with laughter.

'God! I certainly *won't!*'

She's still laughing, as if it's the funniest thing she's ever thought of.

'Have you told your parents yet?' I say, to change the subject. 'About the baby – not having a father?'

That stops her laughing at me for a moment, anyway.

'No,' she says. 'Not exactly.'

'Not exactly … what, then?'

'I've, well, what I've told them is, that I had a one night stand when I was drunk. I thought that might be easier to explain.'

'I see.' I don't, really. Jo's dad's a vicar, and her mum's an R.E. teacher. They're lovely people, but they've got quite firm views, and I don't imagine they ever anticipated the day when their first grandchild would be the result of a casual bonk when their daughter was too drunk to utter either the word *No* or the word *Condom*. 'How did they take that?'

'They were fine.' There's a pause, and then she adds quietly, 'They said they'd pray for me.'

'Bit late for that, isn't it?'

'You can mock, Sophie, but they're very sincere.'

'I know they are. I'm not mocking. But you're lying to them!'

'Well, what am I supposed to say? I think they'd be shocked by the truth – that I couldn't find a man of my own.'

This is so ridiculous, I can't even be bothered to argue.

'Well, at the end of the day, they're your parents, you obviously know what's best,' I say.

'Yes. And one day, when I finally meet The One …'

'The one what?'

'Oh, Sophie, you're impossible! *The One*, you know – the man for me. When I finally meet him, and he marries me and adopts my baby, then everything will be perfect.'

I just shake my head. Well, I'm sorry, but it's like listening to a politician describing his dream of world peace. You can't really believe in it, but he makes it sound so plausible, you can't come up with an argument against it.

'OK,' is all I can manage.

'And speaking of *The One*, how was last night – with *Oscar*?' she purrs, saying his name in a silly coy voice, like we're thirteen year olds having our first crushes on boys in our class. Any minute now she'll be writing down our names together and ticking off the letters: *Love, Friendship, Hatred, Indifference; Love* ...

'Fine,' I say briskly. 'Great. And he's not The One, so don't start getting ideas.'

'No. I suppose he's just, you know, a Getting-Over-Charlie thing, is he?'

'No!' I feel cross, now. 'No, he's not. He's not anything. We're just spending a bit of time together.'

'Mm. Seeing him again tonight, are you?'

'Yes, as it happens.'

'Aha! Not serious, though?' she says, teasingly.

'No!' I sigh. 'Look, *you* don't want to go out drinking because of the baby. Emma doesn't want to go out drinking because of Stefan. Polly doesn't want to go out because of her kids. What am I supposed to do? Sit at home and do my embroidery?'

'You could knit some bootees if you like,' she says, giggling.

'Thanks. Tempting. But I think, on balance, I'd rather have sex with a fit young guy,' I say, smoothly.

At least I've made her laugh.

'I didn't put you off, did I?' says Oscar anxiously as soon as he arrives tonight. 'Talking to you about my kids?'

'No! God, no – not at all! Absolutely not!'

As long as you don't make a habit of it.

'Good. I'd hate to do anything to put you off me – I'm enjoying our time together so much,' he says, deftly undoing my jeans with one hand while he pushes the door shut behind him with the other. Talk about not wasting a moment.

'Me too,' I manage to croak with what little breath he's left me.

We don't even make it to the bedroom this time. Luckily my lounge carpet's quite nice and soft.

'Sorry that was a bit rushed,' he apologises. He's still got his shirt on. 'I've been thinking about you all day. I could hardly wait.'

'That's nice.' It is, too. When you've been dumped by somebody who couldn't wait to get engaged to the nearest long-legged blonde bimbo, a bit of sexual flattery goes a long way.

'Were you thinking of me, too?' he goes on, jumping up from the floor with a youthful zest and vigour I quite envy.

'Yes. Yes, I was, actually.' I smile at him. 'I've been looking forward to seeing you.'

'You don't mind? About me being younger than you?'

'No. I like it. You've got … so much energy.'

'Shall I show you just how much?' he offers, helping me up from the floor – elderly lady that I am – and encircling me with his arms again. Blimey! Twice in the same hour? Is it my birthday, or what?

'OK! But shall we, um, try the bed, this time? My bum's gone numb.'

With which he picks me up, carries me into the bedroom and in one apparently effortless movement, throws me and himself onto the middle of the bed.

Mmm, I'm thinking as he starts kissing me again. *Oh yes. I could really get used to this.*

Charlie? I'm sorry, but Charlie who?

<u>Sunday</u>

Polly's in a strange mood today.

'You managed to get out of bed for long enough to come round and see me, then?' are her first words when she opens the door to me.

'What's that supposed to mean?' I'm holding her by the shoulders, just about to give her a greeting kiss, but now, instead, I hold her out at arm's length and scrutinise her face. 'What have I done?'

'Nothing.' She shrugs me off and leads the way into the kitchen, where Ethan, who's just mastered sitting up properly, is in a highchair, holding something disgusting and wiping it round his face. 'No, Ethan,' she says wearily. '*Eat* the lovely rice cake, don't play with it. I'm trying to start him on solids,' she adds to me, as if I'd have a clue what that means.

'Shall I put the kettle on?' I ask her. 'Where's Gracie?'

'Upstairs, sulking in her bedroom because I wouldn't let her cut up my wedding dress to make clothes for her dolls,' she says tonelessly as if it's an everyday occurrence. Perhaps it is. 'Although, to be honest, I don't know why I'm bothering to stop her!' she adds in a sudden outburst. She sits down abruptly at the kitchen table. 'I don't know why I should fucking care!'

It's not like Polly to swear in front of the kids – even the baby, who can't even repeat *Dada* or *Mama* yet. I get mugs out of the cupboard, fill the kettle, switch it on, before I sit down next to her and ask, gently:

'What's happened?'

She shrugs – a fierce, angry shrug. She picks up the remainder of Ethan's horrible mushy rice cake and starts squashing it back into shape.

'Is he really going to eat that?' I say, lightly.

'How would I know? I'm just a stupid, useless, *mother*, too stupid to do anything apart from change nappies and mop up children's mess ...'

'Polly!' I take the squashed cake-thing out of her hands and hold out my arms to her. 'Come here. What's this all about? Of course you're not stupid, or useless. *I* couldn't do what you do! I wouldn't have a clue!'

She blinks back tears, her lower lip wobbling.

'Is this something to do with Leon, by any chance?' I find it so hard to say his name without grimacing with distaste, I have to bite my lip.

'Yes.' As if I didn't know. 'He's been ... really funny.'

'Or maybe not. You're not laughing,' I point out.

'I don't know what's got into him,' she goes on, shaking her head. 'He's in such a horrible mood all the time. I've tried to work out what it's all about – he won't tell me. At first I thought maybe he wanted more sex. You know, I told you, he hasn't fancied me lately, but perhaps I should try to be more *physical.* More *inviting.* I mean – look at *you!*'

'Me?' I flinch. 'What have I got to do with it?'

'You're at it all the bloody time, aren't you. Every bloody night. Isn't that what they all want, at the end of the day? Should I be doing that with Leon – jumping on him every night?'

'Jesus, Polly – *no!* For God's sake! You've got two kids – a *baby* – you're knackered most of the time! *And* he insulted you, didn't he, saying he didn't fancy you – that's hardly the way to make you feel wanted.' I get up and make the tea, put the mugs down on the table and look at her, anxiously. 'Don't start comparing yourself with me, just because I'm, well, just because ...'

'Just because you're shagging a teenager?' she says, the first flicker of a smile trembling the corners of her mouth for just a second.

'Not *quite* a teenager!' I smile back. 'Seriously, it's only like this because it's new. You know – new and exciting ...' I tail off, seeing the look on her face. That was the wrong thing to say, obviously. Not helpful, inviting comparisons between my *new and exciting* sex and her *old, boring, married* sex. In fact, the thought of any kind of sex with Leon makes me want to puke – if it does the same for her, I wonder she's ever managed it at all.

'I don't know,' she says, with a huge sigh. 'If it's not about wanting more sex, it must be about wanting another baby.'

What? I choke on my tea, spit a mouthful straight out, narrowly missing the remains of the baby's squashed rice cake.

'Another *baby*?' I splutter. 'You've only just had this one!'

'I know. But why else would he be acting so funny about Jo?'

'About Jo?' I repeat, quietly. 'What do you mean, *about Jo*?'

'Ever since I told him about Jo having a baby, and about the artificial insemination thingy, he's been ... well, really funny.' She lowers her voice and her eyes, as if she's ashamed. 'Quite nasty, to be honest, Sophe.'

'He hasn't hit you?' I demand at once.

'God, no. Not that. Just in a horrible mood, and having digs at me all the time. Like he's gone off me,' she adds pathetically. 'Do you think that's what's wrong with him, Sophe? He wants me to be pregnant again, like Jo?'

'Who knows?' I say, crossly. 'But don't even *think* about it – you hear me? You wouldn't, would you? Just to keep him happy – I mean, for fuck's sake ... sorry, sorry Ethan ... for God's sake, Polly – it's *you* that has to do everything, all the feeding and nappies and washing and pushing the pram ...' I can't, for the minute, think what all the other things are that she has to do, but I know there are a lot of them, and none of them are much fun, and Leon doesn't get involved in any of them.

'I know,' she says, sniffing miserably. 'And to be honest, Sophe, I don't think I could cope. Not with another one, not yet.'

'Of course you couldn't! You're still feeding Ethan, anyway, aren't you?'

'Just stopped this week. My milk was drying up. Probably because I've been so upset.'

'Well, you shouldn't *let* him upset you!' I feel so exasperated, I hardly know what else to say. I wish to God she'd leave him. I wish to God she'd never met him, but no point crying over spilt milk. Or dried-up milk. 'If he starts being nasty to you again, just tell him to fuck off.'

'I can't do that, Sophie,' she says sadly. 'I'm too scared – too scared that that's exactly what he will do.'

I'm having fantasies, by the time I go home, of waiting for him in the dark with a sawn-off shotgun. Or maybe that's too good for him. Don't get me started.

So what the hell's his problem? I mean, apart from the usual one of him being a complete prat. You can't tell me he wants another baby – he's never even shown any sign of wanting the two he's already got. Those kids are just lucky they've got such a lovely mummy, because their dad's been a waste of space from the moment of conception onwards. So why the funny mood about Jo? Maybe he sees it as one less supposedly available woman in the world for him to indulge his sick, pathetic little male fantasies about.

Or maybe it's nothing to do with Jo at all. Maybe he's just suddenly become even more of a tosser than he already was. You never know – if he goes on like this, Polly might finally see the light and divorce him. We can but hope.

Don't get me wrong. Even though I'm not the marrying kind, I'm not advocating divorce as a lifestyle choice, either. But sometimes it can't be helped. When my best friend marries a jerk, I have to make an exception. That marriage shouldn't have happened in the first place. He didn't deserve her. Why did she fall in love with him? I'll never understand it. She should have fallen in love with somebody gentle and kind, like her. Somebody who would appreciate her, look after her, treat her properly. She should have bloody *waited* for that kind and gentle person to come along! Or not bothered at all. Better to have sperm from some random stranger, like Jo, if you're that desperate for children, than settling for bloody Leon.

'What's so bad about him?' Oscar asks me tonight, when we're eating chocolate digestives in bed. We haven't had a proper meal together at the table yet – it seems like too much trouble – too long to spend out of bed. I don't know why I've told him about Polly and Leon, really. Well, I suppose I do: I'm still upset about it.

'He's a prat,' I say, dismissively.

'In what way?'

'Oh – too many ways to mention. Sorry, let's not talk about him. I shouldn't have brought it up.'

'No – you're obviously worried, about your friend. He's not violent, is he?'

'No, thank God. Although if he was, at least it would make her leave him.'

He munches another biscuit, looking at me thoughtfully.

'What is it, then? Is he a drunk? A womaniser? Oh!' He must have seen something, fleetingly, in my eyes. '*That's* it, is it? He's been screwing around? And she doesn't know, I suppose.'

I don't say anything. I don't have to.

'She'll find out,' he says softly. 'People always do. And it's better that way. It'll be hard, but she needs to find it out for herself.'

'Are you an expert on this stuff?'

'Absolutely.' He shrugs carelessly. 'It's what happened in my own marriage.'

'You cheated on your wife?' I swallow my biscuit crumbs, staring at him in horror. I don't really know this guy, do I. Anything could be true.

'No! It was the other way around. From day one, apparently, as I found out afterwards. The best man at the wedding – an old friend of mine. Outside at the reception.'

'You're *joking*.'

'Unfortunately not. He was the first of many. As far as she was concerned, she was only getting married because she was pregnant, and it was just about wearing a nice dress and having a lovely party. She never had any intention of being faithful. But it was such a stupid idea, getting married at that age. It was my fault as much as hers.'

I can't imagine how any girl, however young and stupid, could possibly have wanted any more than Oscar. What the hell was she looking for? I mean, sorry to be *graphic*, but multiple orgasms seem to be his specialty. Time is no object. Time and time again seems to be all par for the course. If I'd wandered into Sex Heaven for Girls and asked for their prototype, best-selling model, I couldn't have done any better for myself. And – I know I don't really know him properly yet – but he seems *nice*, too. Why would anyone cheat on him? What was the matter with the girl?

'It's no big deal any more,' he says, smiling at me. 'I'm over it. We've both moved on. We stay in touch, though, of course, for the sake of the kids.'

'Oh. Yes, of course.' I'd managed to forget about the kids. 'I suppose you have to.'

It must be awful. I mean, supposing you had the worst marriage possible – for instance, the worst marriage I can imagine would be with Leon. And supposing you broke up, and still had to keep in touch, and be civilised, because of the children. Wouldn't that be terrible? In Leon's case, of course, I'd hope that if he and Polly break up, she'll just tell him he can't see the kids any more. He wouldn't want to, would he? It's not as though he's exactly been a hands-on father – I've always presumed he'd walk away without a backward glance. Better for everyone.

'Do you still see them, then?' I ask Oscar. 'Your son, and your twins?'

'Of course!' He laughs, as if it's a ridiculous question. 'In fact, that was something I was going to tell you. It's my turn to have them, next weekend.'

'Oh, that's nice for you.'

'You don't mind?' he says, anxiously.

'Of course not!' To be honest, if we carry on at this rate, by the weekend I'll be ready for a rest anyway. 'What do you do with them – take them out somewhere?' I add, trying to sound interested.

'Yes. I was thinking perhaps we could go down to the coast. What do you think?'

What do *I* think? Here we go again – is there no end to my apparent capacity as an advice columnist?

'Oh, don't ask me. I've got no experience whatsoever with kids. I wouldn't have a clue where to take them. It's up to you, isn't it.'

'Well, if the weather's good, that'd be nice, wouldn't it? A day at the beach?'

'I guess so.' I'm getting a bit bored with this conversation, to be honest. 'I grew up at the seaside, so I'm probably a bit biased, but I presume most kids enjoy it.'

'Great. That's settled, then. You're sure you don't mind?'

Bloody hell. We've only been seeing each other for a week, and he's acting like he has to have my permission to go out with his children. This could very quickly get on my nerves, if it wasn't for the fact that he's so gorgeous.

'No, I don't mind – why should I?' I finish the last biscuit and throw the empty wrapper down by the side of the bed. Time to change the subject.

'You're great – do you know that?' he says, reaching over and pinning me down against the pillows. That's more like it. 'You're the best thing that's happened to me in ages.'

'Same here,' I mumble against his hair. An annoying little twinge of conscience surges up inside me for just one moment. *How would Charlie feel, hearing you say that?* demands the annoying little twinge, making me close my eyes and wait for it to pass.

Why would he care? I answer myself. *He's engaged to Horrible Helen – already – not five minutes after dumping me!*

And I'm not going to waste any more time listening to irritating twinges, thank you very much.

The following Saturday

It's Annabel's wedding today – the woman with the rich father and the six bridesmaids – so I've got a busy day, and an early start. Fortunately in a way, I didn't see Oscar last night – the first night off we've had since we met – as he was going to pick up his kids.

'Still OK for Sunday?' he said. 'It'll be fairly early.'

'No problem,' I said, laughing. I presume he's going to drop the kids off home tomorrow morning and come straight round to mine for breakfast. I'll make it worth his while, of course. Meanwhile I've been trying to persuade Polly and the other girls to come out tonight, but honestly, you'd think I was asking them to fly to the moon without a parachute.

'Oh, I don't know,' says Emma, sounding pained. 'I mean, it's not *that* long since last time we went out on a Saturday night, is it? I don't want to keep doing it.'

'Keep doing it?' I stare at my phone, as if it's gone mad. Am I hearing things? 'What do you mean, *keep* doing it? Saturday nights only come around once a week!'

'I know. But if I keep going out on Saturday nights, it's not very fair on Stefan, is it.'

'Why not? Can't he be left? Is he ill?'

'No,' she says, and it's a long-drawn out *no* … more of a *no-o-o-oh* …, as if she's being incredibly patient with me but I really am being difficult. 'He's not *ill*, but he is my *fiancé*.'

'And?'

'Well, Sophie, honestly, what do you think? He expects us to spend Saturday nights together, obviously.'

'Oh! OK. Nice. Romantic. Where are you two off to, then?'

'Nowhere. We're getting a pizza in, and watching *Britain's Got Talent.*'

'Lovely.'

'Don't say it like that, Sophe – so dismissive. We're saving up to get married, you know. Can't go blowing all our money on booze every weekend, any more.'

'No. I suppose not. Can't go having any fun any more, now you're getting married, can you!'

'You'll find out, one day,' she says, giggling as if it's all very exciting, giving up your life to save up, eat pizza and watch crap TV. 'When you decide to marry this new young boyfriend of yours.'

'Don't be ridiculous,' I say, mildly, as this is too ludicrous to even be annoyed about.

'Well, anyway – I'm sorry about tonight, Sophe, but have a nice evening, and I'll see you another time.'

'OK, Em. Next time there hasn't been a Saturday night for a while. Yeah?'

'Yeah,' she says, sounding only faintly puzzled.

Jo's no better – claiming the baby is making her feel tired, even though she hasn't even got a bump yet and the baby must be about the size of a tadpole. Not that I actually know this, of course – I'm guessing – and perhaps I'm being unfair because I suppose if I had a tadpole swimming around inside me all day every day, I might feel seriously shattered too. Just the thought of it makes me come over a bit queasy, so there you go.

And as for Polly – she's got no intention of doing anything that might make Leon even more upset with her.

'It might make him appreciate you a bit, for a change, if you go out and he has to look after the kids,' I say.

'No. He wouldn't like it. You know what he's like.'

I do, unfortunately. But that's another story.

Oh well, I guess it's a pizza and *Britain's Got Talent* for me, too, tonight. I just can't wait.

Annabel's getting married at a huge country mansion in Surrey, and the bridal party are all getting ready at her parents' house – which actually seems to be another huge mansion, also in Surrey. That's why I've had to make an early start, what with driving down here and finding the place – which is down its own drive, behind its own security-protected iron gates with family crests on them.

There's also, of course, the small matter of the six bridesmaids.

'I'll do you first,' I tell Annabel, when I eventually find her. This takes longer than you'd think, as her mother, who's excited but behaving like a very calm, very gracious hostess – I suppose that's all in the breeding – has had to show me up two flights of stairs, down a corridor into a different wing of the house – (how many houses do you know, that have wings? I'm dead impressed) – and finally along another hallway, just to get to the room that Annabel's using.

The room, which was apparently Annabel's bedroom when she lived at home, is enormous – she could have the wedding ceremony in here, to be honest, without too much difficulty – and Annabel is sitting at the dressing-table, staring at herself in the mirror.

'I'll do you first,' I repeat, as she doesn't seem to have heard me. 'Is that OK?'

'Yes, Sophie, of course,' she says in a strangely flat voice. 'Whatever you think best.'

'Well, I always think it's best to make sure the bride's done – after all you're the star of the show!'

I'm bustling about, opening my bags and getting everything out, talking like some sort of cheery holiday-camp entertainer. I think I'm trying to compensate for the fact that she's still sitting there, staring dumbly at her

143

reflection without a flicker of a smile or a hint of excitement. I've seen this plenty of times before, of course – it's usually all down to nerves.

'Now, then – just you relax and make yourself comfortable,' I tell her. 'We've got loads of time, there's no rush, so take some deep breaths and get ready to enjoy the day.'

'We had a row last night,' she says, tonelessly, still staring at herself. 'Jeremy and I – we had a terrible row.'

'Ah, don't worry, love.' I run my comb through her hair, smiling at her in the mirror. 'Lots of couples do. It's the build-up of tension about the wedding, that's all – it'll all be fine today.' Personally, I think this is a very good reason for the old adage about it being bad luck for the bride and groom to see each other the night before the wedding. This nearly always happens, in my experience – the bride's tetchy with nerves, the groom gets drunk, she gets annoyed, he snaps back – suddenly they're talking about calling the wedding off. 'Have you spoken to him this morning?'

'No.'

'Why don't you give him a quick ring, before we start? You'll feel better.'

It's a bit ridiculous that I'm talking to her like I'm her mother. For a start, she's thirty-seven – even older than me – not a sixteen year old. And for another thing, her own mother's here, somewhere, not that I'd ever be able to find her, without a map of the house or a Sat Nav to guide me. Why isn't she here with her daughter, chivvying her along, cheering her up, making her feel better?

'Mum's been saying the same thing.' Ah. 'But I told her to mind her own business.' Aha.

'Well, in that case maybe I should do the same,' I say, lightly, giving her another quick smile and adopting a business-like pose with a strand of her hair between my fingers.

144

'Oh, Sophie! What am I going to do?' she bursts out, suddenly – and starts to cry.

Oh, bloody, bloody hell.

It's not like this is the first time I've had a bride in floods of tears on the wedding day. In fact, if I had a pound for every time it's happened, I could probably afford to live in a house like this myself. Sometimes they cry because they're happy, but more often it's because they're stressed, anxious, having second thoughts, or somebody's upset them. And the number one candidate for upsetting the bride is, of course, the groom.

I think we've got beyond the point of me minding my own business. I pull up a chair and sit down next to her, handing her a tissue and waiting for the crying to subside a little.

'What was it all about?' I ask gently.

She blows her nose noisily. 'The baby thing,' she says, in a dismal voice. 'As usual.'

'Does he realise how upset you are about it? How desperate you are, for a baby?'

'Yes!' she moans, covering her face. 'I've never made any secret of it. I told him, when he asked me to marry him, that I'd only say yes if he agreed to try for a family.'

'And now? He still wants to put it off?'

'He's trying to get out of it altogether.' She turns her tear-stained face to me, and goes on, her voice trembling. 'He's trying to deny that he ever agreed to it! How can he do that, Sophie? How can he *do* that to me?'

'I don't know,' I tell her, quite honestly, since I don't know Jeremy or anything about him. And then, I surprise myself completely by asking her outright: 'Do you think you should call off the wedding?'

You're probably as surprised as I am, that I could be daft enough to ask this particular question at this particular moment. After all, I have a big fat fee promised today, for bridal hair and make-up, plus six bridesmaids who are apparently little angels with long flowing locks. But you see, I do have a shred of integrity, to say nothing of a shred of sympathy for someone whose husband-to-be thinks it's OK to promise one thing and mean the complete opposite. And while I'm the first to admit I'm no expert on the whole baby versus body-clock scenario, the fact is that it's not a thing you can compromise on. You either have a child, or you don't. You can't agree to have half a one, just to keep the peace. And if she wants a baby as desperately as she says she does, and he's not going to play ball, the marriage is doomed already – she must know that.

'I don't know!' she wails. 'How can I cancel the wedding now? After everything my mum and dad have paid for?'

'Annabel, that's hardly the point,' I begin, but she's listing all the expenses on her fingers – the venue, the meal, the dress, the flowers – and shaking her head at the same time.

'I can't do it,' she says finally, sitting up straight and trying to pull herself together. 'I just can't do it to my parents. We'll have to go ahead.'

'You could just postpone – while you and Jeremy talk this over.'

'Talk it over?' she retorts, suddenly seeming to spring to life, like she's made her decision and now she's going to get on with it. 'All we've *done* is bloody talk it over, Sophie – ever since we got engaged. I'm sick of talking – or, rather, listening to *him* talking, making excuses, putting it off, putting it back, and now putting it completely off the agenda. I've had enough. I'm taking matters into my own hands.'

With which she jumps to her feet, runs across the room to where a set of matching, expensive-looking luggage is stacked by the door, obviously ready for the honeymoon departure later, grabs the smallest bag and rummages around inside it until she brings out, with a flourish, a packet of contraceptive pills – which she chucks unceremoniously in the bin.

'There!' She rubs her hands together, a satisfied, slightly maniacal gleam in her eyes. 'That's that!'

'Are you sure that's really a good idea?'

'Abso-bloody-lutely.' She sounds completely cheerful again. 'Come on, Sophie – let's get started, yeah? Or I'll have to walk down the aisle looking like Frankenstein's daughter.'

Well, what am I supposed to say? I'm only the hairdresser, at the end of the day. So I get started on her hair.

The six little bridesmaids, I have to say, are every bit as well-behaved and angelic as I've been led to believe. They're brought into the room in a hushed procession by the bride's mother, just as I'm finishing Annabel's make-up, and are seated in a circle around us, on the floor, looking at Annabel with wide eyes and awestruck expressions. They do, indeed, all have lovely long hair, and there's not a squeak out of any of them as I French-plait them, clip the flowers into their hair and send them back to change into their dresses. If this is how the children of the family turn out, I'm beginning to get a glimmer of understanding about Annabel's obsession with having one herself. Only a glimmer, mind!

I leave just as the photographer arrives to take the family photos, and by then you'd never guess, to look at the radiant bride, glowing with happiness, that a couple of hours ago she was sobbing and considering calling it all off. Or that she's about to embark on the biggest piece of trickery of her life.

It's a slow journey home, the usual chaos on the roads being exacerbated by two idiots from Fathers Fighting For

Fairness threatening to jump off one of the motorway bridges, and by the time I park outside my flat, I'm (a) desperate for a pee, (b) gagging for a drink, and (c) ready to commit brutal and bloody murder if I ever set eyes on a Father who Fights For Fairness. In fact I'm just in the act of accomplishing (a), and licking my lips in anticipation of proceeding to (b), when the doorbell rings.

'Just a minute!' I holler, finishing in the bathroom as quickly as nature will allow, and padding to the front door without any particular hurry. I'm thinking it's most likely a neighbour who's kindly taken in my delivery of hair products while I was out. Or a Jehovah's Witness, or a student selling dusters and ironing board covers. As long as they piss off as soon as I've said No, I don't care who it is. I just want to pour out that wine.

In fact, though, it's Oscar. In front of him, wearing a West Ham shirt and a baseball cap that's on back-to-front, is, presumably, seven year old Benjamin. And on either side of him, holding his hands, are, without a doubt, the five year old twins.

'Hello, Sophie,' he says. 'Say hello, children.'

'Hello, Sophie,' echo the children obediently.

'I thought you might like to meet them,' he goes on, smiling at me as if he's sure it'll be the greatest pleasure he can imagine. 'Before we go out tomorrow.'

'Tomorrow?'

'You know – the day at the seaside – your idea!' he enthuses. 'I've been telling the children all about it – how you used to live by the beach. They're so looking forward to it – aren't you, children.'

'Yes,' they chorus, looking up at me balefully.

A day at the seaside. With a man I haven't yet met in any circumstances that don't involve taking our clothes off, and his three very resentful-looking children.

Oh, boy. Suddenly the takeaway pizza and *Britain's Got Talent* seem like the most appealing things in the world.

Sunday

'I can't come round today,' I'm saying to Polly while I'm pulling on my shorts and T-shirt in the dark. In the dark, because it's so bloody early (for a Sunday), and although I haven't opened the curtains yet, I know the sky's black out there and it's not just raining – it's coming down like stair-rods.

'Why not? Oh – I suppose *he's* staying the whole day, now, is he?' she teases.

'No, he's not!' I sigh. 'He's got his kids with him.'

'What, then? And why are you up so early?' She asks suspiciously, and she's got a good point. Unlike poor buggers like her, who have to get up before dawn to feed, change and do whatever else it is they do to their wailing offspring, I'm normally still tucked up blissfully under the duvet at this unearthly hour of a Sunday.

'We're going out,' I say, sighing again. 'To the seaside.'

'Oh. How lovely. Couldn't you wait till a better day – it's bucketing down out there!'

'I know!' I groan. 'But what can I do? He's promised his kids, now.'

There's a silence, during which I think I can feel the continents shifting. Polly's voice, when she replies, is about two octaves higher than before.

'You're going out with his *kids*?' she squeals. '*YOU*?'

'All right, all right, no need to make me sound like someone on the Sex Offenders' Register. I don't *hate* kids, I just …'

'You're joking! You can't stand them! Bloody hell! I never, ever, thought I'd live to see the day that Sophie Jennings got up early on a Sunday morning to go out with some guy and his *kids*! Well, that's it, obviously!'

150

'That's what?' I say, grumpily.

'You're in love with him, obviously. Must be! Absolutely besotted!'

'Absolutely *not*!' I retort. 'I hardly even know him! All we've done is sleep together. I just seem to have got myself into this. By accident. And I didn't have the guts to back out. Wish I had,' I add peering through the curtains at the deluge. 'Perhaps he'll call it off because of the weather.'

'Oh dear,' she chortles. 'It's *so* obvious you don't have much experience with young children. You can't promise kids a day at the seaside and then cancel it – rain or no rain. They'd make your life a misery for the whole day. Probably a whole week, come to that, or possibly the rest of the year!'

'I don't care – they're his problem, not mine. Oh – *shit* – there's the doorbell! Don't say they're here already? I haven't even had my breakfast!'

'Talk to you later, Sophe. Have a lovely day!' she trills sweetly. 'I'll be thinking of you!'

She's laughing her head off as we hang up. Glad I've brightened up *someone's* day.

The twins, ushered into my hallway by their father, are wearing identical bright yellow macs and identical excited grins showing their missing front teeth. Benjamin, on the other hand, is again wearing a West Ham shirt and back-to-front cap, with a face almost as thunderous as the sky.

'He wanted to go to football,' says Oscar apologetically, patting his son on the back, 'but I told him – no, a promise is a promise, and Sophie's giving up her Sunday to come out to the seaside with us.'

'It's OK,' I say quickly. 'I quite understand, if you'd rather take him to football.'

Football? In this weather? Is he mad?

'No way!' Oscar says at once. 'The girls are looking forward to the seaside, I'm looking forward to it, and I'm sure you are too, Sophie – so Benjamin will just have to get over it and join in the fun – won't you, Benjamin?'

Benjamin scowls and digs his hands into his pockets.

'So – you definitely still want to go? In this weather?' I persist, with my fingers crossed firmly behind my back.

'Of course! Beaches are just *great* in the rain, aren't they!' he exclaims enthusiastically. 'As long as you've got your mac and welly boots – ours are in the car.' He looks at me anxiously. 'You do still want to come, don't you, Sophie?'

What can I say? He's looking at me like an eager young puppy waiting to be taken out for a walk.

'Can I just have my breakfast first?' I say.

'Breakfast? No – don't worry about that! We'll stop off on the way down! It's all part of the fun, isn't it, kids!'

I'm beginning, already, to hate the way he says *fun*, as if he's trying to convince himself. Or convince me, more likely. Me and the reluctant Benjamin, who trails sulkily back out to the car, plonks himself onto the back seat and immediately starts playing some sort of game on his mobile phone.

'I want to sit next to the window!' squeals one of the twins.

'No! It's my turn!' yells the other one, pushing her sister out of the way.

'Deana! Serena!' says Oscar, calmly. 'Whichever one of you agrees to sit in the middle will get an extra-special ice-cream for being so sensible and good.'

'Me, Daddy!' 'No – *me*, Daddy!' squeal Deana and Serena, now competing for the middle seat and the extra-special ice-cream.

'Shut *up!*' yells Benjamin, whose arm has been nudged just as he was about to exterminate an alien or bite the head off a snake or whatever. 'Daddy! Tell them!'

I close my eyes and try to picture my nice warm, dry, cosy bed. I've had enough already, and we're still outside my flat. But just as I'm about to announce the sudden onset of a terrible, very infectious, fatal-for-children type of disease that requires me to go straight back under my duvet, Oscar starts the engine, the children fall silent, either from excitement or from sulking, buckle themselves into their seatbelts and we head off through the downpour towards the glorious beaches of the south coast.

We stop for breakfast at something called a Roadhog Eatery, which is memorable only for the giant statues of pigs at the entrance (ignored by all the children), the screams of toddlers in the Ball Pit in the middle of the restaurant (Why? Why does any civilised society need ball pits in the middle of restaurants?), and the over-use of adjectives and exclamation marks on the garish pink menus:

Giant Hot Spicy Sausages with Scrumptious Saucy Beans!!

Special Smiley Fried Eggs on Delicious Nutritious Wholegrain Bread!!

'I'd like the *Perfect Golden Pancakes* served with *Mouth-watering Sticky Maple Syrup*, please,' I announce, trying to enter into the spirit of things. 'And a coffee.'

'I feel sick,' says Serena.

'So do I,' says Deana.

'You forgot to give them their travel sickness medicine, Daddy,' says Benjamin accusingly, just as Serena clutches her tummy and throws up, straight into a napkin produced by Oscar with split-second timing at which I can only gasp with admiration.

'I don't feel sick any more,' she says, wiping her mouth on the back of her hand as the smell of vomit engulfs the table. 'Can I have fried bread and tomato sauce?'

I end up with just a coffee, having somewhat lost my appetite.

'Would you mind taking the girls to the toilet before we move on?' says Oscar.

'Me?' I stare at him in surprise.

'Well, yes, if you don't mind. Otherwise I have to loiter by the entrance to the Ladies, calling out to them, reminding them not to lock the doors, and to wash their hands, and all that stuff.'

'Oh, yes, of course. OK, then.' I look at the twins, who are even now putting their hands trustingly into mine. I try to ignore the stickiness of their fingers and the lingering scent of sick. I've never taken a child to the toilet before in my life, but how hard can it be?

I soon find out.

'Can I come into the same toilet with you, Sophie?' says Deana as soon as we're through the door of the Ladies.

'No. You go first, and I'll wait for you …'

'*Mummy* lets us go in with *her*,' says Serena indignantly. 'She says we're all girls together.'

'Yes, well. I'm not your mummy, am I.'

'No, but we're still *all girls together*, aren't we?'

'You can go in with your sister,' I tell her, firmly, not wanting to get into the whole topic of the need for privacy. 'And I'll wait outside the cubicle door for you.'

'I wish they'd hurry up,' says Deana, urgently now, starting to wriggle. The queue, as always in the ladies toilets, is slow-moving. 'I'm busting.'

'I'm busting too,' agrees Serena, inevitably starting to do a matching wriggle.

'I'm going to do it in my knickers,' announces Deana.

'So am I,' declares Serena.

'Would you like to let them go in front of me?' asks a nice elderly lady ahead of us in the queue. 'Poor little loves, they can't be expected to wait.'

'Sorry,' says the heavily pregnant girl at the head of the queue, looking back at us apologetically as a cubicle becomes free, 'but I'm desperate myself!'

Silence descends over my two charges as the cubicle door closes behind the expectant mother. Then, in a stage whisper, Serena announces:

'That lady's got a baby in her tummy!'

'I *know* that, S'rena, and I bet you don't know how it got *into* her tummy!' says Deana very importantly.

'I *do*, so there!'

'OK, girls, we don't need to discuss this right now …' I begin, in a panic. They seem to have forgotten the urgency of their bladders for the moment.

'The baby gets *put* there,' says Deana, ignoring me completely. 'When a man and a lady get married.'

'Yes. It gets put there by *God* at their *wedding*. Doesn't it, Sophie?'

'Probably,' I say, with a sigh.

Another good reason for not getting married – as if I needed one.

I won't go into detail about Deana managing to wet her knickers while waiting for Serena to relieve herself, despite the nice lady letting them go first, or about the girls locking themselves in the cubicle – despite my orders to the contrary – and screaming blue murder because they couldn't get out. Or about Oscar having to come into the Ladies to find out what was wrong and calm them down, because they wouldn't listen to me, even when I lay flat out on the horrible damp floor calling to them underneath the cubicle door. Suffice it to say I will *never* allow myself to be talked into taking any children to the toilet again – ever – no matter how dire the emergency might be. I'm utterly exhausted by the time we finally get back in the car to continue our journey to the coast – and the little horrors, perhaps unsurprisingly, are all asleep on the back seat within five minutes.

'The sun's coming out,' says Oscar rather optimistically as we approach the outskirts of Brighton. In fact it's still raining, but it's true that the sky's lightened somewhat and the wipers are now only on single speed. He glances at me hopefully. 'Are you having a nice day so far, Sophie?'

'Mm,' is all I can manage.

It takes us half an hour, from the time we manage, finally, to find a parking space, to get all the kids out of the car, get their macs and boots on, collect up the bags with everything they claim to need for the beach (despite the fact that it's still drizzling), and walk down to the seafront. By the time we get there, Deana is crying that her boots are hurting her feet, and Serena is whining that she's tired and wants a drink. Benjamin's sulking and muttering to himself about football, while Oscar's trying his best to jolly them all up.

'Here we are – the sea!' he exclaims, as if it's a big surprise for us all. 'Come on kids – last one on the beach is a wally!'

Nobody seems the least bit concerned about being a wally. The twins continue to whine, Benjamin continues to sulk, the rain beats down on our heads and nobody's taking a blind bit of notice of the sea.

'Walk on the beach, then – anyone?' says Oscar, clapping his hands together and grinning with enthusiasm.

There's no response. I look at his face, and suddenly I feel really sorry for him. OK, so I didn't want this day out at the seaside. Perhaps I should have been more honest, or more brave, and told him it wasn't how I wanted to spend a Sunday – but I didn't, and now he's gone to all the trouble to drive me, and his three ungrateful brats, all the way here in the pouring rain when perhaps *he'd* rather be relaxing on the sofa with the Sunday papers – or even better, tucked up in bed at my place. I'm seeing another side of him today. Well, to be fair the only side I've seen up till now has been the bonking side. This side is kind, and gentle, and sweet – much kinder, gentler and sweeter than I'm ever likely to be myself, that's for sure. And we're all standing here grizzling and moaning instead of getting on and enjoying ourselves. It's not fair, is it?

'Yes – come along, kids,' I say in a strange schoolmistressy voice that I seem to have suddenly acquired. 'Anyone else for a paddle? I'll race you!' – with which I make a dash down the steps onto the horrible wet slippery shingle, stagger awkwardly to the edge of the water, where I stop to perform the strange one-legged dance necessary to remove boots and socks on a stony beach – and then hobble straight into the sea.

I wasn't *intending*, of course, to actually go *into* the sea. The idea was to put my feet in, squeal and splash around a bit to show the kids how much fun it was, get them to join in and stop being such spoilsports for their poor dad. But something goes slightly wrong at the putting-my-feet-in stage, I somehow slip or tread awkwardly on the horrible sharp stones, and the next thing I know, I'm sitting, fully dressed, in the water, with waves up to my neck, my waterproof jacket billowing out and filling with sea-water and sand and shingle going up the legs of my shorts.

At least the kids are now having fun.

'Sophie!' screams Serena, jumping up and down with excitement. 'You forgot to put your swimming costume on!'

157

'You're really *funny*!' giggles Deana as I struggle to my feet, spitting out sand and pulling seaweed out of my hair. 'Daddy, can we go in the sea with our clothes on, too?'

'Brilliant!' yells Benjamin, who's been taking photos of me on his mobile. 'I'm sending these to my friends!'

'Are you all right?' says Oscar, running towards me with a beach towel. There's concern in his voice, amusement mixed with … something like affection … in his eyes. He wraps me in the towel, pulls me towards him, hugs me and kisses the seaweed-slimy, salt-encrusted top of my head. 'Thank you,' he says gently.

'For what? Making a complete arse of myself?' I retort, rather crossly. First hug or kiss I've had from him all day, and it's while I'm looking like a dressed-up beached whale.

'For being prepared to, to cheer my kids up,' he says. 'It means a lot to me.'

They're all, now, playing happily at the water's edge – re-enacting Sophie Diving Fully-Clad Into The Sea. Oscar doesn't seem bothered.

'I always come out with several sets of clothing for them all,' he says. 'As long as they're enjoying themselves, I don't care about stuff like that.'

Good for them, I think to myself grumpily.

'I haven't got several sets though. I've only got what I'm wearing.' It's actually stopped raining for the moment, not that it makes much difference to me now, and it's a fairly warm day – but I'm starting to shiver.

'You're going to get chilled. You need to get out of those wet things,' he says.

'Didn't you hear me? I haven't got anything else,' I repeat, but instead of listening, he seems to be getting himself undressed. 'What are you doing?' I demand. 'Going in for a swim?'

He's already stepped out of his shorts and tossed them onto a dry towel. He's got swimming trunks on underneath.

'No,' he answers with a smile. He turns and rummages in one of the bags, pulling out another of Benjamin's football shirts, and holds it up briefly against me. 'This should just about fit you. He wears them really baggy – and you're not very big.'

'Thanks for pointing that out,' I mutter, but by now my teeth are chattering so I'm not going to argue. 'And am I supposed to fit into a pair of the girls' knickers?'

'No. You'll have to go commando, I'm afraid – you can wear my shorts. They'll be huge on you, but if you do the belt up really tight …'

A few minutes later, my wet clothes are off, I've rubbed myself dry and I'm feeling warm, if very weird, in a small boy's West Ham shirt and a man's shorts that reach halfway to my ankles and are scrunched up around my waist with a belt that's had extra holes made in it.

'Not the most attractive outfit I've ever worn on a date,' I say ruefully, joining Oscar to sit on one of the remaining dry towels.

'I wouldn't say that.' He smoothes the rather tight football shirt down over my bra-less boobs with a smile of appreciation, puts his arms around me, and I'm just closing my eyes in preparation for a proper kiss at last, when there's a squeal and a giggle from beside me and we look up to find ourselves surrounded by gawping children.

'You were going to *kiss* her, Daddy!' says Benjamin in disgust.

'You've got to *marry* her now!' Serena says. 'Can I be a bridesmaid!'

'And me!' Deanna joins in. 'Will God put babies in her tummy at the wedding?'

159

'I think,' says Oscar, laughing and reaching behind him for the picnic bag, 'it's time for lunch – anyone hungry?'

And it appears that cheese sandwiches and smoky bacon crisps can make five-year-olds forget about weddings and babies in tummies in less time than it takes to unwrap the lunch. Thank God!

Monday

'So it wasn't too bad, then?' says Polly when I finally finish describing yesterday's events.

'No. To be honest, once I got over the whole shock of having children around me for a whole day,' – I ignore her hoot of laughter – 'it was quite good fun. But I suppose that's only because it reminded me of how I grew up,' I add quickly. 'You know – running around on the beach in all weathers, playing in the sea, all that. It's great to see that kids today can still enjoy themselves like that, once they've been torn away from their computers and TVs.'

'So – nothing to do with spending the whole day out with Oscar, then?'

'Yes, of course, that had something to do with it,' I admit, laughing. 'He was so sweet, Polly! He said it meant such a lot to him, that I was prepared to get stuck in and play with his kids.'

I've been thinking about it all day, of course: the way he wrapped me in the towel when I was drenched from the sea, the tender way he held me, the look in his eyes.

'He's coming round later,' I add, looking at my watch. 'To make up for … not having any time to ourselves over the weekend.'

'Oh yes. I see,' she says knowingly. 'I'd better let you go and get ready, then.'

'OK. But how are things with Leon?' I add, spitting his name out with disgust as usual. 'Is he still in a horrible mood?'

'He's just gone quiet now. Not talking to me at all. Like he's sulking about something. I keep asking him what's wrong …'

'Don't bother! For God's sake, he's not a child!' I think, fleetingly, of Benjamin, sulking about his football

161

match. Even he brightened up after a little while, and he's only seven. 'Just ignore him, Polly. He needs to grow up!'

'I know. I know you're right, Sophe – he's not very nice, sometimes.' This sounds like complaining that a snarling tiger, just about to eat you for dinner, has an occasional lapse of table manners. 'But I love him!'

'Why?' I demand, crossly. 'I'm sorry, but he's nasty to you. What's loveable about him?'

'How can anyone answer that? We can't help who we fall in love with.'

I think this is probably the gist of the whole thing. This, basically, is what I don't believe in. I believe in falling in love: I think it's got a lot to recommend it, but what I can't get my head around is this thing about not being able to help it. Why do people (usually women, unfortunately) tell themselves they *can't help it*, even when the object of their unearned devotion is a monster, a pig, a charmless, selfish, bad-tempered moron? Of course they can bloody help it! They can't possibly really love those nasty specimens – even their own mothers couldn't love them – the truth is that they stay with them for other reasons. Whatever the other reasons are – fear of being alone, reluctance to break up the family, financial security, needing a father for the kids – they're all understandable, I *sympathise*, I'm not stupid, we all have needs. But why keep pretending they're still in love and *can't help it*? It makes them sound feeble, and witless, and weak. Men like Leon seem to feed on that kind of weakness – and this is what hurts me, because Polly's *not* actually feeble or weak, and she's certainly not witless. Why does she have to pretend to be?

'Why are you still with James?' I ask my sister Debra, rather rudely, when she calls me straight after I hang up from Polly. 'You never stop moaning about him. You surely don't think you're still in love with him, do you?'

'Why do you ask?' she says, guardedly, instead of answering me directly. I think that says it all, actually.

'Oh, I'm just upset about Polly. I can't stand her husband. I don't know why she puts up with him.'

'Well, love is a very strange thing. There's no explaining it. We don't choose who we fall in love with.'

See what I mean? There's no hope!

'The kids were still talking about yesterday when I phoned them earlier,' says Oscar. It's nearly midnight, he's been here for four hours and we haven't done much talking up till now. We did get out of bed, briefly, to heat up a microwave dinner and pour out a couple of beers, and we did both fall asleep for half an hour or so at one point, but other than that … well, let's just say that if this is always what it's like being in a relationship with a younger man, I'm surprised all the middle-aged women in the world aren't hanging around outside the gates of sixth-form colleges. It seems a bit unfair that this tends to sound even more pervy than older men sniffing around young girls!

'I suppose they're still laughing about my graceful dive into the sea!' I joke, stretching my legs languorously and snuggling up to him.

'No. Not just that! They've all said they had a lovely time – even Benjamin! – and they want you to come out with us again!'

This, of course, is where the Sophie Jennings we all know so well – the cynical commitment-phobe with no maternal feelings who can't even remember the names of her own nieces and nephews – would normally groan and think up some excuses, or more likely, push this child-obsessed daddy-freak out of bed double-quick and never let him darken her door again.

Instead I gaze into his eyes and simper, 'That would be lovely! Your kids are great – just like their dad!'

WHAT???

Where the hell did *that* come from?

I feel sick just thinking about it – what the screaming fuck has got into me? Next thing you know, I'll be saying I want to marry him and have his babies, I'll be telling all my friends I can't go out any more on Saturday nights, I'll be knitting baby shawls and shopping in garden centres and saying I *can't help who I fall in love with*!

'I can't believe I've got so lucky,' Oscar's saying. He's stroking my back gently, making my spine tingle, making my legs tremble and my toes curl. 'I never thought I'd meet someone so beautiful, so sexy and yet such a natural with my children.'

A natural with children? Me? I should be laughing my head off – laughing it off so hard that it falls right off and rolls across the floor! I don't know the first thing about children! I never have any idea what to do with them! I barely understand a word they say!

'Oh … well … I really haven't had much experience with kids,' I try to protest, wanting to concentrate, to be honest, on his back-rubbing and its effects rather than this conversation.

'In that case, it's even more remarkable that you were so kind …so patient … so sweet …' He's punctuating each of these compliments with a kiss to various parts of my anatomy. I'm going to run out of self-control in a minute and leap on top of him.

'Only because they were your kids,' I whisper hoarsely, 'so it stands to reason I'd love them … I'd love them just as much as …' at which point I become incapable of further speech. Which, you might well agree, is a bloody good thing, and only regrettable that it didn't happen sooner. Any time sooner; any time before I got so close to uttering the fateful and much disputed 'L' word. Because that treacherous little word, once it's out, seems to acquire a power all of its own, doesn't it – and there's no knowing where it's going to lead. Seldom anywhere I want to go, in my experience. Seldom if ever.

There's a reason for my distrust of the whole scenario of being *in lurve* – and it's probably about time I 'fessed up to it, before we go any further. I wasn't born this cynical. I had a normal childhood, as we've already discussed – the much-loved eldest daughter of happily-married parents. There was nothing a psychoanalyst could get his teeth into, there. If I had to lie on his couch, being hypnotised and regressed through my life to find out where the rot set in, where my psyche became hard-wired to switch off at the sight of an engagement ring, where I acquired the trigger to my phobia of nappies and knitted shawls, it wouldn't take the shrink long to arrive at the point where I first set eyes on Damien.

Damien was the first man I dated when I moved to London. I believed him to be the embodiment of my dream man – the rock star date I'd fantasised about when I lay in my virginal single bed at home in Devon. Damien wasn't, of course, a rock star, but he was a guitarist with a band who were on the way up – or so they believed, anyway. They played gigs at scummy pubs, with the same half-dozen unkempt druggie fans following them from venue to venue, and with me – for a while – sitting beside them in my rock-chick leather jacket, trying desperately to look as if I understood their music or even enjoyed it. I was young enough, and stupid enough, to convince myself that I was in love with Damien, and he took full advantage of that – persuading me to move into the filthy, smelly room he rented, welcoming my enthusiastic appreciation of his (in retrospect, I realise, appallingly bad) sexual efforts, my childish desire to play house by attempting to clean up his hovel, and cheerfully taking all my wages, while he got me started on cannabis and Ecstasy. Progressing, kind of inevitably, to Cocaine.

I wasn't stupid. I knew what I was doing, knew the risks. Why didn't I feel capable of saying No? For years afterwards, I couldn't think about my easy abandonment of everything I knew was right, and sensible, without clenching my fists and crying. Not crying over my lost love – the love died very quickly, and long before Damien himself eventually did, predictably, from an overdose. No, I cried from frustration and regret at the loss of my self-esteem. I didn't like what I became through using drugs – but it went deeper than that. I'd become someone I didn't like, because I'd *allowed* myself to be changed by a man – a man I'd believed I was in love with, even though underneath it all, I was always aware that he didn't love me back. I was angry and disappointed with myself. With Polly's help, I got clean, got myself a decent job, Polly moved to London and we shared a flat together, and I promised myself I'd never again allow myself to love someone, or imagine I loved them, enough to give up *myself* for them.

And I'd never again make the ridiculous mistake of imagining I wanted a child with anyone. Because it was when I thought I was pregnant, that Damien kicked me out – out of his bed, out of his disgusting grimy bedsit, out of his supply of drugs and out of his life. Of course, in doing so, he did me the hugest favour of my own life. But I don't think I'll ever forget the feeling of utter, physical, suicidal despair I felt at that moment; or the relief that came with my period. It's always felt like a relief, every month, ever since.

And you think that's all going to change now, after all these years – just because Charlie's dumped me and picked up with some big-boobed blonde bimbo? Just because I'm having great sex with someone who happens to have three marginally-cute kids and they think it was fun to see me throw myself in the ocean?

You must be joking. I haven't got where I am today by being sweet-talked into instant step-motherhood. OK, so under extreme provocation, I almost, accidentally, caught myself uttering the 'L' word. I didn't mean it. If I didn't love *Charlie,* who was my soul-mate for two whole years, then I quite obviously don't feel anything remotely resembling it for Oscar. Oscar's only in my life, and my bed, to take my mind off Charlie, right? So it's a bloody good job I didn't actually say it. Because I'd hate him to start thinking I meant it.

A week later – Bank Holiday Monday

Ah, a Bank Holiday. No weddings, no clients, no need to get up early. I can lie in bed as long as I like, as long as Oscar likes, and I don't have to go anywhere or do anything I don't want to. Bliss. I turn over, stretch and smile to myself.

'Cup of tea, Sophe.' Oscar puts the mug down on my bedside table, sits on the edge of the bed and kisses me. 'I'm off now.'

'What?' My eyes fly open. 'Off?'

'Yes!' He laughs. 'Picking up the kids – remember?'

Oh, shit. I'd forgotten. Suddenly the nice blissful holiday feeling is shattered, and I feel irritated and cross. He's got the kids today, even though it's not his weekend, because his ex-wife (the bitch from hell who started cheating on him the minute the ring was on her finger) is going to visit her sick father in hospital. Talk about emotional blackmail. I bet there isn't really any sick father in hospital – probably just a new boyfriend she wants to spend time with.

'Sorry, babe,' he says, looking at me regretfully. 'But you've got this shindig at your friend's place later, anyway, haven't you.'

Oh, double shit! I'd forgotten about that, too. Now I'll *really* have to get out of bed. It was Polly's birthday last week, and it's Leon's fortieth this Thursday, and she's organised a barbecue party in her garden as a joint 'do' for them both. She thinks it's going to cheer him up and make him fall in love with her all over again in gratitude for her thoughtfulness. I really hope it works out, but I've got a horrible feeling it'll end in tears.

'Wouldn't a nice evening out at a restaurant, just the two of you, be better?' I suggested last week when she told me what she was planning.

'No, because I'd have to get a babysitter.'

I closed my eyes, swallowed hard, and said, very timidly and with my fingers crossed: 'I could have the kids. If it helps.'

Polly hooted with laughter, and then went very quiet for a minute before saying, gently: 'Now I really know you're the best mate anyone could ask for. You'd hate it – you know you would. Thanks for offering, but I couldn't put you through it.'

'I'm quite good with kids, now, actually!' I protested.

'Not being funny, Sophe, but one seaside outing doesn't turn you into an Earth Mother. You might cope with Gracie, but with Ethan you wouldn't know which end is up. Anyway, I think a barbecue party will be much more fun. The kids will be part of it – and all our friends – Leon will love it.'

'I hope so,' I said, wishing I could share her optimism. 'But it's *your* birthday party too, and you seem to be doing all the work!' As usual. 'Can I at least help with the food?'

'You're an angel. Yes please. Potato salad? And perhaps a dessert? A trifle or something? That'd be great.'

After Oscar's gone out, I drink my tea and get up, reluctantly, to start working out how to make potato salad and trifle. I don't know what made Polly think I could manage these two particular items. I mean, she's known me for long enough, and in all those years, have I ever produced anything even vaguely resembling potato salad or trifle? Have I, heck. I'm a hairdresser, not a chef, for God's sake. The only thing I make with any regular success is Spag Bol, and even that has an occasional tendency to stick in the pan and end up with burnt black bits stirred in for added flavour. She probably thought I'd just nip down to Tesco's and buy an economy sized tub of the salad, and a couple of ready-made trifles off the shelf. But no! I'm *not* getting out of it that easily. Polly's my best mate, and she deserves better. I'm making them both from scratch, even if it takes all day.

It does.

OK, I do realise the potatoes need to be peeled and cooked, so I get them on to boil, and feel quite pleased with myself. I have no idea what else goes in the potato salad apart from potatoes, which is something of a handicap, so I get on the internet and start looking at recipes. This is all very interesting – I get sidetracked by reading lots of other summer salad ideas and then I have a quick check of my e-mails, my Facebook account and a couple of things I've been watching on E-Bay. By the time I go back to the kitchen, the potatoes are not only cooked, they've turned mushy. But I'm sure that won't hurt. When I drain them, some of the more mushy bits go down the plug-hole but I manage to salvage most of them. So far, so good.

I make myself a coffee while I'm waiting for them to cool down. It's now nearly eleven o'clock, but the party doesn't start till two, so I'm not worried, even though I promised Polly I'd get there early to help her. The potato salad is easy to finish, although the mushy potatoes do disintegrate a little more when I chop them, and pretty much completely when I stir them into the mayonnaise. It's the trifle I'm slightly concerned about. I've bought some trifle sponges – well, you can't make *them* from scratch, can you? – and packets of jelly. I know how to make jelly, I'm not that stupid. I just wish the cubes would dissolve quicker. I did put them in a bowl of hot water, but it's not hot any more, and the jelly cubes are just sitting there, looking red and slimy, at the bottom of the bowl. Then I read the instructions on the jelly packet and find out I should have *stirred vigorously* as soon as I poured boiling water on them. I tip away the cold water, losing only a few of the half-melted jelly blobs down the sink (and managing to rescue them from the plug-hole with a teaspoon), re-boil the kettle, and this time I stir. Vigorously. Success! I pour the hot liquid jelly over the sponges and watch it soak in and disappear. Isn't it supposed to set?

I'm not panicking. It's still only midday so I get back onto E-Bay to give me something to do while I'm waiting. The theory is that when my back's turned, the jelly will set. Half an hour later, I vaguely remember something about using ice cubes, so I chuck a handful of them on top of the jelly mess, and stick the whole thing in the fridge while I go for a shower and get myself ready.

By one o'clock, the only change is that the ice cubes are in the process of melting, spreading their clear icy water into the redness of the jelly-mess, making it even more runny. Well, I'm almost out of time now anyway, so sod it. I open a couple of packets of ready-made custard and splodge it into the dishes on top of the mushy sponge-and-jelly mixture. There – lovely. All I need is the cream on top – I pour that straight on, wondering why it seems to sink into the custard – and decorate it with some sliced-up banana. The recipe on the internet said fruit, and two bananas are the only fruit I've got. They've gone a bit soft but I'm sure they'll be fine.

I have to drive round to Polly's – it's not far, but obviously, with two bowls of potato salad and two dishes of trifle, I'd have trouble walking.

'Did you bring the food?' Polly demands as soon as I arrive.

'Of course I did!' I open the car boot. 'Come and give me a hand.'

We both stare into the boot. Cream, custard and semi-liquid red jelly mixture have slopped over the edges of the dishes onto the tray that I (fortunately) stood them

171

on, and squidgy bits of black banana are floating in the ensuing mess.

'Oh dear,' says Polly, trying not to laugh. 'Are they the trifles?'

'Yes,' I say, sorrowfully. 'They took me ages!'

'Never mind.' She looks at her watch. 'Have we got time to nip down to Tesco's?'

I'll *definitely* stick to hairdressing.

Gracie is wearing a blue party dress with matching ribbons in her hair and is beside herself with excitement.

'Were having a *party*!' she shrieks at me. 'It's for my Mummy's birthday *and* my Daddy's birthday! He's *very* old,' she adds, dropping her voice confidentially. 'Do you know how old he's going to be?'

'Er ... let me see now. A hundred?' I guess.

'No!' She jumps up and down. 'Have another guess!'

'Seventy?'

'No!' She stops jumping, and looks at me suspiciously. 'Is seventy more older than forty?'

'Only just.'

'My Daddy's going to be *forty*! That's very old, isn't it, Sophie!'

'Ancient,' I agree cheerfully.

Leon himself is helpfully watching sport on TV while I'm setting up chairs and tables in the garden and Polly scurries around with plates and glasses, filling the fridge with wine, beer, and lemonade, and trying to pacify a grizzling Ethan at the same time.

'What did he buy you for your birthday?' I ask her.

'Oh, he's going to get me a necklace.'

'Going to?'

'Yes – when he gets paid. You know how it is. I think he's been worrying about money – that might be what's wrong with him, really. Or it could be that he's

172

been a bit depressed: I've heard it sometimes happens to men at about this age.'

True enough. But what excuse is there for those who've been miserable bastards their whole lives?

'I think this party today could be a turning point, you know?', she adds, giving me a bright smile. 'I'm hoping it'll put him back into a better mood.'

Well. It'd be a start if he just got off his arse, turned off the TV and helped out. But the age of miracles is past.

It's standing room only in the garden by half past two. All of Leon's and Polly's friends are here. Emma and Stefan are sitting together, gazing at each other like besotted teenagers, but Jo doesn't seem to have turned up yet. Leon's two brothers are here too – they both look exactly like him and behave just as churlishly, and between them have a whole bevy of children who are now chasing each other in and out of the house, round and round the garden, making themselves (and me) giddy, and screaming with excitement.

'Shut up and sit down, the lot of yer!' roars one of the brothers, aiming a swipe at the retreating rear of one of his own kids – and Leon, who's finally managed to lever himself off the sofa and is now standing, beer in hand, at the barbecue turning sausages over with a fork, says something under his breath that makes the brothers laugh nastily together.

Polly looks tense with anticipation. She's put in so much work – I find myself closing my eyes and praying for Leon to behave and enjoy himself. Already his eyes don't look quite focused, and there's a beer stain on his shirt. I reckon he must have started drinking well before I arrived.

'Hello, darling!' says Jo, who's arrived suddenly and quietly round the side of the house. She pulls Polly towards her and kisses her. 'How's it going? Having a lovely day?'

'Yes – so far, so good,' says Polly, indicating the blue sky and sunshine. 'Get yourself a drink, Jo. The food will be ready soon.'

'I'll get you an orange-juice,' I offer. 'Sit down and rest your … er … womb.'

To get to the kitchen I have to pass Leon, still laughing with his brothers at the barbecue while the sausages turn a carcinogenic shade of black.

'They need turning,' I hiss at him. Well, it's not like it's asking a lot, is it?

He looks up, sharply, probably about to tell me to f off and mind my own business, and he catches sight of Jo, sitting in the shade chatting to Emma and Stefan.

'What the hell's *she* doing here?' he mutters.

Jo's one of his wife's best friends. Why would he *not* expect her to be at the party?

'*What* did you say?' I demand. I mean, whatever he's talking about, it's bloody rude, anyway.

'Nothing.' He's still staring in Jo's direction. 'Fuck off, bitch,' he adds, loudly, to me, 'I'm out of here,' – with which he belches, drops the fork on the ground, and disappears indoors, leaving the sausages burning and the brothers looking after him with open mouths.

There's an uncomfortable silence for a moment, and then all hell lets loose.

'What's going on?' asks Polly, rushing to my side.

'Nothing for you to worry about.' I'm upset and cross, but I'm not about to ruin Polly's day. Leon can do that all on his own.

'What was he swearing about?' she insists. 'Where's he gone?'

'Leave him, he's pissed,' says one of the brothers unhelpfully, trying to touch Polly's arm and getting shaken off so that he loses his balance and almost falls over.

'Yeah, a bloke likes a little bit of a drink for his birthday,' the other brother slurs, leering at her. Christ, it really does run in the family.

'I suppose he's gone for a lie-down!' Polly exclaims, beginning to sound shrill. 'Great! Just great! He'll be asleep within five minutes. You might as well all go home,' she announces to the hushed crowd in the garden. 'Waste of time!' She picks up the nearest item on the food table – which happens to be one of my bowls of potato salad – and begins to march indoors with it.

'No! Look, don't!' I make a grab for her. 'Don't do this! Bugger him, Polly – we can all still enjoy the day, can't we? You've done all this work – let's just carry on, and enjoy it …'

Fortunately it's a plastic bowl. As she shakes my hand off her arm, the bowl flies out of her grasp, landing with a splat, upside down on the patio. Still talking to her, trying to persuade her that Leon or no Leon, the party should go ahead, I bend down to pick it up. And stop, staring in disgust at the mess on the ground. Polly stares at it too.

'*What* is *that*?' she asks in amazement.

'My potato salad,' I admit mournfully.

'It looks … like vomit.'

'I know. The spuds went mushy.'

'You can't fucking cook, can you,' she says, quietly. 'I don't know why I asked you.'

'I know. I'm sorry.'

There's a split second of silence. Then, suddenly, miraculously, she grabs me by both arms, throws back her head, and laughs. Within minutes we're hugging and laughing together – hysteria taking over completely until we're incapable of saying anything other than the odd exclamation of: *Spuds!* and *Mushy!* Random friends and relatives are coming over to see what the hilarity is all about, and one by one, they stare at the pool of potato mush on the ground, grimace in revulsion, and back away quickly as Polly and I are overcome with fresh waves of laughter at the looks on their faces. Leon's brothers, shaking their heads at us, carry on with the cooking and the party continues happily enough … apart from the absence of the birthday boy.

I venture indoors while Polly's talking to some other friends. Leon's not in the kitchen, and he's not lying down in the lounge. I go on through to the hallway. Perhaps he's gone up to bed. The drunken, foul-mouthed, lazy slob: I'm going to find him, give him a piece of my mind, get him to go back out there and apologise to Polly – if he can do it without causing a scene. As I approach the stairs, though, I stop short. There are voices floating down to me. Leon's, raised and angry, and … oh! The other voice is Jo's, low and defensive in response.

'You didn't have to come!' he's saying. 'Are you stupid, or what?'

'I didn't come for you,' she retorts calmly. 'I've come for Polly. She's my friend.'

'Your friend?' He's sneering – and, listening from below, I cringe at that sneer – I hate that sneer. 'Yeah, right! She's your friend, is she? You always sleep with your friends' husbands, do you?'

I don't stay to hear any more. I stumble, shaking, gasping, to the downstairs cloakroom, where I lock myself in and stay, sitting on the toilet, until I feel capable of going back outside and trying to act normally in front of Polly.

I have to do this.

I have to pretend, for the sake of my best friend, that I haven't heard what I've just heard. I don't give a shit about Leon – he can cook himself on his own barbecue as far as I'm concerned, and I won't lift a fork to turn him over. I can't even begin to think how I feel about Jo. I need time for this to sink in; to think it through; to decide whether there's anything I should do.

But today's not the day for it. Today, I just have to smile, and pretend. That, sometimes, is what friends are for.

Tuesday 1<u>st</u> September

'I was pinning my hopes on the party putting him in a better mood,' Polly says when she phones me at lunchtime today. 'But it hasn't. If anything, he's worse.'

'Perhaps he doesn't like the thought of turning forty,' I say, quietly. Actually, I'm thinking he'll be lucky if he gets as far as his birthday on Thursday without me paying someone to murder him.

'What else can I do, Sophe?' Polly asks. She sounds tired, fed up. Defeated. 'I've tried everything. What the hell else can I do?'

I feel like crying. What am I supposed to say to her? I was awake all night last night, worrying about it, changing my mind every five minutes from thinking I should tell her, to thinking I shouldn't.

'Maybe it's best to just completely ignore him. Act like you haven't even noticed he's being an arse.'

'You think so? Is that what you'd do, Sophie? Is that where I'm going wrong – paying too much attention to his moods?'

'You're not going wrong at all, love,' I say, anger welling up in my chest and making it difficult for me to talk. 'Stop blaming yourself. He's just being ...' A bastard. A nasty, lecherous, cheating, lying pig. 'Just being stupid,' I finish, weakly.

It's no good. I can't bring myself to break her heart.

I can't bring myself to talk to him, either.

I'm going to have to talk to Jo.

'What's wrong?' says Oscar when he comes round later. I must look shattered.

'Oh – nothing. Just a bit tired. Didn't sleep much last night.'

178

'Why's that? Missing me?' he says, taking me in his arms at once.

'Yes. Of course.' I can't tell him about Leon. It seems, somehow, disloyal to Polly to tell him without telling her. 'How was your day out with the kids?'

'Not as good as last time. We missed you.'

'Yeah, right!' I laugh.

'I'm serious. It just didn't seem the same. Even the kids said it was much more fun when you were with us.'

'Really?' I'm tempted to be flattered by this. After all, I've had so little to do with kids thus far in my life. My sisters' kids are growing up thinking of their Auntie Sophie as a distant relative who gives them money at Christmas (because I have no idea what toys are suitable for their ages, even if I can work out their ages), and sends cards for their birthdays when she remembers (or is nagged into remembering by their mums). I've seen Gracie most weeks throughout her life, but haven't yet really worked out how to talk to her. And as for Ethan – well, babies are still a complete mystery to me. To be honest, they scare me a little bit. So, to be told that Oscar's children had more fun because I was with them, is very likely to turn my head if I let it. I'm just smiling to myself smugly, thinking how I must be a natural at this whole childcare business after all and maybe it's not as difficult as everyone makes it out to be, when Oscar adds, softly, against my ear:

'I think the children love you as much as I do.'

I freeze. He feels it, and holds me away from him, looking at me quizzically.

'What did I say?'

'*Love*. You mean – love as a friend, as a … well, as a person. Yes?' It sounds stupid now it's out. But I can't help it.

'If you like, yes!' he says, still looking at me with puzzled amusement. 'Am I not allowed to love you, then?'

'As a friend! Of course! I love my friends! We all love our friends!' I'm babbling semi-coherently now.

He nods, slowly. 'OK, Sophe. Don't panic. I'm not about to ask you to marry me.'

'Thank God for that!' I laugh out loud with relief – and then realise from the look on his face that this wasn't entirely tactful. 'I mean … what I mean is …'

'It's too soon.' He smiles. 'I understand.'

I don't think he does. The 'L' word is dangerous territory. It was bad enough that I nearly said it myself the other night – at least I know I wouldn't have meant it. I can't have him saying it to me. It panics me. And for another thing, it reminds me of the night Charlie said it to me. And then dumped me.

I'm enjoying myself with Oscar – of course I am. But it's not because I've got over Charlie or forgotten how much he hurt me. Constant sex, six or seven nights a week, tends to keep you occupied, not to say knackered. But I still think about Charlie a lot. I know this is terrible, but I even think about him sometimes when I'm having sex with Oscar. It's difficult not to, really, when we were together for so long, and our lovemaking was always … well, so lovely. OK, it wasn't always as fierce and desperate as it is with Oscar – but it's different when you've been going out for a bit longer, isn't it. Charlie and I were just so *comfortable* with each other. We didn't always have to have sex – we often just used to have meals together and then fall asleep together. We'd spend a lot of time talking, too. Just talking, and laughing. It was lovely.

I feel a bit tearful now, thinking about it. I shouldn't be thinking about it at all, of course, because Oscar's kissing me and trying to get me in the mood, and it's not working.

'There *is* something the matter – isn't there,' he says, eventually.

'No!' Then I sigh, and admit: 'Well, yes. Just Polly – you know, my friend. I'm a bit worried about her. Her husband's being a knob.'

'The one you told me about. He's still putting it about?'

'Yes.' I'm not mentioning Jo.

'And you still haven't said anything to her?'

'No.'

'There's not a lot you can do, then, is there?' he says, shrugging.

I feel irritated by the shrug. The shrug makes me feel like he's dismissing my concern about my friend as unimportant, in comparison with his expectation of a good shag. I turn away from him and sit down on the sofa. For good measure, I switch on the TV. He's left, standing in the middle of the room, looking puzzled and somewhat lost.

'Don't you want to …?' He nods towards the bedroom.

'No. I don't, actually, tonight, Oscar. Sorry.'

'I've said something wrong, haven't I?'

'No. Look, can we just get a takeaway, and a bottle of wine, and sit and *talk*, for a change?'

He doesn't move. He's still looking stunned.

'Is it the time of the month?' he asks eventually.

'Bugger off, Oscar,' I tell him wearily.

As it happens, we do end up talking; but only for half an hour or so while we eat the curry he buggers off to get, and drink the wine he also buys while he's buggered off. We talk mainly about his children, and what they did on their day out yesterday without me, and how he got held up in a traffic jam coming home. And then we do end up going to bed, anyway – and I'm lying here now, while he's asleep, thinking that perhaps some relationships only work because they're based on sex, and getting on with each other's children, and nothing else. And perhaps, in fact, that's all a lot of marriages are based on so why should I complain?

And I realise what my problem is. I want more, but I don't want enough.

I want more than having lots of sex and being liked by his kids.

But I don't want love, or commitment, or rings on my fingers, or a joint mortgage, or a baby.

What I wanted was what I had with Charlie – the Charlie he used to be, before he turned into someone I didn't recognise any more. In the darkness, I think about Charlie, and I cry a little bit to myself, and then I think about Polly, and realise that's all *she* wants, too – she wants Leon, the way he was when she first met him (or at least, the way she thought he was. In fact he was always a pig, but she obviously didn't know that).

It's not too much to ask, is it – for people to stay the same, stay the way they were when we met them and decided they were what we wanted? Why did Charlie have to suddenly become a different person? Why did Leon have to be a bastard?

It's two o'clock in the morning but I'm not going to be able to get back to sleep. I get up and pad quietly out of the bedroom, into the kitchen and close the door while I make myself a cup of tea. I don't want to wake Oscar up; he'll just expect more sex, and nice though it is, I'm really too tired now.

While I'm waiting for the kettle to boil I pick up my phone and suddenly I know what I have to do. I can't put this off – it's the reason I'm miserable, the reason I can't sleep. I need to phone Jo – and I need to do it now, right now.

The phone rings for a long time before she answers. In fact, it's just gone to voicemail when she picks it up.

'Hello?' She was obviously asleep. Tough. She doesn't deserve to sleep if I can't.

'It's me – Sophie,' I tell her, in case she's too sleepy to read her caller display.

'What the hell ...? Sophe, are you all right? It's turned two o'clock ... I was asleep. Are you pissed, or what?'

'No. I'm not pissed. I *am* pissed off, though.'

'What's happened?' She sounds alarmed, now. 'Is something wrong?'

'Yes. Very wrong.' I'm breathing hard, trying to stay in control. 'Yesterday at Polly's, Jo: you and Leon were talking. Upstairs. I was at the bottom of the stairs. I heard.'

'You heard ... what?' she says, after a moment of silence that speaks volumes.

I put on an approximate imitation of Leon's nasty drawl. '*You always sleep with your friends' husbands, do you?*'

Jo is silent again.

'Well?' I hiss at her. 'Aren't you going to try and defend yourself? Tell me I got the wrong end of the stick? Or that Leon was just telling vicious lies?'

I want her to. I'm actually squeezing my eyes tight shut, screwing my whole face up, tensing, waiting for her to shout at me for being stupid enough to take any notice of anything that slime-ball said. But she doesn't. She doesn't say a thing. She's so silent, in fact, that I wonder if she's hung up.

'Well?' I demand again.

'It was once,' she says, flatly. 'That's all – just the once.'

I gasp with shock, as if I hadn't been lying awake imagining something like this all along.

'And that makes it all right, does it?'

'No. Of course it doesn't. I'm not happy about it, but …'

'*You're* not happy about it? Christ!' I don't know what else to say. I can't think of a single thing I can say to her.

'You won't tell Polly, will you?' she says quickly. 'I … don't think it would be helpful.'

'Helpful to who?' I retort. 'No, I'm not going to tell her, Jo, but not because I give a stuff about either you or Leon. You both disgust me.'

'Look, I know you're worried about Polly …'

'Too right I am! She's been my friend since we were children in Devon. We look out for each other. That's what friends do – real friends,' I add crossly.

'Haven't you ever done anything wrong, Sophie?' she says, suddenly sounding equally cross. 'Or is that why you spend your whole life on the sidelines, watching everyone else's lives instead of getting one of your own – you haven't got the guts to take any risks?'

'*What*?' I say, deadly quiet now.

'Well, it's true, isn't it? Too scared to have a proper grown-up relationship like everyone else, but you don't mind giving out advice to all and sundry, as if you know it all, when actually you know sod all about anything!'

That's it. I've lost my cool. I'm shouting into the phone now, and I don't care if I wake Oscar up. I don't care if I wake the whole fucking street up.

'I *hate* being asked for advice, if you must know – I have no idea why every bugger in town comes to me with their problems – I wish they wouldn't! And while we're at it – *you're* a good one to talk about having a proper relationship! Remind me why you had to go and get a baby by artificial insemination? It sure as hell wasn't because you were in a loving partnership and couldn't conceive, was it!'

'It wasn't artificial insemination,' she says. Her voice is shaking. 'That's the whole point. I made that bit up.'

'You what? What the hell for?' And then, suddenly, belatedly, I get it. I sit down, holding the phone somewhere near my neck now. 'Oh my God,' I mutter to myself. 'Oh, bloody hell.'

'I wanted a baby,' Jo's shouting, defiantly, against my neck. 'I couldn't get a boyfriend – all right? It's all very well for you! It's so unfair! You have men wanting to marry you, and you don't even *want* them. You don't even want *children*! You're so bloody self-righteous, but you have no *idea* how it feels to have nobody – no partner, no husband, no boyfriend, no babies. I wanted a baby, Sophie, and Leon was always coming on to me. So yes – I slept with him. I only had to do it once. Nobody was supposed to find out.'

'Does he know?' I ask coldly. The kitchen door opens, and Oscar appears in the doorway, naked, frowning at me. I shake my head at him and wave him away. 'Does Leon know he was being used as a sperm donor? Does he know the baby's his?'

'I didn't tell him. But he's guessed. He's acting like it's all my fault and he had nothing to do with it. He wanted me to get an abortion!' She makes a strangled noise, like a sob. 'He's told me to stay away from their house, stay away from Polly …'

'Of course he has! You stupid, stupid *bitch*! What did you expect?'

'I never wanted anything from him – I never expected him to support the baby, or anything like that!'

'But supposing he wanted to? And what if the baby looks like him? What if Polly gets suspicious? Leon's right – if you care about Polly, in the slightest, you'll have to stay away from her from now on. For good.'

185

'It's not my fault she's got a fucking awful marriage,' Jo mutters sulkily.

I snap my phone shut and burst into tears.

Thursday

It might be a short week, because of the Bank Holiday, but I'm struggling to get through it. I'm exhausted from lack of sleep, tearful with constantly thinking about Polly and Leon, Leon and Jo, Jo and Polly. Oscar's getting irritated by my miserable mood and I snapped his head off last night for asking me, again, whether it was the time of the month – as if he doesn't know perfectly well it isn't – he's in and out of my body often enough to know what's going on better than I do myself.

'Don't forget I'm going down to Devon for the week, on Sunday,' I told him after I'd apologised for snapping at him. 'Perhaps it'll do us good to have some time apart.'

'What do you mean?' he asked, looking hurt.

'Well – it has been very *full on*, very quickly, hasn't it.'

'Aren't you happy? Are you saying you want to finish it?'

'No!' I sighed, wondering whether in fact perhaps I did. 'No – I just think we've rushed it a bit, and maybe we need a break, that's all.'

He went quiet for the rest of the evening. I felt like I should make an effort to reassure him, but to be honest, I couldn't be bothered with it. I've got enough to worry about without his bloody insecurities.

Now, today, I've got this pregnant bride, Julianne, who's been giving me the whole story about how she only knew her boyfriend for two weeks before she was convinced that he was The One, and that she wanted to marry him and have his babies. Not necessarily in that order. And – wait for it – she's only seventeen. There are so many things I'd like to say to her, but what the hell? I'm not her mother, am I.

'What does your mum think about you getting married so young?' I ask her.

'Oh, she's over the moon!' sighs Julianne. 'She was only sixteen when she married my dad, and had me, you see, and she says that she always felt more like a big sister to me than a mother.'

And? The point is what? That it's better to have a big sister than a mum?

'I see.' I smile at her in the mirror as brightly as I can manage. 'And are they still together – your mum and dad?'

'Oh, no,' she says dismissively. 'Dad walked out when I was still a baby, but Mum always says she didn't care, because she had me.'

'That's nice,' I say, weakly. 'But she's happy for you to be marrying … um … Gary?' I do struggle to keep up with the names of all the bridegrooms. I rarely get to meet them, of course, and there are new ones every week. 'It didn't put her off young marriages – the fact that hers broke down?'

'Nah!' She laughs. 'Mum says *Go for it, girl. If it don't work out, we'll bring the baby up together.*'

'That's nice of your mum. You must be very close,' I say. But you know what I'm thinking, don't you? It sounds like her mum would be quite happy for the hapless Gary to be off the scene as quickly as poss after the wedding. He's done his bit. Now he can clear off as soon as he likes, and leave mum, daughter and grandchild to play happy families on their own.

'Will you be able to do Mum's hair too, on the day?' says Julianne. 'She's got long blonde hair like mine but she wants to wear it up for the wedding.'

I'm just thinking that her mum must be pushing it a bit, having long blonde hair when she's nearly a grandma –

188

when I realise she must, actually, be younger than me. I'm so horrified by this thought that I nearly drop the hairdryer.

'Of course,' I say, shakily. 'Anyone else you need me to do? Bridesmaids?'

'Nah. Not having any. But you can do my Nan, if you like.'

'Sure.' I picture a little old lady with a perm. 'What will she be having?'

'She'll want her hair up too. She's got long ...'

'OK!' I say quickly, before she can tell me that even her grandmother is young enough to have long blonde hair. For some reason it panics the life out of me. But I suppose with the family tradition of schoolgirl pregnancy, she might only be in her mid-forties.

'You're making me feel old, d'you know that?' I say half-jokily.

'Don't worry, Sophie.' She gives me a pitying look. 'There's still time for you to meet someone. And let's face it, women in their fifties are having babies now, aren't they, by that arterial semantic thing.'

I can't even bring myself to answer this. But a very strange thought has just occurred to me. This is a first! My client – a pregnant seventeen year old – is giving *me* advice. Crap advice, of course, but still. Perhaps I'm finally losing my touch as an agony aunt! Can't say I'm sorry!

This evening, just before Oscar's due to come round, I realise I've got a bit of a drive tomorrow to a wedding in Berkshire; and I'm almost out of petrol. So, to save time in the morning, I nip out to the petrol station – and I'm just standing there with the nozzle in the car, as you do, watching the scary figures on the pump clocking up to a small mortgage, when I happen to glance at the person filling up at the pump opposite me, and it's Charlie.

He glances up at much the same moment, and we stare at each other for a minute before grinning and waving, very self-consciously, with our free hands and both calling out 'How are you doing?' at the same time. He finishes filling up before me, locks his car and comes over.

'How are you doing?' he repeats, softly, looking at me with that same old Charlie-look that makes me want to cry.

I should, in response, just say 'Fine thanks!', as everyone does, as everyone always expects everyone else to do, and leave it at that. But something in those soft, brown, caring Charlie-eyes makes my chest tighten with self-pity and … some kind of longing … and I blurt out, instead: 'Not too good, really. I'm seeing someone who's nine years younger than me but has three kids, I'm worried sick about Polly, I'm never talking to Jo again, and I'm *younger* than one of my clients' *mothers* who's just about to become a *grandma*!'

'Bloody hell,' he says, solemnly. We stare at each other for a minute. 'Your tank's full,' he adds, quietly.

I pull the nozzle out and stuff it, awkwardly, back into the pump, and try with shaking hands to put the petrol cap back on.

'Let me,' he offers. Our hands brush as he takes the cap from me and screws it on.

'Thanks,' I say, flustered. 'OK. I'll … see you around, then. Nice to see you.' I give him a silly, fluttery, wave and open the door of my car.

'Aren't you going to pay?' he asks, smiling.

'Oh! Oh, shit! Yes, of course!' I jump away from the car door as if it's burning me, laugh a bit too shrilly and follow him across the forecourt, trying to take deep breaths to calm myself down. What the hell's the matter with me?

'How's your mum?' he asks as we join the queue at the pay desk.

'Oh – she seems to be doing well, thanks. I'm going down on Sunday for a holiday.'

'That's good. I'm pleased to hear it.'

I pay for my petrol and wait for him to finish.

'So what's the problem – with Polly? And Jo?' he asks as we walk outside again.

'Oh – it's a long story. Sorry – I shouldn't have mentioned it. I'm just … look, sorry, it's been a bit of a bad week, that's all.'

'Do you want to grab a coffee? If it'd help, to talk about it?' He's looking at me with that caring Charlie-look again. I can hardly bear it.

'I'd … better not. Thanks. Oscar's coming round in a minute.'

'The toy-boy with loads of kids?' he says, chuckling.

'Only three.' I smile back, ruefully. 'But that's three too many.'

'Sophie, I …'

'Charlie, I …'

We both stop, and look at each other, and laugh uneasily.

'You go first,' he says.

'I miss you,' I blurt out. 'I was just going to say – I still miss you, Charlie! For God's sake! I really miss you!'

He puts a hand on my shoulder, sighs, rubs my back. 'Don't cry,' he says.

'I'm not.' God, I am. How embarrassing..

'Look, I miss you too. But …' He shrugs, sighs again. 'I'm sorry.'

'You're getting *married.*'

'Yes.'

'When? *When* are you getting married?'

'At Christmas.'

'What! *This* Christmas?'

'Yes. She … Helen … she's booked it all. Got a cancellation.'

'You've only just met her,' I tell him, dully.

He just shrugs again and smiles at me.

191

'We need to move our cars, Sophe. The people behind us are giving us evil looks.'

'Oh. Yes. OK. Well … I'll be seeing you, then.'

'You know where I am, OK?' he calls after me as I turn to unlock my car. 'If you ever need to talk, Sophe – I'll always be there for you. OK? I mean it.'

I turn on the engine and put the car into gear, noisily, revving the engine. And drive out without looking back at him. I can barely see for tears, anyway.

'How can he *say* that? All that crap about always being there for me? He *dumped* me! He dumped me and got engaged to some frigging *Helen* almost the next day!'

I'm crying on the phone to my sister Debra. I had to. I had to cry to somebody, you know, and I couldn't burden Polly while she's so worried about Bastard Leon, and I could hardly cry about Charlie to Oscar. I've had to text him, anyway, and tell him to come a bit later – made up an excuse that I've still got a client here – to give me time to pull myself together.

'He probably feels guilty,' she says, calmly. 'But on the other hand, to be fair, it wasn't really just down to him, was it – the end of your relationship? If you'd agreed to marry him …'

'What? So it's my fault he changed his mind? How is that fair?'

'No, I'm not saying it's your fault. But the poor bloke was entitled to change his mind. Most people do, eventually, decide to settle down, Sophie. Face it!' She pauses. 'I just hope, by the time *you* finally make that decision, it won't be too late.'

'Oh, shut up!' I feel like slamming down the phone. So much for coming to *her* for some sympathy! 'You'll *never* understand, will you! I'm not going to change my mind – ever!'

'So you're not serious with this Oscar chap, either, then?'

'No! Did I say I was?'

'Well. Going out for the day with his children … I thought maybe you were getting a bit broody?'

'Well, you thought wrong. I'm not broody, I'm not getting serious with Oscar, my body-clock isn't ticking, and I'm not wishing I'd agreed to marry Charlie. OK?'

'So what's wrong?' she asks, in that know-it-all voice that irritates the shit out of me. 'If you like your life fine just the way it is, what are you crying about?'

'I miss him.' I walk into the bedroom with the phone in my hand and stare at myself in the mirror. I look a wreck. Flushed cheeks, red eyes, hair all over the place, make-up smudged. No wonder Charlie didn't express any regrets. He must be thinking what a lucky escape he had. 'I just miss him, Debs,' I repeat, softly half to myself. 'We were … happy, that's all. We used to be really, really happy.'

She doesn't answer for a minute. Then:

'You were lucky, then, Sophe,' she says, surprisingly gently. 'You were lucky you had that, at least, for a few years of your life. Maybe it was better that it ended while you *were* both so happy. Before it all came crashing down in misery and bloody arguments. Like it always does.'

'I'll see you on Sunday, Debra,' I say, and hang up before she starts telling me her latest string of complaints about James. I'm sorry, but I just can't face it. Not today.

Oscar arrives at nine o'clock, with flowers.

'I thought you'd probably be tired, and stressed, with that client overrunning,' he says. 'So I've booked us a table at Chez Monique. My treat.'

Chez Monique. Our restaurant – mine and Charlie's. Great.

'Thank you,' I say, trying to smile. 'That's really nice of you, but, really, I don't think …'

'No, I insist!' he says, misunderstanding. 'I want to take you out, on a proper date, for once. Not that I've got any problems with spending almost our entire time together in bed,' he adds, looking at me as if he's considering changing his mind, blowing out the restaurant and going to bed instead.

'Well, yes, but …' I feel so miserable, I don't even fancy bed. So I suppose I'll be better off accepting the offer of the restaurant, even if it is going to make me feel even worse just walking in there.

'Get your shoes on, then. And I'll tell you the other surprise,' he adds, looking chuffed with himself.

'Go on, then.' What the hell? He's invited his kids? His ex-wife's joining us? Come on, make my day!

'I've managed to get the week off work,' he says. He grins at me proudly. 'Isn't that great?'

'Which week?'

'*Next* week, of course, Sophie. So we can have a holiday *together*.'

I look at him in confusion. 'But … I told you: I'm going down to Devon. It's all arranged. I've cleared my diary.'

'I know.' He's still grinning. 'I thought I'd come with you. Won't that be great?' He pulls me towards him and, fortunately, holds me so tight that he can't see the expression of incredulity I'm pulling behind his back. 'We'll be able to celebrate our anniversary together – on holiday at the seaside – with your family,' he says happily.

'Anniversary?' Fucking *anniversary*? *What?*

'It'll be one month on the ninth,' he says, softly. 'One month of the most fantastic, passionate, wonderful relationship of my life, Sophie. Shall we start celebrating now?'

194

'No,' I say, my voice coming out hoarse and shaky. 'Let's not be … um … premature, Oscar. It's only three weeks at the moment.'

'OK. We'll save the celebration for Devon. But let's go and eat, anyway.'

Oh God. Oh my God. I have a feeling I won't be able to stomach any food. I might just throw up before we even get there!

Sunday

I've tried every way I could think of, to get out of this. I've tried telling him that because of my mum's illness, it's not really appropriate for him to stay with the family. But he said straight away that of course, he hadn't expected to stay at the house, he'd already booked himself into a B&B. What was I supposed to do? Tell him to un-book it?

'I'll need to spend a lot of time with my family,' I tried next. 'Most of my time, really. In fact, I pretty much need to be with them the whole time. Sorry – it'd be really boring for you. I hardly ever see them, and I feel a bit guilty about it, so …'

'Of course – I understand,' he said at once, annoyingly. 'I'm looking forward to meeting them, Sophie. They must be lovely people, if they're your family.'

What's going on? When did he start talking like this? Did I miss the signs? Did it start – all this yucky romantic stuff – while I was asleep one night, or not paying attention? Too busy concentrating on the sex? And now what? How do I stop it, before it makes me ill?

'They're not!' I said. 'I mean – yes, they're lovely, my parents are lovely, but my sisters … well, they've got problems – terrible problems. Both of them. It's … really difficult. You won't be able to see them. I'll have to see them on their own. Because of their … problems.'

'What sort of problems?' he asked, curiously. 'Are they disabled in some way? It's OK, Sophe – I'm quite capable of meeting people with various problems. I won't do anything to embarrass or upset anyone.'

So what was I supposed to say to that? I was running out of excuses, to say nothing of having invented frightening disabilities for my sisters.

'I won't be any trouble!' he added, jokily. 'You do *want* me to come, don't you?'

I hesitated. This could be my moment: my one chance of ending it, before it gets too serious. Before we have to celebrate a bloody one-month anniversary. But on the other hand – am I really ready to end it? I'm enjoying it, it's taking my mind off Charlie, he's young and fit and good in bed … so I thought: nah, sod it. If he stays in the B&B and keeps out of the way of my family, maybe it won't really be such a problem.

So here we are, driving down the M4 in his rather nice Peugeot, which I'm thinking was another good reason for agreeing to the whole thing, and in fact I'm in quite a good holiday mood, trying to forget the awful wedding yesterday (Julianne – teenage mother-to-be, and her mum and grandma – all dressed in identical shocking pink mini-dresses and wearing enough bling to sink a battleship), and looking forward to seeing Mum and Dad, and Debra and Millie, again.

'I haven't been on holiday with a girlfriend since my marriage broke up,' he tells me cheerfully.

'Have you *had* many girlfriends since it happened?' I ask him, not that I really want to know, I just need to get him away from talking about me as his girlfriend. I don't like the sound of it.

He gives me a quick grin. 'Yeah. But none of them lasted this long.'

'But it's only been …'

'Four weeks now,' he says quickly.

'So you normally have girlfriends that last less than four weeks? They hardly qualify as girlfriends, do they?' I'm purposely keeping my tone light and teasing. 'More of a one-week-stand, by the sound of it!'

He shrugs. 'I suppose so. I never wanted anything more serious...'

'Me too!' I exclaim with relief. 'That's just exactly how I feel, too. I'm not up for a serious relationship, at all

– not with anybody – not ever. I'm *so* glad you feel the same way. I was beginning to worry that we wanted different things.'

'Sophie,' he says quietly, 'I was going to say that I never wanted anything more serious, until now.'

Ah. Bugger.

'I haven't said this to you before,' he goes on, 'because of what you told me about what's-his-name – Charlie. That you broke up because he wanted more from the relationship.'

'Yes. That's right. He did.'

'But I presumed... kind of stupidly, I suppose ... that it was just with Charlie that you had a problem about having a committed relationship. Not the entire male population.'

'I'm sorry. I should have made that clear from the outset. I thought I had. I thought we were both in this ... just for some fun.'

Oh, *bugger*! The sun's gone in, we're driving through a sudden shower of rain, and my holiday mood is rapidly evaporating. *Why* do I seem to be going through this same scenario all over again, already, with another guy? If I wanted to keep on apologising for not wanting a serious relationship, I could have hung around and been mortified some more by Charlie.

'That's all I wanted too, at the beginning,' he's saying very solemnly. 'You're right – that's all I've been doing since my divorce – meeting girls, having fun, having sex ...'

'Well, you do it very nicely,' I joke, trying to lighten things up a bit.

'Sophie, I don't want to spend the rest of my days as a sex object for lonely women!'

So much for lightening things up. Now he looks like he's about to cry, and I feel bloody insulted.

'I'm not a lonely woman!'

'You are! Admit it! All your friends are married, or getting married, and having kids, and you keep on about having nobody to go clubbing with.'

'So? I'm not lonely! I'm quite happy the way I am!'

But something doesn't feel right about this, even as I'm saying it – it sounds wrong in my own ears. Why? I'm only repeating what I've always said! It's still true. I still don't need a husband, a baby, a mortgage – I'm still happy on my own, nothing's changed, nothing's different.

Except that I don't have Charlie any more, of course. But that's irrelevant.

'Well, anyway, I just wanted to tell you – you're the most serious girlfriend I've had, since my divorce,' he says slightly moodily. 'So there you go.'

I cringe again at the word *girlfriend*.

'We still hardly know each other,' I say, gently. I know he's young, but – Christ! He's talking like a ten year old who's walked round the playground twice with a girl and shared his crisps with her, and says they're going out. 'I could have all sorts of nasty personality traits you don't know about yet.'

'True.' He forces a smile. 'Well, all I'm saying is, I like what I've seen so far.'

'So do I,' I agree, laughing and stroking his thigh meaningfully, and then stopping quickly when I remember that he doesn't want to be used as a sex object. What a shame.

'So it's great that we're having this week away together, isn't it,' he says after a minute, seeming to cheer up again. 'It gives us plenty of time to *really* get to know each other.'

Well, what can I say? I don't think it'd go down well, now, if I remind him that I was planning on spending almost the entire time with my family, squeezing him in for sex at his B&B whenever possible and otherwise keeping him pretty much out of the picture.

'Yes – yes, it is,' I say, giving his leg another reassuring stroke. 'We can find out all about each other's nasty personality traits, can't we!'

I know where the B&B is, of course – Sand Bay is so small, I know every B&B in the town and I've been updated, over the years, by Mum or my sisters when any of them have closed down or new ones opened.

'It's right on the front. Let's go straight there,' I suggest as we drive into the town.

'But – your parents will be expecting you, won't they?'

'Yes. Probably looking out of the front room window already!' I say, laughing. 'But it's not far from where you're staying – I can walk back there while you go and check in and get yourself settled.'

'Don't be silly! I'll drop you off – I'm not in any hurry. Mrs Major at the B&B said the room wouldn't be available until three o'clock, anyway. And she sounded quite … strict … about it, on the phone.'

Oh, yes. Prudence Major – I almost forgot about her. Major by name, Sergeant-Major by nature – she won't tolerate anyone arriving at half past two if she's told them three o'clock. She won't tolerate much at all, to be honest – in fact I'm having serious doubts, now I'm thinking about it, whether I'll get away with sneaking in for sex with Oscar while he's staying there. She'll probably phone my parents and report me, as if I was still fifteen and trying it on with the holiday boys.

'West Beach Avenue – this is it, isn't it!' Oscar shouts suddenly as we slow down at the mini roundabout at the top of my parents' road. 'This is where you said they live! OK!' He indicates quickly and swings the car into the road. 'What number?'

And so it is that, much against my wishes, and despite all my plans to the contrary, we're pulling up outside my childhood home, to be greeted by my dad flinging open the front door, my mum squeezing past him on the doorstep to run down the path to hug me, and Oscar climbing out of the car to shake both their hands, introduce himself and get himself invited in to meet the entire family.

'So, Oscar,' says my dad after we've drunk tea, eaten biscuits, described the journey, enquired after everyone's health and that of the neighbours, the cat, the local vicar who had a stroke last month and even my cousin in America, 'Do you live near Sophie in London?'

I can tell they're all just dying to ask a lot more, but trying to control themselves. My sisters' eyes are like saucers, as well they might be. I didn't even tell anyone he was coming.

'Putney. It's ... well, just down the road, really, from where Sophie is in East Sheen,' he says. He's being so charming and polite, he could almost be a Boy Scout, especially in view of his age.

'And ... um ... what do you do for a living, Oscar?' Mum asks brightly – and then suddenly colours and adds quickly, 'or are you at ... um ... college or ...?' She tails off, fortunately, before she adds *school*.

'I'm a sound engineer,' he says, laughing comfortably enough. 'I know I look pretty young, but I'm actually twenty-five. I've got three children!'

'Oh!' There's an audible shifting of consciousness in the room. 'Oh, I'm sorry, I didn't realise you were married,' says Mum. 'So you're ... um ... a friend of Sophie's, then?'

Oh yes, good old Sophie – just another male *friend* tagging along down to Devon with her.

'It's very kind of you, lad, to give her a lift all this way,' Dad's saying at the same time.

I notice neither of my sisters is saying anything, and they're both looking at their shoes. They both know I've been having it off with this *lad* virtually since I stopped having it off with Charlie.

'Oh – no, sorry – you must have misunderstood!' says Oscar at once. He looks at me, slightly puzzled. 'Perhaps Sophie didn't explain? I'm staying down here for the week. I'm booked into Mrs Major's B&B. And I'm not married – I'm divorced. I obviously wouldn't be going out with Sophie if I was married.'

'*Going out* …?' says Mum faintly. Then she recovers herself quickly and adds, 'Oh, I see – yes, we obviously misunderstood, didn't we, John.' She shoots my dad a meaningful look, coughs, blinks, and then adds, 'But Oscar, why on earth would you want to stay at Mrs Major's? Didn't you tell him he'd be welcome to stay here, Sophie?'

I hang my head, feeling like a naughty schoolgirl who's been rumbled.

'I didn't think it was appropriate … bringing friends home … while Mum's still recovering …' God, I even *sound* like a schoolgirl now. How does that happen? Why do I revert to teenager mode whenever I come home?

'But Oscar's hardly just a friend, Sophie,' Mum says reprovingly. 'If you're *going out* together.' She says it a bit coyly, like she really still is the mum of a teenager, who doesn't quite want to think that her daughter and her boyfriend might actually spend time snogging.

'I didn't want to intrude, Mrs Jennings,' says Oscar very politely. 'I'm quite happy to stay at the B&B. I didn't want to put you out in any way, especially in view of your recent illness, and … the other difficulties in the family.'

There's a loaded silence for a moment. Everyone's looking at me: my parents and sisters with suspicion, and Oscar with a smile of satisfaction, obviously imagining I'll be pleased with his tact and diplomacy.

'OK!' Dad gets to his feet, rubs his hands together, and begins, briskly, to gather up the tea things. 'Well, the offer's there, lad – if you change your mind. You're more than welcome.'

'I'll give you a hand with those tea things,' says Mum, following him out of the room.

'No, I'll do it!' say Debra and Millie together, both jumping up and heading for the kitchen too. Debra pauses in the doorway, looks back at me, and shakes her head. But she's grinning at the same time.

'Nice one!' she mouths at me. But I think she's being sarcastic.

'Didn't you explain to your parents?' Oscar asks me quietly when we're left on our own in the lounge. 'About me coming down? About the B&B?'

'I'm sure I did,' I lie, attempting a puzzled expression. 'They obviously didn't take it in. They've had a lot on their minds.'

'Of course. I understand.' He pauses. 'You did tell them about me, though? That we're seeing each other?'

I'm starting to feel rattled. For a start, I've only just been informed, myself, that I'm apparently his girlfriend – never mind announcing it to the entire world. What was I supposed to do? Phone my parents after the first night we spent together and give them a running commentary?

'I'm thirty-four, for God's sake!' I snap. 'My parents don't exactly expect me to give them a list of every man I sleep with!'

'I see,' he says, stonily, looking away from me.

'You see what? Christ! Don't sulk!'

'I mean – I *see*: a list, is it? Of every man you sleep with?'

'No! Oh, God, it was just a figure of speech. I'm not sleeping with anyone else – do I have to tell you that? I wouldn't have the time, or the fucking *energy*, Oscar! And I haven't slept with anyone else for bloody years, if you really need to know. Only Charlie.'

Only Charlie. My heart constricts painfully, making me gasp. He mistakes this for a prelude to bursting into tears, and immediately puts his arms round me and says:

'Oh, I'm sorry, babe! I'm so sorry – I didn't mean to upset you. I should never have asked you that – I've got no right – I really don't know what's come over me. I'm just so desperately ...' He starts to kiss me, fiercely, hungrily, and despite myself I'm just starting to respond when there's a cough at the doorway and Millie, pretending to look the other way, calls out in a giggly voice:

'Another cup of tea, anyone?'

'Clear off!' I shout at her, laughing. 'She always used to do that when she was about eleven or twelve, and I was bringing boys home,' I start to explain to Oscar – and then stop, thinking this might just get him wound up all over again. 'You were saying,' I encourage him instead, wondering if we can, decently, slip off now to his B&B together, 'about being desperate.'

'Yes. I am,' he says softly. He strokes my hair back off my face and studies me, silently, for so long that I start to feel uncomfortable. 'Desperate. Desperately in love with you, Sophie Jennings. Do you mind?'

I think my life just flashed before me.

Wednesday

I'm having a lovely dream about winning the Lottery when my phone wakes me up. I put the pillow over my head and try to ignore it. Must be the wrong number. Nobody I know would think of calling me at whatever unearthly hour in the morning this is. It seems to trill for ever before it goes to voicemail – and just before it does, I suddenly get this terrifying thought: What if it's Polly? I sit up in bed, wide awake now, dreams of Lottery riches fading fast, having a dreadful moment of panic that Polly might need me – she might have found out, somehow, about Jo's baby. Or she might (please God) have decided to leave Leon. Or he might (please God, no) have hit her. Or …

'Good morning, Sophie!' says a very smug-sounding and altogether too jolly-sounding Oscar when I pick up the voicemail message. 'Still in bed, are you, Sleepy-head? Wish I was with you!' he adds in a growl. 'Just calling to wish you a happy anniversary, babe. I'll see you later, OK? Counting the minutes! Love you!'

Counting the minutes? I repeat scornfully to myself, fumbling to look at the time. Half past six. Half past bloody *six* on a holiday morning? Is he mad? He might be counting minutes, but he sure as hell hasn't got the hang of counting the hours. I turn the phone off, crossly, in case he tries it again, and plump up my pillow before snuggling back down again. But it's no good. I can't get back to sleep now, and I bet I never have that dream again. Rats.

I lie for about half an hour, staring at the ceiling, wishing I'd thought to bring a book with me. There's only so much reminiscing you can do about marks on wardrobes from Jason Donovan posters and cracks in mirrors from Ian Wilkins sagas. I toss, and turn, and sigh with irritation about the way things are going with Oscar, and the fact that I'm probably going to have to finish with him when we get

205

home because I can't put up with all this crap he's suddenly coming out with, for much longer. And then I toss and turn some more, and worry about Polly, and hit the pillow with rage about Leon and Jo, and whether Polly's going to find out, and whether the poor bloody baby's going to look like Leon. And then I sit up, and lie back down, and start to worry all over again about Mum, because although everyone says she's doing well, the radiotherapy sessions are obviously taking it out of her and she looks tired, and she's not eating well, and … and I'm frightened. What if the cancer comes back? What if it hasn't really gone? What if she has to have more surgery? What if …

And I can't allow myself to think about it any more, so I have to get up. At seven o'clock. Thanks for *nothing,* Oscar.

Debra calls round just after nine, on her way back from dropping the kids off at school.

'Oh, you're up already,' she says, seeing me slumped on the sofa in front of the TV with a bowl of Shreddies.

'Yes,' I say tersely. 'Mum's having a lie-in. Dad's gone down the shops to get a paper.'

'So tell me,' she says, plonking herself down next to me. 'What is it, with Oscar?'

'What do you mean *what is it* with him?'

'All right, all right,' she says mildly. 'Don't bite my head off. Get out of bed the wrong side, did you?'

'He woke me up at bloody six-thirty, calling to wish me happy anniversary.' I raise my eyebrows at her. 'One month anniversary, for God's sake!'

'Ah. That's nice,' she says.

'Nice? *Nice*? No, it's not nice, Debs, it's just … downright silly! Childish!'

'Well, he *is* quite young!'

'Don't you start!' I sigh. 'Mum keeps talking to him as if he's just done his O-levels, and if Dad calls him *lad* much more I think I'll scream.'

'So what *is* it, with him?' she asks again, looking at me carefully. 'I don't get it. You bring him down here, but you don't seem to want him around. He looks at you like an adoring puppy-dog, you sound like you want to strangle him. And he keeps giving me and Millie funny looks … sort of *pitying*… and nodding patiently whenever we say anything, like we're both a bit slow.'

'Never let it be said, Debs!' I chuckle.

'So what's going on? I thought it was just a fling – a sort of On the Rebound thing, from Charlie?'

'So did I.' I sigh. 'But it's no good, he's got the wrong idea, and it's all getting out of hand.'

'You seem to have a knack for making men fall for you, against your will,' she says, lightly. 'Lucky you.'

'It might be lucky if I felt the same way.'

'Mum and Dad seem to like him!' she teases.

'Well, of course they do! He's behaving like a model schoolboy around them!'

I've tried my best, of course, to keep them apart, but they keep insisting on having him round here. I might just as well have let him stay here, really – he was here nearly all day yesterday, joined us for our picnic on the beach, joined us for dinner, and the only point at which he buggered off was the point at which I'd have liked us to be together – bedtime.

'So why? Why's he treating me and Millie like we're on day-release from a psychiatric ward?'

'Oh.' I smirk. 'Yes, sorry about that. I told him you've both got problems.'

'Problems? What sort of problems?'

'I didn't say. He's presumably drawing his own conclusions.'

'Well, thanks a lot!' she squawks indignantly. 'Why did you say that?'

'To try to put him off,' I admit, with a sigh. 'To tell you the truth, I didn't even want him to come down here. But he's proving a bit difficult to put off.'

'He's rather gorgeous, though, isn't he?' she says, thoughtfully, smiling at me. '*I* would ... if you don't want him any more!'

'Debra!' I gasp, shocked. 'You're *married*!'

'I know,' she says, pouting. 'You don't have to remind me.'

See what I mean? Not exactly an idyllic advertisement for the state of holy matrimony that everyone's always telling me I should aspire to!

'I hope you don't mind, Mrs Jennings,' Oscar says to Mum in that irritating ultra-polite voice he's adopted since we've been down here, 'if I take Sophie out for dinner tonight?'

'Of course I don't mind.' She smiles at him and gives me a strange look. 'Why should I mind?'

'Well.' He smiles back, like they're a couple of conspirators. 'I realise you and the family want to see as much as possible of Sophie this week. But if you can spare her just for this evening ... it's our anniversary, you see.'

'One month!' I explode in exasperation. 'For God's sake, Oscar!'

Oscar flinches, and Mum looks at me in surprise.

'That's very nice, Oscar,' she says. The look she's giving me has become reproving now. 'And of course, all we want is for you both to enjoy yourselves while you're down here. Why don't you go out together for the whole day?'

I'm trying desperately to make eye signals at Mum now, but she's getting into her stride, suggesting all the places of interest around here that I could take Oscar to – all the best beaches, the prettiest villages with the nicest pubs for lunch, the nearest theme parks and farm museums, picnic spots and historic monuments …

'Are you sure you wouldn't like me to stay here and … um … help you with the washing, Mum? Or come shopping with you?'

She stops the tour guide descriptions abruptly.

'No, Sophie,' she says pointedly. 'I'd like you to do whatever *you* want to do. I'll leave you two to decide, then. Have a nice day,' she adds as she goes out of the room.

'If you don't want to spend the day with me,' Oscar says quietly into the silence, 'Just say.'

He sounds hurt, and it's not surprising, really. I'm being a bitch, aren't I. Just because he's making a ridiculous fuss about a one-month anniversary, there's no need for me to be completely horrible to him. He's only trying to be nice, I suppose. And besides – I turn to face him – Debra's quite right. He *is* rather gorgeous!

'I'll tell you what I'd really like to do,' I whisper, putting my arms round his neck.

'What?' he says hoarsely.

'Go back to your B&B and spend the day in bed.'

'I was hoping you'd say that,' he laughs quietly. 'All the time your mum was listing the local attractions, I was wondering whether you were thinking the same as me.'

'Perhaps it's a good thing you didn't take up their offer of staying here, then.' I grin at him. 'I can't help it – whenever I'm under Mum and Dad's roof, I feel like I'm about fifteen again. I could never sneak you up to my bedroom for sex, even if they were out – I'd be terrified they'd catch us at it and ground me for about ten years.'

'Could be exciting, though?' He grins back.

'No. Sorry. I'd much rather go to the B&B!'

'Come on then – we've got an anniversary to celebrate!'

For once, I'm not arguing.

In fact, *celebrating* at the B&B turns out to be a problem. As Oscar pushes the front door open, we can hear the Hoover going in the hall. Mrs Major looks up with annoyance in her eyes as he walks in.

'Wipe your feet!' she shouts. 'I've just done in here!' Then she catches sight of me following Oscar through the door, turns off the Hoover and folds her arms across her massive chest.

'Sophie Jennings!' she bellows. I cower behind Oscar, feeling exactly as I did when I was about twelve years old and being singled out by the headmistress for talking in assembly.

'Hello, Mrs Major,' I respond timidly. 'How are you?'

She ignores this, and, pushing the Hoover to one side, waddles closer to us, jabbing a fat, knobbly finger at me.

'You're not home from London.' It's not a question. Everyone in Sand Bay knows everyone else's business. If I'd moved back, she'd know about it.

'No. Just for a week's holiday,' I tell her. 'To see Mum and Dad.'

'Your poor mother,' she says, shaking her head. 'Poor soul.'

'She's doing OK!' I retort. I'm not having her talking about Mum as if she's passed away.

'Hmm.' She's still shaking her head. 'Only the Almighty knows. Only the Almighty can judge.'

'Fine. Well, in the meantime … nice to see you again, and if you'll just excuse us …'

We start to move towards the stairs. She's watching us, arms still folded, beady eyes sharp in the florid red face.

'Hold it!' she hollers as I'm putting a foot on the first step.

We both stop. I turn and look back at her.

'What?'

'If you think I was born yesterday, Sophie Jennings, you're very much mistaken.'

'Why would I think that, Mrs Major?'

'I'll have you know that this is not a house of ill-repute. I'm a God-fearing, respectable woman.'

'Yes. I'm sure you are.'

'I don't allow *hanky-panky* in my bedrooms, miss, so don't think you can carry on here like you probably do in London.'

'Mrs Major!' says Oscar, giving her the benefit of the nice polite voice he uses on my parents. 'I can assure you, Sophie and I are just going to sit quietly in my room reading our books for a while.'

'You can sit in the lounge, then!' she snaps, pushing the lounge door open with her foot, revealing two elderly ladies sitting on one of the chintz-covered sofas, obviously agog with interest at the discussion going on out here.

This is ridiculous. I've had enough.

'Look – I'm not fifteen!' I tell her crossly, all too aware that she knew me when I was – when she herself caught me once down the alleyway next to her house, drunk on cheap cider and with my skirt up round my waist, against the wall with a Holiday Boy. 'Oscar and I are both adults and we're … in a relationship.'

She snorts loudly at this and mutters something about fancy London expressions for *carrying on together.*

'… and he's paying you the extortionate amount you demand for your crumby room, and if he chooses to have a *guest* …'

'Guest?' She snorts again. 'You're no guest, my girl – you're John and Lizzie Jennings' oldest daughter – and still not married, more be the shame to your poor parents.'

I'm gasping at this, unable to find any words to retaliate. Oscar's trying to intervene with : 'Now look, hang on a minute, you can't say ...' but she's hardly pausing for breath.

'... and if you're carrying on with this young man, who looks like he's only just out of short trousers, then you're no better than you should be!'

I've never understood what the hell that means, but I know for sure it's abusive. I'm not staying here to be insulted any more by this rude old bat. I walk back down her hallway to the front door, my head held high. As I reach the front door, I look back to see Oscar continuing up the stairs.

'Just going to collect my things, Mrs Major,' he calls back cheerfully. 'I won't be needing the room for the rest of the week after all. I've been invited, very kindly, by Sophie's parents, to stay at their house instead.'

'Well! I hope they know what they're doing ...' she splutters indignantly.

'Yes. Well, it's only for a few days, of course, because I'll need to get back to school.'

At this, she makes a kind of choking sound, clutches her throat, and I actually worry for a brief moment that she might be about to vomit on her own spotless floor.

' To collect my three children,' Oscar finishes smoothly.

Mrs Major grabs her Hoover and holds it close to her as if it's all that stands between her and a premature visit to the Almighty. From the lounge, there's a quickly smothered gasping sound – and I look round to see the two old ladies on the sofa holding on to each other, convulsed and shaking with laughter. One of them grins widely at me, while the other raises a thumb enthusiastically. 'Good for you!' she mouths. I lean in the doorway, smiling back at them both, aware of Mrs Major huffing and puffing to herself as she waddles furiously into the kitchen to write out Oscar's bill.

'Well! That was fun! *Not!*' I say, as we walk back down the road after he's packed his bag, paid the old dragon and we've had the door slammed behind us. 'She'll probably be straight on the phone to my parents telling them what a hussy I am! Just like she did when she found me in the alley with that Holiday Boy getting into my knickers.'

'Ooh,' he says, putting an arm round me. 'Tell me more! Where's this alley, then?'

But to be honest, I'm not in the mood any more. I think I'd rather go out to a museum and have a pub lunch.

Saturday

It's strange not to be working, on a Saturday. All over the country, there are weddings going on today, brides panicking and flustered, bridesmaids helping them into their dresses, mothers-of-the-bride pink with excitement, bridegrooms tense with nerves. And for once, instead of being caught up with all that, I'm sitting on Mum and Dad's patio drinking Pimm's and fighting off the wasps while Dad, Oscar and my two brothers-in-law do their manly stuff around the barbecue – poking things with forks and drinking their beers.

It's probably the last barbecue of the season, as the evenings are beginning to close in and become a little chilly, so this family gathering in honour of our final day here is being held early in the afternoon while it's still warm. I'm leaning back in my chair, enjoying the sun on my face, only half listening to the conversations passing between my sisters about the unacceptable level of illiteracy amongst pupils at their children's schools and the worrying prevalence of head lice being discovered. The kids themselves are playing some bizarre game around the trees at the end of the garden, which seems to necessitate one of them crouching on the ground covering their face, while the others run around shouting abuse at them. They're either re-enacting a scene from *Lord of the Flies* or they're playing Mothers and Fathers. Mum, sitting next to me, looks like her eyes are closed behind her dark glasses and I think she's asleep until she suddenly turns to me, while the sisters' voices are particularly strident about falling educational standards, and says simply, nodding in Oscar's direction:

'He's nice. I like him.'

'Oh.' I smile and shrug. 'Yes. He's OK.'

214

'Only *OK*, Sophie?' Her voice is teasing, but I sense something serious behind it, and I don't like it.

'Well – we've only been together a few weeks, and it really isn't anything heavy. He's just ...'

'Just a friend? Again?'

Mum's always had this way with her, of saying something very nicely, very pleasantly, without a hint of criticism in her tone – but you just know there's an underlying disapproval there, somewhere.

'Charlie ...' I begin, wanting suddenly to explain, to confide in her, but not knowing how to begin. 'Charlie and I ...'

She takes off her dark glasses and I can see the concern around her eyes. It stops me dead.

'Let it go, Sophie,' she says gently. 'You have to let it go, and move on.'

'What do you mean?' I say, startled.

'I can tell, just by the way you say his name. He was *more* than a friend to you, wasn't he. He's hurt you. And you still care about him.'

'You seem to know more about it than I do,' I joke. 'What are you – a psychoanalyst? A white witch?'

'No. Just a mum,' she says with a smile.

I'm silent, shaken momentarily by the fact that she can see through me so easily. She always could, but it's scary that she can still do it now I live hundreds of miles away.

'OK, so I'm still somewhat gutted that he got engaged to someone else within weeks of finishing with me, yes. Why wouldn't I be? Even if we *were* just friends,' I add perversely.

'Of course it hurt you. But now you're with Oscar.' She nods in his direction again. 'And he's very nice.'

'It's not *serious*, Mum,' I mutter. The sisters are talking more quietly again now, probably moving on as

215

usual to comparing their husbands' multitudes of faults, and I really don't want them ear-wigging this conversation.

'He seems *very* keen on you.'

'Mm. Well. Maybe.' I'm squirming, here. In a minute she'll be asking me if we're sleeping together. (We haven't been, by the way, while we've been here. He's stayed in Debra's room, and we've kept our doors chastely closed at night. So there.)

'And he says you get on very well with his children? And they've taken to you.'

'Yeah – they're, you know – OK. As children go.'

'Sophie.' She gives me her over-the-glasses look, even though she's not wearing them now. 'Don't mess with their affections, will you. Not the children's. And not his, either.' I'm thinking what a strange expression this is: *mess with their affections*. It sounds smutty, and yet somehow playful. 'It'd be cruel,' Mum adds, wiping these thoughts straight out with that one word. Cruel.

'I'm not messing. I'm not being *cruel*,' I try to protest, quietly, wondering how I can change the subject.

'Well, anyway – it's none of my business, of course,' she says briskly, putting her glasses back on. 'You're old enough to make your own mistakes, I suppose.'

I should leave it at that, and be grateful. But I can't resist asking:

'Mistakes? What mistakes?'

'We've had this conversation before, Sophie,' she says, sighing now as if she's tired of the whole subject. Probably is. 'And you know, I've told you, I respect your wishes, your decision, to stay single. But before you reject somebody who's …' She breaks off and glances at Oscar again. 'Who's intelligent, and kind, and who seems so *right* – just because he might actually *care* about you – perhaps you should ask yourself why.'

Oscar turns round at this very moment, and sees us both looking at him. He smiles, says something to Dad and comes over to perch on the arm of my chair.

'OK?' he says. 'Anyone ready for another drink?'

His bum's inches from my fingers and I'm dying to stroke it, but I manage to resist. It's actually been very different – spending this whole week without any real sexual contact with each other. It has, in fact, given us a chance to get to know each other better. And Mum's right in a way: he is kind, and good, and nice. He is all those things, and I know he does care about me. And his kids like me. And all that stuff. So – OK – as Mum says, why? Why would I reject him? Because I'm scared of having a serious relationship, with all that entails: moving in together, having to share my life and my space, having to consider someone else's wishes as well as my own, giving up control of the TV remote, my free time, my right to do what the hell I like whenever the hell I want to do it. Giving up control, full stop. Because I'm bloody selfish and self-centred, if that's the way you want to see it.

He looks at me, smiles at me again, and suddenly, very weirdly, I feel like I'm seeing myself as other people see me. As my mum, my dad and my sisters probably see me. As Polly and my other friends obviously see me. A spoilt, selfish, self-centred girl – no! not a girl, a *woman*, practically middle-aged, with a body-clock ticking like a time-bomb, who gets gorgeous, good-looking, intelligent, kind, sexy men, practically falling at her feet, but instead of appreciating her luck, she complains about them and pushes them away. Who values her TV remote, and exclusive use of her own microwave, above the love and companionship of an apparently faultless specimen of manhood. Who doesn't, to put it bluntly, know she's born.

Mum's right: it isn't fair. Oscar deserves better. Come to that, he deserves better than being dumped by me just for liking me too much.

217

Just as I'm turning this over in my mind, Dad waves his spatula in the air, and calls out to us all:

'OK, everyone – food's ready! Come and get it!'

But amid the general hubbub – as the kids race up, noisily, from the end of the garden, and Debra and Millie get to their feet and, still chattering, go to help themselves to sausages and chicken – Dad quietly loads a plate with food and brings it over to Mum.

'Here you are, sweetheart,' he says, spreading a napkin on her lap, putting a fork in her hand and offering her ketchup, mustard, salad dressing.

'Special treatment?' she teases him. 'I'm not still an invalid, John.'

'No,' he says, smiling into her eyes. 'But you're still my little princess.'

'Oh, yuck, listen to them!' laughs Debra; and normally I'd be the first to join in, making noises of disgust, pretending to vomit, asking to be spared their embarrassing public displays of affection.

But today, for some reason, I feel my eyes welling up with tears and have to get up, quickly, and walk indoors. And as I'm in the kitchen, pouring myself another drink, Oscar comes in behind me and puts his arms round my waist, kissing the back of my neck.

'Are you OK, babe?' he asks softly.

'Yes.' I turn and kiss him back. 'Just feeling a bit emotional.'

'I'm sure your mum will be fine now,' he says, misunderstanding me. 'And we can come back again, can't we – as often as you like.'

'*We?*'

We look at each other for a moment, weighing each other up.

'I hope so,' he says at length. 'I'd like that. I'd like to be invited again. To be included. But that's up to you, really, isn't it.'

'I'd like it too,' I say. I say it quickly, as if the words might burn my tongue if I don't spit them out. 'I think I'd like us to be together, Oscar. If you would.'

His face lights up. I want to cry again.

'Really? I … God, Sophe, are you sure? I really thought you might be considering finishing it. I didn't think you felt quite the same way as I do.'

'Things have changed, this week.' I touch his face, stroke his hair. He's lovely. What on earth's been the matter with me? He's so lovely! 'I feel like we've got to know each other properly, down here – instead of being in bed the whole time.'

'I hope you're not suggesting we don't have sex any more when we get home?' he says, laughing.

'Wash your mouth out!' I joke, pulling him closer to me – and it's a long time before either of us can talk again.

'I'd forgotten how nice it is – snogging secretly in the kitchen while the rest of the family are out of the way,' I tell him happily when we finally surface.

'I love you, Sophie Jennings,' he says by way of response. He holds me at arm's length and looks at me carefully. 'Is it OK if I say that, now? Or is it still going to piss you off?'

I rest my head against his chest, listening to his heartbeat while I consider this carefully.

'Do you think it's remotely possible to have a relationship like my mum and dad's?' I ask him.

'Looking after each other? Respecting each other? Happy together for ever? Well, it's what I wanted from my marriage,' he says, shaking his head. 'But I married the wrong girl.'

'But you think it's possible?' I insist. 'It's not just a silly, idealised notion? Let's face it, most couples seem to fail disastrously.'

'It might be idealised,' he says, stroking the top of my head. 'But it's still what I'd like to aim for.'

'In that case,' I tell him solemnly, 'then I won't be pissed off. In fact – say it again. Please!'

'I love you, I love you, I *love* you!' he laughs – shouting it, the last time, so loud that there's a whoop and a burst of applause from outside the window. Reddening with embarrassment, I'm nevertheless laughing along, despite myself. The word I've always held in such loathing and contempt suddenly does sound good. It sounds amazing. And I'm not even particularly drunk.

But it's not till later that I realise I never said it back to him. And perhaps I should be worried, because at the time, it didn't even occur to me.

The next Sunday

So this is it. This is how it feels. This is what I've spent my whole life – well, OK, my whole life since Damien – avoiding. Not only avoiding, but fending off so strenuously and vociferously, I could have written the How-To book on it. *How to Avoid Having A Man in Your Life (And In Your Flat)*. He's here. He's in my flat. And the truth is? I'm still not sure whether I want him here.

He started moving his stuff in last night, and finished this morning. We haven't managed to unpack everything yet, so it looks … well, it looks like there's been a takeover. I feel twitchy, and slightly irritable, and like I'm going to have a panic attack every time I see his clothes hanging on the backs of doors or have to step over boxes of his CDs and books in the hallway.

It was my choice. He asked me if I'd prefer to move into his place, but I'd never even considered that option, and I must have looked appalled, because he then pretended not to be hurt, overdoing all the understanding comments about his flat being smaller and scruffier and not in such a nice area. Now I sound like a snob. It's actually nothing to do with the nice area, or the size of the flat (he has a second bedroom where the twins sleep in bunk beds when they come to stay, and a sofa-bed in the lounge for Benjamin, so it's not really any smaller than mine). And the scruffiness could be rectified – most of that is just the result of a man living on his own, nothing a serious fumigation and a spot of redecoration couldn't put right. No – it's just that I can't leave my flat! I can't! The thought of it horrifies me. It's stressful enough giving up *space* in my flat to make room for Oscar. Moving out of it altogether would be a step *much* too far. I'd feel completely adrift. OK, I'll admit it. I'd feel like I'd *completely* lost control.

221

As opposed to … feeling like I almost have.

He's walking around the place grinning like a Cheshire cat. Every time he passes me as he carries something from one room to another, he stops to kiss me.

'There!' he says finally, as he plonks yet another box of crockery on the kitchen worktop. 'I think that's the lot.'

'Oh. Good,' I say faintly. I survey my kitchen with a sinking heart. Where the hell is all this lot going to go?

'It'll be OK,' he says, laughing at me gently. I don't suppose the expression on my face is too hard to read. 'We'll move things around a bit, make some room. Maybe I could put up a couple of extra shelves.'

'No!' What the hell? I don't want him putting up shelves in my perfectly designed kitchen! I don't want him moving *my* stuff around, to make room for his stuff! 'No, that won't be necessary. I'll clear out a shelf or two of one of the cupboards, and you can put your stuff in there.'

He considers this for a moment, his head on one side, still smiling. Still happy, even though he must be wondering whether I'm wanting to keep all his stuff strictly separate from mine in case I throw him out again in a day or two.

'I know it's going to feel a little crowded for a while. Till we both get used to it,' he says. 'But it probably won't be for long, after all.'

The words hang in the air between us like static electricity. He's not planning on it lasting? I get a sudden queasy feeling in my stomach, and I can't, in all honesty, identify whether it's disappointment or relief.

'I mean – we can look for something bigger, can't we. A house, with a garden. With two of us to share the mortgage, we can probably afford to do it already!'

'Oh,' I say, weakly. There's a rush of blood to my head. I reach behind me for a chair, and sit down, heavily. 'Well, let's not hurry things, Oscar.'

'Of course not. I've circled a few properties in the local paper. But we don't need to start looking just yet, if you don't want to. Not till we've put our flats on the market.'

'Oscar!' I feel hot with panic now. 'No! I'm not ready for that! OK? Let's just stop all this talk about moving, and selling, *please*, for the moment – we have to get used to living together first, for God's sake!'

'All right, then. Whatever,' he says, obviously offended now. He wanders into the lounge and turns on the TV. 'How about a nice glass of beer while we watch the football together?' he calls out in a minute, as if this will make everything OK.

'Help yourself from the fridge. I'm going to Polly's.'

'Give it time,' says Polly, hugging me. 'It'll be fine.'

'Will it? Polly, he's been living with me for five minutes, and I couldn't wait to get away from him! I feel like my privacy's been invaded. I don't understand how people ever get used to it.'

She makes the tea, gives the baby something unidentifiable to chew on, and turns to face me, looking serious now.

'In a way, you know, he's got a point. About looking for a house.'

'What? Are you joking? We've only known each other a few weeks!'

'But you evidently felt ready to move in together.'

'Thought I did,' I correct her, morosely.

She ignores this. 'I just think it works better if you both move into a new place. Somewhere that didn't used to be just yours – or just his. I'm not saying he should be rushing you to do it straight away. But I just think it works better like that. That's all.'

Moving out of my flat? Into somewhere new – belonging to us *both*? *Jointly*? I can feel my breathing becoming laboured at the thought of it. Am I about to have a panic attack? Or a heart attack?

'I couldn't do it. It would feel ... like being trapped. Like being married!' I gasp with remorse as soon as I've said it. 'Sorry – I didn't mean it to sound like that. I don't mean that everyone who's married is trapped ...' I tail off, then, and look away from her, because – let's face it – of all the married people I know, I actually do think she's the most trapped, in the worst possible way.

'Well, you have to work at these things,' she says, a bit brusquely. 'It's not going to be perfect straight away. You've been on your own too long. You'll have to adapt.'

I'm not arguing. I want to. I want to retort *Why? Why should I adapt? Why should I change?* – but I know that would be stupid, and childish. Nobody forced me to invite Oscar to live with me. If I'm not prepared to adapt, I shouldn't have done it. That's the bottom line, really, and I know that's what's scaring me: that perhaps I *shouldn't* have done it.

'He didn't like me coming round here this afternoon,' I say instead, sipping my tea, watching Polly's face.

She shoots me a look of concern. I recognise the look. It's the one I give her when she says things like Leon doesn't want her to go out in the evenings.

'Why not?'

'I don't know – I suppose he thought we should spend time together, as he's only just moved in.'

'You could have called me and cancelled. If he had other plans, wanted to take you out, or whatever. I'd have understood.'

224

'Polly, he wanted me to watch football and drink beer with him! I think he's mistaking me for one of his mates from work.'

She giggles. 'Sounds like he's got some adapting to do, too.'

'There's *no way* I'm stopping doing the things I want to do! Especially coming to see you!'

'Good!' she says, lightly. There's a shout from the garden. 'OK, Gracie – I'm coming! I've left her playing in her sand pit,' she tells me as she grabs the baby from his highchair and rushes towards the back door. 'She's probably buried the cat by now.'

'How do you do it?' I ask as I follow her, carrying our mugs of tea. 'How the hell do you manage their conflicting demands? Gracie's, the baby's, and … his – Leon's?'

She shrugs and grins at me. 'God knows. If I stopped and thought about it too much, it'd all come tumbling down.' Then her face suddenly crumples and she adds, almost in a whisper so that Gracie, who's yelling for us to look, look, *look!!!* at the lovely house she's built in the sandpit, doesn't hear: 'Tumbling down even faster than it is already.'

'It's a beautiful house, Gracie,' I gush, at once, to cover Polly's sudden silence. 'Can you build a lovely car now, to go with it?'

She stares at me. I feel myself shrink under the disgusted superior gaze of a four year old.

'Don't be silly, Sophie. You can't make *cars* out of sand!'

Houses are OK, though, apparently. The fact is that we all seem to live in houses made of sand. And they can come tumbling down at any time at all.

It's not like I've stopped worrying and fretting about the Polly/Leon/Jo situation. It's not like the week in Devon, or the whole thing of Oscar moving in with me, has made me forget it, even for a minute. In fact, the worry about it is so scorched into my consciousness, the whole time, it's become almost part of my personality – so that I don't so much *think* about it now, as live it, breathe it, eat it and drink it. Not being able to talk to Polly about it is tearing me into bits. Wondering if she's going to find out about it, and if she does, whether she'll also find out that I knew but didn't tell her, is killing me. But I still can't tell her.

'How have things been?' I ask, without meeting her eyes. We're sitting on her lawn, next to the sandpit, enjoying the September sunshine while it lasts.

'The same. He's so bad-tempered, even Gracie has started asking him what's the matter.' She mutters this with her head turned away from Gracie, hiding her own face behind the baby's, who's chewing his horrible yucky biscuit thing while sitting on her lap, smearing biscuit mess and gooey saliva all over her.

'And what does he say to that?'

'Just snaps *Nothing!* at her, and looks at me like it's my fault she's asking! Like she can't pick up on the fact that something's wrong, on her own!'

'Perhaps there's something stressing him out at work,' I suggest wildly.

She shakes her head. 'I kept asking him that at first – trying to get him to talk to me about whatever's going on there – but it just seemed to put him in an even worse mood. In the end he told me to shut up going on about his job. So I've given up, now, Sophe. I don't ask, any more. I'm trying to do what you said – just ignore him.' She swallows and blinks. 'It's not easy, though.'

'Of course it's not,' I commiserate. I go to take hold of her hand, but Ethan's already holding it, and has squashed the remains of his biscuit into it.

'It's a only a Rusk,' she says, smiling thinly, seeing the look on my face. 'Not anything disgusting. He's teething. It helps.'

I don't see how, when he seems to spread most of it over Polly. But what would I know?

'And to make matters worse,' she says, after moment's silence while she sets the baby down with his toys on the blanket by our feet, 'I feel like I'm losing my friends, too.' Her voice wobbles on the last few words and I look up in alarm.

'You're not!' I say, more loudly than I intend. Gracie, digging furiously in the sand, sings 'Not, not, not!' to herself like a little echo. 'Of course you're not!' I repeat, more quietly, but insistently. 'Polly! Don't say that! Just because Oscar's moved in, doesn't mean anything's going to change. He's not going to stop me coming round to see you! I didn't mean that! It was only because today was a bit difficult, like you said, with us both having to adjust, and …' I break off, floundering, and then add, more calmly, realising the truth of it as I'm saying it: 'Anyway, if it came to it, I'd put you first. You know that. Every time, over any man in the world, I'd put you first.'

She's struggling not to cry, now.

'Come here, you daft thing,' I say, holding out my arms – and then I remember the Rusk and we both laugh, at the same time.

'I'll go and clean myself up. But *you're* the daft one. For God's sake, Sophe – I wasn't talking about you. Not for a minute. I meant the others. Emma hasn't phoned me for ages – she seems to be so caught up with her relationship with Stefan, she's forgotten about everyone else. And Jo: well, I haven't even seen her since the party. And to be honest, I thought she was a bit off with me, that day, too. She left without saying goodbye. And I've tried calling her – she never even returns my calls.' She shrugs and gets up. 'She's avoiding me. I don't know what I've done to upset her, but she's definitely avoiding me.'

I'm glad she goes indoors to wash the Rusk off her, at that point, because I have no idea what to say to that.

I end up telling Oscar a little bit more about the Polly situation tonight. I didn't intend to, but I'm feeling so upset, and it isn't fair to let him think it's anything to do with him.

'I think her husband's definitely having an affair,' I say, skilfully avoiding any specific mention of Jo. I go on to tell him about how special Polly is, how caring and compassionate, what a good friend she is, how she deserves so much better than Leon.

'Poor girl,' he says. 'But thank God she's got you for a friend.'

'No. No – I could never, in a million years, be a good enough friend to her,' I tell him passionately. 'Not compared to what she did for me.'

And to my own surprise I find myself going on to tell him about Damien – the whole story, drugs and all. And how Polly dropped everything to rush up from Devon to be with me, when he threw me out and I thought I was pregnant. How she paid for a room in a hotel for us both, because I was too ashamed to go home to my parents. How she looked after me and helped me to get clean, and then took me back to Devon, to recover from what my family still believe was Glandular Fever. How we decided, then, that we didn't want to be separated any more, and that she would move back to London with me. How Damien had always remained our secret – mine and Polly's.

'Till now,' says Oscar softly, stroking the tears away from my face.

'Yes. Till now.' I look at him in shock, as if I've woken up from a dream. I can't believe I've told him all this. Even Charlie didn't hear all of it, not in the detail I've

228

just spouted to Oscar – because I always thought he'd lose respect for me if I told him about the drugs, about the level of degradation I sank to. About things like Polly having to bath me and dress me, while I was coming off the drugs, because I was shaking too much to do anything for myself.

'Are you disgusted by me?' I ask him, quietly. I look around the flat. While I was out this afternoon, instead of watching the football, he's managed to unpack all his boxes and bags, and put everything – somehow – away in the cupboards without any of them looking unduly messed up. I'm so touched by this, I suddenly, really, don't want him to change his mind and move out again.

'Of course not.' He nuzzles my neck, kisses my damp cheeks. 'You were young, you made a mistake. I'm *proud* of you – for recovering from that, the way you did. And I totally understand how you feel about your friend. If there's anything I can do to help her, I will. I kind-of feel like I owe her something. For helping you to be the woman you are now. The woman I love.'

And I know what you're probably thinking: BLEAH! Yuck!

But right this minute, I guess it's just what I want to hear.

The first Thursday in October

October already. Where did the summer go? It doesn't help that I've been so busy with weddings, I haven't had a lot of time to relax. It's an enjoyable business, when it's busy. The hustle and bustle of lots of weddings, lots of excitement, lots of different people to meet. Well – normally they're different people, but occasionally it happens the way it has today – I have a bridesmaid of one of my previous brides, for a hair trial for her own wedding. And guess who it is? None other than Melissa – one of Hilary's awful bridesmaids. The one who wanted advice about whether to take back the bastard who dumped her two months before her wedding, last year.

'Hilary recommended you,' she booms as she stomps in. 'You did a good job on her.'

She somehow manages to make it sound like a bit of DIY or painting and decorating.

'How is Hilary?' I ask, as I get her settled in front of the mirror. I'm thinking – oh, God help me – I remember this hair. It's an inexplicably strange texture, and the length seems to be different in different places. It'll need a good cut before I can do anything with it at all. I'm not looking forward to it. 'She's your sister-in-law, isn't she?'

'Yes. Daniel's my brother. She's doing OK,' she says, somewhat guardedly.

'So you've decided to follow their example?'

'Pardon?'

'Getting married. You're presumably getting married yourself, now?'

'Oh – yes, absolutely. Next month. Awful month, November – depressing as hell – bloody hate it, but there it is: couldn't be helped. Booking a wedding at short notice, beggars can't be choosers. Could only get a Wednesday in bloody November, have to make the best of it. Hope the bastard turns up this time. If he doesn't, he's had it. I'll break both his kneecaps.'

Somehow I don't doubt it, either.

'So you took him back, in the end?'

'Trevor? Yes – couldn't stand it any more, him whining about being sorry, wanting another chance. Fed up waiting for Mr Right, anyway. Trevor will have to do. Like I say – beggars can't be choosers.'

'Sure you don't mean that,' I say, smiling at her encouragingly, although I have a horrible feeling she does.

'Bloody do!' she retorts. 'Bloody men – all the same! My brother's no better – pissed most of the time, more interested in his rugby team than poor bloody Hilary.'

'Oh!' I stop, mid-contemplation of her hair, startled into asking rather rudely: 'Is it not working out, then – her marriage?'

'No worse than anyone else's, I suppose,' says Melissa. 'Bloody mug's game, if you ask me.'

'But you're ...' I stare at her in the mirror. 'You're doing it too!'

'Yeah. Must be a bloody mug as well,' she says with no sign of humour. 'You? Got yourself a man yet?'

'Kind-of,' I say, faintly, really not wanting to get into this right now.

'Mugs, all of us.' She shrugs. 'OK, get on with it, then. And don't forget – no products. I've got allergies.'

Well, at least it makes a change from being asked for advice!

Oscar's home early this evening. He's carrying a Marks & Spencer's Meal for Two (with wine), a random sad-looking houseplant with pale pink petals that are already dropping all over the carpet, and an airbed. The airbed is, naturally, not inflated, but I can see it's an airbed from the fact that

231

it's in a clear plastic bag that has Super-Deal Air Bed (Double) printed on it.

'What's that for?' I ask him.

He plonks the Meal for Two (with wine) down on the kitchen surface.

'I thought it'd save either of us cooking tonight. It's chicken and mushroom risotto, and …'

'I can see it's a risotto. I meant – what's *that* for?' I nod at the airbed.

'It's for you. It's a Pelargonium. Apparently they can bloom all year round if you put them in a sunny window.'

'Oscar! I'm not talking about the plant. Thank you for the plant. But what's the airbed for?'

He's got his back to me now, positioning the Pelargonium on the window-sill, turning it this way and that, like he really cares what it looks like or how much sun it gets.

'I got it in case we need it,' he says eventually.

'And why would we need it?' I ask, sarcastically. 'Are you planning on sleeping apart from me now that we're living together?'

He laughs, a little too brightly, a little too falsely.

'Don't be silly! In case we need it for *guests*. Overnight guests.'

'Such as?' As if I don't know.

'Well, anyone, really. Friends. Family. My children …'

'No!' I say, too quickly, too loudly. 'No, I can't have the children staying here overnight on a bloody airbed! No way.'

'There's nothing wrong with an airbed, Sophie.'

'I didn't say there was. As long as it doesn't get slept on in my lounge.'

He looks at me in silence for a moment. Then:

'I thought, actually, the spare room would be better.'

That does it. I think we're about to have our first proper row.

'The *spare room*,' I tell him through tight lips, 'is not a spare room. It's my salon. It's my work place.'

'It's pretty big, though. There'd be enough room …'

'Absolutely not!'

'… for the twins to share the airbed in there …'

'No way!'

'…and Benjamin could sleep on the sofa in the lounge.'

'No! No, and that's the end of it! I'm *not* having little children sleeping in my salon – apart from anything else, I keep scissors, and pins, and hair colourants in there. Are you mad? Do you want them to kill themselves?'

'OK. So we could put the airbed in the lounge, then – all three of them could sleep in the lounge, no problem.'

'Hello? Excuse me? Yes, it *is* a problem! Sorry, Oscar, but this was *not* part of the deal when you moved in. You, yes. Your kids, no. My flat is not child-friendly. I'm not having kids staying here. Ever.'

'You knew I had children when you agreed to me moving in,' he says accusingly, as if it's my fault. As if it was me that got pregnant and gave birth to them, God forbid.

'Yes, but you didn't say you wanted to bring them with you.'

'Don't be ridiculous, Sophie. I haven't brought them with me. But I do have them for alternate weekends. You know that. I missed the last one, because I was moving in here.'

'I see. So you're due to have them this weekend,' I say, stonily.

'Yes.'

'And you've left it till now to mention that you were planning on putting them up here?'

'I suppose I presumed that you'd be expecting it.'

I bang my hand on the worktop, making him jump.

'No – funnily enough, I wasn't expecting it! You shouldn't have presumed!'

'But I've told them, now,' he says, hanging his head. 'They're looking forward to it! They're dead excited about the airbed!'

'Then you can blow up the bloody airbed in your *own* flat, can't you.'

We stare at each other. I'm furious. I mean – how dare he? How dare he *presume* I'm going to have his kids running around my flat all weekend?

'So what you're saying is,' he says, slowly, quietly, 'that you want me in your life, but not my kids?'

'I didn't say that. Just not in my flat.'

'I thought you liked my kids? I thought you were getting on really well with them? They love you! They think you're great.'

'For God's sake! This has nothing to do with me liking them. I like lots of people, but it doesn't mean I want them sleeping on airbeds in my *flat*.'

He turns away from me, like he's disgusted with me.

'I'm sorry, but look …' I begin.

'Is this how it's going to be?' he interrupts, swinging back to face me again.

'What?'

'Is this – always – the way it's going to be? You dictating what I can, or can't, do here? Because it's your flat? What's it going to take, for us to be equals in this? Would you like me to pay you rent? Is that it?'

'No!'

'I've told you, I will – if I sell my flat, then obviously I will, but I've still got a mortgage to pay, and …'

'It's nothing to do with paying rent!'

'What, then? I offered to have you move in with *me*, but no – that wasn't good enough for you. You have to stay in *your* precious flat, and keep everything just *exactly* the same, as if I wasn't really living here – all my stuff out of sight, making me feel like a … like a *lodger*. No, worse than that – like a temporary guest! I don't feel like I live here, Sophie! I don't feel like it's my fucking home, if you want the truth. Is *that* how it's always going to be?'

'It's only been two weeks,' I mutter. 'And this is only about your *kids*. I can't have kids here, Oscar – be reasonable. I've got scissors …'

'And pins. I know.' He shakes his head. 'So lock them away. Make an effort, yeah? Otherwise what's the point? What's the bloody point?'

'I'm sorry. I'm not changing my mind.'

'So I'll have to move out for the weekend – is that what you're saying? Go back to my old flat. Good job I haven't put it on the market yet.'

'Don't be ridiculous. You weren't going to put it on the market yet. Of course you'll have to stay there with your children. I can't believe you thought anything else.'

'It seems we had completely different expectations then, doesn't it.'

'Apparently.'

'In that case, I'll move back to my flat tonight, then.'

'Don't be childish. There's no need …'

'I think there is. I'm going to pick up the children straight from work tomorrow evening, so I won't have time to come back here and collect my stuff. I'll do it now.'

'Just for the weekend.'

235

'I suppose so, Sophie. That rather depends on you, doesn't it. Whether you want me back again. Whether you really think you have room for me in *your* flat.'

With which he stomps off to the bedroom, and I hear him crashing around as he packs his bag. And I think: great. Well done, Sophie. A very successful relationship, this is. Two weeks of living together, and he's talking about moving out already.

I eat the whole of the Meal for Two by myself. And drink the whole bottle of wine. And then I lie awake nearly all night, wondering whether this is all my fault. I never wanted a relationship. I lost Charlie because I didn't want a relationship. So here I am – pretty much mainly to please my mum, I've got Oscar living with me, and already we're arguing about it. What the hell am I playing at?

Friday

I'm tired this morning, and depressed, and I've got a busy day – with a new client for a hair trial this morning, and a wedding this afternoon. The hair trial client is booked for nine o'clock – I told her that was the only time I could squeeze her in today. She was insistent on today, as it was the only day she could be spared from her job for a couple of hours – it does make me laugh when people talk like that. What are they – the Prime Minister? A brain surgeon? But like I say, she's a new client, who contacted me through my website, so I didn't want her to go to someone else. Nine o'clock it is, and at nine o'clock, on the dot, she's ringing my doorbell.

I open the door, and we stare at each other speechlessly for a moment. She's tall, and blonde, with green eyes and a figure to die for. And I didn't recognise her bloody name when she made the appointment.

'Helen Hunter,' she says. 'You're … Wedding Belles, then.'

'Yes.' I'm trying not to scowl. 'Um … you'd better come in.'

'I didn't realise it was you, from the website.'

'Charlie didn't mention it?'

I flinch as I say his name. I can't bear it – talking to Hateful Helen about Charlie, her *fiancé*, as if he's just another bridegroom-to-be of just another bride. As if he was never *my* Charlie.

'Don't be silly,' she snorts. 'I didn't tell *him* I was booking my hair trial. He wouldn't be interested.'

I have to stop myself from saying *Really? That doesn't sound like Charlie*. He was always interested in *everything* I did.

'Well, you'd better come in,' I say, again, as she's still rooted to the spot on the doorstep looking like she might decide to turn and walk away. No point losing a potential client just because I hate her. Business is business.

We talk, in a very stilted fashion, about how she wants her hair (up), whether she's having any bridesmaids (two – a sister and a cousin), and what sort of dress she's chosen (lacy, fussy, sounds horrible), while she's getting settled and I'm feeling the weight and texture of her hair. I'm going to keep this impersonal. I'm not going to ask about Charlie.

'So how long have you been doing wedding hair, Sophie?' she asks with ultra politeness and pretending to look interested.

'Five years in my own business. Working in a salon before that.' There's an uncomfortable silence while we both avoid eye contact in the mirror and try to think of something else to say. 'How's Charlie?' I blurt out.

Well, that was good, wasn't it? I managed all of about three minutes without mentioning him.

'Oh – you know what he's like,' she says dismissively.

Is that it? Is that all she can say about the man she stole from me, the man she's presumably so much in love with that she's marrying him within a few months of meeting him? Yes, I do know what he's like. He's kind, and gentle, and caring, and considerate – and if you don't think so too, what the hell are you doing with him, Cow-features?

'How do you mean?' I say instead, aware that my voice is coming out kind-of choked, like I've swallowed a hairclip.

'Oh, I suppose all men are the same. Anyone would think it was all down to me – the whole wedding – all the arrangements: the service, the flowers, the music, the reception, the invitations, the food ...'

238

She's ticking them off on her fingers. OK, OK – it's not exactly like I've never heard this before. It's so common for brides to complain that their fiancé isn't taking much interest in the wedding and they're having to do it all themselves, I actually feel startled when somebody says the groom's arranged something. But if she thinks I'm going to listen to her criticising Charlie, she's got another think coming.

'That doesn't sound like him at all,' I tell her smoothly. 'He was always *terribly* interested when I talked to him about all the weddings I was involved in with my work.'

'Perhaps that's the problem,' she replies equally smoothly. 'Perhaps he got so fed up with listening to you talking about weddings all the time, it's put him off talking about his own.'

She laughs a tinkling, brittle laugh, supposedly to show that this is a joke, but I know it's really because she thinks she's scored a point, got the advantage. She hasn't, of course, because I'm the one standing up, she's the one sitting down, I've got a clump of her hair in my hand and my scissors in my pocket.

'Perhaps he's just not really ready for his own wedding,' I return.

'Oh, believe me, he's more than ready – after all, the whole thing was his idea. He was desperate to marry me. He couldn't bear to wait till next year – he was insistent on accepting this cancellation in December.'

'Really? That's strange. He told me it was you that decided to accept the cancellation.'

She finally meets my eyes.

'When did you speak to him?' she asks, sharply.

Just for a moment, I allow fantasy to take over. I imagine myself replying with a coolness I could never achieve in reality: *Oh, he just mentioned it in passing when he came round for a quick shag last night.* I imagine her stomping out of my flat, getting straight on the phone to Charlie and calling off the wedding. I imagine Charlie phoning me in tears and admitting it was all a horrible mistake, he wants to go back to how we were, he'll be round later, we'll pick up from where we left off. And then I remember Oscar. Things are mixed-up enough between us already, without me inviting Charlie round to pick up from where we left off, even in my fantasy.

'At the petrol station,' I admit. 'We were filling up at the same time. He told me ...' Oh, sod it – what's the point in antagonising her? She's a client. 'He told me how pleased he was that you'd managed to book the wedding so quickly,' I lie.

'Yes.' She smiles graciously, like the queen, aware of her supremacy. 'Yes, he would have done. He's *so* excited about it.' There's another silence, then she reverts to her original story. 'But he's leaving all the bloody arrangements to me.'

'They always do,' I say, with a sigh. I can't help sighing. My heart's doing it all on its own without me asking it to. 'Don't worry about it. It doesn't mean he's not interested.'

She gives me a different kind of look now. I'm not sure if it's gratitude or just acknowledgement that I've decided not to fight her.

'But there are certain aspects he *has* to get involved in,' she says. 'He has to decide about his best man, and the ushers – and choose their suits, and his own! And he has to decide who's going to invited, on his side. Should I keep on *nagging* him to get these things sorted out, do you think? Or should I just assume he's going to do it, when he's ready? What do *you* think, Sophie?'

Well, who'd have thought it? Good old Agony Aunt Sophie to the rescue again, eh? I know every other bugger in the universe wants a share of my amazing wisdom, but I never thought I'd see the day when Charlie's new *fiancée* would be asking my advice about him.

'Oh – nag him, definitely,' I say, smiling confidently back at her. 'No point leaving it to him – it'll never get done. Nag him morning, noon and night till he gets the message. It's the only way.'

'Really? You don't think he'll get fed up with me?'

'Absolutely not. Charlie never minded a bit of nagging. It helps to focus his mind.'

'Well, I'm glad you told me that, Sophie.' She smiles back. There's something genuine in the smile for the first time. She actually thinks I'm being sisterly and helpful, the poor fool. 'I must say, you're being very generous and gracious about all this.'

I nod, generously and graciously.

'And how *are* things with you?' she goes on, trying to adopt a tactful expression, like someone enquiring about a bereavement or a terminally ill patient. 'Have you found anyone, yourself, yet?'

'Oh, yes,' I say, airily. I actually wave my hairbrush, nearly clocking her one on the head with it. 'Yes, I'm living with someone now. He's a lot younger than me. I need that, you see – I need someone young, and energetic. And virile.' I treat her to the smile of someone who's accustomed to being surrounded by energy and virility. Unfortunately it comes out pretty much as the smile of a crazy woman baring her teeth.

'Good for you,' she says rather faintly. 'I'm sure Charlie will be pleased to hear you're … settled.'

Oh yes. I'm sure he *will*. Eat your heart out, Charlie Dawkins. I'm getting plenty of live-in energy and virility – always assuming Oscar comes back after his weekend of childcare and sulking, of course. All *you're* going to be getting is a lot of nagging about suits.

I'm on the phone to Polly as soon as I get home from this afternoon's wedding.

'I did her hair! Hateful Helen's! She was moaning about Charlie! She thinks he's not interested in the wedding! She's having a horrible lacy dress with frills and sparkles and wearing loads of bling, and she wanted to know what *I* thought she should do, and I said to her ...'

'OK, OK, calm down, tell me *slowly*,' says Polly. I can hear her smiling. 'I want to hear this. I need to hear it properly!'

Bless her. Where would we be without our friends?

I don't miss Oscar. That's awful, isn't it? Well, I'd hardly got used to him being here, really. It still felt strange, having him permanently *here*, cluttering up the place with his big old shoes and his dirty underwear and his shaving stuff in the bathroom. Now it just feels more like normal again. I can watch what I want on TV without having to ask, politely, whether he'd prefer to watch something else. I can talk for hours on the phone without being conscious of him being neglected. I can be myself.

'How's it going with Oscar?' Debra asks when she calls me later.

'Oh – fine, fine,' I say breezily. 'He's got his kids for the weekend, as it happens.'

There's a sharp intake of breath on the other end of the line.

'You've got his kids staying? With you? In your flat?'

My sister knows me well. She's right to sound incredulous.

'No. Don't be silly. He's gone back to his own place for the weekend.'

'And you ... don't *mind*?'

I look around my nice tidy lounge. Consider the lack of male clutter, the lack of sport on the TV.

'No, of course I don't mind. It's cool. Everybody needs *space* in a relationship, don't they.'

Hark at me – the relationship expert, now, after two whole weeks.

'Do you think so, Sophie?' She sighs. 'Do you think, maybe, that's where I've gone wrong with James? Should I have allowed him more space? Not expected him to be there for me and the kids all the time?'

Oh, God – I should have known it was a mistake to make myself sound like an expert. It was bad enough, being asked for advice all the time, when I *wasn't* an expert (or pretending to be).

'I don't think you've *gone wrong* at all, Debs,' I tell her, just as I always tell Polly. I hate the way we women always think everything is our fault. 'You *have* given him space!'

'Yes, I have, haven't I,' she agrees sadly. 'Too much bloody space, really. He's never around. Do you think *that's* the problem, then? I let him have too much space? What do you think?'

Bloody hell. I think I'm going back to not being an expert. That's what I think.

Sunday

Oscar hasn't phoned me, or texted me, or probably even *thought* about me, all weekend. I know I'm being irrational; I know I've enjoyed having the flat to myself again, but I'm pissed off that he's being such a big sulker, such a big baby, that he can't even bring himself to talk to me. I know I haven't bothered to talk to him either but I've been *busy* – I've been *working*. I haven't just been on a jolly round of fun with three children.

The phone finally rings just as I'm about to set off to see Polly, and sure enough it's Oscar's number in the display. I have to remind myself to play it cool – after all, it was him that walked out on me in a foul mood on Thursday night, wasn't it.

'Hello,' I say, coolly.

There's a blood-curdling shriek at the other end, making me jump out of my skin.

'It's her!' screams a child's voice. 'She's answered!'

'Let ME talk to her!' screams another, equally ear-splitting voice.

'No – me first!'

'No – me! Daddy! Tell her – I'm talking first!'

I'm tempted to hang up.

'Hello?' I say again, a little more wearily. 'Is that you, Serena?'

'Yes!' squeals Serena.

'No!' shouts Deana. 'It's me!'

'Well, listen. I can't talk to both of you at the same time. Sort it out. One gets to start. The other one gets to say goodbye.'

There's some muted arguing for a few seconds and then a slightly less shrill voice starts again:

'Hello, Sophie.'

'Hello, Deana.'

'No!' She giggles. 'I'm Serena.'

'OK. How are you, Serena?'

'I'm very well, thank you,' she says in her best polite voice. Then: 'Shut *up*, Deana, it's not your turn yet!'

'Have you had a nice weekend with your daddy?' I ask her quickly. I'm getting bored with this already. How much of a conversation can you have with a five year old on the phone?

'Yes, but we wanted to sleep in *your* house but Daddy said we couldn't because of the scissors, but we wouldn't have touched the scissors, and Daddy said your house isn't big enough for children, but we're not very big so we don't take up much room, so can we come to your house next time Sophie?'

This is all delivered on one breath and without the benefit of any verbal punctuation. I'm still forming an 'Um …' on my tongue, as I have no idea how to reply, when there's a crash, a scream, a volley of insults ranging from *piggy-poo* to *horrible-hate-you*, a shout in the background that (thank God) I recognise as Oscar's voice, and then a much more subdued little voice saying:

'Hello Sophie. Sorry about S'rena. She pinched me and kicked me and …'

'Did *not*!' squealed Serena. 'You made me drop the phone on the floor and if it's broken, Daddy's going to *kill* you.'

'Hello, Deana,' I say. 'Look, if you girls are going to keep fighting, I'd better go.'

'No! I haven't had my turn!' wails Deana.

'Quickly, then. What have you and Daddy been doing this weekend? And Benjamin?'

'Daddy took Ben to football and bought us an ice cream cos we were good but I wanted to stay at *your* house Sophie!' Oh no – here we go again. 'Can we stay at your house next time? If we be very very good and don't fight?'

245

'Um …'

'I love you, Sophie,' she adds in her lisping, missing-front-tooth voice.

'I love her more than you do!' comes the inevitable echo.

'Do not!'

'Do!'

'Ow! Don't pinch!'

By now they're both crying. It's such a relief when I hear Oscar's voice next, I almost forget that I was pissed off with him.

'God, how do you stand it? Do they always fight like that? I thought twins were supposed to be very specially close?'

'Close to murdering each other,' he says grimly. 'Sorry about that. The girls were so disappointed not to see you this weekend, I promised they could talk to you. But it was probably a mistake. My mistake. As usual.'

'No, well … it was, um, nice to talk to them,' I lie.

'Look, Sophe – I'm sorry. Sorry for storming off, and … well, being an arse. It's just, well, you know. I was disappointed too.'

'I know. We should have talked this stuff through, shouldn't we. Before you moved in. I suppose we rushed into it, a bit.'

'You're not saying you want me to move out?'

'No.'

Not really. Do I?

'I'll be back later on tonight, then? After I've taken the kids back?'

'Yeah. See you then.'

'Did you miss me?' he asks, softly.

'Yeah.' I take a deep breath. 'Course I did.'

'Love you.'

The correct response, of course, would be *I love you too, darling.* I don't know why I can't say it. The words

246

just won't come. They get stuck somewhere at the back of my throat, like bile that's impossible to vomit.

'Mm. Yeah,' I say, instead, in a mumble.

I'm sorry. It's a poor substitute but what can I do?

Ethan's got a rash, Gracie's throwing a tantrum, and Polly's in tears.

'What did the doctor say?' I ask her, raising my voice above Gracie's yells floating down the stairs. She's apparently been sent to her room to *cool off*. Doesn't sound very cool from where I'm standing.

'It's not chickenpox, or German measles or anything. He thinks it might be an allergy.' She sniffs and blows her nose. 'Look at him!'

The rash has covered the baby's face, arms and legs. He looks like a cartoon character. But of course, it's not funny.

'Does it hurt him?'

'I don't know, Sophie – I can't ask him,' she says irritably. 'But he's not happy. It's probably itching. Or sore. I've got lotion to put on it. But I feel like I'm a bad mother!'

She starts crying again. I put my arms round her, feeling helpless. I have no idea why babies get rashes.

'Why on earth would you think that? You're a fantastic mother.'

'It must be my fault!' she sobs. 'I must have done something wrong! Given him something to eat, that had some additives in. Or let him touch something, or wear something, or … or *breathe* something! I don't know!'

'Look,' I tell her firmly, steering her to the sofa and making her sit down. 'You're being paranoid. Of course it isn't your fault. You can't monitor every breath he takes, everything he touches.'

'That's what I'm supposed to do! I'm his mother, I'm here to protect him! It's my job, Sophie! If I can't even do *that*, what bloody use am I to anybody?'

'You *do* protect him! You're doing a great job.'

'Oh, yeah, sure!' She rolls her eyes sarcastically. 'One child covered in horrendous *spots* and the other one screaming herself sick! Great job, I don't think!'

'What's wrong with Madam?'

'Doesn't want to go back to school tomorrow. Hates me because I've told her she has to.'

'I thought she was loving school?'

She's only been going for three weeks. Every time I've seen her so far, I've had a run-down on the personal attributes of every child in the class, what she's had in her packed lunch every day, and what they've been *doing about* in their lessons.

'She was. But now she's decided she's had enough of it and doesn't want to go any more. She wants me to write to the teacher and tell her.'

'She won't say why?'

'No! Just keeps screaming at me that she's not going any more. I feel ...' Her eyes well up with fresh tears. 'I feel a complete failure, Sophe,' she finishes quietly.

'You're not!' I jump to my feet and run up the stairs, two at a time, and barge into Gracie's bedroom without any warning. The little girl's lying on her bed, yelling, kicking her feet and thumping the bed with her fists.

'Stop this noise!' I bark at her. 'You're not a baby!'

She shudders into silence in pure shock – staring at me and blinking.

'You're making your mummy very upset!' I go on, crossly. I don't suppose this is the politically correct method of dealing with a distressed child, but I can't think any further than my friend's unhappiness. 'Now then! Sit up properly, dry your eyes, and tell me what's the matter.'

'I … don't wanna … go to … school …' she starts to blub again, semi-coherently.

I hold up my hand . 'Stop! I'm not listening until you sit up, stop crying, and talk properly. *Ethan*'s making less fuss than you are, and he's not well!'

The shame of this seems to propel her into a sitting position at least, and stops her yelling.

'Ethan doesn't have to go to *school*,' she points out mutinously.

'I bet he won't make all this fuss when he *does* have to,' I retort, aware that I'm being completely illogical. I can be as childish as the next child, any time. I wait for her to become calmer, then go on, more quietly:

'So what's gone wrong – at school?'

She shudders and sniffs a couple of times. I wait.

'I don't like Rudolph,' she whispers eventually.

'Rudolph?' Blimey, it's only October. Surely the teachers don't start Christmas stuff in school this early?

'He's horrid!' she goes on, pitifully. 'He's big! He's got a big voice! He shouts at me! He took my Jaffa Cakes!'

'A *boy* called Rudolph?'

She nods, wiping her nose with her fingers. 'He's horrid,' she confirms. 'And I have to sit next to him.'

'Why?' She has my sympathy now. I don't like the sound of him myself. 'Why you?'

'Because I'm the best in the class at my letters and my numbers. And he's the worst.'

What? How is *that* fair? Kids get punished now, for being clever?

'I see,' I say, seething inside. 'Well – why on earth didn't you tell Mummy about this, Gracie?'

She shrugs. 'Mummy says I have to be good, and do what the teacher tells me. The teacher told me to sit next to Rudolph. So I'm not going to school any more.'

'We'll see about that,' I tell her calmly.

'Now I feel even worse,' says Polly when I've related the story to her. 'She confided in you instead of me!'

'But that's because I'm *not* her mummy. She probably just thinks of me like I'm another kid.'

'I'll go in with her tomorrow. Talk to Mrs Palmer.'

'Yeah. And make sure Rudolph doesn't get wind of it, won't you. I know what those sort of kids are like. Don't let him pick on her.'

'You *should* have kids of your own,' Polly says, smiling at me suddenly. 'You'd be such a good mum.'

'Don't be ridiculous!' I laugh out loud. 'I'd be terrible! I'm still too much of a child myself.'

'Perhaps that helps,' she says quietly, with a sigh.

She's cheered up a bit by the time I'm ready to go. We've decided Ethan's spots look a bit less red; we've agreed that she should take him back to the doctor if they haven't gone in a couple more days; and Gracie has crept quietly back downstairs and is sitting next to Polly, cuddled up, with her floppy bunny tucked under her arm.

'You need a break,' I tell Polly. 'You look exhausted.'

'Last time I looked,' she says despondently, 'they weren't giving away free holidays on the internet.'

'OK, maybe not a holiday, but a night out, at least. When did you last have a night out? Either with Leon or without him?'

She shrugs. 'It's difficult.'

'Can't you ask your neighbour to baby-sit again? She's done it before, hasn't she?'

'Carol? Yes. But she's got kids of her own.'

'Are we going to Carol's?' Gracie pipes up. 'Can I play with Vicky and Ella? Please, Mummy – can I? Please, please, please! I'll be very good! I won't cry! I'll go to school ...'

Polly and I exchange raised eyebrows.

'Vicky and Ella are Carol's girls. They're ten and twelve. Gracie idolises them,' she explains.

'Well, why don't you ask her – Carol? For next Saturday night?'

'Oh, I don't know. I'm not really interested in the clubbing scene any more.'

'OK, so we'll just go for a drink. Just you and me. None of the others ever want to come out now, anyway. Just a quiet drink in a bar. What do you say?'

'Perhaps,' she says, doubtfully.

'Am I going to Carol's?' Gracie's still bouncing up and down with excitement. 'Am I going to play with Vicky and Ella? Am I, Mummy?'

'We'll *see*.' Polly turns back to me. 'I'll ask her. I'll let you know.'

'Yeah!' shrieks Gracie excitedly.

'But only if you're good,' I remind her. 'And play quietly for Mummy, while Ethan's not well.'

'I will, Sophie,' she says, demurely. 'I promise.'

I go home feeling proud of myself. I seem to have become a Child-Whisperer. Perhaps it's all a lot easier than I thought.

251

Saturday

Everything's been fine again between Oscar and me this week. He's been so apologetic about the whole thing of expecting me to have the kids here, I really can't fault him. He's kept all his stuff tidy, and he's been cooking dinner and even cleaning the bathroom. So what can I say? Maybe it's going to work. Maybe Sophie Jennings is finally growing up and having a proper, live-in relationship at long last. It certainly seems to have pleased my family, anyway. Either Mum, or one of my sisters, seem to be phoning, texting or e-mailing me virtually every day to ask how it's going and say how pleased they are. I feel like I've joined some kind of strange sisterhood; like allowing Oscar to move in with me was a rite of passage, and now I'm being accepted as a Proper Woman. They all seem to be getting a perverse kind of pleasure out of it. Almost more pleasure than I am myself.

Apart from his indisputable stamina and energy in the bedroom, and his physical near-perfection, you'd never guess that Oscar is nine years younger than me. I mean – the way he behaves, and talks. He's not into the things I'd expect a twenty-five year old to like. He doesn't listen to a lot of music, or drive a beat-up old car, or even go out on the piss with his mates.

'The night we met,' he tells me today over breakfast in bed, 'was the first time I'd been clubbing since my marriage broke up.'

'Two years ago?'

'Yeah. It's not really my scene. But some of my mates talked me into it, that night, cos it was someone's birthday. Glad I agreed, though,' he adds, smiling at me meaningfully.

'I used to love going clubbing,' I say, with a sigh. 'But none of my friends seem to be up for it any more. But at least I've persuaded Polly to come out tonight, even if it's only for a few drinks.'

'Tonight?' He frowns. 'What do you mean – tonight?'

'I thought I told you? Polly and I are just going out for a few drinks.'

'But it's Saturday,' he says, still frowning.

'Er .. yes!' I laugh. 'Correct!' He's not amused. 'What's the matter?' I add, as the frown seems to be deepening into a scowl.

'I assumed we'd go out together tonight.'

'Sorry. We can go out tomorrow night, can't we? Where do you want to go?'

'No, Sophie, no.' He sits up straighter in the bed, puts his toast and marmalade down as if he means business. 'Tomorrow night is not the point. Where we *go* is not the point. The point is, I thought I was right to assume that, as a couple, we'd go out together on Saturday nights. Wouldn't you say that was a fair assumption?'

'No – actually, no, I think it's a stupid assumption!' I'm sitting up as straight as him now, and staring back at him, crossly. 'Why would you assume that? *Last* Saturday night you spent with your children, for a start!'

'Oh, I see.' He turns away from me, nodding. 'Like that, is it?'

'Like what?' This is ridiculous. What are we arguing about? 'Like *what*, Oscar?' I repeat, as he's still turned away from me, his mouth in sulk position.

'You're doing this to get back at me, for last weekend.' He states this as if it's a fact. As if that's the end of the matter. 'I get it.'

'*Hello*? No – hang on, don't just turn away again – how old are we, here? What the *hell* are you on about? Last weekend's forgotten, and anyway I didn't mind in the slightest that you were with your kids instead of with me …'

'Oh. I see. I suppose you enjoyed the opportunity to go out *clubbing* with your *friends*?'

'No – I didn't – but I'd have liked to! If any of them had been up for it, I'd have gone like a shot, and I'd have loved it! It sure would've been a lot more fun than playing mothers-and-fathers with you!'

I shouldn't have said that. Of course I shouldn't – but come on: what could he expect? What's the matter with him, all of a sudden?

'Sorry,' I say, quickly. 'I didn't mean that.'

'But you did. Obviously. Or you wouldn't have said it.' He's getting up now, pulling on his jeans, sounding taut-voiced with offence.

'You asked for it. What's got into you? Aren't I allowed to have any friends now?' I'm trying my best to sound placatory here. I'm joking with him – smiling – laughing. 'Aren't I supposed to go out with them any more?'

'Not on a Saturday night, no!' he retorts, without the slightest sign of humour. 'Saturday nights are for *partners*. For *couples*.' He pauses, gives me such a stern look that I want to giggle. The whole thing is just so daft, I can't take it seriously. 'Perhaps you just don't really want to *be* part of a couple, Sophie.'

'Not if it means being your fucking prisoner every Saturday,' I tell him matter-of-factly.

'Thank you!' he says, tersely – and marches out, slamming the door behind him like a bad actor in a bad movie. Not sure what he's thanking me for. My honesty, perhaps? I don't think I gave him the answer he was looking for.

'Sophie, you are awful,' Polly says, laughing. I'm glad I've cheered her up, anyway. 'Poor Oscar. He's obviously far more serious about this relationship than you are.'

'What? I'm serious! Christ, how much more bloody serious can I get – I've let him move into my *flat*! I don't see how that means I have to give up my whole life – do *you*?'

'Well …'. She considers this, turning her glass of wine round and round by the stem for a minute. 'Perhaps he'd been looking forward to taking you out, somewhere special – to make up for last weekend, you know.'

'Then he should have said! Given me advance notice! I'm not about to let *you* down, when we've already made arrangements. He shouldn't expect me to!'

'No. You're right.' She smiles. 'I'm glad you didn't. I'm enjoying this, Sophe. You were right – it's nice to come out for an evening again. Get away from the kids. And Leon,' she adds with a sigh.

'Things no better there?'

She shakes her head. 'We're barely talking. I asked him if he'd come to Relate with me, if I make an appointment. He just stared at me as if I'd asked him to fly to the moon. I think it's got to be another woman. I've asked him straight, but he just tells me not to be stupid. What do you think, Sophie – honestly?'

She drains her glass while I panic quietly and try to think how to answer this.

'I don't know,' I say eventually. 'Would you leave him? If you found out he was seeing someone?'

She's obviously been giving this some thought, as she doesn't immediately get upset, and she doesn't immediately tell me not to be ridiculous, either.

'It would depend,' she says in a very small voice. 'I suppose it would depend … whether it was a one-off. Or how long it had been going on. And whether he was going to finish it.'

255

Or whether he was a serial bloody philanderer who'd also got one of her best friends pregnant, I'm thinking to myself – and just then I look up, and nearly jump out of my skin.

'Hello,' says Jo, calmly. 'What are you two doing here?'

Polly's had several large glasses of wine by now. She doesn't appear to be drunk, but I know she's not used to it any more.

'We're having a drink,' she says, laughing. 'You?'

This is a fairly up-market wine bar – not one of our usual places.

'I'm here with some people from work. We needed to get together to discuss how they're going to cope while I'm off on maternity leave.'

'Oh!' Polly looks puzzled. 'The baby's not due till … February, didn't you say?'

'That's right. But I'm finishing work next month. I need my rest.'

I can't believe I'm listening to this conversation. I'm staring at Jo with my eyes practically popping out of my head. How has she got the gall? How dare she stand here, smiling prettily at Polly and talking about her baby – her baby by Polly's *husband* – without a blink of the eye, a stuttering of the tongue, or the slightest guilty look on her face? She's not looking *me* in the eye, though, I notice!

'Well, I can understand that,' Polly's saying in that gooey voice that mums and mums-to-be use to each other. 'It's a very special baby, after all – you've been to such lengths to get it.'

You can say that again. I try to cover my involuntary snort of disgust by taking a large swig of wine, but it ends up going up my nose and I promptly go into a choking fit and am almost sick. Well, it's enough to make anyone vomit, isn't it.

'Piss off,' I hiss into Jo's ear when Polly turns away to pick up her own glass. She ignores me. 'Piss off,' I repeat a little louder.

'Sophie!' exclaims Polly, looking at me in surprise. '*What* did you say to Jo?'

'I said *it's off*. The wine. That's why I was nearly sick. Don't drink it.'

'Don't be silly! There's nothing wrong with it. It's just you, being greedy, gulping it too fast, as usual!' she laughs. Oh, of course – there I go, silly greedy me. Polly takes another huge gulp, emptying her own glass, to prove her point. She sways slightly on her stool. 'Who wants another one? Sophie – your turn to get a round in, love.'

'No, I don't think so,' I say quickly. I'm *not* leaving these two on their own. How can I trust Jo not to say something to Polly about the baby? I mean, if you can't trust someone not to shag their friend's husband, you can't trust them – full stop.

Polly stares at me. 'Yes it is, Sophe. I got the last one. What's the matter – have you run out of cash? Here you are ... take this ...' She's rummaging in her purse for a ten pound note. 'Come on – don't be silly, take it. You can pay another time.'

'You go and get the drinks, then. As it's your money.'

'What? What's the matter with you?' She's sounding irritated now. 'You're being very *odd* tonight, Sophie.'

'Why don't *I* buy you both a drink?' says Jo. She's still looking at Polly, not me. 'As I haven't seen you for a while.'

'I thought you were with people from work,' I snap.

'It's OK. We've finished our meeting. I was just leaving, actually, when I bumped into you.'

'Don't let us keep you,' I mutter. But she's gone off to the bar to get our drinks.

'What's eating you?' Polly demands. 'Are you in a bad mood because of Oscar? Because of your row?'

'No. I just thought we were having a quiet drink on our own tonight.'

'Don't be childish. We can include Jo, can't we? I haven't seen her for ages. Not since ...' She's frowning, trying to remember. 'Since the party at my house. I suppose she's been busy getting everything ready for the baby,' she adds, smiling happily. 'Ah. It's so lovely, isn't it – her having a baby.'

'Mm.'

'I'm sorry, Sophe.' Her tongue slips a bit on the alliteration. The wine's getting to her. I knew it. 'Sorry, but you really aren't being very nice. I know *you* don't like babies, but Jo's our friend, and I think, honestly, you should ...'

Fortunately, before I can be lectured any further on the deeply insulting subject of how I should be behaving towards Jo, she returns from the bar with our wine and her orange juice, which she proceeds to sip daintily and virtuously as she takes up a safer position on the other side of Polly, away from me.

'I was just saying to Sophie,' says Polly, slurring on my name again, 'How long it's been since I've seen you, Jo. Not since my party.'

'No.' Jo has the grace to look slightly uncomfortable at this. 'I've ... been busy.'

'Yes – ah! – busy getting all the things you need for the baby, eh?' Silly gooey voice again. 'Ah! Have you told your parents yet, Jo? About the ... you know ... the artificial insem ...'

'All right, all right – keep your voice down,' I say.

'It's nothing for Jo to be ashamed about – is it, Jo?' Polly's voice becomes even higher. 'That's what you should tell your mum and dad. Don't you think so, Sophie?

258

She should tell them, it's all perfectly natural, perfectly normal …'

'No it's not!' Oh, Jesus, what am I doing? I *really* don't want to get into an argument about this. I really ought to be just changing the subject. 'How are things at work, anyway, Jo?' I add, weakly, without looking at her. Like I care.

'OK.'

There's an uncomfortable silence. Polly's looking from one of us to the other.

'Have you two had a row?' she says, at length. 'Is that what this is all about?'

'No,' says Jo.

'Yes,' I say at the same time.

'Oh, great!' Polly exclaims. 'So you two have a row – which you don't even *tell* me about, Sophie! – and *I* have to suffer!'

'What are you talking about? You're not suffering!' I'm feeling too shaky, too nervous about what might come out, here, to worry about upsetting Polly. And I've obviously succeeded in doing just that, because her eyes now fill up with tears.

'Well, thank you, Sophie – *friend*!' she exclaims. 'Somehow, even though this is nothing to do with me, I seem to have been ignored by Jo for months, and kept in the dark by you. That's lovely! So now I haven't got *any* friends. I might as well just go home to my poxy husband and be ignored and insulted by him, as usual. Unless he's gone out with his *girlfriend*, of course.'

She stands up, very unsteadily, and at the same time drains the whole of the new glass of wine. She goes cross-eyed and unfocused, burps, and stumbles, clutching at Jo's arm to stop herself from falling.

'What girlfriend?' Jo's saying just before Polly practically pulls her over. Her tone is deadly. I kick her ankle, hard, but she doesn't even flinch. I find it hard to understand how she's concerned that Leon might have another girlfriend, when she only wanted him for his sperm, but I'm too appalled at the course of this conversation to care about her state of mind.

'He's seeing some *bitch*,' Polly spits. She's hanging onto Jo now, both arms round her, slobbering wetly against her face. 'I know he is! I'm gonna *kill* her when I find out who she is. And him,' she adds venomously.

'How do you know?' Jo demands without making any attempt to comfort her.
'How do you *know* he's seeing someone?'

'I've just stopped. Making. Excuses to myself.' Polly's leaning her whole weight against Jo now, regardless of the pregnancy. She's talking in staccato bursts – I suspect she'd be sick if she opened her mouth long enough to make a full sentence. 'Come on.' I'm behind her now, taking hold of her shoulders. 'We're going.'

'No!' Polly protests, still staggering. 'Want another drink!'

'No you don't.' I peel her off Jo, get her leaning on me instead. 'We're going.'

Phew. She's not arguing. She looks too dazed and confused. I haul her towards the door. I'm just about thinking that we've got away before anything disastrous happened, when Jo calls after us – so clearly that people who've taken no notice whatsoever of me dragging my drunken friend out of the bar like a sack of potatoes, sit up with looks of amused interest:

'Tell him from me – if he's seeing someone else I'll have something to bloody say about it! You tell him!'

'What's she going on about?' mutters Polly as I flag down a taxi and shove her into it.

'Search me,' I tell her, my heart banging against my ribs.

I'm beginning to wish I'd gone out with Oscar.

Wednesday

It's cold today – really cold, cold enough for the central heating first thing in the morning, and warm socks under my boots, and a proper warm jacket even in the car. Autumn's really here, and I didn't even notice summer finishing. I've come out shopping today, as I haven't got any appointments until this afternoon, and the shops have got Christmas cards, Christmas decorations and displays of Christmas presents already. I suddenly realised last night that I haven't even had a summer holiday this year, apart from the week down at my parents' – and now it's too late.

'It's not too late if we go somewhere hot,' Oscar said. 'Why don't we look at the last minute deals? The Canaries would still be warm. Or Turkey, or Cyprus. You choose.'

He was being ever so specially nice to me, to make up for sulking for the past few days about my night out with Polly. It had all culminated, eventually, in a massive showdown where I'd told him I wasn't going to put up with him behaving like a spoilt child every time I went anywhere without him, so if he couldn't get his head around me having a life of my own he'd better leave. He left. I actually thought he might have taken me at my word and gone for good, and was just trying to decide how I felt about it when he reappeared with wine and chocolates and protestations of love and apology. So we're back on track once again, and I'm trying not to wonder whether our future together is going to consist of a series of rows followed by wine and chocolates. I suppose it could be worse.

In fact it's silly even day-dreaming about holidays: I can't take any time off work now; but I do stop for a moment outside Thomas Cook and study the Special Offer holidays on display in the window. Tenerife. Malta. Northern Cyprus. Florida. Very nice.

'Not Florida, at this time of year,' says a voice in my ear. 'It's the hurricane season.'

I swing round – to find Charlie grinning at me. And have to stop myself from hugging him. He's almost a married man now.

He says he's got time for a coffee, if I have. He's got the morning off to shop for his wedding suit.

'And have you chosen it?' I try to sound interested.

'No.' He doesn't even sound interested himself.

'Grey's nice for weddings. You look good in grey.' As well as trying to sound interested I'm now trying not to feel sick. The feeling sick is nothing to do with the very nice Cappuccino in front of me; it's much more to do with the picture in my head of Charlie, smart and gorgeous in a lovely light-grey suit, waiting at the front of the church and turning to smile at the bride walking down the aisle towards him. Yuck, yuck, *yuck*. I feel so sick, I want to cry.

'What's wrong with your Cappuccino?' he says, looking concerned as I push it to one side.

'Nothing. I just feel a bit sick.'

'Bloody hell, Sophie. You're not ... are you?'

'Not what?'

'Pregnant.'

At least this makes me laugh. 'Don't be ridiculous. You know me better than that.'

'Well, yes ...' He dips his head for a second, stirs his coffee. 'I *did*. I did know you, but of course, people change, don't they.'

'Do they?'

'Yes! Look at us – both of us. In proper relationships. Who'd have thought, a year ago ...'

'Stop it!' I say, wretchedly. 'Don't! Don't say any more. Please. I *know* where we were a year ago. I liked it where we were.'

He carries on stirring his coffee, silently, frowning into it as if he's not sure what it is.

'I *preferred* it where we were,' I add, recklessly.

He's still silent. Still looking into his cup. The spoon goes round and round, round and round, in the coffee.

'If you weren't with *Helen* ...'

'All right! All right, let's change the subject!' he says abruptly, throwing down his spoon. He looks back up at me then, and there's a moment when I think I see something in his eyes. I shouldn't say what I think I see, because I realise I must be imagining it – after all, he's with someone else, he's getting married, he's almost bought the *suit* for God's sake. 'Let's talk about holidays,' he says, his words tumbling out fast, too fast. 'You were looking in Thomas Cook. Where are you hoping to go?'

'I'm not. I'm too busy with work. I was just day-dreaming'. I can't think about holidays. I can only think about what I imagined I saw in his eyes. I don't *want* to think about it, because it's making me feel shaky and faint and I can feel my heart galloping like I've just run up and down the street.

'That's a shame. It'd probably do you good to get away, somewhere warm, this time of year,' he says, still talking too fast, still fussing with his coffee.

'Where are *you* going?' I catch his eye, and hold it, purposely. 'For your honeymoon?'

He sighs but doesn't look away.

'Florida.'

'But I thought you said ...?'

'It's the hurricane season. But she – Helen – that's where she wants to go.'

'I see. I met her, by the way.'

'She told me. I'm sorry, Sophie – I had no idea she was planning to come to you for her hair.'

'It's OK.' I shrug. 'She's just another client, at the end of the day.'

'And did she ask your advice, like all the others do?' He's smiling now. The smile hurts me somewhere in my ribs.

'Yes, of course she did.' I smile back. 'She asked how to get you more interested in the wedding arrangements.'

'And? You said ...?'

'Oh, nothing much. Just that she should probably nag you a bit.' I give him what I hope is a wicked grin. 'Did she?'

He laughs out loud, and the tension between us has gone. 'You're damn right she did! Why do you think I'm out looking at suits today? She can nag for England – she didn't need any help from you, you cheeky mare.'

And then he stops again, blinks at me, and it's back: the awkwardness, the *feeling* in the air between us. I didn't imagine it. There's something. I don't know what it is, and I'm not sure whether I like it or not. But there's *something*. That's all I'm saying. Something he knows about too. Something neither of us want to mention.

He insists on paying for our coffees. Neither of us have even finished them.

And then, as if I'm not traumatised enough, almost as soon as we've said goodbye, as I'm blundering into the nearest shop, to try to take my mind off it all, I bump into someone else. Annabel.

Remember Annabel? She's the bride who threw away her contraceptive pills just prior to her huge expensive wedding to Jeremy. Jeremy, the groom who decided to inform his bride, the night *before* their huge expensive wedding, that he was never going to want children, no matter how important it was to her.

And here she is. Looking happy, looking radiant. Looking at babygros and maternity bras. Shit! What am I doing in Mothercare?

'Hello, Sophie,' she says in a happy, radiant voice. 'How are you?'

'Fine.' I look around me, slightly panic-struck. I do *not* want to be seen, by anyone else who knows me, browsing the maternity wear. 'I ... er ... sorry, Annabel – I seem to have come into the wrong shop by mistake. Silly me! Um – how are you?'

'Pregnant!' she announces gleefully, as if I hadn't already worked that out. 'Six weeks pregnant, Sophie – isn't it wonderful?'

She must have got pregnant on her honeymoon. Bloody hell – one minute she's chucking her pills in the bin, the next minute she's up the duff. No time for second thoughts.

'Congratulations!' I offer, trying to sound at least half as excited as she does. 'And how has ... um ... Jeremy taken the news?'

Her face drops. 'Actually, Sophie,' she confides, looking around her anxiously as if he's likely to be hiding behind the display of maternity knickers, 'I haven't told him yet.'

'But you're going to? Soon?'

'As soon as I have to.' She looks at me pleadingly. 'Can you understand where I'm coming from? I know I'll have to tell him eventually. And when I do, he's not going to be happy, even if I pretend it was an accident. I don't know what lies ahead, Sophie, so can you blame me for just wanting to hang onto my happiness for a few more weeks ... or months ... just as long as I can?'

'I suppose not.'

I watch her as she turns back to the displays of baby clothes, her eyes lighting up, her smile returning.

'I can't buy anything yet,' she says. 'But I come in here every day in my lunch break. Just to look, that's all. Just to look.'

'Do you still work with Jo?' I ask her, suddenly remembering that this was how I got the introduction.

'Oh, yes – of course. She's getting *very* excited now about her baby, isn't she! Won't be long before she goes on maternity leave. She's having a little boy – did she tell you?'

'No. She didn't.' I close my eyes briefly against the image of an infant version of Leon, screaming in Jo's arms. 'I don't see her very often these days.'

'A little boy,' Annabel repeats longingly. 'She's going to call him Leo.'

She's probably wondering why I've very rudely turned away from her and rushed out of the shop. I make it to the public conveniences in the car park before I bring up what little I drank of my Cappuccino. And then I sit on the toilet seat, shaking all over with shock at what I'm now thinking. Don't get me wrong: I know it's my complete disgust about Jo wanting to name her baby after Leon that's made me vomit. And I also know that it was my strange unease at being with Charlie, imagining something in his eyes and in the air between us, that made me feel too sick to drink my coffee.

But there's also something else – something I didn't think about until Charlie asked the question. It's over a week since my period was due; and I've never been this late before. Never, since that other time, the time when I was with Damien. That, thank God, turned out to be a false alarm ... so there's no reason to think this is any different, is there. I tell myself that all the way home. I phone Polly, and she asks me why I haven't bought a pregnancy test.

266

'Because I'm scared to,' I admit. My voice is shaking. My hand, holding the phone, is shaking too.

'I'll get you one. I'll bring it round, tonight, and we'll do it together.'

'We can't. Oscar will be here.' I groan, at the thought of Oscar, the thought of him finding out that I even *slightly* suspect I could be pregnant. 'I can't have it,' I tell Polly, aware that my voice is rising and I'm sounding a little unhinged. 'If I *am*... I'm not having it! No way!'

'I know,' she soothes me. 'It's all right. If ... if you *were*, I'd come with you – to the clinic. Don't worry. I'm sure it's just – something else.'

I'm sure it is, too. I put it to the back of my mind, try not to shake too much while I'm doing my client's hair a little later. I think about Annabel, keeping her secret from Jeremy. I wonder about Jo, and what the bloody hell she thinks she's doing.

And I don't say a word about any of it to Oscar.

Thursday

I wasn't going to mess about talking to Jo on the phone. I went round there. I left it till eight o'clock last night, when Oscar was watching TV. I didn't tell him where I was going, and he didn't ask. I don't think he dared, after our last showdown.

Jo answered the door wearing some kind of velour leisure wear. The top clung tightly to her bump and didn't meet the trousers. I tried to avert my eyes.

'You can't call him Leo,' I told her without any preamble.

'I can,' she shot back, bristling with hostility. 'And I'm going to.'

There we were, standing on her doorstep, eyeing each other like a pair of fighters.

'Who told you?' she said.

'Doesn't matter. We'd have got to hear about it sooner or later – all of us. *Polly* will hear about it, Jo. Don't you care?'

'He's my baby.' She placed her hand protectively over her bump. 'I can call him what the hell I like.'

'It's *Leon's* baby. And Polly's going to guess. Especially if it bloody looks like him – poor little sod.'

'Well, maybe that'll be for the best. Maybe she needs to know.'

'WHAT?' I stared at her. 'Are you mad? She needs that like she needs a hole in the head. Can you imagine what it'd do to her – finding out that one of her *supposed* friends is having a baby by her husband?'

She shrugged. I wanted to slap her.

'It's not like I was the first. He's been putting it about all over the place, all the time they've been married.'

268

'I know.' I felt, suddenly, weak at the knees. 'Can I come in?' I asked her wearily. 'This is stupid, arguing on the doorstep.'

She stood back, shrugging again, and gestured to her lounge, where I flung myself onto the sofa. She perched at the other end, and waited for me to speak.

'I know what he's like,' I said simply. 'But Polly doesn't. She suspects, but she doesn't want to believe it.'

'Then she's being ridiculous. She's not doing herself any favours, hanging onto a crap marriage. If you're her best mate, why haven't you told her? I would.'

'I don't want to hurt her.'

'Well, it'd be better coming from you. She'll find out, anyway, like you say.'

'Not if you keep away, stay out of her life, keep your baby away from her ...'

'Why should I?' There was a defiant lift to her chin. A different look in her eyes. This was a whole new Jo; I didn't know her any more. 'Not that it's any of your business, Sophie, but I've changed my mind about this baby. At first I wanted to keep him to myself. But now, I've read a lot of stuff in books and magazines. Kids who don't have a father seem to get a bad deal in life. I don't see why my baby should suffer. His dad is going to play a part in his life – I'm going to make sure of it.'

I was starting to feel sick again.

'What does Leon think about that?'

'It doesn't matter what he thinks. He's going to support his child, whether he likes it or not. Whether Polly likes it or not.'

'She's supposed to be your *friend*! And you're willing to completely fuck up their marriage?'

'Don't make *me* out to be the bad guy, Sophie. Their marriage has been completely fucked up for years. She just doesn't want to admit it. She'd better get used to it, because I want Leon to be a proper father to my baby,

269

and what's more, I'd like nothing better than for him to walk out on that ridiculous farce of a marriage and make a proper family with me and Leo.' She narrowed her eyes at me. 'I'm going to work on it.'

'You *want* him? Leon?' I was stunned. 'You're actually making a play for Polly's husband?'

'He's only staying with her for the kids. Once Leo's born, he'll be torn, won't he – between his two families.'

'*You're* not his family! You just had sex with him! Once! You *used* him to get pregnant.'

'I know. But it was good. I fancy doing it again. On a regular basis.' She was actually laughing. I was almost too shocked to speak.

'He's a *pig*!' I spat at her. 'He's a slime ball, a pervert! He tries it on with everyone! He ...'

'Yeah, yeah, I know he likes to screw around. But he'll settle down once I get hold of him. Anyway – look, Sophie, nice of you to call round,' she added sarcastically. 'But if all you came for was to slag off the father of my child ...'

'I can't believe I used to think we were friends,' I told her shakily, getting to my feet. 'I never really knew you, did I. Not at all.'

She opened the front door for me and watched me walk out.

'Actually, Sophie, we're more alike than you realise,' she said matter-of-factly just before she closed the door. 'Neither of us are interested in conventional relationships, are we?'

'We're not talking about being unconventional. We're talking about destroying your friend's life,' I retorted without looking back at her.

The door slammed shut. I turned and gave it a kick, but it didn't help. I cried all the way home.

'Turkey,' Oscar said as I walked in.

'No thanks. Not hungry.' I was being purposely obtuse. I could see the website he was looking at on his laptop. Blue sea, blue sky, white beach, Turkish flag in the corner. He turned to me and smiled.

'It's really cheap, this time of year. Lots of last-minute deals. What do you think?'

'I don't know.' I sat down, heavily, sighing.

'Something wrong?' He looked at me with such concern, I felt my eyes filling up again. 'Have you been crying? What's the matter, babe?'

'Nothing.' I sniffed and wiped my eyes. 'Just a silly argument with a friend.' I couldn't; somehow I just couldn't bring myself to tell him about it. It was too bad. Too unbelievably dreadful to tell anyone.

'Ah, come on.' He put the laptop down and put his arms round me. 'Come on, that's not like you – you're such a good mate to your friends.' This, of course, just started me off crying again. 'Why don't you give her a call and make it up?' he said, 'While I pour you a nice glass of white wine?'

'It's not that simple!' I snapped. 'Sorry. Sorry, but ... it's complicated.'

'Is it Polly? Is it something to do with her husband – the one who's messing her around? Is there anything I can do to help? Have a talk to him – man-to-man?'

The thought of nice, charming, Oscar confronting the horrible Leon for a man-to-man talk about his serial infidelity would have been screamingly funny if the situation wasn't so serious.

'No! No, it's not Polly, don't worry, it'll be fine, I expect. Sorry. I'll sort it out tomorrow.'

'OK – if you're sure. Have the glass of wine anyway. It'll cheer you up.'

It didn't, of course, but I smiled and nodded and said the right things. In actual fact it just made me feel sick again. And that reminded me with a frightening urgency that I have to buy a pregnancy testing kit. Which made me start crying all over again.

'You need a holiday,' said Oscar severely. 'That's what you need. Turkey.'

He's still talking about Turkey over breakfast this morning. I need to put a stop to it.

'I'm fully booked, Oscar. Right up till Christmas. A holiday would be lovely, but I could only manage a few days. A Monday to Thursday, perhaps, towards the end of November.'

'That's no good! Can't you cancel some appointments? I was going to take a week off work – the last week of October. I was going to book something tonight.'

He sounds disappointed to the point of petulance.

'I can't just cancel appointments. These girls have got weddings booked! It's not just like they're having a trim and blow-dry.'

'So what are you supposed to do? Never have holidays?'

'Of course I have them. But I have to book them well in advance.'

To tell the truth, much as I'd love to fly away, right now, to somewhere warm and sunny and beautiful – and *not here* – I don't even think I really want to go away with Oscar. Don't get me wrong: I'm getting used to having him around in the flat, even if sometimes I do still feel like he's in my way. But I can only tolerate it because he goes out to work every day. I don't know if I could put up with being together with someone – anyone! – for twenty-four hours a day. I'd want to spend some of our holiday apart, doing separate things – and somehow I can't see him being very happy with that.

'Well,' he says, huffily, 'maybe we'd better start planning a holiday for next summer then, if that's the only way we're going to be able to do it.'

'Sorry – I can't just drop everything and go away, just like that! I've got my own business!' I sigh. 'You go, if you want. I don't mind.'

He looks at me as if I've just sworn at him.

'Go on holiday without you? Is that what you're saying?'

'Yes. If you've got the time off work, and you can afford it, why not?'

'*Why not?*' he repeats incredulously. 'Because we're *together*, Sophe! I could no more go off on holiday without you, now, than, well, than have an *affair*! It would be disloyal! It would be selfish! And I'd hate it!'

'Would you?' I look at him in surprise. 'But you'd have a nice time, and I'd be pleased for you.'

He stares at me for another full minute, and then he does a very strange thing. He puts down his cereal bowl and spoon, stands up, walks across the kitchen to me and takes me in his arms. He kisses me on the top of my head as if I'm a small and rather sweet child.

'You're the most amazing girl I've ever met,' he says, sounding really choked. 'You're totally, totally unique. Do you know that?'

'So does that mean you're going to Turkey?'

'Absolutely not. I couldn't bear to be separated from you. Not for a single day.'

Men! I'll never understand them.

I nip out to Boots between clients and get the pregnancy testing kit. Polly's already phoned me this morning asking whether I've done it yet. I feel like crying when I hear her voice. It's bad enough knowing that I've got to find a time to talk to her, tell her about Jo, about Leon, about flipping *Leo*, and completely ruin her life – without having her being so caring and compassionate to me, making me feel like a total jerk.

'I've got it now,' I text her when I get home. 'But I haven't got the guts to do it.'

'Shall I come round?' she texts back.

'No. I've got two more clients. I'll do it later. I'll let you know.'

I put in the bathroom to remind me. Apparently it works best if you do it first thing in the morning. I'll definitely do it tomorrow. Once I know, one way or the other, that'll be one less thing to stress about. Won't it?

Just to make sure the whole situation is in my face as much as possible, my next client, Katie, is about eight months pregnant. She's also small and blonde with freckles and a big smile.

'We booked the wedding before I fell,' she says with a shrug. 'What can you do?'

'And the wedding is ...' I check my diary. She's already booked me for the day. 'Oh my God! Three weeks' time!'

'Yeah. Bit of a bummer, eh? But I've got a lovely maternity-trouser-suit for the wedding. It's cream, with a long loose jacket to cover my bump.'

'But aren't you worried that you might go into labour between now and then? Or on the day?'

'Well, I wouldn't mind if it was *now*,' she says, giggling in what I consider to be quite an inappropriate way, considering she's in my flat and I most certainly do *not* want her to go into labour right now. 'Then, at least someone else can hold the baby while I walk down the aisle. But like you say, if it happens on the day, it'll be a right bummer.'

'Couldn't you have cancelled the wedding? Re-booked it for next year?'

'No – it was too late, you see. Too close to the date. We'd have lost our money.' She grins, like she's telling me a naughty girly secret. 'It's my fault. I *knew* I was pregnant, really, but I kept telling myself it was a false alarm. I didn't want to get it confirmed. I left it, and left it, until it was so obvious, I couldn't leave it any longer.'

'Why? Were you worried, about being pregnant?'

'Well, yes, obviously!' she chortles. 'I thought there was going to be hell to pay. I didn't even know if we'd still get married.'

Ah. I'm not sure I want to ask any more. It sounds like little miss Giggle-Pot might have got someone else's bun in the oven. Not her fiancé's. I try to concentrate on her hair and not look like a disapproving schoolmistress. But she's going to tell me anyway.

'Penny and I always planned to have children. We were going to get me done by artificial insanity or whatever it's called. But ...'

'*Penny*?'

'Yes. Oh, silly me – didn't I explain that? Penny is my *partner*. We're having a civil ceremony. We've been together for nearly five years. But I ... well, I shouldn't really tell you this.' (Giggle, giggle.) 'But I got drunk at a work party and had a sort-of a fling with a man. Just a one-off. Didn't like it much.'

'And got pregnant. That was unfortunate.'

'Yes. I thought Penny would dump me, but you know what? She's been fantastic. She says we'll bring the baby up together, just as if we'd had it the other way. She says at least it's saved us the trouble and expense of the artificial whatever it's called. She's an amazing woman.'

'She sounds it.'

'So I was a silly girl, really. I should have got the pregnancy confirmed right at the beginning, got it out in the open, instead of hiding it away and being frightened. I should have known Penny would forgive me one little mistake. That's what you do, isn't it, when you love someone? Don't you think so, Sophie? What do you think? Would you be able to forgive someone for one little mistake?'

I consider this, looking at her in the mirror, my straighteners poised above her head. Why get me involved? Why does everyone, always, get me involved?

'I don't know,' I admit, eventually. Her face drops. I realise this is the wrong response. 'I suppose it depends what the mistake was. And who it might hurt.'

She doesn't say too much after that. Doesn't giggle a whole lot, either.

But the thing with what Jo did, of course, is that it wasn't even a mistake. It was deliberate, scheming and selfish. And now she's compounding it – as if it's not bad enough to have stolen Leon's *sperm*, she now wants to steal *him*. I'd like to say she's welcome to him. I'd like *Polly* to say she's welcome to him. But she won't – she's going to fall apart. And for that, I won't ever be able to forgive Jo. So perhaps I'm not a wonderful woman like Penny the Lesbian.

Friday

Thank God, it's negative. Thank God, thank God, thank God. I feel weak and faint with relief, looking at the stick, looking at the lack of scary coloured lines. That's one worry out of the way, at least. Of course, I've made myself late, sitting in the bathroom for five minutes waiting for the result of this thing – so I've now got a rush to have breakfast and get myself ready before my appointment this morning – for an early afternoon wedding.

'You all right?' says Oscar as I bump into him in the kitchen. He looks at me carefully. 'You were ages in the bathroom.'

'Sorry. I'm fine.' I grab the Muesli packet and pour myself a bowlful. 'You off? See you tonight.' I give him a quick kiss. 'Have a nice day.' I'm trying to compensate for the lack of enthusiasm for Turkey.

A couple of seconds later, he's back. He's standing in front of me, and he's holding something out at me, with a look on his face ... shit. It's the box. From the pregnancy testing kit.

'I just went to the bathroom ...' he says. His eyes are round with amazement.

I grab the box off him, open a drawer and stuff it in there, not that this is going to be remotely helpful.

'It's negative,' I tell him abruptly. 'False alarm.'

'Oh, babe.' He grabs me and hugs me tight. 'Why didn't you tell me? I *knew* there was something ... you've been so uptight and emotional.'

'No point telling you unless there was something to say.' I struggling against the urge to push him away. I need to get on, otherwise I'm not going to have time to eat my muesli, and I've got a long day ahead.

'Are you terribly disappointed?' he says, rocking me in his arms.

277

Disappointed? Is he mad? OK, now I really have got to push him off me. He holds me at arm's length now, looking at me with that terribly-concerned expression that makes me feel so uncomfortable.

'Of course I'm not disappointed! You're joking, aren't you?'

'Well. I know it wasn't what we planned. But I expect, like most women, if it *happened*, you'd be thrilled..'

I can feel my face stretching with horror.

'What! Oscar, I've told you enough times – I don't want children!'

'I know, I know.' He's talking to me soothingly, like I'm frail and sick. 'I know that's what you *thought* – but most women change their minds once they're in a stable, happy relationship. Most women ...'

'I'm not *most women*!' I'm shouting at him now. I didn't want to shout. Bugger, this is *so* not how I wanted today to go. I take a breath and try to calm down. 'Look – we're both running late, this is not a good time to be having this discussion. We'll talk tonight, OK? But please don't go thinking I'm disappointed. I'm not. I'm bloody relieved.'

'OK,' he says, not looking the least like he believes me. 'Have a nice day.'

He goes off to work looking like he's had a bereavement.

This morning's bride, Sara, is in her early twenties, dumb with nerves and looking like she could do with a good night's sleep. But as soon as I arrive at the mother's house where the bride's getting ready, I realise it's not Sara who's going to be my problem today. It's her mother.

'Come on, we're late,' she's squawking at me as soon as I'm over the threshold. She's anorexic-thin, with the very worst blonde bleach I've ever seen, and doesn't

278

appear to have considered having her roots re-done for her daughter's wedding. If I had time, I'd do them myself today just to save my own reputation, in case anyone thinks I'm responsible. 'Come on, get the bride's hair done, quick as you can. I need mine doing, and so does Cara.'

Cara is the bride's older sister and only bridesmaid. I'm almost too stunned by their Christian names – I mean, honestly, who on earth would call their two daughters Sara and Cara? – to take in the fact that she's as obese as her mother is thin. They make quite a startling pair. Cara also seems to be a chain-smoker and when she hasn't actually got a cigarette in her mouth she's coughing horribly all over everyone. I'd like to ask her whether she's heard about passive smoking. I'd like, really, to make her go and smoke her fags and cough her disgusting cough outside in the garden, but it's not my house and they're not my family, thank God.

The whole time I'm doing Sara's hair, the mother's hovering around me, asking how much longer I'm going to be because she wants her turn. Eventually I have to say something. I've tried not to, but I just have to. I think I'm very polite, in the circumstances.

'If you'd like to leave me to it, I'll be done a lot sooner. I don't want to rush Sara's hair. She *is* the bride.'

'*Well*!' huffs her mum indignantly. 'I am paying for this wedding!'

'*I* am, actually, Mum,' says the bride. It's the first time she's spoken. '*We* are – Pete and I. But it was nice of you to pay for my dress,' she adds quickly.

'Yes, Mum,' says Cara, giving her mother a filthy look. 'This isn't all about you!'

'You can keep quiet, Madam, and stay out of it!' retorts the mum. 'You're lucky you've even been invited!'

I can feel my eyes widening with shock. Sara gives me an apologetic shrug in the mirror.

'You're lucky I've bothered to come!' her sister shouts back.

'Well, quite frankly I wouldn't have cared if you'd stayed away!'

'I'm here for Sara's sake – not yours!'

'You think she cares whether you're here or not? It's not like you're doing anything to help her!'

'And what are *you* doing? Bloody interfering, that's all!'

'If you'd stop smoking for five minutes ...'

The bride looks at me appealingly. I'm almost too gob-smacked to speak.

'Ladies!' I try, desperately. 'Please!'

'Mum, Cara – stop it,' says Sara. 'Can't you *please* try and get along together, for just one day of your lives?'

They fall silent, but I can see them, in the mirror, continuing to give each other evil glares behind my back.

'Why don't you both go out to the kitchen, and make us all a nice cup of tea?' I suggest. Anything to get them out of the way. I'd really rather suggest they go and bang their stupid heads together.

'Thanks, Sophie,' says Sara when they've gone. She doesn't seem the least bit shocked by it all.

'Are they always like this?'

'Yes.' She shrugs again and then finally grins. 'I love them both to bits, but they can't stand each other. Isn't it ridiculous? I normally just ignore them, but sometimes I think perhaps I should tell them both to grow up and act their ages. Do you think it would help? Or would that just make matters worse? What do you think, Sophie?'

'I don't know.' I try, desperately, to think of a half-decent snippet of advice. 'I guess some people just can't get along together – even within the same family. It's sad, though – for you.'

'I'm used to it. And anyway,' She gives me a nervous, excited smile. 'Pete's going to be my family now.'

Can't be any worse than the one she's got!

The wedding's at half past two and although I say it myself, Sara looks lovely by the time the photographer arrives, which is when I take my leave – and I've made the best of a bad job with the other two. I've got one appointment this afternoon, for a consultation – which I've agreed to do at the client's house as she doesn't live far from Sara's mother's place. The new client's a very tense, very nervous middle-aged woman who wants my opinion on whether she should have her shoulder-length curly hair cut into a short crop before her wedding in January – and who, surprise, surprise, also turns out very quickly to want my opinion on whether she should invite her fiancé's aunt to the wedding even though she's an unmitigated cow who has insulted her whole family, whether she should go ahead with the wedding in church despite having lost her faith in God when her best friend died in an accident (horrific, freaky story involving a ski-lift and an umbrella – I won't go into details), and whether, in fact, she ought to marry her fiancé at all, as she's only known him for three months and he's the first man she's ever slept with. At this point I decide I ought to stop hairdressing and write a book based on all the relationship dilemmas I unwillingly get caught up in.

'Don't marry him,' I tell her, not that I have a clue what I'm talking about, and despite the fact that I might be throwing away the chance of a nice fat fee, 'unless you can't bear to live without him.'

'But how do I *know* that?' she says, clenching her fists in anxiety. 'What do *you* think, Sophie?'

I think I'm finished here, that's what I think.

It's half past three and I haven't had any lunch, so I spend a pleasant hour on my own in Costa, reading the papers while enjoying a Brie and cranberry wrap and a Hot Chocolate with marshmallows, and feeling a bit like I'm on holiday or skiving off school. Then to extend the feeling, I do a bit of window-shopping and decide, finally, that I'm sufficiently calm to tackle the Big One. I'm going to see Polly.

Of course, this decision alone is enough to turn me from Calm and Chilled, to Stressed Out of My Life. But this is not about me. I have to ignore my own feelings and remember that I need to do this, for Polly's sake. I need to talk to her. And then I need to stay with her, certainly for the rest of the day, probably for most of the weekend, possibly for the rest of my life, while she gets over the shock and distress and gradually comes to terms with the ending of her marriage. It ain't going to be easy, I tell myself with characteristic understatement, but can it be any harder than the way she held me together after the whole Damien thing? Surely not. And also, I can divert her for a while with the fact that my pregnancy scare was just a scare. She'll be glad to hear that.

With this in mind, and with my heart pounding, I knock on her door, ring the bell, peer through the window, call her mobile from the doorstep, and finally have to admit that I'm off the hook for today. She's gone out.

And then I go home. And find her, sobbing her heart out, on my sofa. With a glass of my red wine in her hand and my boyfriend's arms round her.

What's going on isn't the right response to this situation, because I know perfectly well what's going on. I know perfectly well that I've been a rotten friend: that I've missed my chance to talk to Polly before she found out some other way. Shit.

'She told me!' Polly bawls at me. Her face is red and worn with crying, her voice hoarse with distress. 'The fucking cow came round and *told* me! Why? Why, Sophie, why?'

I wring my hands at her. I didn't realise that wringing one's hands was actually a real thing, that people do, but now I know it is, and it hurts.

'WHY DIDN'T YOU TELL ME?' she howls. It's a horrible, ghastly sound, that howl. It makes me shiver from my head to my feet. 'YOU KNEW! She SAID you knew!'

'I'm sorry,' I whisper. 'Polly, I'm so, so sorry. I've just been round your house to tell you, but ...'

'Oh, go away!' she groans. 'Just sod off, go on, go away, leave me alone.'

This is somewhat difficult, as it's my flat, and I don't actually have anywhere else to go. Never mind the fact that my boyfriend appears to be almost in tears himself, and is currently engaged in nuzzling the top of her head and muttering 'Sssh, sssh, it's OK, it's OK,' in her ear like she's a toddler who's just grazed her knee.

'Why didn't you tell *me*, Sophie?' he says, eyeing me accusingly over the top of her tousled head. 'Didn't you trust me? We could have helped Polly together, we could have tackled this as a team, but no – you chose to keep it to yourself, as usual. You really are the most self-centred, stubborn, unsupportive person I've ever ...'

I gasp at the *unsupportive* – gasp so hard it gives me a pain in my chest. For a minute I'm frightened I might be having a heart attack or some sort of fatal allergic reaction. I clutch my hands to my heart and stumble in a wobbly and gasping fashion from the room – and just as I'm about to throw myself dramatically onto my bed and prepare to lie there until I die, or at least until somebody cares enough to come and see whether I'm dead, I hear a little voice behind me saying, very sombrely:

'Mummy's crying, Sophie. She's crying *very* much.'

Gracie is sitting cross-legged in the corner of the bedroom, rocking her sleeping baby brother in his buggy-thing. She looks at me with her big brown eyes and adds, matter-of-factly, 'She put Ethan in here and told me to sit with him, so I'm sitting with him.'

'Good girl, Gracie,' I whisper. My heart is breaking, but at least now I know what I have to do. I was too late, too self-centred and *unsupportive* to help Polly. But at least I can look after her children until she's feeling better. 'Come on,' I tell her, offering her my hand. Let's take Ethan and go for a little walk. Give Mummy a bit of a break. Yes?'

'I'd better tell her,' she says, frowning at me doubtfully.

'No. She's asleep.' I'm going to wonder, for weeks, possibly for months, why I'm telling this lie – but right now, it just seems like the best thing to do. 'Let's not wake her up and make her cry again.'

'OK,' she says, trustingly. She puts her little soft hand in mine, and quietly, ever so quietly, I push the buggy out through the front door and close it behind me.

I don't know where I'm going. But for probably the first time in my life, I'm aware that I now have responsibilities on my hands – responsibilities that I'd fight, kill, or die to protect. For once I'm *not* being selfish.

Saturday

OK, OK, so it wasn't a sensible thing to do. All right, in fact it was a bloody stupid, ridiculous, irresponsible thing to do. But come on, I didn't mean any harm. I was trying, desperately, to help Polly in any way I could, despite her new low opinion of me – an opinion which is now, of course, even lower.

The thing is, however well-intentioned I was, I realised within five minutes of leaving the flat that I still didn't know the first thing about small children or what to do with them. However fiercely I love little Gracie (because I love her mum), I don't really understand four year olds or what they like doing. And however much I was prepared to fight to the death to protect little Ethan, asleep in his buggy, I had no idea what I was going to do if he got hungry, thirsty, or (God forbid), needed a clean nappy. So I took them to the pub.

Look, it's not as bad as it sounds. I'd wandered the streets for about twenty minutes, promising Gracie we were going somewhere nice, and I couldn't think of anywhere. There are places, I suppose, that I could have taken *her* – the pictures, or on a bus or a tube to see a museum, if indeed children of her age like museums; I doubt it – but I couldn't imagine taking a baby, in a pushchair, with us.

'Let's go to the park!' I suggested brightly. 'You could play on the swings! Feed the ducks!'

She looked at me scathingly.

'Have we got anything to feed them with?'

'Well, no, but I could get something.'

'I'm hungry,' she complained. 'And thirsty. And Ethan's waking up.'

Oh, bugger. It was too soon to go back. I wanted Polly to have a chance to recover a little bit, and, OK, if

I'm honest – to appreciate what I'd done for her. And just then, we turned a corner and I spotted, like an oasis rising out of the desert, the Red Lion pub. *Children welcome. Bar snacks available. Beer garden at rear.*

We were there for maybe an hour. I bought chips and lemonade for Gracie, and gave Ethan one chip at a time to squash and wipe round his face, which Gracie assured me was quite normal.

'Shall we go back now?' she asked me when all the chips were gone. 'I'm cold, and Mummy might be getting worried.'

So we trundled slowly back home, with Ethan singing to himself in baby language all the way, and Gracie chatting to me about bully-boy Rudolph in her class and how she doesn't have to sit next to him any more because he's been put on the Naughty Table. And we got home just as the police car pulled up.

'Ooh,' Gracie said, watching with awe as the two police officers marched up to my front door and rang the bell.

'Can I help you?' I asked. I thought, to be honest, they were probably ringing the wrong bell and wanted Jamie in the upstairs flat – lots of people make that mistake – and I was just wondering what the quiet, peace-protesting, sandal-wearing Jamie might have got up to, when one of the officers said, looking me up and down and taking in the two kids:

'Are you Sophie Jennings, by any chance?'

'Yes, that's me.' I felt my heart leap into my mouth. 'Is there a problem? Oh, God – what's happened? Has anything happened to Polly?'

'Shall we go inside, Miss? Get the children in the warm?' was all he said. He was looking at them both carefully, like he was inspecting them for damage.

'Yes,' said Gracie helpfully. 'I am *very* cold. I did tell Sophie, at the pub, that I was very cold.'

And that was what took a bit of explaining.

Nevertheless, I'm still upset that they felt they needed to call the police, even if Polly did end up telling the officers it was all a misunderstanding and I hadn't, after all, abducted her children.

'*Abducted...*!' I protested, close to tears, after the police had gone. 'Polly, how could you even *think* such a thing?'

'What was I supposed to think?' she raged. 'You *sneaked* out with them without a word, without telling me you were going, or where, or why. You took my *babies* out to a *pub*, Sophie, in the middle of a cold, dark, winter night!'

'It was six o'clock! And it's October! And – dark? It's never dark in London! You can see the light of it from outer space! And we weren't *in* a pub, we were sitting in a perfectly nice pub *garden.*'

'We had chips, Mummy!' Gracie put in, excitedly. 'With tomato sauce! And lemonade!'

'Junk food!' Polly exclaimed dramatically. 'How dare you feed my babies junk food without my permission?'

'Polly – this is all ridiculous. They were perfectly fine, perfectly safe!'

'To be fair, Sophie, we couldn't *know* that,' Oscar said quietly. He was looking at me like I'd suddenly sprouted horns. 'We had no idea where you'd gone. You weren't answering your phone.'

'Oh. I must have left it at home.'

'It was pretty irresponsible,' he said.

'Well, I'm so *sorry*!' I wanted to stamp my feet and shout with frustration. I'd failed. I'd failed miserably at supporting my best friend, failed to tell her the horrible truth about her husband and Jo, left her to find out herself, in a much more hurtful way. And then I'd even failed when

I tried to be helpful with the children. Let's face it, it seemed like I was just an all-round failure. 'I was doing my best,' I said, miserably.

'Well, if that was the best you could do, at the very worst time of my entire life, it wasn't much bloody good, Sophie!' Polly said angrily. At least she seemed to have stopped crying.

'You told me to sod off and leave you alone,' I reminded her. 'What was I supposed to do?'

'Even *Oscar* was more use than you, and he's a man!' Oscar was trying, quite obviously, not to look smug at this rather back-handed compliment. She shook her head at me. 'Come on children – we're going home.'

'What are you going to do?' I asked her quietly.

'Throw him out, of course,' she muttered under her breath. 'He can go and live with *her*. Or do whatever the hell he wants. I don't want him anywhere near me, or the kids. Ever again.'

'If I can help ... in any way at all ...' I started, but she just turned away, shaking her head again, before taking the children and leaving without another word.

'What did you expect?' Oscar commented, without looking at me. 'I can't believe what you did.'

I went in the bedroom and slammed the door behind me. He slept on the sofa.

And now, today, I've got to concentrate on doing the mad hair of a mad bride who's so hysterical with excitement she can't sit still, and keeps bursting into song. I wouldn't mind but it's all dreary love ballads and she's got a voice like a cat being strangled.

'Michael wants us to think about moving to the country after the honeymoon,' she confides in me eagerly when she finally seems to run out of songs. 'But I'm not sure. What do you think, Sophie? Should I agree? Or not?'

'Absolutely,' I tell her. I really couldn't care less if she moves to the Moon.

'Ooh, do you really think so? Thank you, Sophie. You're *so* helpful.'

Glad someone thinks so.

This evening I make a bit of an effort with Oscar. I cook his favourite dinner – well, OK, I buy it from Tesco's – and I don't say anything when he puts the football on the TV without asking if I want to watch something else. He's still barely talking to me. I can't work out what he's most pissed off with me about – the fact that I won't fly off on holiday with him at the drop of a hat, the fact that I'm not pregnant and not sorry about it, or his apparent belief that I abduct little children and take them out on the razzle with me.

While he's watching football, grumpily, and drinking beer, grumpily, I sit in the bedroom and phone Polly.

'How are things?' probably isn't the most sensible thing I could have said.

'How do you think?' she snaps back.

'Have you done it? Thrown him out?'

'I was just warming up to it, Sophie, when you called.' She sounds grim. No wonder.

'Sorry. Is there anything I can do?'

'Not unless you want to hold the knife while I twist it.'

'Don't ... Polly, don't do anything silly.'

She sighs. 'What do you think I am? Unfortunately he's my children's father. Much as I'd like him dead, I'll have to make do with getting him out of my sight.'

'Shall I come round? Give you a bit of moral support? Look after the children?' Whoops. I suppose that wasn't a good idea. She still seems to be annoyed with me about yesterday.

'You must be joking,' she says. 'Don't worry about it, Sophie. I'll manage.'

When I hang up the phone, I sit for ages on my own in the darkness of my bedroom. I think about all the stuff Polly and I have been through together, over the years – how we've always been there for each other and supported each other. And now, now the worst possible thing has happened to her, she doesn't want me around – and it's my own fault. I can't even cry. I think I've gone beyond tears.

I'm still sitting here when the football finishes and Oscar comes in to bed. He glances at me without any sign of affection, undresses and gets under the duvet.

'G'night, then,' I say, quietly.

He doesn't even answer.

Sunday – a week later

'How are things with Oscar?' trills my sister Debra. 'Still loved-up and wonderful, eh?'

'Leave off,' I growl.

It's nearly eleven o'clock and I'm still in bed, feeling sorry for myself.

'Ooh, sorry – have I interrupted something?' she carries on, giggling suggestively. 'It's been so long since I indulged in lazy Sunday morning shag-ins ...'

'We're not shagging. He's out with his kids. I'm in bed on my own.'

'Ah. Never mind. I expect when he comes home he'll be pleased to see you,' she says coyly. 'Lucky you – enjoy it while you can, Sophe – once you're married, with kids ...'

'Debra! How many times do I have to tell you?' I explode. 'I'm not getting married! I'm not having kids! I'm not ...' I stop, realising what I was just about to say. And then I think – sod it, I might as well say it anyway. 'I'm not even sure that we're going to stay together.'

There's a heavy silence. Then, in a completely different tone, she says:

'You've had a row? It happens! God, Sophie, it's *normal*. Don't start thinking, just because you've started arguing ...'

'No. We're not arguing. We're not even talking.'

'But that's normal too!' She's laughing, sounding relieved. 'Is that all? What did you expect? That you'd go on forever having lovely cosy chats together – all of that stops once you're living together. Nothing left to talk about, is there!'

I sigh. I'm wasting my time, I know – why am I trying to explain to her? How can I make myself understood to anyone whose passionate belief in the desirability of marriage – marriage even to someone who quite obviously doesn't make her happy – defies common sense?

'I don't think he likes me any more,' I say, quietly.

'Of course he does! He's just being an arse! You know what men are like. Take no notice.' She sniggers. 'He'll soon change his tune when he wants something. When he's ready for a bit of action. You know – when he fancies ...'

'Yes, all right, I get the picture,' I say irritably. 'But why should I put up with that? Ignoring me, acting like I'm in the way – in my own flat! – and then expecting me to roll over and be nice to him? No, I'm sorry, I'm not having that! No way!'

She tuts her disapproval. 'You always were too stroppy for your own good, Sophie. Men don't like that.'

'Well, in that case, men can fuck off!' I retort in childish exasperation.

It's been a bad week. I spent a couple of days trying to improve Oscar's mood – I even tried apologising to him, which wasn't easy as I don't actually understand what I've done wrong. I then lost my temper and told him pretty much what I've just told Debra – that if he's going to carry on like this, he can fuck off.

'That's what you want, then, is it?' he said in an annoying sneery voice. I don't know why I haven't noticed before that he has a tendency to sneer annoyingly.

'I didn't say it was what I wanted. I said you might as well, if you're not happy being here with me – which you don't appear to be.'

'I need time, Sophie. Time to recover from my disappointment.'

Disappointment? What frigging disappointment? He was looking like he'd invested all his money in Icelandic banks.

'You're disappointed because I made a stupid error of judgement with my friend's children? What's it got to do with you?' I spat at him. I mean, it was bad enough that Sophie didn't want to see me or speak to me. I take two kids out for a treat, and suddenly I'm a pariah.

He sighed, and shook his head, and turned away from me like I was being completely ridiculous. I wanted to hit him.

'I'm disappointed,' he said eventually in the voice of someone who's struggling to be patient with a hopelessly thick child, 'that we don't seem to be as well attuned as I thought we were.'

Well attuned. What a choice of expression. It made me think, fleetingly, of an orchestra with all the instruments twanging and screeching together madly.

'So maybe you should be talking to me about it. Your *disappointment*. Instead of just being grumpy and bloody non-communicative.'

'Don't try to blame *me* for all of this, Sophie. *I'd* have liked us to go on holiday together, like normal couples do – that would have given us the chance to *communicate*.'

So there you go. It was all my fault. Wouldn't you just know it.

By the middle of the week, with no word from Polly, who wasn't answering her phone, or responding to text messages, and who was never in when I called at the house (several times a day), I was feeling sick with anxiety about her. I put a note through her door, asking her to call me and apologising (again) for my stupidity with the children. Nothing. In desperation, I took to hanging around outside Gracie's school when the kids came out, risking being carted off as a potential child-abductor. Again. But Sophie was nowhere to be seen, and nor was Gracie. I asked one of the other mums, who was collecting a little girl I recognised as one of Gracie's friends. 'She's away,' she said. 'Gone down to Devon for a few days, apparently.'

Feeling more miserable and worried than ever, I mentioned this to Oscar in another attempt at reopening communication between us.

'I suppose she's gone to stay with her mum,' I sighed. 'To give Leon time to get out of the house.'

'Yes. She has. She phoned earlier on.'

'What!' I stared at him. 'When? Why didn't you tell me?'

'Before you got home from shopping. I'd have told you if you were speaking to me.'

'I'm *trying* to speak to you, for Christ's sake! What did she say? Oh – forget it! I'll call her back.'

I was actually dialling her mobile number when he took the phone out of my hand.

'She won't answer. She doesn't want to speak to you.'

I was so stunned, I had to sit down.

'She told *you* that she didn't want to speak to *me*?'

'That's what she said. She thinks she needs some space from you, for a while.' He shrugged. 'You've got to respect that, Sophie, if you're really her friend.'

How dare he!

'Don't talk to *me* about really being her friend!' I screamed. Yes, I screamed. I'd lost it, flipped, completely. Can you blame me? 'I've been her friend since we started school! What would you know about it? You've been around for five minutes, you know nothing!'

'So it seems,' he said, in that annoying sneery voice I mentioned earlier, which I now seem to be noticing more and more.

I sat, gulping for air, trying to calm myself down. I couldn't believe it. I *didn't* believe it. Polly wouldn't do that! She'd never say she wanted some space from me –

especially not while she's going through such a traumatic time.

'So why would she phone here, then, if she didn't want to speak to me?' I demanded.

He gave me a superior stare. 'To speak to me.'

Oh, yeah, like *that* was likely! I actually laughed at the very idea of it.

'Don't kid yourself,' I muttered when I'd stopped laughing. But he was still giving me the superior stare.

'We developed a rapport,' he said haughtily. 'Last week, when you *absented* yourself with her children. I was there to support her. When you weren't.'

Later, in the bedroom with the door shut, I found Polly's mum's number in my old address book and called that.

'Hello Sophie,' said her mum, wearily. 'Yes, she's here, with the children. I'm sorry, love, but she's told me she doesn't want to speak to anyone.'

'Anyone?' I asked. My voice sounded hollow in my own ears. 'Or just me?'

There was a long enough pause for me to know the answer.

'She's not talking to Leon either,' she said eventually. 'Or Jo.'

'Of course she's not! They don't *deserve* to be talked to!' I was trying not to cry. Trying without much success. 'But I ... I only want to help..'

'I know, Sophie,' her mum soothed me. 'Look, she's very unhappy right now. Very depressed, and confused. I'm sure she'll come round. Just give her time. It's Gracie's half-term holiday next week, so she'll stay down here till after that. When she comes back, she'll need you again, I'm sure.'

'Will you tell her I called? If it doesn't make her feel worse?'

'Of course. I'm sorry, Sophie, love. This has all been so upsetting – for all of us.'

I cried myself to sleep. When I woke up halfway through the night, I was still on my own. Oscar had slept on the sofa again.

And then, yesterday, he announced that he'd be going out all day today with his kids. To be honest, the thought of having him out of the flat for the day came as such a relief, I nearly told him not to bother coming back. I *so* nearly said it, that it brought me up sharp. Was this it, then? Was this how we were going to finish – simply because neither of us could be adult enough to try and sort it out?

'Would you like me to come out with you all?' I offered, trying to sound jolly and cheerful about it. 'Shall we go to the seaside again? I'll drive, if you like.'

There. I couldn't be much more conciliatory than that, could I? I waited for him to smile his thanks and appreciation, to take me in his arms, admit that he'd been a bit of a pig lately, and apologise. Some nice make-up sex might help to cheer me up.

Instead, he looked at me coldly like I'd suggested something disgusting.

'I don't *think* so,' he said. 'I don't actually think I can trust you around my children after what happened last week.'

And that was when I decided, in my own mind, that we're probably not going to stay together. I just haven't told him yet.

There's one very specific reason why I haven't told him yet. Apart, of course, from the fact that I think he ought to work it out for himself. I mean, I shouldn't actually have to throw him out, the way Polly's having to do with Leon. It's not like *we're* married, with a mortgage and a couple of kids and all those complications to sort out. It's not like one of us has been unfaithful. He just moved into my flat, a mere few weeks ago, and it's a simple matter of him moving back out again. I shouldn't have to spell it out. He should just go.

But maybe not quite yet. The one very specific reason, is that I still haven't got my period. I've done another test, and it's still negative – but everyone knows that happens sometimes: negative doesn't always mean negative. Of course, it might be the stress of all this business with Polly – stress affects some people's cycles, doesn't it. Not mine, not normally, but there's a first time for everything. I can't, in my heart of hearts, believe I'm pregnant. I don't *do* pregnant! I don't feel pregnant – not that I even know how it feels to be pregnant. But until I know, for sure, I feel like I'm living in a kind of limbo. Because if, God forbid, there actually is a baby, and I actually have to do something about it – Oscar needs to be around to support me – right? That's the least he can do, isn't it. Before he moves all his stuff, and himself, out of my flat again.

Two weeks later

We're into November, and all the Christmas stuff seems to have been in the shops for so long already that I'm beginning to feel like spring should be just around the corner.

I've only come into Boot's to buy a deodorant but the queue at the pay-desk is too long, and I'm standing here, wondering whether to give up and walk out, when the piped music changes abruptly from *Deck the Halls with Boughs of Holly* (fa la la la lah, etc), to *A Child is Born*. And suddenly, I can feel a panic attack coming on. It's as if the song is being played specifically to me, to torment me. A child is born? No! Stop it, shut up, stop singing about it! I don't want to think about it! I throw the deodorant back on the shelf – any shelf, I don't care, in the middle of the Christmas chocolates is just fine – and hurtle out of the shop. I've got to talk to someone.

I tried talking to Oscar last night, but it was difficult. The timing was bad. He was packing up his things.

'So you're definitely moving out, then?' I said, quietly, standing in the bedroom doorway and watching him.

He'd been talking about going for a couple of days, and I'd been trying to bring up the pregnancy-threat thing (gulp) – but I couldn't seem to get the words out. And now, he seemed to have made up his mind, and there I was still struggling to say anything about it.

'I don't see the point in prolonging this, really, do you?' he said, sighing.

He sat down on the bed to zip up one of his holdalls, and I suddenly had a mental image of him sitting on the bed, just like that, such a very short time ago –

unzipping it. Unpacking. How have we managed to get it so wrong, so quickly?

'I know it's probably all my fault,' I said. 'I know you think I'm selfish, and irresponsible, and ...'

'Sophie, I think the time for blame and argument has past.'

I fought back the urge to say *Well, get you, Mr Maturity*. He was right. What was the point in provoking another row? Instead, and without realising I was going to do it, I burst out:

'I might still be pregnant.'

There was a long silence. I waited for him to put his arms around me, like he did before, and talk about how I might really be thrilled even though I didn't know it yet. All that stuff. Instead, he sighed again and said:

'Is that your way of trying to make me stay? You're going to pretend you're pregnant?'

'What?' I stared at him. 'Oscar, I'm not pretending!'

'You said it was negative. A false alarm.'

'But I still haven't got my period.'

He sat back, then, and looked at me carefully, as if he was trying to work out from my face whether I might actually be having a baby.

'Have you got any other symptoms?'

'Well, how should I know? I'm not a doctor, or a nurse, or anything. I don't have a clue about being pregnant. I have felt sick sometimes, though,' I remembered suddenly.

He shook his head, like he thought I was making it up.

'Go and see your doctor, if you're worried,' he said calmly, getting back to his packing.

'Is that all you can say?'

'Well, what am I supposed to say? You've made it clear you wouldn't want it – if you *were* ...'

'But wouldn't you want to help me? Support me?'

'Give me a call,' he said wearily, standing up and picking up the bag. 'If you need anything.'

So here I am. I've now missed two periods. I don't know if I feel sick or if I'm just imagining it. I feel tearful, and frightened, but I don't know if that's just because I haven't got anyone to talk to. I've lost everyone. I know it's my own fault, and I know I'm feeling sorry for myself, but how has my life gone so wrong in such a short time?

One thing's for certain: I can't ignore this situation any longer. It's a Monday, I've got a free afternoon, and I've made an appointment at the doctor's.

And it's in the waiting room that I meet up with Polly.

We catch sight of each other over the heads of Flu Jab queue, most of whom are elderly and seem to be treating this as a social get-together. For a moment, neither of us reacts. Then she gives me a very small nod of her head, like she's just about admitting she recognises me. I give her a nod back, and try a little lift of my eyebrows, like I'm merely wondering how she is. She manages a half-smile in return, and then looks away. I sit here, wondering whose move it is next. I'm so desperate to make up with her, I don't want to mess it up. I've got to do it right. On her terms.

A few seconds later she looks over at me again, and half-smiles again, and gives a little shake of her head, like she doesn't know what to make of things. So this time I smile properly, and wave to her, and then feel stupid because who waves to each other when they're only a few yards apart? She laughs. I laugh back. We both get up at the same time, and I kind of hurtle at her, meeting her halfway, completely overwhelming the orderly seating arrangement of the Flu Jab queue, some of whom look like they're going to topple out of their chairs with shock.

'Polly!' I gasp.

'Sophe!' she says.

And we're both hugging each other and laughing like crazy things. Thank God. Oh, thank God.

While we're waiting to be called in to see the doctor, we establish that she's sorry, and I'm even more sorry, and no – she's much more sorry than me ... and then we give up, hug again and start filling in the gaps. She's left Ethan with her neighbour this afternoon while she sees the doctor for a follow-up about her depression.

'Depression?' I say, horrified.

'It's nothing. I'm better. I'm here to check I can come off the drugs. I just needed a bit of help to get through the separation.'

'*I* should have been around to help you!'

'Yes, but I wouldn't let you, would I. I've been horrible, Sophe – horrible to everyone, but mostly to you. I didn't seem to be able to help it.'

'I suppose it was the shock.' I hang my head. 'I should have told you about Leon and Jo. I tried ...'

'I know. None of this is your fault, Sophie.' She looks at me sadly. 'I know you never liked Leon. I should have listened to you all along. Perhaps that was why I resented you. You were right, weren't you. He's a complete pig.'

'You deserve so much better. You'll get through this.'

'I know. I have to, for my kids' sake.'

'How are they taking it?'

'Ethan's too young, but Gracie misses him, of course – he hasn't exactly put himself out to see much of her. But most of her little friends at school have daddies who only see them for visits, so she feels quite normal.' She sighs. 'Makes you wonder where we're all going wrong, doesn't it?'

But before I can reply, and argue that she's not going wrong, has never done anything wrong apart from marrying that plank of a husband – I get called in to see Dr Barton.

'I haven't asked you why *you're* here!' she exclaims as I get up to go.

I try to tell her, but suddenly my mouth has gone dry with nerves, and no words come out.

'Jesus, Sophie,' she hisses at me quietly. 'You're not ... you're not ...?'

'Sophie Jennings for Dr Barton?' calls the receptionist again.

I turn and hurry off to the consulting room, leaving Polly watching me with her mouth open.

'He says it could be any number of things.' We're sitting in my car, outside the doctor's surgery now. I'm still shaking with relief. I'm not pregnant. He's sure I'm not pregnant. But he's sending me for some blood tests to find out what's going on.

'It could just be – you know, one of those things. Stress, anxiety, emotional stuff ... . Or I might have something wrong with me.'

'What sort of something?'

'Well, I don't know. He didn't exactly say. Hormonal things, I suppose. Gynae things.' I shrug. 'I don't care. As long as it's not a baby!'

She hugs me again.

'I'm so relieved for you, Sophe. If I'd realised you were still going through all this worry, on your own ...'

'You had far worse stuff of your own going on. Look, let's just be glad the doctor has brought us back together again – yeah?'

'Yeah. Thank God.'

'I've missed you so much,' I add with a smile.

'Me too. Want to come round later, when the kids are in bed? I'll open a bottle of wine. We ought to celebrate.'

'Me not being pregnant? Or you coming off the anti-depression pills?'

'Both. And just being back together.'

'I'll certainly drink to that.'

I'm thinking, while I'm microwaving my dinner tonight before going round to Polly's, about the other thing that I haven't told her. That I've never told her. And thinking that maybe it's time I did. There was never a reason to, before, and at least a million reasons not to. But now ... well, I'm thinking it might just reinforce everything she now knows.

I'm so tense with thinking about telling her, I'm hardly through the door before she asks me what's up.

'There's something else I want to tell you,' I admit. 'And I think it'd be best to get it out of the way right now, in case you want to throw me out without giving me a drink.'

She's pouring out the wine already, and her hand shakes a little bit when I say this, so that she spills a drop on the kitchen counter.

'Don't be daft,' she says, handing me the glass of wine and visibly squaring her shoulders. 'Let's go and sit down, then, and get it over with.'

'About Leon,' I say, when we're sitting in the lounge. I look into my wine glass instead of at her face. 'You knew I never liked him. But you never asked why.'

She shrugs. 'Nobody likes everybody. I know you thought he didn't help me enough with the children ...'. She stops, and I can hear her breathing in the silence. 'I suppose he's had affairs before, has he?' she says flatly. 'I suppose you knew.'

'Yes.'

'How did you know?'

'He told me.'

'He *what*?' Now she's put her glass down, and I'm having to meet her eyes. 'He *told* you?' she repeats incredulously. 'When?'

'The first time he mentioned it,' I say, slowly, carefully, watching her face, 'was when you were in hospital having Gracie.'

She'd been admitted for a Caesarean at thirty-seven weeks because Gracie was in the breech position. They kept her in for a couple of days before the op, hoping the baby might turn at the last minute, and then she was in for several days afterwards.

'I came round to tidy up and put some shopping in the fridge for you, before you came home.'

'I know. You didn't trust Leon to do it,' she remembers, with a faint smile.

'He came home while I was there. He ...' I pause, swallow, feeling wretched. Was this really such a good idea? After all this time? 'He said how nice it was that we were alone in the house together.'

She gasps. 'He tried it on with you. That's what you're trying to tell me? While I was in hospital, having our baby – we'd only been married a few months! Is that what happened, Sophie?'

I nod, miserably. 'He seemed to think I'd be glad of the offer. I was so disgusted – I couldn't believe what I was hearing. It was so unbelievable, I actually thought he was joking at first, but he ... tried to ...'

'Don't give me the details,' she says, horror etched into her face.

'I'm really sorry, Polly. I practically raised the roof. Screamed at him, threatened to tell you – he just laughed in my face. Told me not to worry, there were plenty of girls who were up for it – *gagging for it* – and he'd already had three different ones while you were in hospital so he'd just go and have himself another helping of that, as I was obviously either frigid or a lesbian or both. Walked out and slammed the door.'

'Oh ... my ... God,' she says, in a whisper. 'Sophie. Poor you.'

'Poor *me*? No – it was *you* I felt so sorry for!' I squawk, indignantly. 'I was so angry! I wanted to run after him with your bread knife! I wanted to cut off his ... well, I wanted him out of your life, to be honest. But what could I do? You, bringing home your beautiful new baby, thinking everything was wonderful ... how could I ruin that for you? What was I supposed to do?'

'Oh, Sophie,' she whispers again, shaking her head.

'The next time I saw him on his own, I told him if he ever said, or did, anything like that again, I'd tell you and you'd leave him.'

'And did he care?' she asks, still shaking her head.

'What do you think? He obviously found it hilarious. Every time he saw me after that, he'd make some disgusting comment about his latest shag, or ask me if I'd told you yet. He knew I wouldn't. He knew I didn't have the guts.' I look down at the floor, close my eyes. 'Some friend I've been to you.'

She grabs me round the shoulders so suddenly I nearly drop my drink.

'Don't *ever* say that again!' she says, fiercely. 'You've been the best friend in the world! You've kept that horrible, horrible secret from me all this time – and it wasn't because you didn't have the guts, it was because you didn't want me to be hurt! I know that! *He* knew that – the bastard! If he hadn't gone too far this time – with my own bloody *friend*, getting her *pregnant*!' She practically explodes on the last word, throwing herself back against the sofa as if she's been shot. 'If it hadn't been for that,' she repeats more quietly, 'I'd probably never have thrown him out.'

'I wish I'd told you. I do. I wish you'd known about this years ago – it would have all been over, you'd have been over it by now.'

'And never had Ethan?' she puts in quickly. She's smiling. I can't believe it. I thought she'd have either been crying, yelling, or throwing me out by now. 'Sophie, don't you think I had my suspicions over the years? I'm not completely stupid. I knew he was a crap husband – I just didn't realise quite how crap. I don't know why I thought I loved him,' she finishes sadly.

'You kept hoping he'd improve?' I suggest.

'I suppose so.'

We both pick up our wine glasses at the same time, take a sip, and put them down again, sighing. We look at each other and laugh.

'I'll top up your glass,' she says, going to get the bottle. 'You're not driving home. You can get a cab, or stay the night.'

'Good idea.'

'We haven't got drunk together for ages, have we? And now you know you're not pregnant ....'

'Don't remind me!' I shudder. 'And now that Oscar's moved out ...'

She fills our glasses, raises hers and announces: 'Here's to the New Us. Both single and starting over.'

'Men!' I say ruefully, clinking my glass against hers. 'Who needs 'em, eh? Who bloody needs 'em.'

The next Tuesday

Today, I think, has been a turning point in my life. I did something very out of character – and I didn't even think about it till afterwards. This is what happened.

This morning I was doing a new client's hair, and she'd brought along her friend who's going to be her bridesmaid. They were both nice girls: Jennie and Lou. Both about my age, both been married before.

'I don't know why I'm doing it again!' Jennie laughed at one point in the conversation. 'Must be mad!'

'That's what I keep telling you!' Lou said, laughing back. 'Completely bonkers! It must be love, I suppose!'

'Yeah.' Jennie smiled to herself in the mirror. 'He's *so* different from my ex. Second time lucky, I hope.'

'I hope so too,' I said, smiling back at her.

'I suppose you see quite a lot of girls getting married for the second time?' she asked me curiously.

'Yes. And third, sometimes.'

'I bet you feel like telling them not to bother, don't you, Sophie?' Lou jokes.

'Of course not. I'm only here to do their hair,' I say.

'You don't ever hand out advice? With all your experience of brides and weddings?'

I look round at Lou. She's smiling at me expectantly, waiting for me to tell her some stories about all the advice I've given to all the brides over the years. I look in the mirror at Jennie, also smiling at me, expecting something similar. At least they're not asking for advice *themselves*, for once. And suddenly – perhaps because they seem so nice, so friendly, so easy-going and happy and *normal* – I find myself blurting out the truth.

'I get asked for advice, yes – all the time. But I can't understand why. I'm the worst person in the world to

307

ask for advice about relationships! I haven't got one myself – the only one I've had, I've messed up completely because basically, I didn't really want to be in it. I only let him move in with me to please my family and to stop everyone thinking I was weird. I like being on my own! I've never wanted to get married, or have babies, and I can't understand why people seem to mind that. I mean – I'm happy for them to live their lives the way they want to, more than happy – I love other people's weddings, why else would I be doing this job? But nobody seems to like me living the way I want to live. Why do you think that is? Do you think I'm peculiar? What am I supposed to do – live the way they expect, marry someone just to keep everyone else in the world happy? What do you think?'

There's a stunned silence, which isn't altogether surprising. I'm horrified at myself as soon as I've (finally) finished speaking. What on earth am I thinking of? This is just not the way I'm supposed to behave! *I'm* supposed to be here to answer *their* insecurities – not the other way around!

'I'm sorry – I'm so sorry!' I gabble, smoothing Jennie's hair frantically as if I've just been tangling it up in the excitement of my oration. I hope I haven't. 'I don't know why I said all that ... I never normally ... God, I don't know what's come over me ... please, just ignore me ... just forget I ever spoke!'

'Don't be silly!' says Jennie at once, her eyes wide with concern. 'Sophie, of course we're interested in your life, in your problems – aren't we, Lou!'

'Of course we are!' Lou echoes, a little too enthusiastically. 'Of course you should feel able to confide in your clients, Sophie – why should it all be one-sided?'

'Yes – why should you have to stand here, day after day, offering up wisdom and advice to us brides, and never get your own stuff off your chest?' Jennie joins in. 'Come on, Sophie – tell us all about it. What happened with this relationship, then?'

'Personally, I think it's awful,' says Lou, 'that anyone should make you feel under pressure to conform. If you don't want to live with anyone, or get married, you have a perfect right to stick to your guns, Sophie. Doesn't she, Jen?'

'Absolutely!' agrees Jennie stoutly. 'So what happened, Sophie? Obviously it wasn't ever going to work, was it – moving in together just to please your family! So you ended it? Good for you!'

'Yeah, good for you!' says Lou. 'Marriage isn't for everyone, is it! It's your life – live it the way you want, girl. Anyone who disagrees is just plain jealous!'

'Jealous of your freedom!' agrees the girl who's just about to give herself away in matrimony for the second time. 'Jealous of your independence!'

And before I know it, I'm having the whole story of Oscar cajoled out of me, bit by bit, to a resounding chorus of approval at every stage. And I'm being thanked for the privilege of accepting their very welcome advice, paid a handsome tip and promised a very good booking for the wedding day.

I think I've been doing this job wrong, all these years. I'm not giving out advice any more, I don't care how much they beg and plead. I'm going to tell them all my own crappy life story and ask for *their* advice. It's a lot more rewarding!

So I'm on a high, of sorts, when Debra phones this evening.

'You haven't called for ages,' she starts off, accusingly. 'And I keep leaving you messages. And you keep ignoring them.'

'I know. I'm sorry. I've had a few issues.'

'It's over, is it? With Oscar?' Her disapproval bounces over the wire at me, all the way from Devon. 'He's gone for good? It wasn't just a walking-out-in-a-huff thing? He hasn't come back?'

'No, Debs – and I wouldn't take him back even if he did. Which he won't. We both know it's over. We're not sorry. I'm not upset. I'm happy about it.'

'*Happy*?'

'Yes – happy. Remember that?' I laugh, and then feel really guilty. 'Sorry, Debs. I didn't mean ...'

'*I* am *perfectly* happy with *my* relationship, thank you very much,' she says stiffly.

'I know. I know you are, and I'm happy for *you*. But look, you know me. You know I was always happier on my own. It was a mistake, ever letting Oscar move in with me. It's just not me, having someone living with me. You know that as well as I do.'

'I suppose so.' She sighs, as if she's just had to accept a very difficult character trait in a wayward child. 'I guess we can't all aspire to the same achievement, can we.'

'No,' I say gently, suddenly having no desire to argue, no desire to gloat, even to myself in my own mind, about the desirability of my lifestyle compared with hers; the futility of her self-delusion about her marriage. 'No, Debra – we're not all capable of the same aspirations.'

'Well, as long as you're happy, love,' she says equally gently. 'That's the main thing.'

'I am. And thank God, I'm not pregnant,' I add, teasingly.

'Pregnant?' I bet she's almost swallowed the phone, her mouth has probably gaped so wide. 'What! Was there a chance ...? Did you think ...?'

'I had a bit of a scare, yes. But it's OK. It was nothing.'

'Well. Well, I suppose that's a relief for you, then. Of course, we'd all have rallied around, you know, if you had been ....' She tails off for a moment, obviously trying to conceal the regret in her voice. 'I mean, I know it wasn't what you wanted. But if you *had* been, we'd all have supported you, Sophe. We'd all have been there for you. You know that.'

'I know.' I'm smiling to myself. I'm not going to upset her by telling her I wouldn't have wanted to keep the baby. What's the point? It's not going to happen anyway. I know she only wants to be allowed to care for me, in her own way. They all do.

'I love you, Debs. I love you all. However it might seem, sometimes. OK?'

'Love you too, you silly cow,' she says, sounding surprised. 'What's the matter? Feeling a bit low?'

'Maybe. Sometimes I miss you all, you know.'

'We miss you too. Can't you get home before Christmas?'

'Probably not. I'll be home for the whole week then, though. I'm looking forward to it. Don't worry – I'm fine. I've got Polly. We're both fine.'

Absolutely fine, I repeat to myself after I've hung up.

Just ... absolutely, totally fine. As always.

It's only a month now till Charlie marries Hateful Helen. Not that I'm thinking about it, particularly. She's just another client in my diary, you know. A 2pm wedding on the Saturday before Christmas. Lovely. It'll probably be freezing cold and everyone will be shivering in the wedding photos. Not that I care.

If I cared, I'd be drinking a lot more than I am. A lot more than the few little glasses of wine I'm having on my own in front of the TV in the evenings. I'm only having them to warm me up, you know, on these chilly November evenings.

Don't you just hate November? It's such a mournful month. Everything's dead, and damp, and dull. It's enough to drive a person to drink, just living through it.

'Are you drinking like this *every* night?' Polly asks me tonight, which is one of our re-invented evenings together at her house. Always at her house because of the kids. Always with me getting a taxi home because of the wine.

'Like what?'

'This amount.' She nods at the empty wine bottles on her table. 'Not that I mind, obviously, but I just wondered.'

'I haven't drunk all that on my own!' I protest. 'We've drunk it together! Between us!'

'But I only ever have a couple of drinks, Sophe. Because of looking after the children in the morning.'

'Fine!' I shrug, laugh. 'I don't have that problem!'

'No.' She smiles her gentle Polly-smile at me. 'As long as you're not getting any other kind of problem. Eh?'

I feel a bit offended, and drink twice as much as usual, just out of pique. I think she's probably just gutted that she can't get stuck in, herself. Can't blame her – it must be a major pain in the arse, getting up to feed babies and wipe bums and so on in the morning. Bad enough getting myself up and dressed!

And then she says something, quietly – something she seems to drop into the conversation from nowhere, like she's only just remembered to tell me. Except that I know from the way she looks at me and looks away again quickly, and the way her voice quavers just very slightly as she says it, that she's found it difficult to broach it.

'Oscar called me last night.'

Glances at me, glances away again. There's a little bit of pink in her cheeks.

'Oscar?' I say, in an *Oscar Who* tone of voice that doesn't fool either of us.

She shrugs and looks at the carpet. 'Yes, just for a little chat.'

'Oh.' I let this register, turn it over in my mind. It doesn't help that I'm a bit drunk. Oscar called her for a little chat? How come? Unless ... oh, of course: he's called her to see how I'm getting on without him! He's obviously thinking that'd be better than phoning me direct. I smile back at her.

'That was nice of him. Did he sound concerned? Did he ask about the pregnancy thing? Did you tell him it's all OK?'

'Er, well ... oh, yes, sure. I told him you're fine.'

'And did he sound like he's missing me? D'you think he has any regrets? Did he say anything, you know, about being sorry the way it ended? Did he ...?'

She's looking at the carpet again. Her cheeks are very pink.

'To be honest, Sophe, we didn't talk about you a lot.'

'You didn't ...?' Oh. I stare at her. 'What did you talk about, then?'

'Just this and that. His kids. My kids. You know.'

I don't, but then again, nothing's going to make too much sense till I've slept off the wine.

'I don't want to keep anything from you, Sophie,' she says quietly. 'I don't want us ever to have any secrets from each other any more. Right?'

'Right,' I agree. Secrets? Who's talking about secrets? I suddenly feel like perhaps I ought to go home and lie down. Everything's beginning to feel very muzzy.

'I'll call you a taxi, love,' she says.

Good idea. But I've no idea why she's looking at me like I'm an invalid, or someone in need of special care. I'm fine, me. It's everyone else who suddenly seems to be acting very strange.

Wednesday

I get a call from the doctor's surgery just as I'm about to start work. The bride, a timid-looking girl with bright red hair that reaches to her waist, listens to me quite openly as I argue with the receptionist.

'I don't need to see the doctor again. He told me I'm OK. I'm not pregnant.'

'But he needs to see you again. At your convenience,' says the receptionist smoothly.

'Well, it's not convenient. I'm working. I'm not ill – I'm fine. Why does he need to see me again?'

'He's got your blood test results back.'

Oh. I forgot about those. I kind-of presumed that because the nice man who stabbed me with a needle and extracted about a gallon of my blood and put it in lots of different coloured pots hasn't phoned to say I had anything wrong with me, it meant I was normal. Normal, just not pregnant and not menstruating either, but otherwise normal.

'Results?' I say, dismissively. 'And are they all good results?'

'I can't actually discuss the results with you. You need to see the doctor.'

'But you know what they are, right – the results? Can't you just tell me whether they're OK or not? It seems like a waste of the doctor's time, for me to come in and see him, if I'm OK.'

'The doctor has looked at your results.' She's sounding slightly strained now. 'And he has indicated that he needs to see you, to discuss them.'

'You can't just give me a little clue?'

'If there was nothing to discuss,' she says, pointedly, 'the doctor would have just asked me to call you and tell you that.'

This sinks in. Slowly.

'So there's something wrong with me.'

'I didn't say that. I just said ...'

'The doctor has something to discuss with me.'

'Yes.'

'So there must be something wrong with me.'

'Look, you mustn't jump to conclusions; you really do need to make an appointment, come and see the doctor, and he'll explain everything. OK?'

'OK.' My heart's racing now. I wonder how long I've got. I wonder if I'll live till Christmas, live to see my family again. My eyes are filling up with tears and the red-headed girl's staring at me in horror. 'I'd better come quickly, then, hadn't I,' I tell the receptionist shakily. 'In case.' I don't need to explain the *in case* to her. She knows. She must have to deal with bad news, people with bad test results, all the time.

'Can I come tonight?'

'We...e...ll,' she begins. 'We're pretty full tonight ...'

'Please!' I shout. 'Please, if I've got to find out what's wrong, then the sooner the better, wouldn't you say? I'd better get it over with, hadn't I? You said yourself, I needed to discuss it. Well, I won't be able to sleep. Or work. Or eat,' I add, dramatically.

'Well, all right, I could fit you in at the end of surgery, half past seven. Can you make that?'

'Yes. Thank you, yes. I'll be there.' I put down the phone and stare at it for a minute.

'Are you OK?' asks the red-headed girl anxiously. I'd forgotten about her.

'Oh! Yes. Well, no – but, hey, nothing for you to worry about.' I blow my nose and blink back the tears of self-pity. She's looking at me as if she's considering making a run for it.

'Do you want to cancel?'

'No! No, the show must go on. Gives me something ... to take my mind off things.' I'm aware that this isn't exactly what she will be wanting to hear. 'I mean, you know – of course, I want to concentrate on making you look beautiful, um, Valerie.'

'Vanessa.'

'Vanessa, yes, sorry, Vanessa. OK. So – how are you going to have your hair on the Big Day? Have you got some ideas?'

'Some. But I was rather hoping you'd have some suggestions of your own.'

'Of course! Well, look, here we are – these are all my styles for long hair. Have a look through, have a good old browse, eh? While I make myself ... sorry, while I make you a cup of coffee? Or tea?' I'm actually thinking I need a good strong slug of brandy. 'And then we can try a couple of styles out. No rush.'

No rush at all. I need about two hours to calm down and compose myself. I need to talk to Polly. And my mum. No! Not my mum! How could I do that to her, of all people, when she's so recently been through something equally awful herself? Oh, God, now I know – now I really know – how Mum must have felt. How scared, how terrified, how *alone.*

I leave Vanessa looking through the style book and go to the kitchen to put the kettle on, and while it's boiling I quickly call Polly's number.

'I'm sick,' I whisper, shakily. 'I think it's really bad.'

'What?' She's trying not to laugh. 'Sophie – what's wrong? You've got a hangover?'

'Hangover!' I shout, forgetting Vanessa in the next room, for a minute. 'Polly, I'm not kidding – this is serious. The doctor wants to see me. Urgently! Tonight!'

'He's got your test results back?'

'Yes. And the receptionist woman wouldn't tell me what they were.'

'They never do. The doctor has to explain them to you.'

'But she hinted ... Polly, listen, honestly, I'm not imagining it. I'm not exaggerating. She definitely hinted that he's looked at my results and that they're not OK.'

'You're really worried? Sophie, I'm sure it's nothing. Like you said before, probably just some hormonal blip, you know?'

'It's worse. I just know it. I don't even feel all that good, to be honest.'

'Well, I'm not surprised!' She sniggers again. 'The amount of wine you've been putting away.' She stops. Then: 'Sophie, are you crying? God, Sophe – I'm sorry. I didn't realise you were *that* worried. Look, don't panic, I'm sure ... Sophie, please don't worry. I'll come with you. What time is your appointment?'

'Half past seven,' I sniff. 'But you'll have the kids in bed.'

'Carol next door will look after them. Of course I'll come. I'll drive you. OK? Come on, cheer up, I'm *sure* it'll be OK. Are you working?'

'Oh! God, yes – I'd forgotten about her. Thanks, Polly. I'll see you later, then.'

I make two coffees and carry them through to the salon.

Vanessa's gone.

She phones me a couple of hours later to apologise.

'I've changed my mind,' she says quietly. 'I tried to tell you, but you were on the phone.'

'I'm *so* sorry, Vanessa. I'm not usually so unprofessional. Please don't go elsewhere – I'll make you another appointment and give you a free blow-dry. I'll do your bridesmaids half-price on the day. I promise you'll be happy with my work. I just had a slight personal crisis today.'

'I know. It's not anything to do with you, Sophie. I meant I've changed my mind about getting married.'

'Oh!' I'd laugh, if I wasn't so ill. 'Vanessa, every bride goes through these little doubts. I completely understand. I'm sure, when you've had a chance to think it over ...'

'No. I'm a hundred percent certain. I'm calling it all off. I've told Neil already. It's off. Definite. Final. That's it. The end. Over. I'm emigrating to New Zealand.'

'Blimey.' I sit back in surprise. For someone who had no idea what to do with her hair, she's certainly sounding decisive. 'What brought this all on, if you don't mind me asking?'

'It's my hair. He doesn't like my hair. He's never liked it. I don't know why he wanted to marry me really – I mean, it's quite a big part of who I am, you know what I mean? Being so long, and so ... red. He wanted me to have it cut short, and bleached blonde. I was going to do it for the wedding. And then you gave me all those pictures to look at, of all those beautiful girls with their lovely long hair – blondes, brunettes, *and* redheads. And I thought – what the hell am I doing? He should either love me the way I am, or not at all. Don't you agree, Sophie?'

'Yes. I do'. And I'm also amazed that she can talk so much, and so fast, and so confidently. This morning, she seemed like she was scared of the sound of her own voice. 'You're right. I'm sorry you've had to cancel your wedding, but ...'

'I'm not!' she retorts. 'I always wanted to go to New Zealand, and then I met Neil, and he didn't want to,

318

so I ... just pretended it didn't matter. But it does. *I* matter. I don't know how I let him make me forget that.'

'People do. Unfortunately. Good for you, Vanessa. I really hope it all works out well for you.'

'And you, Sophie. I hope ... well, good luck at the doctor's. I'm sorry, I couldn't help overhearing. I hope it's not ...' She breaks off and coughs, then adds quietly. 'I hope you're OK.'

'Thanks.' The panic is rising up in me again, and it's only half past four, and I haven't got any more clients, and there's only one way I'm going to last out the next three hours without having a total nervous breakdown. 'Bye, Vanessa,' I add quickly before dropping the phone and pouring out a large measure of red wine.

That's the first one.

By the time Polly picks me up, I've had several more. I've actually lost count. But hey, can you blame me? I needed the drink to calm my nerves. I'm still nervous, but I haven't got time to drink any more now. Polly's actually taken the bottle out of my hand as I'm getting in the car.

'You can't bring that with you,' she says gently. 'Come on. I'm sure it's all going to be OK.'

In the waiting room, she prattles away to me about lots of things. The weather, the government, Christmas, her children, even football, bizarrely, which neither of us are interested in. I know she's just trying to keep me from thinking about the doctor, and what he wants to see me about. But it's not working, obviously. When my name's called out, I jump out of my seat like I've been scalded.

'It'll be OK,' says Polly again, squeezing my hand. 'Go on.'

Dr Barton looks up at me over his glasses.

'What can I do for you?'

'You wanted to see me,' I say in a squeak. 'About my blood test results.'

'Ah.' He taps something into his computer, adjusts his glasses and squints at the screen. 'Ah, yes. Hmm.'

I'm practically wetting myself by now.

'Come and sit down,' he says.

I hadn't realised I was still standing in the middle of the room. I'm trembling with nerves. So much so, that as I reach the chair next to his desk, I have to hold onto it to steady myself. The chair tilts. I lose my balance. I end up falling over, across the chair, and banging my head on the desk.

'What ...? Are you all right?' he says, jumping up and coming round the desk to help me up. 'Goodness. Here, sit down. Do you want a drink of water? Do you feel faint?'

I do, a bit. But I'm not sure if it's nerves, or the wine I drank before I came here beginning to take effect.

'I'm OK,' I say, weakly. 'I just need to know. About the results.'

'Of course. Yes.' He's feeling my forehead, looking into my eyes. Never mind about all that, let's get the diagnosis over with! I breathe out, heavily, and he recoils slightly. Whoops. Probably got a whiff of my wine breath. 'You've been drinking,' he says. It's not a question.

'Only a little bit of Dutch courage.'

'OK.' He's frowning, but he doesn't actually look too cross. 'Not a good idea really. Using alcohol as a prop – not the best way of coping with these things.'

I fidget in my chair. This isn't what I came here for. I suppose he's putting off talking about what's wrong with me because it's going to be hard for him, too.

'Is everything all right?' he goes on, looking at me with concern like a friendly uncle. 'You're not depressed, or anxious? Having trouble sleeping? Eating?'

'Only since yesterday. When I got the phone call about these results.'

'Ah. Yes. Your blood test results.' He looks at the computer screen again and sighs. 'Well, you know, life doesn't always go the way we expect. Things happen, and we have to find ways of coping with them.'

'Yes,' I whisper.

'But alcohol isn't the answer.'

What the hell? Is he obsessed with alcohol, or what?

'I know. I do realise ...'

'Here.' He reaches across his desk and takes a couple of leaflets from the shelf. 'Take these away with you. You just might find them helpful.'

I shudder. Here we go. I suppose they'll explain how I'm supposed to cope with my frightening disease, whatever it is. I turn the leaflets over and look at the covers. *Your Drinking – Is It Safe, Is It Sensible?* And *How To Stop: Your Guide to Alcohol Abuse.*

I stare at him. OK, I'm annoyed now.

'I didn't come here to discuss my drinking!' I protest. 'I was only drinking because I was so bloody scared! I want to know! I need to know what's wrong with me! Please! Just tell me!'

'I was coming to that,' he says, calmly. Once again, he taps the screen. Once again, he looks at me over his glasses. 'Now then. You originally came to see me because you thought you might be pregnant. Were you hoping you might be?'

'No! You're not saying ... please don't tell me you got it wrong? I'm not ...?'

'No, no – you're definitely not pregnant. Were you in fact planning on having children? At some point?'

'No. No, I don't want children. I didn't want to be pregnant.'

321

'In that case,' he says, looking up and giving me a faint smile, 'this diagnosis might be a bit easier for you to take on board.'

'MENOPAUSE?!' I shout at Polly once we're safely back in her car. 'That's for *old* people! It *can't* be that! He's got it wrong! He's talking out of his arse! I want a second opinion! For God's sake!'

She starts the car.

'SAY something!' I demand.

'I don't know what to say.' She turns the engine off again, turns and looks at me sadly. 'I'm sorry, Sophe, I know it must be a horrible shock. But just think how much worse it could have been.'

'Worse? How? How could it be worse than being told my life is over, I'm finished, on the scrap heap, as good as dead?'

'You could have been told it was cancer. Or something equally awful. You know that's what you were worried about. That's what *I* was worried about. Sophie, I'm *glad* this is all it is.'

'You're glad? That I'm on my way to becoming a shrivelled, sad old wreck with no hormones? That no man will every look at? I've got to take HRT, Polly – HRT! It's what poor old ladies take for their hot flushes!'

'Have you started getting them, then?'

'What! No, I haven't! I ... oh, great, I suppose that's the next thing I've got to look forward to.' I throw myself back against the seat as she starts to drive away from the surgery. 'Well, that's it, I suppose. I might as well stay at home, buy a cat and take up knitting.'

I screw up the leaflet on *Early Menopause – Your Questions Answered* that Dr Barton gave me and throw it, along with the two on alcohol abuse, onto the back seat. Quite frankly it looks like drinking's going to be the only pleasure left to me.

Thursday

Polly turns up at lunchtime, just as I've finished a colour and style on a bridegroom. Yes, a bridegroom. First time for everything. He's got longer hair than most of the brides, anyway.

'Oh! Come in,' I tell her, as she passes the newly bleached and blow-dried young man in the doorway. 'I was just about to make myself a sandwich. Want one? Does he ...' I indicate Ethan, wriggling in her arms, 'want one, or is he still only eating mushy stuff?'

'That'd be nice, if you've got time. I'll make the coffee. How are you, Sophe? Feeling any better about ... things?'

I scowl at her. 'If you mean, about becoming middle-aged and past-it overnight, no, I don't feel better, particularly. Would you?'

She turns on the kettle and perches on one of my kitchen stools, still jiggling Ethan in one arm. Amazing.

'Well. Let me think,' she says. 'How would I feel about not having to put up with the misery and inconvenience of monthly periods for the next twenty years or so? How would I feel about not having to worry about contraception – if I ever get into another relationship, that is? About taking the Pill and worrying about what it's doing to my body, or using some other unreliable method and worrying every time I have sex? Hmm, well, hard to know how I'd feel about that.'

'All very well for you to say that. It hasn't happened to you.'

'I know. Honestly, Sophe, I do understand what a shock it must be. But if it had to happen to anyone, thank God it's you.'

'What's *that* supposed to mean?' I gasp, halfway through buttering a slice of bread.

'Just think about it. If it happened to Emma, for instance – she's getting married soon, they're going to want a baby. Or if it happened to one of your brides, who haven't had kids yet. It'd be a disaster.'

'Oh, I see. So good old Sophie, everybody's favourite maiden aunt – who cares if *her* ovaries pack up while she's still in her thirties? Who gives a stuff if *her* skin goes all dry and wrinkly, she puts on weight and gets osteoporosis and turns miserable and grumpy and ... all right, all right.' I try to force a smile. 'I know, I'm being miserable and grumpy already.'

'I don't blame you, love, honestly. But in time, when you've started to get over the shock, I think you'll see this isn't such a disaster. You didn't want babies anyway.'

'No. I also didn't want to get old before my time.'

'You won't.' She jumps down from the stool and puts her arms around me. 'Trust me. You won't, as long you're sensible and do what the doctor says.'

'Take the bloody HRT.'

'Yes. And ... cut down on the drinking.'

'What!' I push her away, crossly. 'Have you been talking to him? Why are you both on my case about drinking, all of a sudden? What the hell?'

'I found the leaflets. You left them in my car. The doctor must have been concerned, Sophe. And so am I ... a bit.'

'I don't drink that much! It's only been since I've had all this worry! Out of the corner of my eye, I catch sight of the box of empty wine bottles waiting to go out in the recycling. I sigh. 'Well, OK, since I split up with Oscar. I've been a bit ... you know.'

'Down.'

'Yes.'

'You miss him? You wish you were still together?' She's looking very intently at the bread I'm buttering. She's gone a bit pink again.

'No! God, no. I'm relieved it's over, to be honest. It wasn't working. I'm much better on my own.' I pause. 'I suppose I just felt – a bit of a failure. And when you and I weren't talking either ... there didn't seem much to do apart from having a drink.'

She hangs her head.

'Not that I'm blaming you!' I add quickly.

'I know.'

'So you really think I am? Drinking too much?'

She shrugs. 'I don't know. I just think you should perhaps be careful. You know how easy it is, Sophe, don't you.' She looks back up at me, pointedly. 'To get addicted to something.'

A scene flashes into my head. I'm lying on a bed, drenched in sweat. I hurt, everywhere: my eyes, my limbs, my chest, my stomach. I feel hot, and cold, and I'm shaking so hard I'm having to be held in somebody's arms just to stop me throwing myself off the bed. I want to die. I want *never* to have taken drugs.

'Jesus,' I mutter shakily. 'How could I ever forget?'

The arms that were holding me, back then, were Polly's. Surely I'm not about to put her through the ordeal of getting me over another addiction?

'I'll stop,' I whisper. 'I'll stop drinking. I mean it.'

'Just be careful, that's all I'm saying,' she says, gently. 'Just be aware.'

'No. I'll stop. I'd rather have a cup of tea, anyway.'

Much more suited to someone who's becoming middle-aged, wouldn't you say?

'You know,' says Polly later when we've finished lunch and I'm getting cleared up ready for my next client, 'what I asked you? About Oscar?'

'If I was sorry we'd finished?'

'Yes. There's a reason I asked. Apart from the obvious reason about how you are, yourself.'

'Go on.' I suppose he's been ringing her again. I hope he's not making a nuisance of himself. Perhaps he's nagging her to find out whether he's got any chance of coming back to me. Using her as a kind-of go-between. *Not very subtle!*

'He's called me a couple more times.'

I knew it. I feel myself smirking.

'Oh yes? Not hoping to get back together with me, is he?'

She falls silent.

'Is he?' I persist, starting to laugh.

'No, Sophie. He just calls me for a chat. He likes ... we like talking to each other, that's all. We're ... well, you know. We've both got children. We're both on our own, now.' She tails off, looking very uncomfortable. 'We just chat.'

'Oh My God.' I stare at her. It's slowly sinking in. 'You want to start seeing him. Don't you! That's what you were on about the other night – all that about not having secrets from me! Why didn't you *say*?'

'There isn't anything to say. Not yet. And not at all,' she goes on hurriedly, 'If it was going to upset *you*, Sophie. I promise, I've already told him – I won't even *talk* to him any more if you don't like it, if it hurts you. I haven't even seen him, he's just called me a couple of times ...'

'It's all right.'

'He called me, and I said I wasn't sure if it was a good idea, I didn't want you to be hurt, I'd have to tell you. And we just chatted, that's all, and then when he called again ...'

'Polly, it's all right!'

326

'... he said perhaps we could go out somewhere for a day, with the children, all of them, just as friends – some time – in the future, you know, maybe next year or I don't know, maybe the year after, when it's all less ... raw ...'

'Polly!' I grab her arm and shake her gently. 'I *said*, it's all right. I don't mind.' I smile at her. 'It seems kind of weird, but I'm pleased, really. You'll be good for each other. He's a lovely guy. I just wasn't the right person for him.'

'We're only talking about a day out with the kids! Possibly!'

'I know. And why not? Go for it. I want you to be happy. Him, too.'

'You're sure it wouldn't upset you? Make you feel even more ... down?'

'I'm absolutely sure. As long as ...'

'What? Anything! What?'

'We'll still see each other, won't we? You won't let him *take you over*? You know – stop you seeing your friends, or ...'

She just shakes her head at me, and we both smile.

'Don't be bloody ridiculous!' is all she says.

If I'm honest, of course, I do feel kind of odd about it. I meant what I said – I want her to be happy. More than anything, I want her to meet someone who'll treat her properly, love her the way she deserves. She needs that – God, she needs a lifetime of it, to make up for being with bloody Leon for all that time. And if Oscar turns out to be the right person to do that for her, then I'm glad – I am, really glad. I can just picture the two of them together. I think it could work. He's lovely, she's lovely, they've both got kids, they both like being in a relationship. I can imagine them going out for jolly days at the seaside together, with all five kids. Yikes. And taking the kids on jolly picnics and having jolly fun in the park together.

So I mustn't be selfish. Because all I can picture for myself is a future of loneliness, HRT, and no sex. Some of which is my own fault, I know. But not all of it, surely? I think I'm entitled to feel a *little* bit sorry for myself?

I'm feeling sorry for myself when I call my mum this evening. I know – I *know* I don't call her as often as I should. But who else does a girl turn to when she's upset and feeling sorry for herself? That's what mums are for – right?

She only has to utter the magic words – 'How are you, darling?' – for me to start blubbing about how awful my life has become.

'I'm all alone! Nobody cares about me! I haven't got any friends, apart from Polly, and now she's going to end up marrying Oscar and they'll spend their whole time together and she won't have time for me any more, she'll probably have another couple of babies and ...' I take a deep breath. 'And I couldn't have any, even if I wanted them. I've been robbed of my fertility, Mum – in the prime of my life! I'm having an early menopause – can you believe that? I'm peri-menopausal, that's what the doctor called it. I might have some more periods, I might not. I'll never know. I might go for years without them, and then get one, suddenly, in the middle of something – no way of knowing. How cruel is that? I'm going to get old, and withered, and dried up, and nobody will want me.' I stop for a good sniff. 'I'm finished, basically. I'm on HRT, like I'm middle-aged, older than you! How unfair ...'

'Oh, *stop* it, Sophie!' she says.

I feel like I've been slapped.

'What?' I thought she'd be sympathetic. Mum, of all people, was supposed to feel sorry for me, comfort me, commiserate with how crap my life was turning out to be.

'Stop whining! Do you *know* what you sound like? Honestly – I've never heard so much rubbish. Cruel? Unfair? You have *no idea* what you're talking about!'

'I ... but I ... I'm *menopausal*, Mum!'

'Yes, I heard you, and I'm sorry this has happened – it's unfortunate.'

'Unfortunate?'

'Well, it's hardly the end of the world, is it, Sophie? I'd even say it's tantamount to an act of God.'

'A *what*? How can you say that?'

'You've made it very clear, all your life, that you don't ever want children. Perhaps God's answered your prayers.'

'I don't even believe in all that!'

'No. Maybe you don't need to believe, to get what you ask for. I'm not an expert.' Her voice softens slightly. 'But I *do* know that there are worse things that can happen to a woman than an early menopause.'

'Yeah right,' I mutter. 'I'm only thirty-four. I should have had another twenty years of being a *woman*, a proper woman, being – you know – *fertile* and *wanted*.'

'Take the HRT, Sophie, and you'll still be sexually attractive till you're drawing your pension. If that's all you're worried about.' She's sounding weary, now.

'Sorry. Sorry if you think I'm whining,' I say, moodily. 'How are you, anyway?'

'Oh, not too bad, thank you. Just getting over the last lot of radiotherapy. Mustn't complain,' she says, pointedly.

Shit.

Oh, shit.

'Mum. I'm so sorry. What a complete *cow* I am. I was going to ask ... that was going to be my next question.'

'It's all right, darling. I know it must have been a shock for you – this menopause thing. I'm shocked to hear about it myself.' She pauses. 'No mother, ever, wants to hear that there's anything upsetting their child, Sophie. Even when the child is in their thirties. It still hurts. It hurts me to know that *you're* hurting.'

'But I'm being so selfish! Whining about my problems.'

'Well, that's part of my job, isn't it. To listen to your whines. Just like the tantrums when you were a little girl! Doesn't mean I have to encourage you to wallow in it!' She laughs.

'I should have stopped to think that you've gone through something so much worse,' I admit. 'So *much* worse! When I was waiting to see the doctor, I was frightened that I might have had something awful like that myself. And then – when he said those words, *Early Menopause* – all that went straight out of my head. I should have been grateful, I know I should – but all I could think of was how unfair it is.'

'It is. I know. But if life were fair ...'

We're both silent for a minute.

'Sorry, Mum,' I say again. 'You're right. It's not really a problem, is it. In some ways, it could even be seen as a blessing. In the circumstances.'

'That's the best way to look at it, Sophie. Even if you don't really believe it – try to convince yourself. You'll soon get used to the idea.'

So that's my mantra for the rest of my life: get used to it. It could be a lot worse. I've got to stop whining. At least I've still got my mum.

I'm thinking about all this as I'm settling down in front of the TV. Without my customary glass of wine. No booze, no man, no hormones – shit. The phone rings again and I probably sound a bit gloomy as I answer it.

'Hello,' says a male voice. A voice I recognise only too well. 'I need to cancel an appointment please. A wedding hair appointment.'

'*Charlie!*' I breathe, sitting up straight, my eyes wide with surprise. '*Cancel?*'

'That's right.' He sounds even more gloomy than I feel. 'Cancel.' There's a fraction of a second's hesitation before he adds, quietly, 'Can I come round?'

Friday

I feel like I'm half-asleep, working in a dream. Thank goodness today's wedding is a nice straightforward one – a bride with a graduated bob, blow-drying and straightening, one bridesmaid with a short crop, washing and waxing.

Charlie and I talked till half past two this morning, and after he'd left I couldn't sleep. I feel like I might never sleep again.

'It's all off,' he'd told me before he was even through the front door. 'I finished it. She's gone.'

'Oh, Charlie.' I took him by the hand, led him into the lounge and put my arms around him. We actually stood like that for ages, just holding each other, not speaking. It felt ... like coming home. Like snuggling into your own bed. Like relaxing into a warm, scented bath. It felt wonderful. But I couldn't even tell whether he might be crying. 'Are you OK?' I asked eventually.

'Yes.' It was spoken on a long, long sigh. We sat down, still holding hands. I never wanted to let go. Never, ever again. 'Yes, I'm OK. I just feel a complete prat.'

'Why? For falling in love with someone?'

He laughed – a short, bitter laugh. He wasn't smiling.

'Love? What a joke. How did I ever talk myself into believing *that* was what it was all about?'

'What happened?' I asked him softly. 'No – wait. Let me get you a drink first, then you can tell me all about it.'

'Can I have a coffee, please, Sophe? I've been drinking too much lately.'

'That's a relief. I'm trying to stay off the booze, but if you were having one I'd have to join you.'

He laughed again then – a proper, nice laugh this time like the old Charlie.

'Why are you off the booze? That's not like you!'

'Long story.' I went out to make the coffee and said, when I returned with it: 'You first.' I sat down and took hold of his hand again. 'So what happened – with Helen?'

He shrugged. 'Just one big mistake, from beginning to end. I can't think, now, what the hell I ever saw in her.'

'Can't you?' I said, sniffing. Boobs, legs, face, where did we start?

'I hope I'm not *quite* that shallow,' he muttered, not looking at me. 'OK, she was attractive, but ... I don't know. Perhaps she just came along at the right time.'

'As in – after you finished with me?' I tried to say it lightly, as if it didn't matter, didn't bother me in the slightest, but he winced a bit and shook his head.

'As in – just as I'd decided I wanted a relationship. Possibly a marriage. All that.'

'And it was obviously what she wanted too. So ... what? You think you rushed things?'

'Of course we did. She wanted to get married quickly; I got caught up in it all. I can't imagine what I was thinking of. Christ! Thank God I found out what she was like, before it was too late.'

Four weeks before the wedding. Certainly cutting it fine somewhat.

'And?' I prompted again. 'What *was* she like?'

'Controlling. Demanding. Spoilt. Domineering. Bad-tempered. Spiteful. Vicious.' He takes a breath. 'Jealous. Possessive. Neurotic.'

'Bloody hell.' I gave him a quick grin. 'Not all bad, then?'

'She was a fucking nightmare,' he admits, shaking his head. 'I must have been out of my mind.'

'What made you finally realise?'

'Found out she'd been reading my e-mails. Checking my phone. All that stuff. Wouldn't have been so bad, but she refused to see why I was annoyed. I had a sudden vision of my future life – I wouldn't have just been *married* to her, I'd have been her bloody prisoner. She wanted to choose my clothes, pay my bills, keep my diary, control my life! Shit!' He shook his head again. 'My mum gave me more freedom when I was ten years old than Helen wanted me to have!'

'Sounds like she's got some problems,' I said. I thought, carefully, about how to phrase the next bit. 'You don't think, perhaps, you should feel sorry for her? Like – if she got some help, some counselling or whatever – she might have got better? It might have worked out?'

'I was wondering about that myself, a few weeks ago. I suggested it to her. I offered to make her an appointment, go with her, whatever she wanted.'

'And? She didn't like that, I suppose?'

'Understatement of the year,' he said ruefully. With which he rolled up his shirtsleeves and showed me the scratches and bruises.

OK, I might have overreacted a little at that point. I suppose that threatening to go round her house and beat the crap out of her wasn't entirely helpful and could perhaps make me look as bad-tempered and vicious as her. Perhaps.

'She took me by surprise,' he admitted. 'Flew into such a rage, I didn't have time to defend myself. By the time I'd grabbed her wrists to stop her, she'd got in the first slaps and dug in her nails.'

'Why? I can't understand! You were only suggesting ...'

'Turns out I was the third or fourth boyfriend to make the same suggestions. And the third or fourth one to end up calling off the wedding. She's desperate.'

'Well, if she's that bloody desperate, perhaps she should take the suggestions on board and get herself sorted out!' I ran my fingers over his poor scratched arms. 'Stupid cow,' I added in a whisper.

Next thing I knew, he had both arms round me and was saying, over and over, in a kind of groan: 'Oh, Sophie, Sophie. Oh, Sophie!'

'It's OK,' I said. 'Come on, it'll be OK, Charlie. You'll get over her. You'll move on. You'll forget her in the end.'

'Forget her?' he retorted, sitting up straight again and staring at me. 'I've forgotten her already. Get over who? Helen who?'

'You're obviously going to feel upset, and confused, for a while, but ...'

'I'm not confused, in the slightest. I'm only upset because ...'

'I know, I know,' I soothed him. 'It must have been awful for you. I'm sure you tried your best, but in the end, when things don't work out – well, nobody wants to end a relationship, but ...'

'Sophie, you're not hearing me! I was *glad* to end it! It was a crap relationship! It was a relationship that should never have happened! If I hadn't been feeling so vulnerable at the time, when I met her ...'

'Because of wanting to get married. All that,' I nodded, trying to sound mature and sympathetic.

He took hold of my face in both hands, turned me to look at him.

'Because of wanting to marry *you*,' he said. There was a little quiver in his voice. 'Because I'd been such an idiot, Sophie; because I thought I wanted to get married, more than I wanted *you*. I'm sorry, Sophie. I know I hurt you. I'm so sorry!'

And we were kissing before I'd even realised it.

'Shit!' he said. Eventually. 'Bugger! Oh my God – sorry! I didn't mean to do that!'

'Didn't you?' I said, feeling a silly, happy grin stretching my face. 'Why the hell not?'

'Because ... you know! Because of *him*! Where is he, anyway?' He looked around the room, like Oscar was likely to be hiding behind the curtains. 'Out?'

'We're not together any more. Didn't I tell you? It wasn't working. My fault, probably. I'm just ... well, as you know. Not cut out for living with somebody. Relationships. I'm useless at them.' I shrugged, sadly. 'Obviously.'

'That makes two of us, then, by the looks of things.'

'So it seems,' I said. 'Two of a kind.'

I don't know how long we just sat and looked at each other. Maybe a few seconds, maybe half an hour. But when we started to kiss again, it felt like everything was different. I didn't have to tell him how much I'd missed him; how much I'd longed for us to be back together like this. He didn't have to say it either – although he did try, in between kisses. We both just knew it was right; we were right together. We should never have split up.

We didn't even go to bed together. It was almost like everything was too fresh, too new-again, and magical, and sweet, like we'd only just met and needed to work up to having sex again after a few dates.

But just as he was leaving, just as he was kissing me goodnight for about the sixth time, and neither of us could wipe the soppy grins off our faces and even before he'd gone I was trembling with excitement at the thought of seeing him again – just at that moment, I opened my mouth and said it. The thing I'd always refused to say; the words that had stuck in my throat, every time I'd thought about saying them in the past. The words I should have been brave enough to utter before.

'I love you, Charlie,' I said.

What the hell had I been I waiting for?

'Guess what!' I'm shouting now, as soon as Polly answers the door to me. It's three o'clock and I've come straight from doing my afternoon bride. 'Guess what – I'm in love!'

She laughs. As well she might.

'You?' she says, grinning. 'You're in love?'

'Yes! Quick – let me in, make me a cuppa, I've got to tell you all about it!' Her grin falters a bit as I practically shove her out of the way to barge into the house. 'What's up, anyway? Had a bad night with the baby?'

She's still in her dressing gown. To be honest, she looks a bit of a wreck. Poor thing, I wonder what I can do to help her. Shouldn't Ethan be sleeping better by now? How old is he again?

'No: to be honest, Sophe ...' She's following me down the hallway. She sounds a bit agitated. 'The baby's next door. Carol's looking after him.'

'Needed a break, did you? Oh, Polly – poor you. Why don't you sit down and put your feet up. I'll make the tea.'

'No. I'll do it.' She's steering me away from the kitchen. 'You go and sit in the lounge and ... and you can tell me, in a minute, all about it – who you're in love with, and ...'

'Who?' I look at her as if she's mad. 'Who? Charlie, of course! Don't be ridiculous! Who else would it be? What – you think I've suddenly decided I loved Oscar all along? Ha! As if!' I try again, to move her aside so that I can get into the kitchen to put the kettle on. 'I mean, Oscar's a lovely guy, we had great sex, I can't fault him in any way at all, except that ... Jesus, Polly, the thing is – he was never Charlie. That was all that was wrong with him. You see?'

'I see,' she says, although I don't think she's actually been listening to me. There's a look of panic in her eyes all of a sudden. And she's shaking her head, desperately, at ... at someone behind me. Behind me, coming out of the kitchen. I swing round. Who ...?

'Hello, Sophie,' says Oscar, sheepishly.

It's not just Polly who's undressed at three in the afternoon and looking like she's been dragged through a hedge backwards. Or, come to think of it, like she's been given a thoroughly good seeing-to. They're both staring at me in muted horror.

'We didn't intend ...', Oscar starts, awkwardly.

'This wasn't what we planned,' says Polly, trying to sound apologetic and yet, at the same time, seeming unable to take her eyes off Oscar, who's wearing a towel that barely covers his decency. 'Oscar just came round for a cup of tea.'

'We were just having a friendly chat,' Oscar goes on. 'It wasn't ... um ...'

'Planned. It wasn't planned,' Polly finishes, looking at me pleadingly. 'Sophie, honestly, I don't want you to think ... you know ...' She tails off. 'Oscar – maybe you should go?'

'No!' I start to put out a hand to stop him, but think better of it. Somehow it seems terribly wrong, now, to even think about touching him, especially when he's wearing so very little. I give them both what I hope is a reassuring smile, even though the situation is so weird, I know it'll take a bit of getting used to. 'No – don't rush off on my account. I shouldn't have turned up without phoning. You don't have to explain, or apologise: it's OK. Honestly.' I nod, vigorously, to show how OK it is. 'Honestly, I'm fine with it. I'm happy about it. I actually only came round to tell Polly all about ... um ... someone.'

'Charlie,' says Oscar, with a hint of a smile. 'I overheard.'

'Sorry.'

'No. I should be ... well, I am, pleased for you. We should both be – you know.'

'Pleased for each other,' I say, doing the nodding thing again. 'Yes.'

'Yes.'

There's a rather uncomfortable moment where we all three stand there, nodding at each other like those dogs people have in their rear windscreens. Then he turns to Polly and says, 'Well, anyway, I'd better ... um ... nip back upstairs and get dressed. And I'll see myself out – OK? So you and Sophie can chat.'

'OK. It was nice of you to come,' she says, and then goes bright red and he smothers a snort of laughter, and I rush into the kitchen and turn on the kettle, humming very loudly to myself so that I don't have to hear them saying goodbye. Or whatever.

'Well!' I say when she finally joins me, holding her dressing-gown around her and looking like the naughty girl who's been caught snogging in the playground. 'That was a surprise!'

'To me, too,' she admits. She giggles, then stops, and says, guiltily: 'Oh, Sophie – I'm so sorry. After all I said, about taking it slowly, and just being friends. Are you upset with me?'

'Course not, you daft moo! Come here.' I pull her towards me for a hug. 'Phew – you smell of his after-shave.' Now we're both giggling. 'Good, isn't he,' I whisper mischievously.

'Bloody amazing,' she laughs. Then she stops laughing and adds: 'But it only happened ... like that, so quickly ... because I like him so much. I really do, Sophie. I can't believe ... so soon after, you know: Leon. I can't believe I'm feeling like this about someone else, so soon.'

'It's great. You deserve it. And now, let me tell you ...'

'About Charlie!' she squeals. 'Oh, wait – here, take your tea, let's both sit down – I want to hear this properly! Carol's picking Gracie up – she'll be home soon and I ought to get dressed, so tell me quickly. What *happened*?'

I think about this before I answer. What happened? It's a good question.

'What happened,' I say, slowly, stirring my tea, 'is that I didn't know a bloody good thing when I had it. I didn't know I loved him, Polly. Why didn't you *tell* me what an idiot I was?'

'I tried,' she protests.

'I nearly lost him. So nearly lost him for good, to hateful Helen.'

'But you didn't. He's called off the wedding? He's finished with her? And you're back together, now?'

'Yes.' I smile, and the warmth seems to flood my whole body. I feel so good, I want to jump up and down and sing and shout about it. 'We're back where we started. Isn't it wonderful?'

'And – and does he still want to live with you? Marry you?'

My face drops slightly. 'We haven't discussed that yet.'

'But is he happy ...' Her voice is softer now. 'Is he happy, now, about not having children?'

OK, don't spoil the moment.

We haven't discussed that either. But he'll have to be, won't he? I'm afraid, now, that he's just going to have to be.

Christmas Eve

Another bloody difficult head of hair. Another awkward madam who wants miracles performed.

'I need the back blow-dried first, and the ends straightened, OK? Are you sure you know what you're doing?'

'You're trying my patience now. Sit still! Look, if you don't trust me, do it your bloody self, why don't you!' Debra puts the brush down in exasperation. 'Honestly, Sophie, I might not have your expertise and diplomas but I *can* do a bit of blow-drying.'

'Sorry.' Well, it's frustrating, you know – being the one in the chair, for once. Knowing how tricky my hair is, and how Debra messed it up last time I let her loose on it. OK, she was only about eleven at the time but I had nightmares, to say nothing of a dodgy fringe, for weeks afterwards. 'Sorry – I'll shut up and sit still.'

'Bloody hairdressers,' she mutters good-naturedly.

'I know. I suppose it's like a doctor being confined to bed and told what medicine to take.'

'Tell me about it,' she says gloomily. 'James is a pain in the neck if he's ill.'

'Only if he's ill?'

She shrugs. 'Well, he hasn't been too bad lately. Maybe it's because it's Christmas, you know – goodwill and joy and peace, all that.' There's a pause. 'Or maybe he's got another woman.'

'Oh, come on, Debs – you don't really think that, do you?'

'I've wondered about it for ages.'

'I know. But do you *really* believe he'd do that – leave you and the kids for some bit of stuff? He loves his children!'

341

'I know. And I don't think he would *leave* us. He's greedy enough to want it all.'

I wish we hadn't got into this. I don't want to be unkind, but I don't really want to be discussing Debra's difficulties with James today, of all days. She gives a guilty little start as if she's suddenly realised this herself, smiles thinly and says in a determinedly cheery voice:

'Anyway, you're probably right, it's most likely all in my imagination. At least he's being nice at the moment.'

'Good.' I smile back at her. 'Let's not have any unhappy vibes today.'

'No. Oh – Sophie!' She puts down the hairdryer and hugs me from behind, smiling at me in the mirror. 'I'm *so* happy for you!'

'Never mind all that,' I say teasingly. 'Get on with straightening the ends, can you? We haven't got all day!'

'Your wish is my command,' she laughs. 'But only for today, mind!'

Today's going to be very special. My parents have made sure of it. Christmas down here in Devon is always magical: Mum's always loved entertaining, having the whole family together, decorating the house, the Christmas tree, cooking all the special Christmas goodies and buying lavish presents for all the kids. This year, though, she hasn't had quite as much energy as usual, so Dad and my sisters have been doing most of the preparations – and the result is just amazing. The tree is bigger, brighter and more spectacular than ever, with blue and white lights twinkling like stars, beautiful wooden decorations and miniature chocolate treats tempting little fingers but out of bounds until tomorrow. There are beautifully wrapped parcels stacked under the tree, and the kitchen cupboards are groaning with homemade cookies, puddings, cakes, sweets, chutneys, relishes and every type of seasonal treat you can imagine. In the lounge there are decorated bowls of fruit and nuts – bright juicy Satsumas, fat sticky dates, walnuts and Brazil nuts in their shells, bunches of red and green grapes. Bottles of sherry, Whisky, wine and brandy are lined up on the sideboard. The very best Christmas crackers are already on the table for tomorrow. Mum says she hardly had to lift a finger – it's all been done for her this year. And about bloody time, too.

'I should have been here to help,' I said when we arrived last night.

'Another time, perhaps,' she murmured, hugging me tight. 'This year, you're the guest of honour.'

Blimey. Where's the red carpet?

Charlie and I have been back together for over a month now. We've had a few things to sort out. A few issues to get out of the way.

'I need to tell you something,' I told him, shakily, after the first night we spent together. 'Something serious.'

'You've decided you prefer girls?' he teased, tracing a finger along my arm. 'Or ... younger men?'

'Ouch!' I laughed. 'You're not jealous, are you? About Oscar, just because ...'

'Because he's barely out of nappies ... no, no, why would I be jealous? Why – are *you* jealous about Helen?'

'Yes,' I admit. 'Because she sounds such a bitch, and she hurt you.'

He was silent for a moment. 'I guess that's why I haven't really got a problem with Oscar. He's basically a nice guy – and he's making Polly happy, so I can just about forgive him for taking my place in your bed.'

'Only to stop me pining for you!' I joked. And then I sighed. 'Anyway: that's not what I wanted to talk to you about.'

'Go on, then. What's up?'

'You remember when you told me about the shawl in the attic?'

'My mum's famous baby shawl. Yes – I know I told you about it. I seem to remember it caused some hysteria.'

'Well: I think it kind-of triggered our ... separation, Charlie.'

'The shawl did? Not the fact that I overstepped the mark and expected you to fall in love with me?'

'We've been through that already,' I said, stopping to kiss him. 'I *was* in love with you. I just couldn't admit it. It was all my fault.'

'Well – let's not argue about it! As long as we're in agreement now!'

'I hope so.' I paused, sighed again.

'So what is it?' He sat up now and took hold of my hand. 'Something's worrying you. You know I'm not going to put any pressure on you, babe – about getting married, or anything – we're both happy as we are, now. We've agreed ...'

'But we haven't discussed the baby thing,' I said, all in a hurry, looking away from him. 'The shawl ... your mum wanting a grandchild ... your cousin having a baby ... that was all part of the problem, wasn't it. Part of why you left me for somebody who might be up for the whole *maternity* package.'

He stared at me. 'Sophie – love – what the *fuck* are you talking about?' he said, quite calmly.

'Babies. Having a family. Making your mum a grandma. It's obviously something you decided you'd like. You went so quiet, after you visited her that time, and she told you all about your cousin's baby, and showed you the shawl, and ...'

'Are you mad? Where's all this coming from? I was probably quiet because I was a bit upset. I actually spent most of that visit telling Mum she'd have to get used to the fact that I wasn't going to give her any grandchildren. She didn't take it very well. It was all quite upsetting, but she's

344

come round to it since. Apparently my cousin's got to go back to work when the baby's a year old, and Mum's going to help out – look after the baby occasionally – so she's getting over me being such a disappointment to her.'

'Oh, Charlie. You never said.'

'Well. I suppose it all got overlooked in the ... shock of everything else. Breaking up with you.' He stopped, suddenly, and looked at me with surprise in his eyes. 'Why? Have you changed your mind? Is that what you're saying? You *do* want babies, now?'

'No! No, I ...'

'Because, look: it's not what I had in mind. I've never seen myself as a father; I never wanted that. But Sophie, I want *you*, I never want to lose you again, and if it was what *you* wanted, I'd do it – for you – I'd get used to it, I'm sure – everyone else does, don't they, even if it isn't what they thought they wanted.'

'Calm down,' I said. I was smiling now. 'It's OK. You haven't got to learn to change nappies.'

'Phew.' He laughed, uneasily. 'So ...?'

'So we're both off the hook. I probably wouldn't be able to have any, anyway. I've left it too late.'

'Hardly! Lots of women have babies in their late thirties, forties ... we'll still have to be careful, if we're both agreed that we don't want any.'

'Yes. For a while. But not as long as you might think.' I'd been worrying for days about how to tell him, and now, suddenly, the tension got too much. I burst into tears.

'Hey!' He held me at arm's length, looking alarmed. 'What is it? Tell me! Whatever it is, it can't be so bad that we can't work it out – together.'

And with that, it all spilled out. How I was going into the dreaded *change of life* before I was even thirty-five, how my body was going to gradually collapse on me, how my skin would sag and my boobs would shrivel and

I'd grow hair on my chin and have hot flushes and bad moods and ...

'But you said the doctor's started you on HRT?' he interrupted me just as I was getting going on how bad my moods were going to be.

'Yes. HRT, at my age! It's mortifying! I feel like an old woman!'

'You don't *look* like one,' he said, gently, kissing me. 'You don't *act* like one.' He kissed me again. 'You don't make *love* like one.'

'Huh. That'll be the HRT, I suppose.'

'So bring it on!' he said with a laugh. 'Sophe, it must have been a shock for you. It's probably a lot to take on board – mentally. Not what you expected. But does it really change anything?'

'You don't mind?' I whispered.

'Mind? Why should *I* mind? As long as you're OK – as long as the doctors are going to look after you and make sure you're all right – God, Sophe, there could be so many much worse things.'

'That's what my mum said.'

'And she should know,' he reminded me gently.

'Yes.' I grinned at him, relief suddenly making me feel weak. 'No babies then – ever. It doesn't bother you?'

'It's the best news I've heard for a long time!'

Debra's finished my hair. She brings me another mirror so I can check the back view.

'Hmm – not bad!' I joke. Actually I'm amazed. Perhaps I should take her on as a trainee.

'Good. Glad you approve, madam! Well – it's nearly time – shall we get changed?'

Millie arrives while we're changing. She clatters up the stairs to join us and the three of us shut ourselves in my old room, chatting together, while we dress, about similar occasions in our teens when we were doing just this, preparing ourselves for nights out at the local nightclub (there was only one, and it was crap, but we didn't care – Saturday nights there were the highlight of our week). Every now and then I hear the front doorbell, and excited voices, Mum and Dad calling out hello to people, footsteps in the hall downstairs.

'Everyone must be here by now!' I exclaim. 'It sounds like half of Devon have turned up!' I glance at Debra. 'It's only the family, isn't it? And Charlie's mum – I know she was invited. Mum hasn't asked all the neighbours in or anything?'

'No.' She hesitates. 'Not the neighbours.'

'Who, then?' Just then there's a squeal of laughter from downstairs and I look from one of my sisters to the other in astonishment. '*Polly's* here?'

'She's staying at her mum's. With Oscar, and the kids.'

'Ah! It's *so* sweet of them to come all this way.'

'You surely don't think your friends would have missed this, for the world?'

'Friends? Why ... who else?'

'Emma and Stefan are here too. Staying at Mrs Major's.'

'At Mrs Majors? Blimey! Has the old battleaxe allowed them in without a marriage certificate?'

'Yep. The engagement ring probably got them through the door!'

'And a couple of Charlie's friends, too ...' Millie joins in. 'They're all here.'

I have a sudden, horrible thought.

'Please don't tell me,' I begin, in a panic, 'that you invited ...'

'Don't be daft,' says Debra calmly. 'Jo's name's not even in our address books any more.'

None of us have heard from Jo since she told Emma, several weeks ago, that she and Leon were moving out of London.

'You can move to the moon for all I care,' Emma told her stoutly. 'You haven't got any friends around here any more.'

Apparently, Jo's parents were disgusted with her too – bad enough that she'd had sex with a married man and broken up her friend's marriage, but the stupid stories about artificial insemination she'd originally spread around had come home to roost and her parents were hurt and upset about the lying too.

'So what? We'll make a new start,' Jo apparently told her. 'Me, Leon and the baby.'

'How very cosy.'

'We might even go abroad. To the States.'

'Good idea.'

'So I'll say goodbye, then?'

At which point Emma had lost her temper and said that there was no point Jo contacting any of us again unless it was to apologise to Polly for what she'd done – not that Polly wasn't one hundred percent better off without Leon – and Jo had promptly hung up.

'I think she was crying, though,' Emma added with some satisfaction.

'Perhaps she'll be sorry one day,' I suggested.

I think being in love has made me a bit more mellow.

When we're finally ready to go downstairs, I can hardly believe how quickly my parents' lounge has been transformed. It's six o'clock – pitch dark on a cold December afternoon – and the curtains are drawn, with dozens of scented candles alight on every surface. The chairs have been pushed back around the walls; there's soft background music playing, and as we walk in, everyone, including the children, falls silent and turns to look at me.

Ridiculously, my eyes fill up with tears. I look at Charlie, who's sitting waiting for me in the middle of the circle of chairs, and the lump in my throat is so enormous I don't know whether I'll even be able to speak. I feel so emotional – so excited and yet so strangely nervous; so happy and yet so weepy.

I feel like a bride.

But this is not a wedding. This is something of our own – something we both wanted to do: a celebration, with our families – and friends, as it turns out! – of the fact that we're back together. And more than that. It's ... OK, I know this is unbelievable. It's not what you'd ever have expected from Sophie Jennings. But it's an expression of commitment. Yikes. No second thoughts: I really mean it.

Oh, don't get me wrong – I haven't *completely* caved in! We're not living together ... well, not all the time, anyway. We've decided to keep both our flats. We're both too independent to give up our own space on a permanent basis, even though we're spending most of our time together now. And – marriage? Legal contracts? No – that's not for us. Not in the foreseeable future, anyway, and probably not ever. But I never want to risk losing Charlie again. Or hurting him. That's what today's all about.

The words we've chosen are very simple.

'*Sophie,*' he begins, as the music is turned off and the silence in the room is so intense that I can hear my heart beating. '*Sophie, I'm making these promises to you in front of all these people we love. I promise that I'll always treat you with honour and respect. I promise always to be your friend, to care for you and support you, whatever you choose to do. I love you, Sophie, and I hope our love will last for ever.*'

Mum's crying. My sisters are both sniffing into tissues and even Dad is blinking very hard. I look around the room, smiling like an idiot. Polly's smiling encouragement at me, and beside her, holding her hand, Oscar's nodding at me as if to say it's all good, it's all worked out well. Deana and Serena, sitting at his feet, are beginning to fidget.

'Is Sophie getting married, Daddy?' Serena stage-whispers into the silence. 'Is God going to put a baby in her tummy now?'

There's a ripple of laughter around the room.

Sorry, Serena. God's made a much better job of things than that!

'Go on, Sophe!' Polly whispers as everyone falls silent again.

Perhaps she thinks I'm going to chicken out at the last minute. You couldn't blame her, could you – with my track record? But no. Not this time. Sophie Jennings isn't getting married – not now, not ever; but perhaps even the most dedicated single girl needs something in the end. Something I was always too proud to admit to.

'*Charlie,*' I begin, turning to him to repeat the chosen words. My voice comes out clearer, firmer than I expected. This is good. I need this to be heard. '*I'm making these promises to you in front of all these people we love. I promise that I'll always treat you with honour and respect. I promise always to be your friend, to care for you and support you, whatever you choose to do*'. I pause, smile at him, and then continue, slowly, deliberately: '*I love you, Charlie. And I promise to love you forever.*'

'You changed it!' he murmurs as he kisses me, to the accompaniment of whoops and squeals of delight around the room. 'You changed the words ... you said you *promise ...*'

'I know. I'm sorry. Do you mind?'

'*Mind?*' he exclaims. He doesn't need to say any more. He's too busy kissing me again.

And what more can *I* say?

Except, perhaps, that if anyone ever needs any advice on their relationships, husbands, boyfriends, weddings, children, parents, friends, whatever ...

Don't ask me!

Ask your own hairdresser.

Printed in Great Britain
by Amazon.co.uk, Ltd.,
Marston Gate.